ADDIE
PRAY

JOE DAVID BROWN

G.K.HALL &CO.

 Boston, Massachusetts

1971

Library of Congress Cataloging in Publication Data

Brown, Joe David.

Addie Pray.

Large print ed.
I.   Title.
[PZ3.B8167Ad3] [PS3503.R81936] 813'.5'4 70-38103
ISBN 0-8161-6009-0 (1.print)

Published in Large Print by arrangement
with Simon and Schuster

Set in Photon 18 pt Times Roman

for Gilbreth

ONE

They say my mama, Miss Essie Mae Loggins, was the wildest girl in Marengo County, Alabama. I couldn't say about that. There's not much I remember about her at all. What I can recall are mostly little things. Like how after she put polish on her fingernails, she would spread her fingers wide, hold out her arms, and go waltzing around the room while it dried. I used to try to do the same thing and we both would laugh and laugh because I would get dizzy and tumble down. I remember one time a man she didn't like came to the house, and she took off her shoe and chased him right out the door.

I've heard tell that little memories are the fondling kind. Maybe so, but I'm glad I have one memory about Mama that I know is important and worth keeping. It was the last time I saw her. That was two days before I was six years old. I was in the backyard with Callie, the colored girl, when she came out to kiss me goodbye. Maybe I

1

only made it up, but I've always told myself I remember her exact words: "Be a good girl and mind Callie, and I'll bring you home a baby rabbit for your birthday." I do know she was wearing a green dress and had on a perfume that smelled like cape jasmine. When I smell cape jasmine today I think of her.

She was killed in an automobile wreck the next night, coming home from a house party down on the Black Warrior River. A man named Joe Clay Powell was driving the car, and he was killed too. He was a married man, so there was a big scandal. That's what started me traveling around with Long Boy Pray and helping him do business. But that's a long story, and I'll tell you about it later.

The time I'm talking about, mind you, was a few years before and after Franklin D. Roosevelt was elected President for the first time. I know you've heard about the Depression we had back then. Well, I don't think times were nearly so bad as some people put on. For one thing, in those days folks in small places were accustomed to being poor and didn't expect to get rich, like they do now. For another, when people are working hard for the grit essentials — like enough to eat, and clothes for their kids, and a roof that's tolerably sound — they're apt to be goodhearted and understanding of one another. It's only when they start flogging themselves to get things they don't really need — like big cars, and fancy clothes, and a house bigger than the one next door — that they get aggravated and mean. At least, that's the way it appears to me.

Besides, lots of people did have some money in those days. I don't think there was hardly a place Long Boy and I went that we couldn't find somebody to do business with. Anybody who was working usually had a cash reserve of some kind, and that's sure not true today.

Long Boy and I never stayed more than a couple of days in one place. We traveled in Alabama mostly, but Long Boy was liable to strike out in any direction. The only thing I could be sure of was that at least once a month he would head toward Decatur. I didn't like it, but there wasn't much I could say, being a girl and all. The first time I let

3

him know I knew what was going on was when I was eleven. I don't know what possessed me, but I reckon I just was cranky and out of sorts. That happened a lot when I was eleven. It was the year I became a woman, and for a long time it scared me nearly to death every month when you know what happened. There wasn't anybody around to explain to me what was going on.

Anyway, on this day, Long Boy was tooling the old Hudson up Route 31 toward Decatur. He was humming and looking pleased with himself. It must have been late summer because there were a lot of big old wagons on the road hauling cotton to the gin. It seemed like every mile or so we would pass a bunch of men working on WPA. Every time, Long Boy would say something like, "Lookit them pore scutters," or "I wouldn't work with a shovel less'n I was drown'ding in manure." I was used to Long Boy talking this way. He never had much use for anybody who did ordinary work for a living.

Finally, he turned to me and said, "How

much money we got in the box, honeybunch?"

"Enough for you to get your pole greased, I reckon," I said.

He couldn't have been more surprised, like the old saying goes, if I had hit him in the face with a wet cat. He got red in the face and blinked his eyes and forgot to shut his mouth. He yelled, "Where'd you hear that kinder talk?"

"I heard," I said.

"You oughter be shamed of yourself, talking thataway," he said, "a ten-year-old girl."

"Eleven," I said. "You talk that way."

"I ain't never . . ." he started. He worked his mouth like he always did when he couldn't think of what to say. "You ain't too big for me to take a hickory to, missy," he said.

"Poo!" I said.

That made him mad. "I swear," he said, "I'm gonna do it for sure! I'm gonna put you in a home! You need a good woman to take the sass outer you."

I didn't say anything, just sort of scooched down in the seat and looked out the window at the red dirt and pine trees. It was five, maybe six, minutes before he spoke again, like I knew he would.

"Hon," he said, sounding sorry, "I didn't mean that about the home. I was just a-talking." He coughed and made clearing noises in his throat. He said, loudly, "Sure, I go to Aunt Kate's now and then. Lots of men go to Aunt Kate's, specially men that ain't married. Ain't nothing—well, you ain't old enough to know about it, hon. . . . One of these days you'll understand."

If I hadn't been out of sorts, I might have giggled. I had been knowing about Aunt Kate's house ever since I was seven. One night when Long Boy was there, I went and stood across the street. I never will forget how disappointed I was. Aunt Kate's looked like the other houses in the block, except all the lights were on. Somebody had told me houses like that had a red light out front. But that wasn't so. I had a lot of imagination in those days. I suppose I expected to hear a lot of laughing and singing and carrying on. Except for the katydids, all I could hear was a victrola playing real low, and I couldn't be sure it was in Aunt Kate's.

I wasn't about to tell Long Boy all this. I just turned and stared at him like I did when I wanted to make him uneasy.

He got red in the face again. "Well, now . . ." he said, opening and shutting his mouth. He bent over the wheel and peered at the road, like he couldn't see three feet ahead. I let him wiggle a little before I turned and looked out the window again.

After a while he reached over and gave my shoulder a little push. He tried to sound like nothing had happened. "What say I buy you a little ol' new dress in Decatur? You like a new dress, Addie sugar?"

"Ain't enough money," I said.

"Why, shoot," he said, "that ain't no problem. We'll just do a little business this afternoon. A little quick business before the stores close."

"What kind of business?" I asked right away. I couldn't help it. Everytime we talked about business, I got that little crawly feeling of excitement.

Long Boy knew it, too. He cut his eyes at me and grinned. "Well," he said, "we've

7

still got some picture frames, ain't we?"

"Ten," I said.

"And Bibles?" Long Boy asked, making talk, because he enjoyed seeing the way I was perking up. "We must have some old Bibles left?"

"We got five," I said.

"Any white Bibles?" he asked, just like he didn't know.

"One's white," I said.

Long Boy pretended to think that over. "How much money did you say was in the box, honey?"

"There's twenty-three dollars and eighty-seven cents, " I said. I always knew to the penny how much money was in the Roi Tan cigar box under the seat.

"Well, then," Long Boy said, "we oughter add ten, fifteen dollars to that easy. We'll just take that old white Bible and put some golden initials on it and do a little business."

I swallowed hard. "You think we can, Long Boy?"

"I don't know why not, " he said.

"I ain't helped you do business but one

8

time with a white Bible with golden initials,"
I said.

"I know," he said.

"That time in Demopolis," I said.

"I know," he said. "You done fine."

It made me smile to think about it. I said, "You remember, she had tears big as horse turds running down —"

Long Boy yelled, "Don't talk thataway!"

"You said it," I said.

"Not to you I didn't," he said. He was red in the face and scowling.

I scooched up in the seat and looked out the window. After a little while he gave my shoulder a nudge and asked, "You hungry, Addie honey?"

"Not much," I said.

"Wouldn't you like a coney island and a Nehi?" he asked.

"Well, I wouldn't mind," I said.

He laughed. The old fool. He knew there wasn't anything I liked better than a coney island and a strawberry Nehi.

It was in the middle of the afternoon when we got to Decatur. Long Boy drove right to the newspaper office. I waited in the car while he got all the newspapers for the

9

last week. He divided them up and we began to read through the death notices. It didn't look too promising. It's not easy to do business with a Bible with golden initials. You've got to have just the right kind of information. Finally, Long Boy slapped the paper he was reading and said, "Got it!" He started reading off the important facts, "Amos Huff . . . died suddenly . . . at home . . . baggage master, Frisco Railroad . . . deacon, First Baptist Church . . . married former Edna Richards."

He reached in the glove compartment and got out the kit he used to put initials on things. I had the white Bible all ready, but before I handed it to him I had doubts. I asked, "Do you think we ought to, Long Boy?" White Bibles cost us three dollars apiece even when we bought them by the dozen. Putting initials on a Bible raised the price but they were ruined if you couldn't do business with the right person.

Long Boy just grinned and started work with the thingmajig that pressed initials in the cover of the Bible. I never knew him to take so long. After he dabbed on glue and sprinkled on a little golden powder I saw why. Instead of initials, he had put on a whole name: *Edna Huff.* He blew on the name, squinted his eyes to study it, and said, "That oughter hold the old biddy!"

I never could understand how Long Boy could be so calm when we did business. Even if we did go through the same thing two or three times a week, I always felt like everytime was the first time. You never knew what was going to happen. Why, one time I—but I'll tell you about that later, too. As we drove out to the Huff residence, I was feeling like I always did. Excited and a little scared, and feeling like maybe I would wet my pants.

"Now, don't talk too fast," Long Boy said.

"I won't," I said.

"Don't let her see the Bible till I get there," he said.

"I won't," I said.

"Be sure you got her hooked afore you call me," he said.

"I will. I will," I said.

It was the kind of medium-size, neat house I expected. There were some petunias and hollyhocks outside, and the grass looked like it had been cut blade by blade.

11

Long Boy sat in the car with the motor running. I walked up the front walk and climbed the front steps slowly, holding the box with the Bible in it like an angel's-food cake. The front door was open and through the screen I could see the living room was as prim and clean as a cat in mittens. As soon as I tapped on the door jamb with my toe, I heard a woman call out, "Coming."

It was the widow, all right. New widows all look the same, kind of washed out and put upon, like somebody they trusted had done them a dirty trick. Mrs. Huff was plump and pretty old, about fifty, but kind of sweet-looking. It surprised me when she gave me a smile that was almost natural. "Well, hello, child," she said.

I pushed the box forward a little and said, "I've got something for Mr. Amos Huff, C.O.D., ma'am."

Her smile died. "Well, I . . . I . . ." She fumbled around for a moment or two before she said sadly, "Mr. Huff has . . . has passed away, dear."

"Oh," I said. Still holding the box up high, I backed away and looked at my feet, then toward the car.

"I'm Mrs. Huff," she said. "Maybe if you—"

I backed away a little bit more and said, "It's for Mr. Huff, C.O.D."

"I know, hon," she said, "but maybe I can—" She unlatched the screen door and pushed it open.

I waited until I was sure she was coming outside, then said quickly, "I'll call my daddy." I went to the edge of the porch and yelled, "Daddy! Daddy!"

It was hard to beat Long Boy when it came to doing business. He climbed out of the car and came up the walk, looking good-natured but a little impatient. He took his hat off and smiled at Mrs. Huff. "Evening, ma'am." He looked at me, but I just shuffled my feet.

Mrs. Huff said, "I was telling your little girl that Mr. Huff has . . . has passed away."

Long Boy let his jaw sag. "No!" he said. He shook his head slowly. "I just can't believe it!"

"It was his heart," Mrs. Huff said.

Long Boy looked at her. "Oh, I'm so sorry to hear it, ma'am," he said. "Why, it was only a week, ten days ago—"

13

"We had the funeral Tuesday," Mrs. Huff said.

"—he was as healthy as me'n' you," Long Boy said.

"He was sitting reading the paper," Mrs Huff said.

"I jus' can't get over it," Long Boy said, shaking his head.

"He just put his paper in his lap and smiled and—and went away," Mrs. Huff said. She had found a handkerchief somewhere and was dabbing at her eyes.

"Such a fine man," Long Boy said. He shook his head some more before he said, "Well, I guess you know, ma'am, I'm with the Dixie Bible Company, and Amos ordered this here deluxe Bible for—"

"Bible?" Mrs. Huff asked, surprised. "Why, we have—"

Long Boy cut in. "He wanted it as a gift for somebody, ma'am." Before you could blink, he had the box out of my hands and open. He held up the Bible. The name *Edna Huff* looked like it was printed in molten gold.

Mrs. Huff's face purely dissolved. She sure cried tears big as horse turds. They

poured down her face. She grabbed the
Bible and hugged it to her breast like it was
her lost child. "Oh, that blessed man," she
said, "that dear, blessed man!"

"Yes, ma'am," Long Boy said
sorrowfully. After a while he said,
" 'Course, if you don't wanter keep the
Bible, ma'am, I'll be glad to give you back
Amos's dollar deposit, and —"

"Oh, I want to keep it!" Mrs. Huff cried.
"Of course I want to keep it. Oh, that sweet,
blessed man!" Before I knew what was
happening, she had reached out her free arm
and pulled me close. I stiffened a little at
first, but I can't say I really minded. She felt
warm and comforting, and I couldn't even
remember when I had been hugged last.

Long Boy nodded understandingly. "Yes,
ma'am, I can see why you'd wanter keep
Amos's last gift." He pulled out an order
book, and while he flipped through it he
said, "I told Amos I could sell him a
cheaper Bible. But, no, he naturally wanted
the best. The deluxe edition with the name
printed in golden letters and the words of
Jesus printed in red. Ah! Here it is, ma'am.
Amos paid me a dollar deposit, so the rest

15

due is twenty-four dollars."

I must have jumped. That price shook me. I thought Long Boy had lost his mind. But Mrs. Huff didn't seem to give it a thought. She sniffed and said, "I'll get my purse." She leaned down and smiled at me with her face all woozy. "How old are you, hon?"

"Eleven, ma'am," I said.

"Do you like gingerbread?" she asked.

"Well, I . . . I'm not hungry, ma'am," I said.

"Of course you are," she said, squeezing me hard. "You come in the house with me and I'll give you some gingerbread while I get your daddy's money."

There wasn't much I could do. She held me so tight I had to walk sideways as she pulled me into the house. The living room was close with the smell of flowers, like it always is after a funeral. But it wasn't a bad smell, and it gave me the funniest feeling that I had been in this house before. I wondered if I felt that way because it was the kind of house I sometimes wished I lived in.

It had the nicest kitchen I had ever seen,

all yellow and white, and everything in its right place. There was a big spicy-smelling pan of gingerbread on the kitchen table. Mrs. Huff pushed me toward it. "You help yourself, child," she said. "Take all you want."

I didn't, of course. I just stood there and looked around while Mrs. Huff went to a cupboard and took out her purse and counted out Long Boy's money. When she came back, she gave a little laugh and picked up two or three big pieces of gingerbread and handed them to me. It was still warm. Then she did a funny thing. She put her hands on both my shoulders and turned me around so she could study me, smiling sadly. "What's your name, hon?" she asked.

"Addie Pray, ma'am," I said.

"Well, Addie," she said, "one time I had a little girl just like you. I used to make her gingerbread men." Her chin began to tremble and big tears ran down her cheeks. She sobbed, "She went away, too, Addie." She leaned over and put her wet cheek next to mine for the longest time. Then she pulled me close to her side and began

17

dragging me along again.

We had almost reached the front door when I realized why the house seemed so familiar. Out of all that heavy smell of flowers, my nose had somehow picked out the odor of cape jasmine. It made me feel awful, all choky and teary. Partly it was because I was reminded of my mama, of course. But then it hit me all of a sudden that mostly it was because of another feeling I had. It was awful. Nothing like it had ever happened when I did business before. It made me feel so confused and terrible that I don't remember much of what happened until Long Boy and I were back in the car.

"Oh, man alive!" he was saying. "You don't come across many as easy as that old sister." Suddenly, I began to cry as hard as I could. You wouldn't believe how surprised Long Boy looked. "Whoa! Whoa, honey!" he said. "What's got into you?"

About a block from the house I began to get mad at Mrs. Huff for making me feel so ashamed. I threw the gingerbread out the window. "That old wabble-jawed bitch," I sobbed. "That fat old egg-sucking slut!" I

18

cussed and cried and cried and cussed. And for once I didn't pay any attention when Long Boy kept yelling at me not to talk thataway.

TWO

To this day, I don't know whether long Boy was my daddy or not. That sounds right peculiar, I know. But it was on account of my mama being — well, fast and all. Miss Katie Lou Bishop, who was Mama's very best friend, told me that Mama always used to laugh and say that any one of three men could be my daddy, but if I was real fortunate I'd never find out which.

One of the men was a baseball player named Boggs, or Bloggs, who was in town for just one summer. I believe he was from up North somewheres like St. Louis. I never bothered to find out. Somehow I never felt like he might be my daddy.

Another one of the men was Mr. Thad Bledsoe, who worked down at Burchfield's drugstore for the longest sort of time. I always thought he bore a strong resemblance to Gary Cooper, because he was tall and quiet and had a long sad face. He always wore a dress white shirt and a black bow tie. I never spoke to him but once. It was maybe a year or two after Mama was killed. I went in Burchfield's for an ice-cream cone, and after he served me he stood wiping his hands on a towel and staring at me. "Ain't you Es Loggins' little girl?" he asked.

I said I was.

He came out from behind the counter, still wiping his hands and looked me up and down good. Finally, he said, "I liked your mama. It tore me up when she got killed." He turned and walked back behind the counter.

The third man, of course, was Long Boy. I can't remember when Long Boy wasn't around. Not all the time, because Long Boy was never one to stay in one place for long. But he never was away for such a spell that I forgot him even when I was tiny. I think Mama was always as glad to see him as I was. I can remember she seemed to laugh all the time he was around. He did the craziest things. If he showed up on Christmas, he always had his car filled up with presents. If it was Thanksgiving, he always brought three or four turkeys. One Fourth of July he brought enough fireworks

21

to hand out to all the children in the neighborhood.

I don't mean to say Long Boy was always flush. You could tell how much business he was doing by the kind of car he drove. Sometimes he showed up in old rattletraps that looked like they were about to fall apart. One time I remember Mama was on the porch talking with some people about one of Long Boy's old cars, and she said Long Boy's business wasn't so good. I piped up and asked, "What does Long Boy do, Mama?" Everybody nearly died laughing when Mama made her voice sound country and said, "Jes' any pore ole soul he kin, sugar."

Mama was always poking fun at Long Boy's countrified ways, but she did it fondly. Long Boy was a country boy clear through. His family was grub-poor, and he was raised on one of those forty-acres-and-a-mule farms down in Coffee County. His real name was Moses Pray, but everybody started calling him Long Boy because he shot up to his full height of six feet three when he was only twelve or thirteen years old.

But Long Boy wasn't nearly as country as he pretended. There was his gold tooth, for instance. When Long Boy was doing business with small-town people, selling Bibles and such, that gold tooth was always shining in the front of his mouth. But it was just a gold crown, and Long Boy slipped it off and put it in his vest pocket when he was doing bigger business with smarter folks.

Let me tell you, Long Boy wasn't hiding in the canebrakes the day they handed out brains. He could be as slick as they come. He could even roll out quality talk if he had a need to. I guess I was the only one who could make a fool out of him on a regular basis, but it was natural for him to underestimate me. I'll be telling you later about Major Carter E. Lee, who was one of the smartest men doing business in the country. Major Lee sometimes did business for thousands of dollars. Once he told me he didn't know what he admired in Long Boy the most. Whether it was because Long Boy looked so honest and acted so honest and had so much larceny in his heart, or whether it was because he could look so dumb and act so dumb and be so smart.

The only thing about Long Boy was you had to watch him every minute. When it came to doing business, he had no more sense of right and wrong than a tom polecat at rutting time. I know he felt loving toward Mama, but that doesn't alter the fact that one reason he was there johnny-on-the-spot after she was killed was that he saw a chance to do some business for cash. He needed a little cash pretty bad just then so he could do some business for a new automobile. He was driving an old beat-up Ford pickup that would barely run and couldn't climb a grade that had as much slant as a cow's face.

I was supposed to be sent off to live with my aunt, Mrs. Billy Joe Griggs, up in Anniston. Before anybody knew what was happening Long Boy had taken charge of getting me there and was talking big about how he was going to buy me lots of clothes first. You might wonder how I know so much about this and what followed, me being so young and all. Well, I didn't know it all at the time. Some of it I figured out by putting things together. Long Boy and I talked about a lot of it later on. Besides, I've helped Long Boy do business for two automobiles since then.

Anyway, Mama was hardly laid in her grave when Long Boy had me in the old pickup and heading toward town. I remember that well enough. "I've got to do a little business afore we go to Anniston, baby girl," he said. "Do you reckon you could he'p old Long Boy?"

"Sure," I said.

"Well, I'm taking you downtown to see a man," he said. "I want you to be real quiet and not say a word. Will you do that?"

"Sure," I said.

The man we went to see was a brother to the man who was driving the car when Mama was killed. I never did learn his full name or what business he was in, but he had an office downtown. I sat in the outer office while Long Boy went inside. After a while he came out again and took me by the hand and led me inside. A fat bald-headed man was sitting at a desk. He just looked at me with a sour face and didn't say a word. Long Boy took me outside again and peeled me a stick of juicy-fruit gum and told me to be a good girl and wait.

Pretty soon I heard Long Boy and the man going at it hot and heavy. They yelled and slammed things and I began to get scared. But after a time they quieted down. A few minutes later Long Boy came out, all red in the face and not looking too pleased. Well, the man just wasn't having any of Long Boy's soft talk that he owed me something because it was his brother's fault I was a poor homeless orphan. Long Boy finally had to squeeze two hundred dollars out of him by threatening to go to a lawyer and tie up his brother's estate.

Long Boy never did like fighting for money. I don't recall he spoke a word as we drove down to the post office. But after he bought a money order and sent off most of the two hundred dollars to the Mercantile Bank in Eutaw where he always managed to keep an account of some size going, he seemed more cheerful. "We're going to get us a real humdinger of a car to go to Anniston in, sugar pie," he said. "Just you wait and see."

That must have been on a Thursday or Friday. We went over to Mrs. Agnes Keller's boarding house and stayed either one or two nights. I liked it there. Everybody was always hugging me and calling me poor baby and making a fuss over me.

On Saturday morning Long Boy and I headed for Walesburg in the old pickup. It wasn't far, just over the county line, but it seemed to take us forever. Every few miles the pickup would get so hot it wouldn't run. Long Boy would groan and cuss and get out and use a rag to unscrew the radiator cap and let the steam blow out. When he wasn't fussing with the car, he kept telling me how to act when we did business. "Now, remember, baby doll, you're going to play like I'm your daddy. Don't forget that."

I would promise I wouldn't. I was tickled with the whole idea, especially when every so often Long Boy would ask, "Now, who am I?" I would laugh and say real loud, "You're my daddy!"

Even with all the trouble with the pickup, we made it to Walesburg before noon. That meant we had about an hour to kill. One of the things you have to be careful about when doing business for a car is to be sure the banks are closed tight. We went and had ourselves some coney islands and Nehis, and then walked around a bit. Walesburg is the county seat, and it being Saturday, it was crowded. I believe it was the first time I had ever seen so many people in one place before.

About one o'clock we went back to the pickup and drove to the biggest automobile agency in town. There was a big sign outside that said SEE CLIFF HATHAWAY — DRIVE A BARGAIN AWAY. A man came up to wait on us but Long Boy said he wanted to see Mr. Cliff Hathaway personally.

Mr. Hathaway was a prissy-looking man with gold-rimmed glasses and a collar that was too tight. Long Boy gave him his biggest country grin. "Me 'n' my little girl been reading yo' signs," he said. "I got this old hunk o' junk and a hunnerd and fifty dollars. Let's swap."

Mr. Hathaway did his best to be jolly. "All right, neighbor," he said, "let's see what you got here." He walked around the car slowly and then shook his head. "I'll have to pay somebody to haul it away," he said.

Long Boy laughed. "You sho might at that."

Mr. Hathaway took us to the back lot and showed us an old Ford coupe that had a sign on it that read: *A-I, $200.* "I won't make a penny, neighbor," he said, "but I'll let you have this one because it's a cash deal."

Long Boy was still grinning and acting the fool. He looked the car over and said, "I'll tell you what, fill 'er up with gas, and you sold yo'self a car."

Mr. Hathaway agreed, of course, and we went inside to make out the papers. Long Boy waited awhile before he took out his checkbook and began waving it around. Mr. Hathaway stopped writing and asked, "Whereabouts you bank, neighbor?"

Long Boy told him the Mercantile Bank in Eutaw.

Mr. Hathaway shook his head. "We don't take checks on out-of-town banks. I'll have to have cash."

"Good Lawdamighty," Long Boy said, "I don't carry that kinder cash money around—a fella could get hit in the haid! Call the bank. I'll pay the charge."

29

Mr. Hathaway put his fountain pen down and said, "The bank's closed. Today's Saturday."

Long Boy acted like he was getting mad. "What kinder crook you take me for anyhow! You think I'd come in heah with mah little chile and give you mah pickup if I was gonna give you a no-good check?" Long Boy pulled out his big old wallet that was always bulging with fake cards. "Why, looky heah, man," he said, "heah's mah Woodmen of the Word card, mah burial insurance card, mah . . ." He stopped and looked at Mr. Hathaway. "You a Mason?"

Mr. Hathaway blinked a couple of times. Long Boy grabbed his hand and gave him the secret Masonic handshake he had learned somewhere.

"Well, all right," Mr. Hathaway said. He finished making out the papers.

I sure was disappointed in that car, but I didn't want to hurt Long Boy's feelings. As we drove out of the lot, I said, "Well, it's lots nicer than that old pickup."

Long Boy looked at me and laughed. "Why, shoot, honey, this ain't the car I promised you. I'm going to get you a real pretty car. This car ain't fit for nobody. I'm going to drive it around a little bit, and then we'll sell it."

That's exactly what we did. Long Boy stopped at a curb market and got us a big bag of boiled peanuts. We rode around Walesburg for about an hour, looking at things and spitting out peanut hulls. Then he headed for Cold Springs, a little town about six miles away. He must have known where he was going. There was only one used-car lot in town. Long Boy drove in, and when a man came out he said, "How much you give me for this old heap, cash on the barrel head?"

The car man looked the old Ford over. "It's in real bad shape, mister."

Long Boy grinned. "Brother, you said it!"

The car man took out a pad and pencil and started figuring. Long Boy said, "Tell you what's fair. Give me eighty-five dollars and drive me 'n' my little girl over to Bailey's Hotel in Walesburg, and the car's yours."

"Seventy-five," the car man said.

"All right," Long Boy said. He and the car man went into the little shanty on the lot to make out the papers. Everything was

31

signed, and Long Boy and I were getting in a car with the colored helper who was going to drive us back to Walesburg, when the car man came hustling out of the shanty. He had just realized what date was on the bill of sale. "Hey!" he said. "You just bought this car today."

"That's right," Long Boy said.

"Then why're you selling it?" the car man asked.

"'Cause I want the money," Long Boy said.

The car man frowned and was about to say something else, but Long Boy slammed the car door. He said to the colored man, "Let's go. I'm in a hurry."

Bailey's Hotel in Walesburg was the first hotel I ever stayed in. It makes me sad to think how dumb I was in those days. I thought it was real nice. As soon as we got to our room, Long Boy sat on the edge of the bed and took both my hands in his. "Now, look, baby doll, in a little while some men are going to come busting in here. They'll be saying lots of mean things to Long Boy, but don't you fret. It's a kinder game men play when they do business. We'll have to go off, so's I can sign some papers and things, but it won't take long. Just keep on acting like I'm your daddy. You won't be scared, will you, sugar pie?"

" 'Course not," I said.

"That's my good girl," Long Boy said.

Long Boy took off his coat and vest and stretched out on the bed. I sat on the floor and worked on a coloring book he had bought me when we stayed at Mrs. Keller's boarding house. It was well over an hour, maybe closer to two, when somebody started pounding on the door. Long Boy smiled and winked at me. He got up and started putting on his vest and coat. "Who's there?" he called out.

"Open the door!" somebody yelled.

Long Boy took his time buttoning his vest. "Who's there?" he asked again.

"Open the door, or we'll break it down!" somebody yelled.

Long Boy took his time walking to the door and turning the key. Three men came charging in the room like billy goats headed for clover. Two of the men wore badges and carried guns. They were deputy sheriffs. The other man was Mr. Hathaway. When

33

he saw Long Boy, he began to bounce up and down. "That's the man! That's the one!!" he hollered.

Long Boy just stood there, looking like he couldn't believe what was going on.

Mr. Hathaway shook his fist at him. "You crooked sonofabitch!" he screeched. "I oughter bust you right in the nose!"

Long Boy got red in the face. "Now, looky here, don't you talk thataway in front of my little girl."

"Don't be telling me how to talk, you thieving, no-account bastard!" Mr. Hathaway yelled.

"Now just a min . . ." Long Boy began. He took a couple of steps toward Mr. Hathaway. The biggest deputy, a mean-looking man with a purplish face, grabbed him and slammed him up against the wall.

That scared me. I ran at the deputy and began to hit and tussle at his leg. "You stop that!" I screamed. The deputy reached back with one big hand and gave me a push. I went sailing halfway across the room and landed on my behind. I began bawling.

They took us downstairs and loaded us in

a car and drove us to the county jail. Long Boy sat with his arm around me and kept patting me to show me it was all right. All he said was, "I sure wish somebody would tell me what this here is all about." The deputy with the purplish face glared at him. He was a mean man. I sure did hate him. When we left the room, he reached up under Long Boy's coat in the back and grabbed hold of his belt, so he could push him along. He did the same thing when we got out of the car and went into the jail. Mr. Hathaway came in his own car and met us there.

It was when we got in the jail that Long Boy first realized he had miscalculated. It was the first time it ever happened, and you can bet it was the last. It still makes me laugh to think about it. Long Boy had naturally expected to be charged with auto theft. He had fifty dollars in his pocket to give a bail bondsman to stand his bail. He had no way of knowing what a nasty-spirited, conniving little mouse-fart Mr. Hathaway would be. Why, he swore out warrants for Long Boy for everything he could think of—auto theft, grand larceny, selling stolen property, fraud, and I don't know what all.

Long Boy's face was some sight to see when he heard all those charges. Then he began to get mad. He looked at Mr. Hathaway level-like and said, "Mister, you're sure going to be sorry you ever clapped eyes on me!"

Mr. Hathaway was smirking like a possum floating in cow plop. "Why, you must be the dumbest goober-grubber I ever saw," he said. "What made you think you could put something over on me?"

They made Long Boy empty out his pockets. They put everything he had in a big brown envelope and made him sign his name across the flap. Then they took him upstairs and locked him up.

I know you're wondering what happened to me. Well, I went to jail, too, you might say. In those days, the head jailer and his family always lived on the ground floor of the jail house. In some little places they still do. They turned me over to the jailer and his family to take care of until Monday when it would be decided what to do with Long Boy. The family was named Tucker. I think they were kind of common but not a bit trashy. They treated me real nice.

On Monday morning they took Long Boy and me over to the courthouse for what's called a preliminary hearing. That's when they decide whether or not somebody should be held for trial and how much bond to set and all. I thought Long Boy would cry when he first saw me. He was that glad to see I was all right. The old fool. He looked about as nice as I've ever seen him. He had his hair all combed back, and he must have put his pants under the jail mattress and creased them up.

The judge who heard the case was named Beasley. He was real young to be a judge, but his hair was thin and he was pale and sort of clammy-looking. His eyes were red and he kept taking off his glasses and rubbing them. I know now he must have been suffering because he was on a toot the night before. But then he got my back up because he seemed so uninterested in what was going on. He didn't even look at Long Boy when he read off the charges and asked him if he had a lawyer.

"I don't need a lawyer, Judge, your

honor," Long Boy said, " 'cause I ain't done nothing."

Judge Beasley raised his eyes a little. "You plead not guilty?"

"I sure do, Judge, your honor," Long Boy said. "I don't know what these folks think I did."

Judge Beasley fished around in the papers in front of him and found Long Boy's check. He held it up and said, "Do you want—"

That was as far as he got. Just then the purplish-faced deputy came in the courtroom and something came over me. I know part of it was I wanted to get back at him. I guess, too, I was afraid for Long Boy and thought the judge wasn't paying enough attention to him. It might have been that nobody was noticing me at all. I never did like that when I was little. Anyway, I stood up and pointed to the deputy and screamed, "That's the one there! That's the man that hit me!"

Judge Beasley made a face. "Hush that child up," he said.

That did it. I began bawling as loud as I could. "He did hit me!" I yelled. "He did so! He knocked me down!" I twisted around and rared my bottom up and pointed to a bruise I got when a swing bumped me. "See where he hurt me! He knocked me down!"

That sure stopped things. Judge Beasley stared at me, then crooked his finger and said real kindly, "Come here, sis." Still sobbing, I went over and climbed up behind the bench. He patted my shoulder and said, "Now what's all this fuss about?" I began making hiccuping sounds and pointed my finger at the deputy. "That there man knocked me down." The deputy's ugly face turned purple as an eggplant.

Long Boy said, "He did hit my little girl."

Judge Beasley snapped, "You keep quiet!" His face was red and his eyes had turned real mean. He looked at the deputy. "Well, Deputy Mays, what do you say about this?"

The deputy had trouble finding his voice. "Why, I . . . I never did," he said. "I never did hit that chile!"

"You did so," I said, "right here!" I was about to turn around and show my bottom again, but Judge Beasley stopped me. "Now, now," he said. He gave the deputy another dirty look, then slid over in his chair and motioned for me to sit with him. "Now, you sit quiet, hon, while we find out what this is all about." He found the check again and held it up and looked at Long Boy. "Did you write this bad check?"

"Why, that check ain't bad, Judge, your honor," Long Boy said. "It's good as gold!"

Judge Beasley looked at the deputies and a man who was some kind of county prosecutor. "Well?" he asked. They just stared straight ahead. Judge Beasley looked at Mr. Hathaway, who was sitting in the front row. "What do you say, Mr. Hathaway?"

Mr. Hathaway got red in the face. "Of course the check's bad," he said, practically quivering he was so outraged. "Ask him why he sold the car."

Judge Beasley looked at Long Boy. "Why did you sell the car?"

"'Cause I needed the money," Long Boy said. "My sister called me long distance from up in Birmingham. She said they was hiring in the mills up there. I needed the money more 'n the car, so's me 'n' my little girl could travel up there and get settled."

"Well, why didn't you sell it back to me?" Mr. Hathaway hollered.

Long Boy turned to face him and looked real mad. " 'Cause you misrepresented it to me as being worth two hundred dollars. I thought I could get that much somewhere else. It wasn't till I got ready to sell it that I discovered you cheated me." He turned to the judge. "Look, Judge, your honor, that check ain't bad. Just call the bank. I'll pay for the call."

Judge Beasley didn't say a word. He motioned for the bailiff and handed him the check. "Use my phone," he said.

While the bailiff was gone, he opened the drawer in front of him and found things for me to play with, like an eraser and magnifying glass. Pretty soon the bailiff came back and leaned over and whispered in his ear. "How much?" Judge Beasley asked. The bailiff leaned over and whispered again. Judge Beasley's eyes got real mean again. "There's more than enough money in this man's account to cover this check," he said in a hard voice.

Well, I want you to know he then proceeded to lay them out. I wish I could use all the big words and legal terms. He started with the purplish-faced deputy. He said if he ever heard of him hitting a child again, he'd clap him in the penitentiary. He said he hoped my daddy would bring charges against him. Then he turned on Mr. Hathaway and said he was purely irresponsible. He had put a man in jail who didn't belong there, and he hoped he would learn he couldn't get by with it. Then he hit his desk hard and said, "Case dismissed."

I scooted over to Long Boy. He had walked over to Mr. Hathaway, and I heard him say real low, "You're gonna get yours now, you little jaybird turd."

"Now, wait a minute," Mr. Hathaway said. "How was—"

"Get outer my way," Long Boy said in a gritty voice.

"But listen, neighbor," Mr. Hathaway said. "I'm sure if you—"

Long Boy took my hand and said real loud, "Let's go back to the hotel, sugar. I wanter call up the best lawyer in this here town." We left Mr. Hathaway standing there.

We were walking across the courthouse

square before Long Boy began to laugh. "Hot diggety dog!" he chortled. "Did we ever cut their water off!" He squeezed my hand. "Honey, you was just wonderful. You must be about the smartest little girl I ever heard of."

"Did you see that old deputy's face?" I asked, beginning to walk slew-footed I was that proud.

"I sure mortally did, you little imp," Long Boy said, about to choke with laughing. "You pert near yanked all his short hairs out."

Long Boy and I laughed all the way back to the hotel. We went into the dining room and Long Boy ordered me up waffles with syrup, and he just stuffed himself with eggs, biscuits, and grits. He said the jail food was so sorry he could hardly touch it. We were still at the table when Mr. Hathaway and a wrinkly old man in a high stiff collar found us.

Mr. Hathaway showed his teeth like a hog that had swallowed a corncob sideways. "Why, hello, little girl," he said, trying to make up to me, "you enjoying your breakfast?"

I made a face at him.

Long Boy said, "Git outter here while we're eating!"

The wrinkly man said, "Mr. Pray, if you will be reason —"

"Git!" Long Boy said.

They were waiting for us in the lobby. Mr. Hathaway said, "Now, neighbor, just give us a minute to talk to you." The wrinkly man kept humphing in his throat and saying, "Let's be reasonable . . . let's be reasonable."

Long Boy had made his eyes as hard as two taw marbles. He didn't say a word or even look at them as they followed us up the stairs and down the hall to our room. Finally, at the door he put his hand on my head and said, "You wait out here, honeybunch, while I talk with these men."

I waited, but you can bet I put my ear to the door. The first thing Long Boy said was, "Now, you listen. I'll tell you straight I'm gonna sue your ass raggedy. An' when I get through with you, it ain't gonna be a question of you not having a pot to pee in. Brother, I ain't gonna leave you no tallywhacker to pee with!"

44

"Now, now," Mr. Hathaway said, trying to be soothing, "going to law's no way to settle this. Ask Judge Suggs here. He's my lawyer."

The wrinkly old man humphed and said, "That's right, Mr. Pray. Let's talk this here thing out like reasonable men. We can settle it amongst ourselves."

"Settle! Settle!" Long Boy said, sounding like he was about to explode. "I reckon you think I'm some holey-pants plow-pusher that can be bought off with some money or a new car. How you gonna settle for slapping a sweet little child clean across the room? How you gonna settle for putting an innercent man in jail?"

"It was all a mistake," Mr. Hathaway said.

"You bet your little dusty butt it was a mistake!" Long Boy said.

They went on and on from there. After a while I sat down and leaned back against the wall and tried not to fall asleep. It was the longest time before the door opened and they came out. Mr. Hathaway and the wrinkly man looked frazzled out. Long Boy was sulky. "C'mon, sugar pie," he said,

45

"Daddy's got to go down to the car place for a little while."

Well, the other details aren't important. But I tell you this, when we left Walesburg late that afternoon, Long Boy had his check back in his hip pocket. And we were tootling along in a Model-A Ford Deluxe sedan that had been a demonstration car and didn't have but five hundred miles on the gauge. It looked brand-new, and it had the gas tank up on the hood, fringe on the window curtains, and even two cut-glass vases to put roses in. It was a free and gratis gift.

Long Boy grinned at me. "Didn't old Long Boy tell you he would take you to Anniston in a new car?"

"I ain't going," I said.

"What you mean you ain't going?" Long Boy said.

"I mean I ain't going to no old Anniston."

"But, sugar pie," Long Boy said, "who's going to take care of you?"

"You're my daddy, you're supposed to take care care of me," I said.

"Aw, honey," Long Boy said, "we was just making believe."

I looked at him. "Ain't you my daddy?"

Long Boy turned red. "Well . . . now, well . . . now." He began opening and shutting his mouth.

I scooched up in the seat and turned my head toward the window and pretended to cry like my heart would break.

"Aw, honey," Long Boy said. "Aw, Addie, baby . . ." After a while he reached over and pushed my shoulder. "Lookit, honey, suppose we take a little trip for a few days. Heck, there ain't no reason why we have to go to Anniston right away, I reckon. Maybe after a few days you'll . . ."

I didn't pay any attention after that. I was getting sleepy, and I knew I wasn't going to no old Anniston. When it came to dealing with me, Long Boy just didn't know B from a bull's foot.

THREE

It was only natural, I guess, him being a normal conceited man and all, but it took quite a while for Long Boy to realize what a help I could be to him. He seemed to think what happened in Walesburg was only a lucky accident. Why, when we first started traveling together, he tried to leave me at the hotel or park me in a picture show when he went out to do business. I soon put a stop to that by sobbing and acting like I was losing my breath. He started taking me along, but for a month or so he always made me wait in the car.

In those days he was doing business mostly in Bibles and pictures of the deceased. I've told you how we did business with Bibles. The procedure with pictures of the deceased was pretty much the same. Long Boy would buy up a batch of back issues of the local newspapers and go through the death notices. After making a list of what seemed to be fairly well-to-do citizens, he would go to the local photographer and see if a picture of them was on file. In most little towns there wasn't but one photographer, or, at the most, two. It's a funny thing, but photographers never seem to throw away negatives, even when it looks like they would from pride if nothing else.

If the deceased had lived in those parts long enough, there was nearly always some kind of picture of him to be had. Sometimes we got wedding pictures that went back thirty years or more. Then there was always graduation pictures, pictures taken in all sorts of uniforms, and pretty often one of those stiff, plop-colored pictures photographers call studio portraits. Long Boy usually could get a print of a picture for $1 or $1.50. He stuck it in a fancy-looking gray plaster picture frame that cost seventeen cents when ordered by the dozen from a place down in Mobile. Of course, Long Boy did business with the deceased's widow by claiming her husband had ordered the picture before he died. Most times he could get $5 or $7.50 for the picture. If the widow bawled and carried on enough, he sometimes raised the price to $10 or even $15.

What really got my goat good was Long Boy thought I was too dumb to understand what was going on. When we would pull up in front of a house where he meant to do business, he would say, "Now, you slide down in the seat and be quiet like a good girl. Folks don't like to be bothered with chillun when they do business."

All that foolishness stopped one day up in Silura. Long Boy had called on a widow and was trying to do business with an ordinary old black Bible when it turned out her brother was visiting her. He came out on the porch and it was plain he was a lawman of some sort. There was an empty pistol holster on his belt and a big blackjack was sticking out of his hip pocket. I could tell by the way the back of Long Boy's neck changed color that he was having a hard time. He was talking away with his hands sixty to the minute, but he kept easing toward the edge of the porch. I opened the car door and went running up the walk. I heard the lawman saying, "Wal, I don't see how. He didn' go nowheres near the shop for more 'n a month afore he died."

I made my voice whiney-sweet: "Daddy,

can't we go? I'm getting tired."

Well, Long Boy clutched me as gratefully as a baby calf grabs a sugar tit. "We sure can, honey pie," he said. "Daddy's jus' fixin' to leave." He smiled at the widow and her brother. "This here's my little girl." The widow gave me a sad pinched smile. Her brother stuck out his bottom lip. He had eyes like a sneaky pig. Long Boy whipped out a dollar bill and pushed it into the widow's hands. "I'm sure sorry to hear about Jim Bob, ma'am," he said. "Maybe I did get the dates a little mixed up. Anyhow, here's the dollar deposit he give me. Let me know if there's anythin' we can do."

You can bet we were down the steps and out to the car as fast as we could make it without running. Before Long Boy could get the motor started, the brother hollered from the front porch, "Hol' on there! Wait one minnit!"

Long Boy and I just sat there, not stirring, while he waddled down the walk. But what he said was "Mah sister might wanter keep that Bible. How much is it?"

Long Boy sounded as relaxed as could be. "Well, friend, the price is supposed to be six

51

dollars, but seein' as how I was so partial to Jim Bob, I reckon I won't charge no commission. You can have it for five dollars even."

The man scowled and shook his head. "Naw, sir. You gotta make a livin' same's everybody else." He gave Long Boy back the crumpled dollar bill he had given his sister. Then he dug in his wallet and found a $5 bill and handed it over. When Long Boy passed over the box with the Bible, the lawman smiled a little, as if to show he was sorry for the way he acted. "Thankee kindly," he said. "This heah's gonna be a comfort to mah sister."

Long Boy said, as solemn as a preacher, "That's what the Good Book's for, brother."

Long Boy didn't exactly sigh as we drove away, but he did kind of ooze down into the seat. He didn't say a word about what I had done, but several times I caught him looking at me in a funny way. Finally, as we were getting ready for bed and he was turning back the covers on the cot he always had brought to our room for me, he asked, "Addie, honey, could you tell old Long Boy was in trouble back at that house today?"

"Sure," I said.

"How could you tell?" he asked.

"Well, how do you think!" I said, getting cross because he thought I was so dumb. "When that old lawman came out, I was afraid he might haul your butt off to jail."

Long Boy got a little red in the face and I thought he might tell me not to talk thataway. But he just stared at me and shook his head. Then he grinned like he would split and said, "Well, if you don't beat all!"

After that, Long Boy always took me by the hand and we went up to the front door together when he did business. Long Boy just couldn't get over what a difference that made. I guess nobody was ever suspicious of a man who showed up holding a tiny child by the hand. Before long, Long Boy decided it softened up widows even more if I went up to the door first all alone. For one thing, he had this notion that if he could get a widow to unlatch the screen door and step out on the porch, she was as well as hooked. I don't know how he figured it out, but it sure worked.

To my way of thinking, there wasn't

much about salesmanship Long Boy didn't know. When he was wound up right he could sell doodle bugs for dooknobs. Like most good salesmen he was self-taught, or maybe you might say natural-born. He had gone to hear a lecture on salesmanship back some time or other, but the only thing that impressed him was the speaker had used a long word he never forgot — ramification. He twisted that word around to suit himself. When we were getting ready to start out in the morning, he might say, "Well, let's go ramify 'em, honey," or when we stopped in front of a house, he would say, "Go ramify the ol' sister, Addie sugar."

Doing business with Bibles or pictures wasn't always easy. I think I mentioned before that you never did know exactly what to expect. Like the time I went to call on the widow of a head steward of a Methodist church down in Sylacauga. She was a tall, skinny white-leather kind of woman with a mouth as tight as a spring trap. She came to the door wearing a long yellow wrapper. As soon as I said I had a C.O.D. package for her husband, she pushed open the door and snatched the box out of my hands. When she ripped it open and found a Bible, you could have heard her scream two blocks away. "A Bible!" she yelped. "Why, that whifflecattin' ol' hypocrite! That two-timin' ol' grab-ass!" She raved and carried on so I thought she might run amuck. She dropped the box and Bible on the floor, hiked up her long wrapper and kicked them down the front steps. She turned to me with her face all twisted and said, "Now, honey chile, I'll tell you what! You march right up to Bethel Cemetery with that Bible and ram it up his no-account ass!"

She was the only widow that ever got really violent. But quite a few would listen to what I had to say, then snap, "He's dead!" and slam the door in my face. Sometimes they tried to be funny and would say things like "Well, if he ordered it, dig him up and make him pay for it," or "You'll find him up at so-and-so cemetery."

Once a widow with the sweetest face listened to what I had to say, and without changing her expression a bit she made her voice cold and hard. "You see that house over yonder, hon," she said, pointing across the street. "You take your package over there and ask for Miss Poontang Tate. Tell her Mrs. Bishop sent you." She gave a mean little laugh and shut the door.

When I told Long Boy what she had said, he sighed and threw the Bible in the back seat.

Doing business with pictures in some ways was even more unpredictable. You'd be surprised how many times we had the picture of a prosperous-looking, well-set-up man that the papers had described as a "prominent farmer" or "leading citizen" and it turned out he had lived in a miserable old shack that was about to fall down. The widow of a "young civic leader" might turn out to be an undernourished, washed-out little biddy thing, living in a pigsty of a house, with young'uns glued all over her like leeches.

No matter how poor the surroundings, Long Boy and I always tried to get at least the cost of the picture and frame. Most of the time we could. Sometimes, though, a widow would grab a picture and hug it and sob that she didn't have a cent. But if they were accustomed to being dirt-poor, folks would say, "You'll hafter trust me fer a while," or "You'll hafter come back later t' git paid." That has always been the poor folks' way of saying they they don't have any money and don't have any prospects of getting any. If we saw they really couldn't get up even a dollar or two, Long Boy and I would take the picture out of the frame and give it to them.

Like with Bibles, some widows still were raving mad at their deceased husbands. Once, down near Union Springs, Long Boy handed a woman a picture of her husband that had been killed in a car wreck and she spit on it. A nice-looking, well-to-do widow in Selma laughed when I showed her a picture of her late husband. "Well, if he ordered it, I'll pay for it, baby doll," she said. "But you take it with you. I wouldn't have it in the house."

Most people weren't like this, of course. I guess, all told, Long Boy and I succeeded in doing business with about 90 percent of the widows we called on. Sometimes we hit it real lucky. Once when we called at a big white house, also near Selma, with a picture of a young man killed in a sawmill accident, it was filled with relatives who had stayed on after his funeral. We sold the picture we had for $10 and filled orders for seven more at the same price.

We made anywhere from $50 to $75 a week doing business with Bibles and pictures, and back in those days that was good money. Even after we branched out and started doing other kinds of business, we always kept a few Bibles and picture frames in the car in case we needed some cash in a hurry. It was a good steady way of doing business. After a while we just discovered ways to make more money faster.

Long Boy had always been real good at doing business with cashiers. Almost every time we stopped somewhere to eat or he bought a cigar, he made $5 on the deal. It was so easy and he was so slick that he almost never got caught. Even when he did, it was always laughed off as a perfectly natural mistake. I don't recall he ever did get caught when the cashier was young and kind of dumb and he flustered her a little first by flirting and telling her how pretty she was.

What he did was pay for whatever he

bought with a $5 bill. After he started away, he would turn back with a grin and say, "Look, my ol' wallet's getting kinda full. Give me back that five and I'll give you five ones." The cashier would get out a five and lay it on the counter. Long Boy would count out five ones slowly, giving her a little more sweet talk. When the cashier picked up the five ones, Long Boy would say, "Well, heck, I might jus' as well take a ten." Still grinning, he would toss her back the $5 she had just laid out. Without a thought, the cashier would stuff the $5 bill and five ones back in the cash register and hand him a ten.

Long Boy found doing business this way so simple and profitable that some days we didn't do anything else. We might stop at as many as ten or even fifteen drugstores and cafes. It was fun at first, and some days I just sloshed I was so full of Nehi and Orange Crush and Nu Grape. Finally, I got to where I couldn't stand soft drinks of any kind. I took to waiting in the car while Long Boy went inside for a cup of coffee or a cigar. Naturally, I didn't like this much. I think it was because I began to get so peevish as much as anything else that caused Long Boy to work out a way I could start helping him do business again.

Our big day for working together was on Saturday, when the stores were crowded. Most folks have forgotten what a big day Saturday used to be in small towns. Whether he intended to shop or just gawk, it was the day when nearly every farmer would put on a pair of clean overalls and head for the nearest town. Most of the time he brought his family with him. Not every farmer owned a car in those days either. It was a common sight to see whole families going to town in a wagon, with the women sitting in cane-bottom chairs in the back and the young'uns perched on the tailgate dangling their legs.

The streets of little towns were just thronged. Farmers with nothing else to do would hunker down with their backs to the buildings and whittle and spit, or eat boiled peanuts, and watch the crowds go by. The areas around farm mercantile stores put you in mind of a carnival. Vendors were hawking all sorts of things to eat and drink. Farm women, dressed fit to kill in their best weekday ginghams, bustled in and out of the stores, or flocked together like old hens to giggle and gossip. The menfolks moseyed along looking over the rows of plows and cultivators of various sorts set out back of the stores, stopping now and again to howdy old friends and swap stories.

Long Boy and I would do business in any store that was crowded, but we liked five-and-ten-cent stores the best. For one thing, there was always a lot of activity. But mostly it was because they always hired big dumb old girls straight off the farm who didn't have no more presence of mind than ewe sheep.

The way we did business was simple. We would go in the store separately. I'd follow along behind Long Boy, looking over things and paying him no mind until I saw the clerk he had picked to do business with. He would usually buy something he really needed, like razor blades or toothpaste or shaving soap. He would pay for it with a $20 bill. While the girl was still counting out his change, I'd saunter over to the same counter and pick out something that cost less than a dollar, like maybe a bottle of toilet water.

Most of the time one or two people would be ahead of me by the time I could get to the clerk. That always made me real nervous. I kept expecting somebody to pay for something with a $20 bill. But nobody ever did. There weren't that many $20 bills around in those days.

Anyway, when my time came I paid with a $5 bill. After the girl counted out my change, I'd turn away a little but not so far somebody else could get the girl's attention. I'd turn back and hold out the change in my hand and say, "Lady, you made a mistake." Usually that alone was enough to make her dumb, painted face get a little red. "Why, no, I didn', hon," she would say. "You give me a five."

"No, ma'am," I'd say, "I gave you a twenty-dollar bill."

Well, she'd really get blotchy red then, particularly if people were gawking. She'd open the cash register and look in to see if she had put a $20 bill in with the fives. "No, you give me a five," she'd say.

"No, ma'am," I'd say firmly. "It was a twenty-dollar bill. I know 'cause it was a birthday present from my Uncle Harry, up in Birmingham. He wrote 'Happy birthday, Dolly' across the end of it. You just look and you'll see!"

She'd look in the $20 compartment. When she saw the bill, she'd get so red and flustered that she'd just shove it at me, without saying as much as I'm sorry or kiss my foot. I'd walk out of the store looking put upon.

Every now and again I'd run across a clerk who was too dumb or too stubborn to admit she had made a mistake. I kind of enjoyed that. I'd march to the back of the store, working up tears as I went. By the time I reached the manager I'd be sobbing out loud. I'd gulp out my story to him, and he'd go back to the counter with me. When he found the $20 bill, just like I'd said, he'd give it to me and usually give the girl a dirty look or bless her out for making a mistake.

Now, I think the strangest thing about all this was that, 99 times out of 100, neither a clerk or a manager would ever think to ask me to give back the change for the $5 I had been given. It meant that instead of swapping a $5 bill for a $20 bill, what we really did was make $20, less the price of the few things we had bought.

If we started early enough, we could work three or four little towns, and maybe ten or twelve stores, on a Saturday. The money sure did start to roll in. Every Monday morning Long Boy would send off a sizable money order to the bank in Eutaw, keeping back a few dollars in the Roi Tan cigar box. He always figured we'd make enough to live on doing business as we went along.

Long Boy was kind of peculiar about money. He certainly wasn't a tightwad, because he was as generous as could be when I wanted something. But I guess I never did want much, and neither did he. I'd let him buy me a new dress now and then, mostly because he thought it tickled me, but I really didn't care much for clothes. He didn't either, and besides he didn't think it was good for business if he dressed too fancy or sported a diamond ring, and things like that. Long Boy just loved money. What he talked about most was getting together enough money to do business in a big-time way. He had the notion, and I sure couldn't find fault with it, that the thing that impressed people most was money.

"I know folks like to pretend different,

Addie baby," he said, "but it's gospel truth, all the same. If you don't believe it, you jus' take a real smart college professor an' some dumb ol' fat coot who never did nothin' except inherit a farm they discovered maybe five million dollars' worth of oil under. Jus' send them both around to the same places, and watch which one folks suck up to. It's easy enough to pass judgment on how folks should act, but like the man says, that don't he'p the houn' dawg catch the rabbit. It's how they do act that really counts. An' folks jus' mortally do kowtow to a rich man. Women 'specially act like he smells so sweet he don't need to spread lime when he goes to the outhouse."

Of course, Long Boy's conscience never pinched him at all when it came to doing business. "Most folks don't know a bloomin' thing about how business works anyway," he said. "Now you take the ordinary man, he thinks something's illegal if it's against the law. Why, that jus' don't make sense. Everybody knows those Big Mules up in Birmingham, and in places up north like Wall Street, hire lawyers full time jus' to show them how to bend the law or sneak aroun' it. There ain't nothin' illegal when it comes to business less'n you have the bad luck to get caught at it."

All the same, Long Boy was particular about staying clear of people who were doing the same kind of business we were. Traveling around like we did, we ran across them all the time. "Fool aroun' with crooks an' folks'll take you for one," he always said. About the only one Long Boy would even pass the time of day with was a funny-looking little man they called Fat Moe. Fat Moe sure was fat and not much taller than I was. When he sat in a chair in a hotel lobby his feet wouldn't touch the floor. He was always chewing on a cigar, and before I got to know him I thought he looked like an ugly little hop toad with a stick in his mouth. But Fat Moe really had the sweetest brown eyes, and he was real nice to me. He knew how much I liked coney islands, which he always called hot dogs. Some evenings when Long Boy was out and he saw me down in the hotel lobby alone, he would come over and say, "C'mon, kid, let's go down to the corner and get a dog."

Fat Moe's business was selling railroad timetable advertising. All he did was take a timetable and paste white paper over the ads to make what he called a dummy. He took this dummy around to stores and offices and sold the advertising space. Of course, he had no connection with the railroad, and after he did all the business he could, he simply blew town. Long Boy and I ran into Fat Moe in various towns for two or three years. He finally disappeared. We never did know whether he was caught or just moved on to another state.

There were lots of people around doing business with household appliances, like vacuum cleaners or electric toasters and percolators. They went around knocking on doors, offering whatever they were doing business with at about half the regular price, on any terms a housewife said she could pay. After squeezing out a down payment that could be anything from fifty cents to ten dollars, they made out a fake contract promising delivery on the appliance within ten days. Naturally, by that time they had moved on to another town.

People who did business like this were

generally sorry, no-account drifters, considered down at the bottom of the slag pile. Sometimes Long Boy and I stayed at the same hotel with somebody who was way up on top, like Judge J. B. Domingus. People said Judge Domingus had been a circuit-court judge down in Louisiana. For all I know, this could have been true. He was a wispy, frail little man who wore white suits both winter and summer, and he had the most beautiful manners. He rode around in a big old LaSalle car with a colored chauffeur named Chauncy.

Judge Domingus had been doing business with pecan trees for as long as anybody could remember. He called on well-to-do farmers and represented himself as the president of the biggest pecan-processing plant down in New Orleans. Judge Domingus even had a little booklet that showed a picture of his huge plant and told all about how it supplied pecans to markets all over the world. The biggest problem with his business, Judge Domingus told farmers, was getting enough pecans to supply the demand. If they would agree to put in a grove of pecan trees, he showed them an ironclad legal contract he was prepared to sign that guaranteed them two dollars a bushel for all the pecans they produced. Furthermore, he would pay half the cost of getting them as many fast-producing pecan trees as they needed at a special discount price of two dollars ,apiece. Some farmers were so impressed by Judge Domingus's big car and chauffeur, not to mention the fake booklet and contract, that they gave him the money to order as many as two hundred pecan trees. Big orders like that must have made Chauncy, the chauffeur, really groan. For as Judge Domingus and he went along, it was his job to cut sticks off pecan trees, tie them in bundles, and send them off to the Judge's customers.

Of all the people we met doing business, I think I was most impressed by the McGuire brothers. It may have been because I thought they were the best-looking things I had ever laid eyes on. They came from up north somewhere, and they were so clean-cut and firm-looking around the jaw that they reminded me of those young executives you see in magazine ads. The McGuire brothers did business by pretending to be government agents. They always called on the managers of the biggest stores and markets in a town. After showing fake credentials, they said they were on the trail of a gang that was passing counterfeit $10 and $20 bills. They asked the manager to let them take a look at all the bills of that size he had on hand.

One of the McGuire brothers had a little dab of a special kind of green ink on his thumb. As the manager watched, he began to lay out the $10 and $20 bills, stopping to rub one corner of about half of them with his thumb. This always made a little green smear like the ink on the bill was rubbing off. The brother would say, "Aha, thought so!" and put this bill in a separate pile. Naturally, the manager of the store was always horrified that he had been taken for so much. But the McGuire brothers assured him he didn't have anything to worry about. One of them took out an official-looking brown envelope and sealed the smeared bills in it. Before handing the manager this envelope, they impressed on him how important it was to keep it locked up tight until they could get to the nearest federal court and get an impounding order. They promised that when they returned the next afternoon with the impounding order and took the envelope, they also would reimburse him for his losses.

Of course, this gave them time to do business with all the big stores before they left a town. Sometimes a store manager would wait almost a week before he got suspicious enough and tore open the envelope. All he found inside were some neatly cut pieces of newspapers. The McGuire brothers switched envelopes while they patted him on the back and assured him he didn't have anything to worry about.

As we traveled around, we were always bumping into the same crews of hotel hustlers. When I was real small I was a regular pet of theirs. Why, some evenings when Long Boy and I reached a town late and came in a hotel lobby to register, you wouldn't believe the commotion it caused. "Girls, lookit, it's little Addie!" one of them would squeal. They would all come rushing over, fussing and exclaiming over me, like I was foreign royalty. Long Boy would stand there holding my hand, making an effort to grin, but flushed in the face and mortally looking like he could sink through the floor.

I don't recall Long Boy ever saying anything to me at all about hustlers. When I was real young, naturally, I thought they were the sweetest and cutest bunch of girls I had ever seen. They were always talking about "parties," how many "parties" they had been to the night before, or how many "parties" they had planned. For a long time, I had this vague notion that all they did was dress up pretty and run around to parties. Even after I got older and knew why they went sashaying around hotel lobbies, or why they spent so much time in fancy kimonos while bellboys brought men to their rooms, I don't think I gave it much thought.

What I remember most is the nights they would get arrested. I used to enjoy that. You see, in those days, crews of four or five hustlers worked a regular circuit. They would stay in the smaller places only a night or two before moving on. But in the bigger towns they might stay around for a week or more. In practically all the towns, they had an agreement with the police that they

72

would be arrested on a regular basis, usually once for every seven days they worked. The police would come and herd them down to the police station, then drive them back to the hotel after they had posted a $25 cash bond on charges of soliciting or disorderly conduct, or something similar. This cash bond was always forfeited, of course. It was a kind of license the girls paid.

The police were considerate about waiting until the night's work was over before they came around. This was usually late Saturday night, or rather real early on a Sunday morning. It seems to me I always woke up when the police came stomping down the hall and started knocking on doors and rounding the girls up. There was always a lot of joshing and squealing and laughing as they went off with the policemen.

But the best part was when the girls came back alone. As they walked down the hall, they used to cut up and try to outdo each other in things they said about the police. I used to lie there listening, and it was about all I could do to keep from giggling out loud. You just wouldn't believe some of the things they made up to say. If I had believed just a little part of what I heard, I sure would have had some queer ideas about how men are put together.

The hustler I liked best was a black-eyed girl named Juanita Pritle. She must have been good at her business considering the way the other girls deferred to her, but she wasn't a bit pretty. She was short and a bit on the dumpy side, and she had this hoarse, kind of breathless way of talking that made it sound like she had just run up some stairs. She just couldn't resist pretty clothes. I remember she had one dress with real monkey hair on the collar. Juanita always laughed and said clothes were the cause of her downfall. I guess it was because she was deprived as a child. The way she told it, her daddy was a well-off cotton grower and a lay preacher in the Holiness Church, but real stingy. She used to say she went around in tow-sack drawers until she was sixteen years old.

I think Juanita was kind of sweet on Long Boy, but he shied away from her like she had a stinger in her tail. One reason may have been that she always was low-rating him because of the way he took care of me. If she thought I wasn't getting to bed early enough, or if she saw me doing something like eating hot tamales real late at night, Juanita would bawl Long Boy out. "You don't know no more about raisin' a chile than a wall-eyed mule," she would say. "If you got to drag this little thing all over creation, you might at least watch after her proper." Naturally, I was just at the age where I loved to have somebody make a fuss over me, especially a woman. I would push up close to Juanita and try to look sickly and mistreated.

The truth, of course, was that Long Boy looked after me as well as he knew how. The thing that worried him most was that I wasn't in school. During the first few years we started traveling together, he was always trying to convince me how happy I would be in a boarding school somewhere. Somehow I had learned about orphans' homes. If he pressed me too hard, I would sob and carry on and accuse him of trying to put me in a home. I put on a good show, I guess, because finally Long Boy seemed to forget the difference himself. At least, when he got provoked at me he tried to scare me by threatening to put me in a home when he really meant a school.

As I got older I found a better way to deal with him. I guess I was lucky because I couldn't even remember when I didn't know how to read. By the time I was seven or eight, I was buying magazines like *True Story* or *Fact Detective* and reading them from cover to cover. I had always been interested in writing well. If I saw a handwriting I liked, I would practice copying it until I could do it letter perfect. Naturally, just doing business taught me to figure.

When Long Boy would start on me about school, I would say, "I can read and write, can't I?"

"Sure you can, hon," he would say, "but you—"

"I can figure as quick as you, can't I?" I would ask.

"Well, yeah, hon, but . . ." he would begin.

"Then what's the use of me going to school?" I would ask. "What can I learn in some old school?"

76

Long Boy would just hem and stammer
and sigh. I guess he just didn't know.

FOUR

For a long time I guess I nursed it in the back of my mind that Long Boy and I would settle down someday. I can't explain why really. Maybe it was because of this lonely, wistful feeling I used to get when we would drive through some quiet, pretty little neighborhood along about nightfall. You probably remember what it was like. The menfolks would be out in the stilly gloom-light in their shirt sleeves hosing down the lawn, while their wives rocked away on the front porch and the children ran in and out of the bushes, laughing and yelling as they played Tar Baby and Hide-and-Seek. It seemed like such a good, peaceful life that I always felt choked by a yearning to be part of it. I reckon it stirred the woman in me.

That all changed after Long Boy and I made a trip up to Birmingham to see Franklin D. Roosevelt. What happened up there finally made me realize the truth that Long Boy and I just weren't cut out from the same pattern as ordinary folks.

Going to Birmingham was my idea. I had learned somehow that Franklin D. Roosevelt's special train was going to make a stop there. I don't recall the exact occasion, but I think he had been out West somewhere and was on his way to Warm Springs, Georgia. Anyway, I made up my mind I would just die if I didn't go up to see him.

At first, Long Boy laughed at the idea. "What you wanter see that ol' booger for, baby doll? he asked. "He ain't nothin' to you."

"He's the President of the United States," I said.

"Well, shoot, hon," Long Boy said, "that don't signify nothin' 'cept he's a Big Mule politician. I wouldn't drive two hundred miles to see aller politicians in the world strip down naked and do a toe dance. They's all crookeder than a washtub of snakes anyhow."

"Franklin D. Roosevelt's no crook," I said, getting mad. "He's a great man."

Long Boy hooted. "Great man, my foot! There ain't no such thing, leastways not living. Why, you oughter know that. Ol' Roosevelt climbs into his britches one leg at a time, same's anybody else."

"Well, he's helping the poor folks," I said.

"Aw, go on, sugar," Long Boy said. "Don't go believing all that stuff. They's jus' foolin' the people with all that alphabet doasey-do about WPA an' NRA an' such. Why, ol' Roosevelt's a millionaire, from up in New York somewhere. He's never had to hit a lick o' work in his life. He wouldn't know a pore man if one walked up and bit his nose."

Of course, I finally had my way. I had to cry and pout, and Long Boy grumbled some, but on the day before Franklin D. Roosevelt was due we headed toward Birmingham.

Let me tell you, that town was some revelation. I don't mean because I was a little country girl and it was the first big city I ever saw. Oh, it seemed big enough, with big old yellow streetcars making an echoing sound as they ran between the high buildings, and traffic going every whichaway, and people thronging the streets. I mean I was surprised how people acted. Like everybody else, I had always heard that the steel mills and iron and coal mines around Birmingham attracted people of a rough and common nature. Well, it just wasn't so. I never ran across sweeter, nicer people in my life. They turned themselves inside out to be polite. Why, once when Long Boy and I tried to cross a street in the middle of the block, traffic just came to a halt as drivers stopped their cars and smiled and waved us across.

Long Boy said people were so nice because Birmingham had been hit so hard by the Depression. "They're wallowin' in the same misery together, hon. They've just plain got enough troubles without wantin' to be mean to each other."

We stayed at the Thomas Jefferson Hotel up there. It was big and clean and nice enough, but I wasn't too impressed. I had reached the point where I took hotels as they came. My big disappointment came the next morning when we started down to the L & N train depot to see Franklin D. Roosevelt. We thought we had allowed ourselves plenty of time, but it didn't look like we could get near the place. I never saw such a crowd in my life. Why, people had stopped their cars in the street and just walked away from them. I wanted to sit down somewhere and cry, I was that heartbroken.

But something like that never fazed Long Boy. "You jus' hol' my hand tight and stay close, sugar pie," he said. He made his voice real loud and official. "Step back, please!" he said. "Coming through, please!" When he spoke, people just moved aside and let us pass. When we finally reached the station, Long Boy walked right up to the first policemen he saw. He spoke like he was a G-man or something. "This little girl is Judge Smith's daughter. Judge Smith is on the train with the President. We got to get out to the platform." I thought I would die, but the policeman said, "Yessir, follow me." He began to shoulder through the crowd, saying, "Open up! Stan' aside!"

The policeman took us right out to the platform where there was a band and all the important people with badges were waiting around for the President. He pointed to some white marks on the platform. "The

President's car oughter be stoppin' right about heah," he said.

"Thank you, Officer," Long Boy said. "Can I ask your name?"

"Ware, sir," the policeman said. "Henry Ware."

"Thank you, Officer Ware," Long Boy said. "I won't forget this."

Officer Ware got red in the face and looked like he was trying to wag his tail. "Jes' let me know if I can he'p some more," he said. After he went away, Long Boy squeezed my hand and gave me a smirky wink. The old fool.

I wish I could tell you something historic about Franklin D. Roosevelt. I guess no child ever got a better look at a President. After his train finally came in, Long Boy lifted me down on the tracks and I was right at the foot of the observation platform where he stood. I almost could have reached out and touched him. I could even see the hairs growing out of his nose and ears. If I had wanted to, I could have counted the big old liver spots on his hands.

Mind you, I knew how lucky I was. I was so excited I could hardly breathe when he first came out on the platform. I kept telling myself I had to remember every single little thing I saw and heard so that when I got to be an old lady I could tell my grandchildren all about it. But then I got distracted by Franklin D. Roosevelt's poor feet. I guess everybody knows he was crippled. That's why he went to Warm Springs, Georgia, all the time. But nobody ever talked about how crippled he really was, probably because it wasn't a nice thing to do. Maybe it still isn't, but I want to tell the truth. I was just shocked.

Why, he couldn't walk a step. He was leaning on a man, and he would kind of shift his body and let his feet swing forward in a shuffle. My head was right even with his light tan shoes. They didn't have any marks or creases, but looked stiff and unnatural, like shoes on a dummy in a department store. There were two cruel shiny steel braces running alongside each shoe. I know I must have heard what Franklin D. Roosevelt said that day, but I can't recall a word. What I remember most is those stiff, unmarked shoes and how shocked and sad I felt. It was a good thing I didn't get a chance to talk to him. I'm sure I would have started crying and blurted out, "Mr. President, I'm so sorry about your poor feet. It shouldn't have happened to a man as great and good as you."

It's funny how two people can feel so different about the same thing. After Franklin D. Roosevelt's train pulled out, I felt like I wanted to go off by myself and think on what I saw and maybe cry a little. But Long Boy hadn't been the least bit impressed. I doubt if he paid much attention to Franklin D. Roosevelt at all. All he kept doing was looking over the crowd and trying to think of some way to cash in on the enthusiasm. "Man, oh, man!" he said. "There oughter be some way of doing business with a pack of people like this."

He found a way, too. As we were leaving the station, he spied one of the posters that had been put up all over the place. I think it said, WE ARE BEHIND YOU ALL THE WAY, MR. PRESIDENT. In the center was a real good drawing of Franklin D. Roosevelt, with some furled flags and an inscription in old-timey print that said, OUR PRESIDENT. Long Boy stopped so quick he almost yanked my arm off. Long Boy studied the poster a minute, then went over and got the printer's name off the corner. When he turned around, he was grinning.

We didn't even go back to the hotel for the car, but took a taxi out to the printing plant. It was a messy little one-man operation in a rundown section of town. Long Boy asked the printer, "You got any more of those Roosevelt posters?"

"No, sir," the man said, "but I'm still all set up. I can run you some off."

"How much you askin'?" Long Boy said.

"Seein' as how I'm all set up, ten dollars a hundred," the man said.

"How about jus' the picture?" Long Boy asked. "On a piece of cardboard ten by twelve."

"Well, I'll have to trim down the regular stock," the man said. He picked up a pencil and figured awhile and said, "Seven dollars a hundred's the bes' I can do."

"I'll take two hundred," Long Boy said. "I'll pick them up first thing in the morning." He counted out the man's money and asked, "Whereabouts can I find a good picture-frame company?"

The man sent us to a big picture-frame company near the center of town. Of course, getting plain black ten-by-twelve frames was no problem. Long Boy got a gross and a half for about twenty-two dollars.

That's how we started doing business with pictures of Franklin D. Roosevelt. We sat in the car the next morning and stuck maybe thirty or forty pictures in frames before we started calling on stores. It was the most amazing thing. Most of the time we wouldn't even have to say a word. As soon as a storekeeper saw the picture we were holding, he'd say, "How much?" We'd say, "One dollar." He'd go to the cash register and punch it *ting-a-ling* and get out a dollar bill and hand it over. Before we left the store, he'd be hanging the picture behind the counter.

After a couple of hours Long Boy said, "We ain't chargin' enough. Start askin' a dollar and a half." That didn't make the slightest difference. About mid-afternoon Long Boy said, "We still ain't askin' enough. From now on they's two dollars."

A few storekeepers balked at that price, but not enough to matter. It was plain Long Boy had really hit on something. We sure did sell those pictures.

But it was hard work. We dragged ourselves back to the hotel that evening just fagged out. I was so tired and my feet ached so that I hardly ate any supper. Long Boy's appetite wasn't much better.

We started out again early the next morning. The pictures sold as fast as ever, but I was beginning to realize the big problem in doing business that way. It just involved too much walking, and it took too long to go from store to store. Besides, it was hot, and Long Boy and I both had worn holes in our fingers pushing the little nails back in the picture frames after we put in the pictures. We began getting cross and cranky when we talked to each other.

As the day went on, things got worse. We began to run out of stores right in the downtown area, and we had to shift to the outskirts where stores were even farther apart. About two o'clock, I came back to the car for more pictures and found Long Boy sitting in the front seat, scowling and making figures on the back of an envelope. He turned on me like I was bad luck. "You know how many pictures we've done sold?" he asked.

"A lot," I said.

"No, we ain't" he said, sounding real aggravated. "I figger no more'n ninety-one or nintey-two."

"Well, that's a lot," I said.

"No, it ain't," he said. "It's plumb miserable, I'm thinkin'.'

"Well, how we going to sell them any faster, Mr. Smarty?" I said, getting mad myself. "I near about walked my legs off as it is."

"Now, now, honey," Long Boy said, "don't go flarin' up. I wasn't pickin' on you. I was jus' tryin' to give you the facts." He pointed to the envelope. "Lookit, we've taken in a hundred and thirty-nine dollars. When you deduct the cost of the pictures and frames, you can see we've pert near kilt ourselves for somethin' like a hunnert dollars."

"That's not so bad," I said, still feeling a little sulky.

"It's bad when you consider we're

wearin' ourselves down to a nub walkin' aroun' this way," Long Boy said. "That's the trouble with doin' business legitimate. There ain't no sense people killin' themselves when they can make jus' as much money easy as fallin' off'n a log."

When I just sat there, not saying anything, he asked, "Well, is there?"

"No, I reckon not," I said. I had been thinking. He didn't mention it, so I didn't either, but as far as I was concerned the worst thing about doing business legitimate was that there was no excitement to it. I think I could have stood the drudgery if selling a picture of Franklin D. Roosevelt gave me the same kind of tingle I felt when I did other kinds of business.

Long Boy turned to me with a big grin. "You know what I'm gonna do?"

"What?" I asked.

"I'm gonna go outer this business right now," he said. "I think it's kinder beneath us. Besides, it ain't any good for my disposition, an' it sho is about to ruin my feet."

Of course, that's what we did. We put the picture frames in the trunk of the car and tied the pictures of Franklin D. Roosevelt in a bundle. When we got to the edge of town, Long Boy stopped the car and heaved the bundle down into a big ravine. We didn't say anything about it, maybe we didn't even think about it at the time, but I guess we both knew that put an end to doing business legitimate as far as we were concerned.

We spent that night in Tuscaloosa. Maybe it was because we were so tired that we both had trouble sleeping. I lay awake for the longest sort of time, and I heard Long Boy turning and punching his pillow and muttering to himself. Finally, just as I was about to drop off, I heard him say softly, "Addie, honey, you asleep?"

"Just one eye," I said.

He cleared his throat. "Well, I been thinkin', honey, that maybe it's time we quit all this two-bitting aroun'. We oughter commence doin' business in a big way."

"What kind of business?" I said, coming awake fast.

"Well, business for big money," he said. "I mean real folding money. 'Course it means we gotter take more risks."

"That don't scare me none," I said.

91

"They can't put a little chile like me in jail."

"Don't make jokes about it," he said.

"I'm not joking," I said. "What kind of business?"

"Oh, there's several kinds," he said, "but I think maybe you 'n' me could work best doing business with dropped wallets.'

"How do we go about it?" I asked.

"Well, I'll tell you," Long Boy said. "First off you gotta find somebody . . ."

FIVE

I'll tell you the honest truth. When Long Boy first explained to me how to do business with dropped wallets, I thought he must have left something out. It just didn't seem reasonable that anybody with the brains of a piss ant could be taken in so easy. Of course, I didn't have any experience then of how dazzled the ordinary person becomes when he thinks he's getting something for nothing. This is especially true if you look around and find somebody with one-way pockets who's not too honest to begin with. Give folks like that a whiff of free money, and they get as shortsighted as a hog at the slop trough.

We started out by dropping wallets that didn't have but $100. For a week or so, I picked old ladies to do business with. They were easy to find, out shopping and all, but I guess, too, I was partial to old ladies. They always seemed to take a shine to me and weren't hard to handle. Long Boy didn't say anything, at first, because mostly we were practicing and getting things down pat anyway. But, finally, he had enough. "I don't wanter waste time with no more old sisters," he said. "I don't care how simple they look. You gotter commence pickin' men with fat pockets, baby doll. We ain't gonna get money if we don't go where it's at."

Well, I started picking men after that, and I can't say they appeared to be any harder to deal with than old ladies. May be they were even easier, because they didn't seem inclined to balk at all at the idea of taking what they thought was money belonging to somebody else. They acted like it was just smart business. In no time at all, we were doing business with wallets that had $250. After a week or two, we raised this to $300, then $400, and, finally, hit on $500 as just the right amount when doing day-to-day business.

I can't begin to remember all the towns we worked the balance of that summer—Marion, Centreville, Brent, Prattville, and even some tiny places like Boligee and Bogueloosa. We made some bad mistakes, I'll tell you. Sometimes it seemed like nothing went right. But we didn't miss but twice, and I don't think they were outright failures. What happened was people we were doing business with went to the bank to get the money, and when they didn't come back within ten or fifteen minutes, Long Boy and I just hauled freight out of there. Long Boy never took chances with the police. "I promise you, honey," he always said, "if we get caught, it won't be while we're a-standin' still."

He was sure slick at doing business with dropped wallets. He had taken to using what I guess you might call disguises. He had different kinds of work clothes, and he passed himself off as everything from a railroad man to a state road inspector. A couple of times he put his hat square on his head and stuck on a pair of five-and-ten-cent-store glasses and pretended he was a Baptist preacher. Of course, I didn't do so bad either. After all, I had to pick the people we did business with all by myself.

Toward the end of the summer, we drove down to southeast Alabama. The big money crop down there was peanuts, and by all reports it was real good. Long Boy had been raised down that way and he knew all the best towns to work. We decided we would start at Dothan, which was a county seat and had some of the biggest peanut-oil mills. We got there late one afternoon and scouted around in the car so Long Boy could show me the street where the peanut-oil mills had little offices. Like always, we also carefully went over what we were going to do when we did business the next day. Then we headed for Enterprise, about thirty miles away, to spend the night. We never stayed at a hotel in a town where we did business with wallets. That was so if the police came looking for us later, there wouldn't be anybody to give a description of us, or maybe tell what kind of car we were driving.

As we drove along, Long Boy said real casual, "I reckon we'll use a wallet with fifteen hunnert dollars tomorrow."

At first I thought he was kidding. When I saw he wasn't, all I could do was stare at him.

He laughed. "What's the matter, cutie? Cat got your tongue?"

"You're plumb crazy," I said. "That's too much money."

He grinned at me. "No it ain't," he said. "Why, shecks, hon, I know these ol' goober farmers down here. Hard times or no, lots of 'em 'll cash in mill vouchers for a thousand dollars or more. An' they'll be totin' the whole wad aroun' in their pockets. Lots of 'em don't trust banks, but even those that do like to walk aroun' town with their money for a while, so they can run their fingers through it and squeeze on it.'

"Well, how am I supposed to know who they are?" I asked.

"Oh, you'll find one," Long Boy said. "You can smell out money like a honey bee smells out woodbine."

I smiled at that. The old fool.

Long Boy said, "Jus' don't bother with no stooped-over, sun-cured ol' farmers with deep gullies acrost the back of their necks. Take your time, an' walk aroun' till you find a big old pink farmer with a bay window wearin' a clean suit of overalls. One that's lookin' like he thinks he's flat-footed wonderful. That's the kind that has the money. Or he'll be able to lay his hands on it. Don't you worry about that."

But I did worry. Especially that night

97

after Long Boy took a fifty-cent wallet and aged it up some by rubbing it across the bathroom floor and then filled it with $1,500 in fifties, twenties and tens. I believe it was the most money I had ever seen in one pile up to that time. It sure did make some play-pretty to dangle in front of a goober farmer.

When we got in the car to go to Dothan the next morning, I felt nervous as a cat with deaf kittens. But Long Boy was as unconcerned as could be, humming and whistling away like it was an ordinary day. A mile or two outside Dothan he stopped the car and slipped into the kind of striped overalls with a jumper that railroad men wear. This time he even put on an engineer's cap and tied a bandanna around his neck. We drove on to Dothan and parked the car near the courthouse. He handed me the heavy old wallet and grinned. "Let's go ramify a big fat farmer, honey," he said.

Well, I did some walking that morning. Just up and down the block. Lots of farmers were going in and out of the peanut-oil-mill offices, but none of them seemed right. I guess I walked better than an hour, but it seemed longer. Long Boy must have felt the same way. Every now and then I caught a glimpse of him up in the next block, moseying along looking in windows.

Finally, the right kind of man did come out of one of the offices. Why, Long Boy had described him almost to a T. He had a pink face and enough of a potbelly to hitch up his clean overalls in front. He looked like the kind of farmer who owned a commissary and rode around in a pickup truck telling field workers what to do. He took off spraddle-legged up the street, and I was right behind him. He stopped at the corner and leaned back against Blumberg's Department Store, standing on one foot with the other one back against the wall to prop him up. He seemed to be surveying the world like he owned it.

I stayed as close to the buildings as I could. When I was about ten feet from the man, I made sure he wasn't looking my way, then let the wallet slip out from under my jacket onto the sidewalk. I made a loud little noise of surprise and pounced on it. He heard me all right. When I straightened up, he was looking at me. Like men always did, he gave his pocket an automatic pat to be sure the wallet wasn't his. I just stood there holding the wallet, looking like I didn't know what to do. I held it out and walked toward him. "Mister," I asked, "did you drop this?"

He just looked kind of superior. Both his eyeteeth were gold and he wore rimless eyeglasses. "Why, no, I did'n', little lady," he said. "It ain't mine."

I looked helpless. "Well, I found it," I said.

"So you did," he said. He held out his hand. "Well, le's see if we can fin' out who it b'longs to."

As soon as he felt the wallet, his expression changed. When he opened it and saw all that money, he looked like he stopped breathing for maybe half a minute. He just stood there stone-still. Then he stuck out the tip of his tongue and ran it across his lips, and, you won't believe it, the first thing he did was count the money. He took his time about it, too, making sure none of the bills stuck together. When he finished, he stood there with a dazed look in his eyes.

"What do I do, mister?" I asked.

"Oh," he said. For the first time he began to examine the wallet to see if there was a name in it. When he couldn't find one, he said, "Well, now, I reckon . . . I guess, er . . ."

Just then Long Boy came swinging around the corner, looking like he had just parked his locomotive. I gave a little squeal and said, "Here's my daddy!" I ran toward Long Boy. "Daddy, I found a man's wallet with some money it it!"

Long Boy smiled and made his voice humoring. "Well, did you now." He grinned at the man like he was asking him to forgive a child's foolishness. "Howdy," he said.

"Howdy," said the man, not cracking a smile. Without a word, he handed Long Boy the wallet.

Long Boy took it and his own grin flickered out. "Lawsey mercy!" he said in a shocked voice. "This here thing's fulla money." He ran his thumb over the bills. "Why, there mus' be four, five hunnert dollars."

"There's fifteen hunnert even," the man said, real solemn.

10

"Naw!" Long Boy let his jaw sag. He gave a low whistle. He thought that over a second or two, then he began to tear into the wallet like he was looking for a name.

"There ain't no name, er no cards, er nothin'," the man said. "I done looked."

"No name!" said Long Boy, sounding shocked. "Why, what kinda durn fool . . ." He shook his head and looked thoughtful. Finally he said, "Well, I reckon we oughter . . ." Suddenly he stopped and looked over his shoulder. Some people were passing. He cut his eyes around like he wanted to be sure nobody was watching. He made his voice low. "What say we go somewhere and talk 'bout this. Le's walk up t'wards the courthouse."

"Suits me," said the man.

As we started across the street, Long Boy stuck out his hand. "My name's Sam Renfrow. I engineer for the Short Line."

The man took his hand. "Goolsby. Tom Goolsby. I do a little farmin'." He hadn't taken his eyes off the wallet.

When we reached the stone fence around the courthouse square, Long Boy stopped. "I reckon what we oughter do with this here money is take it to the police," he said. He looked at Mr. Goolsby. Mr. Goolsby just looked back for a while, then nodded.

"The big trouble," said Long Boy, "is I really don't trust them sorry sapsuckers much. More 'n likely they'll jus' divide it up amongst themselves."

"That's what I was a-thinkin'," Mr. Goolsby said.

"I sure don't want nothin' that don't b' long t' me," Long Boy said. "I jus' ain't that kinder man. But if nobody claims this wallet, I think it's only right mah little girl is entitled to seven hunnert and fifty dollars. Reckon you feel the same way 'bout yo' share?"

At this point people sometimes made a show of protesting that I had found the money and it was all mine. But it was plain Mr. Goolsby had dealt himself in from the start. "I sho do," he said. "Right's right."

Long Boy gave a little laugh. " 'Course, I don't feel too much sympathy f' no durn fool that toted aroun' this much money in a billfold with no name on it. Looks t' me like he was askin' for trouble."

"Probably was drunk," said Mr. Goolsby.

"Might have stole it," Long Boy said.

"Wouldn't put it pas' him," said Mr. Goolsby.

" 'Course, I ain't one for courtin' trouble neither," Long Boy said. "I never been in no trouble with the law in mah whole life, thank th' Lawd. I try t' do right."

"Same with me," said Mr. Goolsby. "I ain't so much 's had my foot inside a jail."

Long Boy sort of sighed and put his hand on my head. "I wouldn't mind seein' mah little girl get seven hunnert and fifty dollars, though," he said.

Mr. Goolsby cleared his throat. "Well, like the feller says, finder's keepers."

Long Boy gave him a slow smile, then shook his head and stuck out his bottom lip and seemed to be pondering. After a while he grinned and snapped his fingers. He turned to me. "I know what I'll do, honey. I oughter thought of it sooner. I'll call Cousin Aaron."

I made a big grin like I was tickled silly. "Cousin Aaron'll know what to do," I said.

Mr. Goolsby was looking at us kind of

sour. Long Boy turned to him. "Reckon you know Aaron Renfrow," he said, naming the biggest lawyer in the county. "He's mah first cousin."

"I've heered of him," Mr. Goolsby said. He hesitated a moment, then cleared his throat. "I ain't trying to tell you yo' business, but if you get tangled up with them lawyer fellows, it —"

"Aaron?" Long Boy cut in, laughing. "Don't worry none. Ol' Aaron's the bes' frien' I got in the world." He pushed the wallet into Mr. Goolsby's hands and gave me a pat on the head. "Now, you wait here with Mr. Goolsby, sugar," he said, "while I go in the courthouse and use the phone to call Cousin Aaron."

Mr. Goolsby sat down on the stone fence and began fondling the wallet. I climbed up beside him. "My daddy's a train engineer," I said.

"So he tol' me," Mr. Goolsby said.

"We live up in Cottonwood," I said. "In a brick house."

"Is 'at so," he said.

"Whereabouts you live?" I asked.

"Out near Ardilla," he said.

"My daddy's treasurer of the Methodist church," I said.

"Is 'at so," he said.

"That's why we's in town," I said. "Daddy had to come in and draw some money out of the church fund at the bank. They got to put a new roof on the church."

"Is 'at so," he said.

"Whereabouts you go to church?" I asked.

"Why, we go t' th' Pentecostal church," he said.

"They's nice people," I said.

By the time Long Boy came back, I had Mr. Goolsby telling me about his children. Long Boy was grinning. "Reckon it pays t' have a lawyer in the family," he said. "That money's as good as our'n."

"How's 'at?" asked Mr. Goolsby.

"Well, ain't nothin' to it, really," Long Boy said. "Aaron says the law's plain as can be. All you gotta do is post a bond for the same amount as the money you found to prove you ain't no crook or nothin'. Then you advertise in the paper that you foun' it. If it ain't claimed in seven days, the money's yours, free and legal." He gave Mr.

Goolsby a big wink and laughed. "Only thing is, th' law don't specify where you gotter advertise. Cousin Aaron's gonna put an ad in a little bitty paper 'way up in Troy."

For the first time Mr. Goolsby smiled a little. It looked like he was about to squeeze out a tiny laugh. "Well, God dog," he said, "if that don't beat all!"

Long Boy stopped smiling and looked embarrassed. "Mr. Goolsby, I don't mean no offense," he said, "but Cousin Aaron said I oughter do this. He won't be back in his office until four o'clock this afternoon, an' I got a run scheduled for two o'clock. I'll be highballing some ol' engine along down aroun' Quincey at four, so I'll have to give you mah share of the bond now. It means I'll . . . well, it means I'll have to trust you with a lot o' money. It jus' makes sense t' ask you to show me some kinder identification—jus' to prove you're who you say you are."

This was what Long Boy always called the cruncher.

"Why, sho," Mr. Goolsby said. "Business's business." He reached in his pocket and pulled out a worn old wallet.

"Heah's mah Houston County Livestock Breeders card" he said, "mah VFW card . . . mah tax receipt . . . mah—"

"That's enough," Long Boy said. He smiled kind of shame-faced. "I wouldn' asked you at all, 'cept t' tell you the truth, th' money I'm gonna give you ain't really mine. It b'longs to mah church, but I reckon they won't need it for a few days. It's lucky I had it on me."

"Well, it takes money t' make money," Mr. Goolsby said.

"I'm thinkin' you'll be wantin' t' go to th' bank?" Long Boy said.

"No, sir, I can manage mah share," Mr. Goolsby said.

Long Boy looked amazed. "You mean y' carry much as seven hunnert and fifty dollars 'roun' with you?" he asked.

Mr. Goolsby looked smug. "Sometimes I do," he said.

Long Boy looked real impressed. "Well, we gotter put the money we foun' and our cash bond in an envelope, seal it, and sign it acrost the flap," he said. "When you see Cousin Aaron he'll put a seal on it and notarize it. Then you can leave it with him in his safe, or take it home with you — only please don't lose it, Mr. Goolsby."

"How much's he gonna charge us?" Mr. Goolsby asked.

"Cousin Aaron?" Long Boy looked surprised. "Why, nothin', man. I tol' you he was mah bes' frien'." He laughed. "Oh, I reckon we'll have to pay for the newspaper ad."

Long Boy turned to me. "Run in the courthouse, honey girl, and ask the folks in the county clerk's office t' give you the biggest envelope they got. Jus' tell 'em it's for Daddy."

I ran into the courthouse and found a kind of dark place behind the big old staircase. I hiked up my dress and pulled out the envelope I was carrying next to my belly under the elastic on my pants. After waiting around about a minute, I ran back outside. Long Boy already had his money in his hand. Mr. Goolsby reached in his overalls pocket and pulled out a small roll of brand-new bills. He counted off seven crisp $100 bills and one $50. Long Boy emptied out the wallet and put all the money together and stuck it in the envelope and licked the flap. After sealing the envelope, he hefted it and grinned. "Man alive," he said, "that's sure some pile!'

Long Boy asked Mr. Goolsby for his pen. He put the envelope on the stone wall to sign it across the flap. "This ain't smooth enough," he said. He laughed. "Turn aroun', Neighbor Goolsby, an' let me use your back." Mr. Goolsby turned around, and quick as a wink Long Boy had slipped the envelope into his pocket and pulled out one just like it we had stuffed with pages cut out of a Sears, Roebuck catalogue. After he signed, he laughed some more and turned around and let Mr. Goolsby use his back.

Long Boy smiled at Mr. Goolsby. "Now you be at Cousin Aaron's office in the First National Bank Building at four o'clock sharp. I'll keep in touch with Cousin Aaron, but I reckon we'll be meetin' there about a week from today to divide up the money." He stuck his hand out. "I sure ain't gonna forget you, Mr. Goolsby," he said.

Mr. Goolsby shook his hand and tried another little smile. "I reckon we brought one another luck," he said.

SIX

Long Boy always liked to brag that we finally got too big for Alabama. But that's not completely true—in fact, I don't reckon there's any truth in it at all. I've always felt we probably could have gone on doing business in Alabama for the rest of our lives if Long Boy hadn't made a big fool of himself over Miss Trixie Delight. It's sure a fact that if Long Boy hadn't been showing off in front of Trixie he never would have bought a fancy yellow car that made us as conspicuous as two turds in a punch bowl. Maybe if he hadn't been mooning over Trixie we never would have landed in the mess that made us run for the state line.

I wish I didn't have to tell you about Trixie. She was just plain bad luck. Besides, I can't say I'm exactly proud of how I got rid of Trixie. That's not to say I'm ashamed of it either. Watching after a man is a hard, worrisome thing. Any woman who hopes to do the job right can't be too particular about the methods she uses.

It all began when Long Boy and I drove up to Cullman for the big tri-county fair they hold there. Strawberries are the main money crop up that way, and we were hoping to do business with a wallet or two. After walking around the fairgrounds just once, we saw there wasn't much chance of that. Most of the big strawberry growers are Germans, and I guess you know Germans are cautious, barkbound folks, especially when it comes to money. They sure had taken some precautions against crookery. Everywhere you looked there was a big nosey old special policeman. If you had so much as stooped over to pick up a wallet, I guess a couple of them would have stumbled over you. Long Boy sized up things and was ready to leave, but I pleaded with him to stay.

I can't explain this exactly. Nothing aggravates me more than to hear some sentimental old fool gushing about the joys of childhood. Anybody with a speck of honesty knows better than that. Growing up is a downright painful experience, and being real young is plain humiliating. Still, I reckon there are a few bonafide joys of childhood, and maybe a child's first fair is one of them. Or maybe it was just me. Maybe that fair sort of made up for the fairy tales I had never been told and the children's books I had never read. Anyway, the noise and the smells and the sights of that little old fair just knocked me lopsided with wonder. To this day, whenever I smell sugar browning in a pan I can close my eyes and remember plain as day how disbelieving I was when a skinny little redheaded woman took a paper cone and spun me up my very first gob of pink cotton candy. I remember the first time I ever tried to bite into a candied apple on a stick, and how my heart almost jumped out of my mouth the first time a ferris wheel stopped and left me swinging right up at the very top.

I was lucky, of course. Not many children, especially during those hard times, ever got all the money to spend at a fair that they wanted. Long Boy gave me any amount I asked for. Let me tell you, I did that fair thoroughly. I saw everything at least once, and I rode everything two or three times. I was usually there when the gates opened, and I didn't leave at night until a short, bowlegged man climbed a tall, shaky ladder up to a tiny platform and did a backward somersault into a tank of water that had gasoline burning on top. I remember he called himself the Great Sinbad. Every night, when he climbed out of the tank grinning and waving his arms, a big pretty girl, twice his size, came rushing up and wrapped him in a robe and kissed him.

It's funny what people paid good money to see in those days. Why, one of the big attractions on the midway was the Living Stone Man. You paid a dime and went inside, and there, stretched out on a folding cot, was a poor wasted old man, wearing a kind of diaper. It was easy to see he was suffering from some kind of horrible disease that had paralyzed him solid. After enough people had gathered, a fat, sweating man came inside and picked up a little wooden mallet and tapped the paralyzed man on different parts of his body, *thunk, thunk.* "Do you feel that, Living Stone Man?" he would call out. "Do you feel me hammerin' on you?" The old man answered in a hoarse croak, "No, I don't feel a thing. My body is solid stone."

In another tent there was a man who had had part of his head sheared off in an accident. I've forgotten what they called him, but there were big paintings outside showing a man with his whole brain exposed and signs that said, SEE A LIVING HUMAN BRAIN. Of course, it wasn't like that at all. You went inside and there was an ordinary-looking man, wearing a black skull cap, sitting down and reading a newspaper. After a while, he put his paper aside and stood up and gave a spiel about how he was the world's greatest medical oddity, how big doctors had come from all over the world to study his brain. Then he took off his skull cap, and sure enough you could see a part of his brain bulging under a thin layer of skin.

But the biggest attraction of all was the Half Man, Half Woman, SEE NATURE'S MISTAKE—A GENUINE HUMAN HERMAPHRODITE. Well, people sniggered and giggled at this, but they paid their dimes and thronged in anyway, expecting to be cheated. They weren't, though. Oh, I don't mean they saw anything like the pictures outside—you know, a beautiful woman and a handsome man joined together. But it always had seemed to me that show was awfully unusual, considering the times and how nicey-nice everybody was expected to be. I guess one reason they got by with it was because there was a canvas partition down the center of the tent. The men and boys went on one side and the women and girls went on the other.

There was a platform at one end of the tent, and after a while a plump little gray-haired man, wearing a plain blue robe, climbed up on it and began to speak in a soft voice. He said he was fifty-four years old and had been born with the sexual organs of both a man and a woman. He said that up until the time he was fifteen he had dressed and lived as a young girl, but then, because he began to feel he was more like a man than a woman, he had switched to male clothes. He said doctors were always curious about him, and lots of them had examined him and studied him, but none of them knew how to help him. After that, he slipped off his robe and stood there stark naked. He sure looked like a woman, all right—a young woman. His plump, white little body, with its small protruding breasts, didn't seem to bear any relation to his white hair and fifty-four-year-old face. After everybody got a good look, he reached up inside himself and pulled out his male organs—a tiny little peter and two balls.

Nobody was still giggling when they left that show. They had seen almost exactly what they paid to see, but they weren't happy about it. I guess that's human nature. Most folks had rather be cheated than see something that makes them uncomfortable.

Maybe one reason I remember the Half Man, Half Woman so well is that he was living at the same hotel where Long Boy and I were staying. I used to see him in the dining room every morning at breakfast and sometimes in the lobby late at night when he came back from the fairgrounds. He was a neatly dressed little man, with his long white hair carefully combed, except where it scraggled around his collar. He kind of scurried along when he walked, never raising his eyes, but looking down at the floor. I felt so sorry for him. One morning when he was coming out of the front door of the hotel and I was going in, I spoke to him without thinking. "Good morning, mister."

You'll never believe what a pleased, grateful smile he gave me. He stopped and looked around, like he was hoping everybody had seen me speak to him. "Why, good morning to you, young lady," he said. He was still smiling when he scurried across the sidewalk and got in a dime taxi that was waiting at the curb.

I've always regretted I almost lost track of Long Boy during the week I spent at that fair. He was always around close at hand, of course. I just didn't keep my eye on him like I should. Naturally, I knew he was spending a lot of time hanging around a show on the midway called the Sultan's Harem. But that didn't seem strange. Lots of men were hanging around the Sultan's Harem, especially after ten o'clock at night when every other show was for men only. What I saw of the Sultan's Harem sure didn't appeal to me—a bunch of big old girls thumping around in sleazy costumes. I knew, too, that Long Boy sometimes went out at night after he dropped me at the hotel, but I was used to that.

It wasn't until the night before we left Cullman that I knew something unusual was up. After clearing his throat like he always did when he was up to something, Long Boy said, "Er . . . honey, I promised a lady a ride down to Mobile when we leave tomorrow. A lady and her maid."

That surprised me. "Mobile!" I said. "I didn't know we were going to Mobile."

"Why, sure," he said. "I been meanin' to go down that way a long time. We can do lotsa good business in Mobile."

I knew that was a lie. I could always tell when Long Boy was lying. The bigger the lie, the more sincere he sounded.

"What's the lady's name?" I asked.

"Uh . . . Miss Delight," he said. "Trixie Delight."

"That's a funny name," I said.

Long Boy gave a little laugh. "Aw, that's jes' a stage name. People in show business always have fancy names, sugar. She's a dancer."

"The Sultan's Harem?" I asked.

I didn't change my expression. I made sure I didn't. But Long Boy got a little red in the face. "Now, hon," he said, "don't go

119

gettin' any wrong ideas about this girl. She's a real lady. That's one reason she's leavin' the Sultan's Harem. She thinks the folks out there are kinder common an' ordinary. This girl comes from a good family. Why, she's got a high-school diploma."

Well, the next morning Long Boy and I drove out to a boarding house near the fairgrounds to pick up Trixie Delight and her maid. We had to wait a couple of hours while Trixie got out of bed and got dressed, of course. Trixie was never on time for anything in her life. But I guess that didn't seem so important at the time. And I won't tell you a lie—when Trixie finally did get dressed and came out to the car, I was just bowled over. I won't say I thought she was the best-looking woman I ever saw, but she was sure the most striking.

For one thing, Trixie had platinum blond hair. Maybe you've forgotten how unusual that was in those days. Only a few women were brave enough to fool around with their hair, especially to lighten it. Those that did used peroxide or henna. I never did find out how Trixie learned to bleach her hair platinum, but as far as I know the only other woman who had hair that color at the time was Jean Harlow, the big movie star. Trixie's skin was as creamy white as a magnolia bud. She made it look even whiter because she dyed her eyebrows and used so much mascara that her dark brown eyes seemed black.

Trixie had a good figure, a little on the heavy side, but I don't guess most people looked past her bosom. Oh, my, that bosom! If Grant had met up with breastworks like that, he never would have taken Vicksburg. You've heard about women looking like they were poured into their clothes? Trixie looked like she had been pumped into hers. She liked to wear tight sweaters, and when she walked along everything from her waist up seemed to joggle and strain at the moorings, like she suddenly might float right up to the ceiling.

Now, I don't want to give the impression that Trixie was a great beauty. After you studied her awhile, you could see that her nose was a little too thin and pointed and her eyes were too close together. Besides, she had a mouth that was kind of loose and stupid. But when Trixie walked in somewhere, women would nudge each other and men would pop their eyes and sit up straight. It was easy to see why Long Boy thought she was really something on a stick.

I'll give Trixie credit for one thing. She never did make a big fuss over me because she thought it would impress Long Boy, like some girls did. As far as she was concerned, I was just part of the scenery. Anyway, I wore a skirt. Trixie was one of those women who are bored and listless when a man's not around. You know the kind I mean. When Trixie and I were alone, all I could ever get out of her was a "Yeah, that's right," or "I guess so, kiddo." She would yawn and scratch herself or buff her nails and champ away on a cud of chewing gum. But let Long Boy, or anybody else in pants, come in and she would perk up and laugh and talk and bat her eyes. Trixie needed a man to prime her pump.

On that first morning when she came out to the car she rushed up to Long Boy with a big toothy smile and squealed and gushed about how sorry she was to keep him waiting. When Long Boy introduced me, she nodded absently and said, "Hullo, kiddo." Then she just stood by the front door of the car, waiting, while I sat there gawking at her. Finally, Long Boy cleared his throat. "Addie, baby, maybe you'd better ride in the back seat awhile."

Naturally, I didn't like that. I didn't see why giving Trixie Delight a ride to Mobile entitled her to my seat. But I just nodded like a polite little girl and climbed into the back seat with Trixie's colored maid.

The maid's name was Imogene. She was a little bitty girl, with big eyes, and skin exactly the color of an old penny. She was so tiny, in fact, that I wondered if she might be stunted until I found out later that she was barely fifteen. Imogene and I got to be good friends later, as you'll see, but, I swear, for a while on that first morning I thought she was about the dumbest, most sullen thing I had ever seen. If I asked her a question, she just grunted and mumbled. If I made a comment about something, she would turn and whittle me up with her big, unblinking eyes, then turn away.

It was about an hour before I realized Imogene might be sullen, but she sure wasn't dumb. Trixie was rattling away to Long

Boy, as usual, about what a great dancer she was and how folks at such and such a place had adored her, when Imogene suddenly leaned forward and said, "Tell 'im 'bout the time 'at man tried to crack open yo' haid wif a bottle, Miz Trixie." Imogene settled back in her seat with a mean gleam in her eye.

For a moment Trixie sounded as if she had swallowed her tongue. Then she squealed, "Why, Imogene, you silly ol' thing. You know that's not true. That ol' country boy wasn't goin' to hit me with no bottle." She made a scoffing sound. "He was jus' horsin' 'round." She looked at Long Boy archly. "Ask me nice, an' maybe I'll tell you 'bout that sometime."

Imogene sat quietly and waited until Trixie got wound up again. I was watching this time and I saw that gleam come in her eye. She leaned forward. "Tell 'im 'bout the time you almost got throwed in jail, Miz Trixie."

This time Trixie didn't try to laugh it off. She turned around, and if looks could kill, Imogene would have been deader than Stonewall Jackson's horse. "Shut up,

Imogene," she said curtly. Trixie turned back to Long Boy and gave a little laugh. "I declare, that girl makes up the biggest stories. She makes me so mad! I don't care what ol' Abe Lincoln said, one of these days I'm jus' goin' to give her a good whippin'." Imogene just sat there, looking satisfied with herself. I made up my mind right then that Imogene and I were going to have a good long talk.

I had my chance when we stopped at a barbecue place for lunch. Long Boy and Trixie ate inside, but I took some sandwiches and drinks for Imogene and me out to the car. After a while I asked, "Whereabouts you from, Imogene?"

Imogene gave me a sulky look. "Ain't from nowheres. I jest allus goin' somewheres."

"Well, you had to be born somewhere, didn't you?" I said.

Imogene chewed on her sandwich for a while before she decided to answer. "Down near Troy," she said.

"How long have you been working for Miss Trixie?" I asked.

Imogene shrugged. "I dunno. I ain't kep'

count. Long time — 'bout a year."

"What kind of dancing does she do?" I asked.

"She take off 'er clo'es," Imogene said.

I laughed. "Doesn't she dance, too?"

Imogene made a snorting sound. "Some folks call it dancing, I sposen. She waggle 'er hips an' shake 'er ol' behind a li'l bit."

I asked, "Why did she leave her job in Cullman, Imogene?"

"They want 'er to put out," Imogene said. "Boss man try to make 'er put out for 'is frens."

I thought about that. I was disappointed, I guess. "Well, you can't blame her for leaving," I said.

"Oh, she don' min' puttin' out," Imogene said. "Onliest thing is, she 'spect to get paid extry when she put out. She don' believe in puttin' out for free — not for nobody."

"Does she put out much, Imogene?" I asked.

Imogene turned and gave me that cutting, unblinking stare, like she was asking how anybody could be so dumb.

I asked, "How much does she charge?"

Imogene shrugged. "Most she can get, I

126

spose. She allus asks for five dollars.''

"That's a lot," I said. It was, too. I knew a good hustler like Juanita Pritle didn't charge but three dollars. After a while I asked, "Why are you so mad at Miss Trixie, Imogene?"

Imogene's eyes flashed. " 'Cause she won't give me my money. She sposed t' give me fo' dollars every week. An' she never give me nothin', 'cepting a nickel or dime sometimes."

"Why don't you quit?" I asked.

Imogene turned on me furiously. "Quit! How I gonna quit? Whut I do if I quit? Got no money t' git home t' my mama—an' whut if I do git home? They got hard 'nough times as it is." Imogene's lower lip began to tremble. For a moment I thought she was going to cry, but Imogene was tough. She gave her mouth a hard swipe with her hand and the trembling stopped. She clenched her hands in her lap and looked down at them. "My mama say, 'You go t' work for this white lady an' she take good ker o' you.' " Imogene gave a snort and looked at me with blazing eyes. "You wanter know whut I thinks? You know that lil' white speck on the top o' chicken doodle? Well, I thinks that's the kind o' white Miss Trixie is. She jest like that li'l white speck on th' top o' ol' chicken shit!"

For about twenty-four hours I guess I had some hope that we would take Trixie to Mobile and tell her goodbye. Not much hope, but some. Then I just had to face the truth. As far as Long Boy was concerned, Trixie was a permanent fixture in our lives. His good sense had gone bird nesting for sure. Every time he looked at Trixie, he got a silly, bleary grin on his face. Sometimes when Trixie went strutting through a hotel lobby or restaurant, while heads swiveled, he would nudge me and whisper, "Ain't that girl sump'in?"

Once or twice it was about all I could do not to tell Long Boy what a cheap little hooker Trixie really was. It must have been instinct instead of good sense that warned me he wouldn't believe me anyway. You see, it was two or three days before I discovered Long Boy and Trixie weren't bedding down together. That really scared me. It was plain that for some reason Trixie had convinced Long Boy she was saving her goodies for her husband. I wasn't sure what Trixie was up to, but it seemed to me anytime she wanted to crook her finger Long Boy was primed about right to slap a wedding ring on it.

Looking back, I find it hard to remember all the places we went and just exactly what we did during the twelve days Trixie was with us. We just zigzagged along. We didn't do any business at all. I mentioned this to Long Boy once or twice, but he put me off. "Aw, sweetie pie, forget about doin' business for a while," he said. "We been needin' a vacation a long time. Le's jus' relax and enjoy ourselves."

We never got under way until 'way past noon. Trixie always slept late, then spent three or four hours slopping around in her teddies, primping and eating chocolate-covered cherries and reading movie magazines. She ran poor Imogene ragged. "Imogene, wash these hose." . . . "Imogene, run downstairs and get me a Coke." . . . "Imogene, press this off for me." . . . "Imogene, I got a rip in the seam of my blue dress." Trixie was too lazy to hit a lick at a snake.

After we did get started, Trixie was in charge. Sometime the first few days she had started calling Long Boy "Daddy" and she would squeal like a little girl. "Oh, Daddy, stop and get me one of those," or "Oh, Daddy, can't we go there?" Trixie must have had a bladder the size of a peanut. There was a garage somewhere in Alabama at that time named Winfield's. It was run by a man whose initials were P.P. He gave away black tire covers that had printed in big red letters P.P. AT WINFIELD'S. Trixie thought those tire covers were the funniest thing she had ever seen. She screamed and pointed every time she saw one on the back of a car. So when she wanted to go to the toilet, which was about once every hour, she would giggle coyly and say, "Daddy, baby's got to go to Winfield's again." That meant we had to stop at the next filling station and wait fifteen or twenty minutes while Trixie used the rest room and took her time putting on fresh makeup.

Long Boy didn't mind anything Trixie did. All she had to do was look at him and he got that silly, dazed grin that made him look like a tom cat being choked to death with cream. Because Trixie claimed she had an uncle who went there, we drove down to Tuscaloosa and looked around the University of Alabama. Because Trixie had heard it was a pretty place, we drove down to Hale County and poked around the Indian mounds. We didn't pass a roadside stand that had a two-headed calf or a six-legged pig, because Trixie claimed she loved museums.

All of this time, of course, I was doing my best to figure out some way to get rid of Trixie. I thought about it so hard that my head ached. Imogene and I always shared the same room, and every night when Long Boy and Trixie went out to get sizzling steaks and shoestring potatoes because that was Trixie's favorite food, that's all we talked about. Imogene tried, but she wasn't much help. "You kin poun' up some glass real fine an' put it in 'er cawfee," she said once. Another time she said, "Ol' 'oman down home say you take a lil' bitty piece of a 'oman's monthly rag an' hide it inside a man's hatban', he nevah looked at 'at 'oman agin." At least, Imogene had some ideas. I simply couldn't think of any.

I really got desperate when Long Boy bought a new car. Ever since we had left Cullman, Trixie had been yelping and passing remarks when she saw a flashy roadster or some other fancy open car. "Oh, isn't that the cutest thing!" she would say, or "Yum-yummy, wouldn't you jus' love to have that!" Sometimes she was even more pointed. She would bat her eyes at Long Boy and say, "A big man like you oughter to have a pretty car like that, Daddy." I honestly don't remember I thought too much about this. There were too many more important things I held against Trixie. Then, one afternoon in Sylacauga, Imogene and I were waiting outside the hotel for Long Boy and Trixie when they drove up in a brand-new canary-yellow Cadillac V-8 touring car. Long Boy was grinning like an idiot and Trixie was looking as pleased and contented as a hen that had laid a corkscrew egg. I was just speechless.

Long Boy climbed out of the car. "You like it, Addie, baby?"

All I could do was look at him. Finally, I

found my voice. "You mean you *bought* it?" I asked.

" 'Course I did," he said, just as if he had never done business for a car in his life.

"How much did it cost?" I asked.

"Twenty-one hundred smackers," he said proudly. "They give me a good deal on the Hudson." He took my hand and led me around the car, showing me how the top went up and down and how there was a second windshield between the front and back seats.

I wasn't really listening. All I wanted to do was run off someplace and bawl my eyes out. It wasn't that I minded Long Boy buying the old car with our money. What really hurt was he had taken Trixie with him instead of me. That didn't leave any doubt in my mind that Trixie came first with him in everything. I made up my mind right there and then that I had been too easy on Trixie. I swore I was going to watch her night and day until I found some way to fix her big swinging butt for good.

Fortunately, I had some good luck the very next day. We drove down to Montgomery and stayed at the Exchange

Hotel. I suppose they've fixed the old Exchange up now. In those days it was pretty much like it had been in Civil War times. You know, old heavy leather furniture in the lobby, with lots of potted plants, and big, high-ceilinged rooms with transoms over the doors. Imogene and I had a room right next to Trixie's. There was a heavy oak door connecting the two rooms, but it was locked. The transom over the door was painted over, but I fiddled around and managed to open it a little. I could hear everything Trixie said or did.

I really didn't have any clear idea what I hoped to accomplish. I had just swore I was going to keep tabs on Trixie 'round the clock, and I did. When she left her room, I would stand at my door listening until she caught the elevator, then I would follow her. Luckily, we were on the second floor, because it was a long corridor. But if I ran real fast and hurried down the one flight of stairs, I could get to the lobby right behind Trixie. If she was meeting Long Boy, I would sit down and wait until she came back. A couple of times, though, Trixie went out by herself. I followed along behind her, stopping when she did, and ducking in doorways, just like a detective.

It didn't seem much, but I did learn one little thing by following Trixie. It was plain she didn't have any money. She did a lot of looking and admiring in the stores, but no buying. For the first time it dawned on me that, while Long Boy bought Trixie anything she wanted, he never gave her any hard cash. That was the way it was in those days. Nice girls didn't take money from men. As long as Trixie was pretending to be nice, she couldn't take money from Long Boy and he sure wouldn't offer her any.

There was one other thing. The clerk at the cigar counter in the lobby of the hotel was a man named Floyd, and he really thought he was something. You probably know the kind of pea-patch Romeo I mean. He had a tiny pencil-line moustache, and he wore his long black hair slicked back, except for a big false wave in front that he was always pushing in place with the heel of his hand. He couldn't wait on a woman without cutting his eyes and getting flirty. He always put on a special little show when Trixie went to the counter to buy candy and chewing gum. Once when he was handing Trixie a pencil so she could sign for what she had bought, he waited until her fingers closed on it, then smirked and yanked it back. Another time he held out his hand like he was handing her some gum, but when she reached for it his hand was empty, and he made a motion as if he was going to grab her hand. Both times Trixie giggled and pretended to slap at his hand and said, "Oh, you!"

After watching this for the second time, I went up to my room and lay on the bed a long time, thinking. Finally, I got up and hauled out the old Roi Tan cigar box I had been carrying in my suitcase since Trixie started traveling with us. I wanted to be sure I wasn't mistaken about how much money was inside. There was sixty dollars and some change. That night when Imogene and I were alone I asked, "Imogene, what do you suppose Miss Trixie would do if somebody offered her twenty-five dollars to put out?"

Imogene said, "Who-eee! You crazy?" She giggled. "For 'at much money 'at 'oman drap her pants down in the middle o' th' road."

"That's what I figure," I said. I told Imogene the plan I had. She listened, her eyes growing wider every minute. She shook her head, "Uhh-uhh! Not me, no sireee! You gonna git us kilt!"

"Look, Imogene," I said, "you want to get away from Miss Trixie, don't you? If you help me, I'll give you enough money to go home."

"How much money?" Imogene asked.

"Thirty dollars," I said.

"Le's see th' money," Imogene said.

I got the Roi Tan box and counted Imogene out thirty dollars. It was all in ones, and in Imogene's tiny hand it made some pile. Imogene's eyes bugged a little. She looked at that money and she looked at me. Finally she said, "Aw right."

I was standing right up against the door listening the next morning when Imogene came back from downstairs with Trixie's breakfast. I could hardly breathe I was so scared Imogene might get things mixed up, but Imogene was a natural-born actress. She said, "Miz Trixie, you know 'at man down at the cigar counter—th' un they call Mistah Floyd?"

Trixie was still in bed. I heard the springs squeak. She gave a big yawn. "Yeah, I know him," she said. "What about him?"

"Well," said Imogene, "he tell me he pay twenty-five dollars t' have a good time wif you."

"What!" Trixie yelped. "Why, that little two-bit bum! The nerve of that guy!" She sounded so indignant that my heart sank. But after a while the bed springs squeaked again and Trixie's voice sounded almost as if she was thinking out loud. "Twenty-five bucks. Huh! Why, I bet that little john don't make that much in a week. Where would he get twenty-five bucks?"

"I dunno," Imogene said. "All I know is whut he tole me."

"Twenty-five bucks, huh!" Trixie said again, disbelievingly. There was a long pause before she said, "Well, I'd sure have to see the money to believe it."

That was all I needed. I went down to the lobby and waited until a couple of customers left the cigar counter. I went over and asked for a pack of juicy-fruit gum.

Floyd handed it to me and said in that smirking way he had, "Here we are, my little beauty. Want I should chew it for you?"

I laughed like that was funny and gave him a nickel. I said, "You know that blond lady that comes down here—Miss Trixie Delight? Well, she thinks you're real cute."

He was so surprised he almost lost his silly grin. He narrowed his eyes and studied me to see if I was kidding. "Oh, yeah," he said. "Sez you and who else?"

"No, honest," I said. "She says you're better-looking than Warner Baxter."

He wet his lips and fingered his tie. "She did, eh?" he said. "Well . . ." He gave a smart-alecky grin and tried to wise-crack, "Well, the lady's sure got good taste, eh?"

I laughed again and said, "I just thought you'd like to know." I turned to walk away.

"Hey, jus' a minnit," he said. He reached on the shelf behind him and got a half-pound box of chocolate creams and handed them to me. "Give these here to the lady—tell her they're with Floyd's compliments."

"Oh, she'll like that," I said, acting

thrilled. I had a sudden thought. "Maybe you should write her a note," I said.

"Yeah," he said. "What kinda note?"

"Oh, I don't know," I said. "I thought men always wrote ladies notes when they sent them presents. Maybe you should ask her for a date. That sure would tickle her."

He preened his little moustache and grinned. "Yeah, maybe I oughta." He reached under the counter and got a piece of paper and a pencil. He started to write, then stopped. "Say, she's not married or anything, is she?"

I laughed like that was the funniest thing I had ever heard. "Of course not," I said. "She doesn't even have a regular boy friend. That man you see her with sometimes is my daddy. He's her manager. She's a dancer."

"Well, whatta you know," he said, puffing up like a rooster about to crow. "A dancer, eh? Y' know I figured she was something like that. Whereabouts does she dance?"

"Oh, lots of big places," I said. "She's a star."

"Now, how about that!" he said.

I could hardly wait to get up to my room

to read this note. It read: *Some sweets for the sweet ha-ha. Some girls say I am a pretty smooth dancer myself. Hows about trying me out some nite soon. Floyd.*

It wasn't hard to copy his sprawling old handwriting. After about an hour I had written a note that would have fooled his mother: *Some sweets for the sweet ha-ha. Theres lots more where this came from. Will be up in 15 minutes. Floyd.*

I took the twenty-five dollars that was left in the Roi Tan box and wrapped the note around it. Then I sealed it all in a hotel envelope and put a rubber band around the envelope and box of candy. I hid the package away in the bottom drawer of a bureau.

The hardest part of my plan was still to come. I won't pretend I wasn't scared. If one single little thing went wrong, I knew I was in for real trouble. That night I made Imogene go over her part so many times that she finally got mad and wouldn't talk to me. I didn't think I would sleep a wink, but I did. I guess I was worn out from racing my brain so much.

At nine o'clock the next morning I

knocked on Trixie's door. When she finally opened the door, yawning and scratching herself, I said, "Miss Trixie, Long Boy asked me to tell you he had to run over to Hayneville today. He won't be back until suppertime."

"Huh? . . . Why, wha . . ." Trixie said.

"I think he had to go to the bank to get some money," I said. "He'll be gone all day."

"Yeah . . . well, er, oke, kiddo," Trixie said. "Oke."

I waited a few minutes before I went downstairs to have breakfast with Long Boy, like I sometimes did. At least I had a doughnut and some coffee while Long Boy ate. I felt like I had a bullfrog hopping around in my stomach. In about fifteen minutes Imogene came up to the table looking as cool and starched as could be in her maid's uniform. "Mistah Long Boy," she said, "Miz Trixie don' feel so good. She say t' tell you she gonna stay in bed today. She say she see you at suppertime."

Long Boy looked worried. "She's sick," he said anxiously. "Sick in bed? Better go up there." He started to get up. I turned cold all over. I hadn't figured on anything like this.

Imogene, bless her heart, saved things. She said, "Oh, she ain't real sick. Ain't nothin' t' worry 'bout. She's jest got th' curse."

Long Boy got red in the face. "Oh . . . I see," he mumbled. "I see . . ." He cleared his throat. "Well, tell her I'll see her this evenin', Imogene."

After Long Boy had settled down in the lobby to read the paper, I took the elevator back up to my room. I tried to lie down on the bed and be calm, but every few seconds I would get up and go to the door and listen through the transom to check on Trixie. After I was sure she was wide awake and had finished her breakfast, I took a deep breath and went to the bureau and got out the box of candy and envelope. I wanted to run, but I made myself walk slowly down the corridor and down the stairs. I stood near the foot of the stairs in the lobby so Long Boy couldn't see me until I caught a bellboy's eye. I motioned him over and gave him a dime to take the package up to Trixie's room. As soon as he headed for the elevator, I turned and scooted back up the stairs to my room.

I was standing under the transom, listening to Trixie boss Imogene around, as usual, when the bellboy knocked at the door. I heard Trixie say kind of peevishly, "Well, what's this—what's this?" before there was a crackling sound as she tore open the envelope. There was a long silence. I held my breath and shut my eyes. If Trixie had yelped or rattled the telephone, I do believe I would have fainted. Instead, the silence went on and on. Trixie cleared her throat. "Imogene, let that go for now," she said. "You can run along. I'll call you when I need you."

I didn't care if Long Boy did see me going to the cigar counter. He didn't anyway. He was still slumped down in a chair, reading the paper. Floyd gave me a big smirking grin. "Why, hello, cupid," he said.

I gave him my best little-girl's smile. "Miss Trixie wants to see you," I said. "She says it's real important—room two-thirty-three."

"Oh, she does, does she?" he said. He wiggled his shoulders like he was settling his coat and tugged at his tie. "When?"

"Right now," I said.

His grin faded. He shot a glance around the counter. "Well, I don't . . ."

"She says it's real important," I said. I rolled my eyes. "You won't be sorry."

He beamed again. "Well . . ." He hesitated a moment, then said, "I guess I can go up a few minutes. What's that room number?"

"Room two-thirty-three," I said. "She's waiting for you."

He laughed and looked smug. "Okay, you tell her I'm on my way up, sweetheart."

I walked across the lobby like I had all the time in the world, but when I reached the stairs I ran as fast as I could. Imogene was sitting on her bed when I reached our room.

I did a little jig and whispered excitedly, "He's coming! He's coming!" Imogene just stared at me with her big eyes and shook her head mournfully.

We both were pressed up against the door under the transom when Floyd came up the corridor. He was whistling "My Blue Heaven." When he knocked on the door,

Trixie called out in a voice dripping with sugar, "Who is it?"

"The Sheik of Araby," Floyd said.

Trixie giggled and we heard her cross the room and open the door. Floyd must have been taken aback by whatever Trixie was wearing, because there was a long pause before he gave a little whistle and said, "Hey, hello there! An' don't you look pretty!"

There was another pause, and Trixie said a little impatiently, "Well, c'mon in, honey." We heard the door close, and Trixie said, "Say, you're some fast worker, aren't you? You don't give a girl much time."

"Oh, I manage to get around," Floyd said. I could almost see his smirk.

"I just bet you do," Trixie said. She gave a kind of hoarse laugh I had never heard her use before. "I just bet you do!" There was a silence and I knew she must be giving Floyd her old eye-batting treatment. "There's just one thing we gotta straighten out, honey," Trixie said. "You're not one of these fellows that goes aroun' blabbin', are you?"

"Whatta you mean?" Floyd asked.

"Oh, you know the kinda fellow I mean," Trixie said. "He goes out and has a good time with a girl, then goes aroun' telling everybody in the hotel about it. Most of the time I don't mind. But it's important to me right now not to get talked about."

"Look, do I look like that kinda fellow?" Floyd said. "Say, sweetheart, I been around in my time. I don't talk about nothin' to nobody. Anything me and you do, baby, is between the two of us."

"Okay, honey," Trixie said. "I believe you. I just wanted to get it straight."

"How's about tonight?" Floyd said. "Say I pick you up about seven?"

"Oh, I couldn't tonight, honey," Trixie said, "really I couldn't. If you wanna do it, we'll have to do it now."

I guess I would have paid a hundred dollars to see old Floyd's face at that moment. But he recovered pretty fast. There was a scuffling sound and Trixie gave a little squeal. "Say, you are a wild one, aren't you?" she said. Then her voice got sharp. "Hol' it! Hol' it! Wait a minnit! You're gonna tear it! Let me slip it off."

I looked at Imogene. Her eyes were wide

and solemn. "I'm going," I whispered. I held out my hand and she reached in her apron pocket and handed me the key she had to Trixie's room. I was almost out the door when she said, "Don' leave me!" She was right behind me as I ran down the corridor. When we were about halfway down the stairs, I turned to her and said, "Wait for me here."

Wouldn't you know Long Boy wasn't in the lobby? When I saw his chair was empty, I almost got sick on the floor. I ran across the lobby and looked in the dining room. He wasn't there. I ran to the front door and looked up and down the street. I ran over to the house phones and called his room. I suppose I wasted about three minutes, but it seemed an hour before I saw Long Boy coming into the lobby through the garage entrance. My face must have been a sight. When I went running up to him, his mouth dropped open. "Why, Addie, sugar," he said, "what ..."

I handed him the key. "You better go up to Trixie's room right away," I said.

"Why, what ... what ..." he stuttered. "Is she sick?"

"No, she's not sick," I said. "Just go on, like I tell you. Don't knock. Use the key." He stuttered some more, but I gave him a push toward the elevators.

I climbed the stairs slowly. Imogene was sitting down on the step where I had left her. I sat down beside her. I didn't feel well at all. My stomach was churning, and my heart was beating so fast I was afraid it might stop. After a while Imogene said, "Yo' daddy gonna kill 'at man, I reckon."

"Don't be silly," I said. But do you know, that was the first time I had ever given such a thing a thought? I suppose I simply didn't think Long Boy would be so foolish. Yet, when I did begin to think about it, I wasn't so sure. I began to get scared.

"I 'spect he cut him purty bad," Imogene said.

"No, he won't," I said. "He doesn't have a knife." Then I remembered Long Boy did have a knife. It was a tiny penknife but I realized it could do a lot of damage. Besides, Long Boy did have a terrible temper. He was crazy about Trixie, so suppose . . .

"Down home," Imogene said, "man

149

come home from wuk and heered man inside house in bed wif his wife. He jus' walk 'round t' woodpile and git his dubble-blade ax. He go inside and chop 'em bofe t' li'l pieces. Folks say he chop 'em up lak kindlin' wood."

"Hush up, Imogene," I said. The longer I thought, the more panicky I got. I tried to think about something else—anything else. It was no use. I jumped to my feet and ran up the stairs.

I shouldn't have worried. Long Boy was coming down the corridor. His face was flushed, but, oh, his poor eyes! He looked like a load of bricks had been dumped on his head. His voice was tight, "Get your things, Addie, dear," he said. "We're leavin'."

"Now?" I asked.

It was some trip Long Boy and I took the rest of that day and most of the night. He headed the car north and just drove and drove. I didn't ask where we were going, because I realized he didn't know. He stared straight ahead, not talking, but drawing his breath in big sighs from time to time.

We never talked about Trixie but one time. It was late that night and I was half asleep when Long Boy heaved one of his deep, shuddering sighs. "I swan," he said in a sad tone, half talking to himself, "I don't know why that girl did such a thing to me. Why, I would've done mos' anything for that girl. It jes' ain't fair."

I said, "From now on you ought to buy it. It's cheaper that way."

He sounded shocked. "Honeybunch, don't talk thataway. It ain't nice."

"I've heard you say it," I said.

"Well, I didn't mean for you to hear," he said.

He drove awhile and he said, "I reckon she'd been carryin' on a long time."

"From the start," I said.

"You mean there were other men?" he asked.

"Lots of them," I said.

"Why, dadblammit, hon, why didn't you tell me?" he asked.

"I knew you wouldn't believe me," I said.

He sighed again. "Baby doll," he said mournfully, "I want you to promise me jes' one thing. When you grow up, don't be the

151

kind of woman who goes aroun' deceivin' men. Promise me that."

I tried to hide a yawn. "I promise," I said. The old fool.

SEVEN

In case you don't know, a two-timing woman can do lots more damage to a man than break his heart. Most times she knocks the squeal right out of him. For more than a week after we left Montgomery, Long Boy moped around like a little shoat pig that had just paid a visit to the cutting pen. He acted so meek and unsure of himself that it almost made me sick.

Naturally, I tried to pretend nothing was wrong. Every morning I would ask, "We going to do some business today, Long Boy?" He would sigh and roll his eyes and mumble excuses.

"This place is too small, hon," or "I don't think we better take any chances 'round here, baby doll."

Once when we left a cafe I said, "You could've done some business with that dumb old cashier."

Long Boy looked pained. "Aw, Addie, sugar, you know I don't feel up to sweet-talkin' no woman right now."

There was some truth in one of Long Boy's excuses. We were drifting aimlessly around north Alabama, and most of the towns we hit really were too small to do business in. Especially since we were driving that big bright yellow Cadillac. New cars of any kind drew glances in those hard times. In poor farm regions, fancy sports cars were as rare as eight-teated cows. Every time we stopped in some tiny, dusty one-street town to eat or gas up, a crowd would gather to gawk. Even so, there were plenty of places in north Alabama, like Huntsville and Florence, where we could have gone without being noticed. After a few days I began to suspect that Long Boy was avoiding big towns deliberately. When he drove into Winston County I was sure of it. Later on, of course, I realized I was doing Long Boy an injustice. Driving into Winston County just proved he wasn't himself.

Now, what can I tell you about Winston County? Back in the thirties, I guess any little child in Alabama knew you didn't go poking around up in Winston County unless you had pressing, legitimate business. Even then it was best to go around with a smile on your face and take pains not to step on somebody's foot. For one thing, Winston is a mountain region, and everybody knows mountain folks are as clannish and touchy as honey bees on the swarm. But Winston folks got a special reputation for being hotheaded, mistrustful of outsiders, and pure cussedly mean at the outbreak of the Civil War. There weren't any plantations in the county and nobody owned slaves, so the people decided the fight didn't concern them. They said that if Alabama could secede from the Union, they could secede from Alabama. They set up an independent government and called it the Free State of Winston. The Confederate government sent troops riding into Winston several times during the war, trying to get provisions or conscript men. Most times the mountain men took down their long rifles and fought them to a standstill.

I must say, at first look Winston didn't seem to be the rip-snorting, hot-blooded place I had always heard it made out to be. It was hardscrabble poor country, of course. There weren't any paved roads to speak of, and as we rode along, churning up big clouds of dust, we almost never saw any substantial farm houses. Sometimes we would pass whole families walking along the road barefoot. The men always wore overalls and beat-up old hats, and the women all looked alike in long, flapping Mother Hubbard dresses and poke bonnets. The skinny little children were dressed in any kind of raggle-daggle odds and ends that came to hand—flour sacks and cut-off overalls and ragged hand-me-down dresses. But being dirt poor wasn't an unusual condition in Alabama right then, and it struck me that the mountain folks of Winston did have some real advantages over poor farm families who were trying to scratch out a living down in the hot, dry flatlands. Dense green pine forests went meandering off in all directions, and practically every time we turned a curve, there was another little stream rushing down a mountainside. The mountain air was cool and sweet.

The little towns in Winston, like Double Springs and Haleyville, were pretty similar to towns anywhere else, except maybe the people weren't as outgoing. Nobody in

Winston seemed to smile much, and they used words like they cost ten dollars apiece.

I was surprised when we found a hotel that wasn't bad at all. Actually, it wasn't as much a hotel as a game lodge, a rambling, fairly new place, located on the edge of a state forest and game reservation that covered miles and miles. The lodge catered to hunters during the winter months, but a CCC camp was being built in the reservation, and while we were there it was filled with government engineers and surveyors.

During our very first evening at the lodge I noticed a tall, freckled-faced man sitting by himself on a sofa in one corner of the lobby. He wore a cream-colored Stetson hat and a business suit, but somehow I knew he was a Winston man. I didn't like his face much. It seemed cold and calculating and he had a kind of mean look around the eyes. From time to time men would come in the lodge and walk over and talk to him. He wouldn't say much, just listen. Sometimes he would take a black notebook out of his pocket and jot something down. A couple of times he got up and went out the back entrance of the lodge with the men. He would always come back within a few minutes and take his seat on the sofa, staring into space and twisting an unlit cigar between his lips. I decided he was connected with the lodge in some way.

The next morning when I was coming down the stairs to meet Long Boy for breakfast I glanced over the banister. Standing in the shadow of the staircase so he couldn't be seen from the lobby was the same man. He was holding about the biggest roll of money I had ever seen. Somebody must have just handed it to him, because he was counting it slowly and deliberately.

Long Boy had already ordered breakfast when I got to the dining room. As soon as I sat down I said excitedly, "I just saw a man with a wad of money big enough to choke us both!"

Long Boy looked interested right away. "What man?" he asked.

"Over by the stairs," I said. "Wait awhile and I'll show him to you." In a minute or two the man came walking across the lobby headed toward the sofa in the corner. "There he is," I said.

Long Boy sized the man up. *"Hummmm,"* he said musingly, *"hummmm.* How much money you think he had?"

I was so pleased that Long Boy was showing an interest, in something that I exaggerated a little. "Oh, lots — two or three thousand, maybe."

"Hummmm," Long Boy said again. *"Hummm."*

I told him what I had noticed about the man the night before.

"Bootlegger, mos' likely," Long Boy said.

"Bootleggers don't have that kind of money," I said, thinking of the dime taxi drivers I always saw slinking around hotel hallways.

"They do if they got a big enough operation," Long Boy said. He was still looking at the man thoughtfully.

"You think we might do some business with him, Long Boy?" I asked. "Maybe if we took a wallet — "

Long Boy shook his head. "There's better ways t' do business with bootleggers, honey."

"What ways?" I asked.

"Oh, heaps o' ways," Long Boy said. He studied on it a minute. "Well, I'll jes' see if I can't get a line on that ol' boy. Then we'll see."

I didn't see Long Boy until suppertime. When he came in the dining room, he was grinning and looking like himself again. He knew I was dying to hear what he had found out, but he ordered a sizzling steak and waited until the waitress served it before he began to talk. "Our friend's name is Jess Hardin. He's a bootlegger all right — leastways he wholesales to pert near all th' bootleggers in the county. His brother's deputy sheriff in this district. Far's I can make out, between 'em they run jes' about everythin' worth runnin'. They own mos' of this place."

I thought that over "Do you think we—"

Long Boy didn't let me finish. He gave me a big grin. "I sure do, baby doll. I think we can do ourselves some real business. All we got t' do is watch our p's and q's."

I must have wiggled I was so pleased. Long Boy laughed. He leaned across the table. "Now, lookit, th' first thing we gotter do is find out where ol' Jess stashes his goods. I reckon you can do that better 'n me. After we finish eatin', we'll go out and sit down in the lobby an' act like we're enjoyin' ourselves. If ol' Jess gets up an' goes outside, I want you to kinder mosey out to th' side verandah over there. Try to see where he goes. Be real casual about it.'

"I will," I said.

"Th' main thing is—don't let 'im see you," Long Boy said.

"I won't," I said.

We sat in the lobby for about twenty minutes before a man came in and went over to Jess Hardin. He said something and Hardin gave a nod and stood up. They walked across the lobby toward the back door. Long Boy looked at me and blinked his eyes.

I stood up and stretched, like I was tired of sitting down. Pretending to be looking for something to do, I wandered across the lobby until I reached the double doors opening onto the verandah. I stepped outside and looked around to be sure it was empty. Then I ran toward the end of the verandah. All I had to do was lean forward and crane my neck to see behind the building. Hardin and the man were standing in front of some sort of bin just a few feet from the back door. As I watched, Hardin lifted the top of the bin and the man reached inside and took out four or five bottles with straw wrappers. He gave Hardin a nod and began walking up the driveway toward the front of the lodge, staying in the shadows.

I could hardly wait to get back inside, but I took my time. When I told Long Boy what I had seen, he asked, "What size bin?"

I thought that over and was about to answer when Jess Hardin came back in the lobby. For the first time I noticed he held himself so straight that he looked a little sway-backed. I waited until he had taken his seat on the sofa before I said, "Pretty big — about three times bigger than the trunk on the car."

Long Boy smiled sweetly, like he was saying something nice to his little girl. "That's not it, honey. Not big enough. Jes' keep watchin'."

During the next couple of hours four or five men came in and talked with Hardin. He got up and went outside with two of

162

them. I follwed him both times. It was always the same. Hardin went to the bin and lifted the top. The men reached inside and loaded their arms with bottles and walked away.

It was about ten o'clock and I was beginning to get bored and sleepy when Hardin suddenly stood up. He gave a little yawn and walked across the lobby to the reception desk. He said something to the clerk, and when he turned away it seemed he was headed for the stairs. Instead he kept on walking and went out the back door. I looked at Long Boy. He was blinking his eyes. I stood up and got out to the verandah as fast as I could without seeming to be rushing.

Hardin had the lid to the bin open and was looking inside. When he closed it he turned and started walking toward three outbuildings about fifty yards behind the lodge. He disappeared in the shadow of the biggest building, which was about the size of a one-car garage. After a couple of minutes he reappeared carrying two bulging croaker sacks, one in each hand. I guessed it was whiskey, and I was right. After stopping to rest once, he lugged the sacks up to the bin and lifted them inside.

I was still crossing the lobby when Hardin came in the back door. Without looking right or left he went up the stairs. When I told Long Boy what I had seen, he grinned and said, "That's my girl!" He looked toward the stairs to be sure Hardin was out of sight and stood up and stretched. "Well, baby doll," he said loudly, "how 'bout a little walk before we go to bed?"

Getting out to the outbuildings was no trouble. We walked down the driveway of the lodge for a short distance, then out across the grounds and made a wide circle until we were directly behind them. When we reached the shadow of the building Hardin had entered, Long Boy stopped and whispered, "Watch the hotel, honey. If you see anybody comin', cough real low. I'm goin' inside."

I said, "It may be locked." My heart was thumping, but Long Boy sounded cool as an oyster.

He chuckled. "Shucks, folks in th' country never lock anything."

He was right. I heard the door creak as he

opened it and went inside. I heard him fumbling around, and I thought my heart would stop, because I heard him strike a match. But as soon as it flared, he blew it out again. He gave a low whistle and said, "Lawsy, mercy." He fumbled around some more, and in about a minute I heard the door creak again and he was outside. "Le's go," he said.

As I followed him along in the shadows toward the front of the lodge, Long Boy said, "You wouldn't believe it! Why, honeybunch, that ol' boy's got enough whiskey in there to float the Chattahoochee Ferry."

It wasn't until we reached the driveway that I saw he had two bottles of whiskey, wrapped in straw, under his arm. That surprised me, because Long Boy didn't drink. I asked, "What you want with those bottles?"

Long Boy grinned. "These here are my samples — in case I need samples." He took me by the arm. "C'mon, I'll leave them in th' car. When we reached the car in the parking lot behind the lodge, he said, "Slide in a minnit, honey, an' we'll talk." When we were in the front seat, he pushed back the straw wrappers and looked at the labels on the bottles, then put them in the glove compartment. He turned to me with a big grin. "Well, all we gotter do now, sweetie pie, is sell ol' Jess Hardin some whiskey."

"We don't have any whiskey," I said.

Long Boy laughed. "We don't need any. What I'm aimin' t' do is sell ol' Jess some of his own whiskey." When I just looked at him, he said, "Look, hon, it's real simple. I'll go to Jess an' sell him an order of whiskey. I'll promise to deliver it to him at a place somewhere near here at — oh, le's say seven o'clock in the mornin'. Well, sometime before sun-up — maybe four or five o'clock — I'll slip out t' that little warehouse of his. I'll take what whiskey I need an' drag it down to th' edge of the road. Then you an' me get in the car an' drive by an' pick it up. We take it to th' place we've arranged to meet Jess and stash it away in the bushes. We wait aroun' until he shows up with th' money — then we take off like big birds."

"What if he finds out his whiskey is missing?" I asked.

Long Boy smiled. "He won't, honey. He won't even if he looks — which ain't likely. Leave that to ol' Long Boy. Mos' times it's bes' to stuff some croaker sacks with paper to leave in the place of the ones you take. But the way that shed's stacked up, I won't even have to do that. I'll push a few things aroun' an' ol Jess might not ever find out he's bought the same batch of whiskey twice."

"How much you aiming to sell him?" I asked.

"I figure twenty cases oughter be about right," Long Boy said.

"Suppose he won't buy it?" I said.

Long Boy said, "Oh, he'll buy it right enough. I'll offer it t' him so cheap he can't refuse."

"How cheap?" I asked.

"I reckon about twenty-five dollars a case," Long Boy said.

"That's five hundred dollars," I said, thinking out loud. I grinned at Long Boy. "I reckon it'll work."

He laughed. " 'Course it'll work. Why, I was doin' business with bootleggers when I was a shirt-tail boy."

The next morning Long Boy and I got in the car and went looking for a place to stash Jess Hardin's whiskey. It didn't take long. The countryside around the lodge was so overgrown and untamed, if we'd had a mind to we could have hid away a herd of Jersey cows. We looked at several places, but settled on a dry gully about two miles from the lodge. It was only a few yards off the road and easy to locate because it was near a big pine tree that had been ripped by lightning.

It was such a pretty day that we decided to ride around for a while. Long Boy started taking back roads and pretty soon we were in wilderness so deep and silent and beautiful that I was just awed. We saw so many deer that I lost count. Most of the time they went bounding away, holding their white tails up high, but sometimes they just stood looking at us with their big sad brown eyes. Once, down in a little glade, I saw an old tom turkey in full strut, herding along a flock of hens and poults. It seemed to me that forest must not have changed any since before the time of man. I told Long Boy so, but he smiled. "Oh, I wouldn't say that, hon. Somebody's cookin' up a powerful lot of whiskey in these woods."

"How do you know?" I asked.

"There's signs — if you know what t' look for," he said.

Long Boy seemed to dawdle over his supper forever that night. I sat there waiting with that crawly, goose-bumpy feeling I always got before we did business. Finally, he finished his last crumb of blackberry pie and gave me a wink. "Le's go ramify ol' Jess, sugar." We left the dining room and, like it was the most natural thing in the world, walked over and sat down in two chairs facing Jess Hardin's sofa. He didn't give the slightest sign he noticed us. He was looking straight ahead, as usual, rolling his cigar in his mouth with his fingers. After a minute or two Long Boy went over and sat down beside him on the sofa. "Yo' name Hardin?" he asked.

Hardin turned his head just long enough to give Long Boy a short, hard look. "Thass right," he said.

"Jack said I oughter come see you," Long Boy said.

"Jack who?" Hardin asked.

Long Boy gave a wise little laugh. "Oh, jes' Jack's good 'nough, I reckon."

"Don' know no Jack," Hardin said, looking straight ahead and rolling his cigar.

"Well, you oughter get acquainted," Long Boy said. "He's runnin' the biggest wholesale business in th' state."

Hardin sat silently, seeming to ponder this. "You sellin'?" he asked finally.

"Thass right," Long Boy said.

"Ain't interested in no shinny," Hardin said.

"Ain't offerin' no shinny," Long Boy said. "All I handle is bonded goods."

"What kind?" Hardin asked.

"All kinds," Long Boy said. "Can give you a special price on some Three Feathers."

"How much?" Hardin asked.

"Depends," Long Boy said. "Take twenty cases an' I'll let it go for twenty-five dollars per."

"Too much," Hardin said.

Long Boy gave a snorting laugh. "Ain't too much. Can't buy it 'at cheap where they sell it legal."

"Ain't legal heah," Hardin said.

"All the more reason you're gettin' a bargain," Long Boy said.

"Give you twenty dollars," Hardin said.

"Can't do it," Long Boy said. "Price is set down in Birmingham."

Hardin thought that over. "How long 'fore delivery?" he asked.

"Late tonight or early in th' mornin', if you want it," Long Boy said.

For the first time Hardin turned and looked at Long Boy. He took his cigar out of his mouth. "Got it in th' county?"

"Thass right," Long Boy said.

Hardin thought some more. "Sounds all right," he said. "Set it up with you in th' mornin'."

As soon as we were in our room, Long Boy gave a little chortle. "Didn't I tell you, honey? Ain't nothin' easier than skinnin' a polecat."

I grinned, but I couldn't help showing I was a little disappointed. "I was hopin' we could do business tomorrow morning," I said.

"Why, shucks, baby," Long Boy said, "don't be in such an all-fired hurry. Ol' Jess needs some time t' get our money, don't he?"

"Reckon we'll have to spend another night here," I said.

Long Boy smiled at me. He knew how I hated waiting. "Well, I don't see why," he said. "Suppose we jes' deliver ol' Jess his goods late tomorrow night. We could be down the road an' clean outer sight by midnight. How would that suit you?"

He burst out laughing when I gave him a big smile and said, "Oh, I'd like that fine."

Altogether the rest of that evening was pretty much like it had been before we ever met up with Trixie. Long Boy was as relaxed and cheerful as I had ever seen him. Doing business always did soothe his nerves.

After we went to bed, I was almost drifting off to sleep when I thought of a question I had meant to ask. I called over to Long Boy, "You asleep?"

"Not yet," he said.

"What's shinny?" I asked.

"Moonshine," Long Boy said. "Reg'lar ol' corn likker."

"Oh," I said. I smiled, thinking of something else. "Ol' Jess Hardin was sure surprised when you told him you could deliver him his whiskey so quick."

"Yeah," said Long Boy. "Yeah . . ."

It didn't seem any time at all before Long Boy was shaking me and saying, "Addie . . . Addie, baby . . . Wake up, honey!" I opened my eyes and blinked. The light was on and Long Boy was dressed, except for his coat. He had an anxious look.

"What is it?" I asked.

"Get up, honey," he said. "Hurry an' get dressed. We're leavin'."

"Wha . . . Why . . ." I said. "What time is it?"

"A little after three," Long Boy said.

"Are you crazy!" I said, so sleepy I couldn't see.

"Please, baby," he said. "This is real serious. Don't make a fuss. Be a good girl an' do like I ask."

"Well, I . . . I . . . never—you . . . you . . ." I got up muttering and spluttering and groped around for my clothes. I was simply cross as crabs. Long Boy had been acting peculiar ever since we left Montgomery, but I decided this was too much. I was too sleepy to think straight, but I had this vague idea that Long Boy had lost his nerve and

173

was running away so he wouldn't have to do business with Jess Hardin. He pretended not to hear my mumbling and fussing. He looked worried as he packed our packs and fastened the straps. As soon as I buttoned my shoes, he had me by the arm and practically dragged me out of the room and down the hall.

A sleepy old man was behind the desk in the darkened lobby. But as he fumbled around making out our bill, he came awake and began asking questions—where were we going, what road were we taking? Long Boy gave him short answers, and soon we were out in the cool night air and into the car.

I was wide awake now. "Will you tell me what this is all about?" I asked.

Long Boy started the car and headed down the driveway. "What it's all about," he said bitterly, "is I've made a dadblamed fool outer myself. Why, I could even a gotten us both kilt! I been layin' up there thinkin' about it all night. Ever since you mentioned it." He shook his head and made a clucking sound. "Doggonit, I don't see how I coulda been so nutty."

"What are you talking about?" I asked.

174

"I'm talking about tellin' that weasel-eyed Hardin that I had some whiskey stashed away in this county," he said. "I don't know what I was usin' for brains! I ain't never overplayed my han' like that before. Why, I—"

I tried to interrupt. "Well, I still don't—"

"Lookit, honey," he said in the same disgusted tone, "don't you understan' what I've done? Hardin runs things 'round here. This here is his territory! When I pretended I'd brought whiskey in here, I was in bad trouble right there. Folks have been kilt for less—lots less. In the second place, I—"

"He didn't seem to mind," I said.

"Oh, no, he didn't seem t' mind," Long Boy said. "Oh, no! That's where he was smart—smart enough t' make a sap-suckin' fool outta me. He didn't have nothin' t' worry about. When we met him to deliver that whiskey, the least he had t' do was take it away from us an' send us high-tailin' it for the county line. That's the very least! Mos' probably that deputy-sheriff brother of his woulda come outer th' bushes an' throwed me in jail. On the other han', lots worse could've happened. We jes' might never

175

have been heard from again. I mean it! I wouldn't put nothin' pas' that crook. He's colder 'n a sidewindin' snake."

We had reached a crossroads near the lodge. Long Boy stopped the car long enough to read the signs. When we were under way again he said, "I jes' wasn't thinkin' straight. Now we jes' might've done some business if I'd tole Hardin it would take a couple o' days t' bring the whiskey in. He jes' might've figured it was a bargain an' paid off. But th' more I think about it, th' more I doubt it. Why should he pay good money for a shipment o' whiskey when all he has t' do is take it? Th' minnit a batch of whiskey shows up aroun' here, far as he's concerned it's his."

"Well, he has to buy whiskey somewhere," I said.

"Yeah, but he hauls it himself, honey," Long Boy said. "He ain' agoin' t' let anybody that wants to start bringin' whiskey into his territory. Why, it would ruin his business. I guess he's mean enough t' do near about anythin' t' prevent that."

"I guess so," I said, "but you told me you used to do lots of business with bootleggers."

"Aw, I was messin' 'round with ol' country bootleggers," Long Boy said. "I used t' find out where they kep' their goods an' sneak away a few gallons and sell it back' t' them. But that was shinny—plain ol' 'shine. They used t' keep it in fruit jars an' I'd fill up fruit jars with water t' leave in place of th' ones I took." He shook his head and made a face. "Doggonit, my head needs an oil change for sure. I don't know how I thought I could do business with Jess Hardin the same way." He looked at me. "You see, hon, back then I wasn't invadin' nobody's territory when I went 'round to a bootlegger t' sell him whiskey. Anybody with an ol' car radiator, a few sacks o' corn, and a few dollars to buy sugar and yeast could set up a still and cook up some corn whiskey. Nobody cared. Might be the same today, far's I know. But sellin' bonded whiskey is somethin' else again. There's lots of money in an operation like Jess Hardin runs, an' he ain't about t' let anybody cut in."

"Well, I was sure hoping we could take some of his old money," I said.

"There'll be other days, honeybunch,"

Long Boy said. "Some things jes' ain't worth no amount of money—like windin' up in a ditch dead."

I leaned my head back against the seat and thought about that. For the first time I noticed how dark the night was. The sky was so black that I had to strain my eyes before I picked out a few stars here and there. The moon was a pale sliver. As I watched, an ugly black jagged cloud began to swallow it. I made a little shiver.

Long Boy noticed. "You cold, honey? Want me to stop and put the top up?"

I shook my head. "I'm not cold." I sat and watched the narrow road rushing towards us in the car lights, and I realized I was glad we were leaving Jess Hardin and Winston County. I said, "I like to ride at night."

"So do I," Long Boy said. "Seems like the car runs better." He laughed. "You probably were too little to remember, but one night—" He stiffened and broke off.

"What's wrong?" I asked.

Car's behind us," he said. His eyes kept darting to the rear-view mirror, and by the light from the dashboard I could see his face

178

was more tense than his voice had sounded.

I turned and looked back. "I don't see any lights," I said.

"He's not usin' lights," Long Boy said. "Keep lookin'."

For a long time all I could make out was a swirl of dust rising at the back of the car. But as we hit a stretch of straight road, I saw a black shadow following along maybe sixty yards behind us. "I think I see it," I said. "Now, what do you sup—" Then it hit me like a jolt. I turned to Long Boy. "You don't think it's Jess Hardin?"

"Him or his brother," he said. His voice was calm. "Think we're in for some trouble, honey."

"Aw, it couldn't be," I said, not wanting to believe it. I looked back again. "How would they know where we were?"

"Been watching probably," Long Boy said. "Hopin' we'd lead them t' those twenty cases of whiskey. Maybe the hotel clerk called them."

"Aw . . ." I said, still trying to convince myself it wasn't so. I was suddenly scared. "Aw, I bet it's some old country boy in a rattletrap."

179

"We'll fin' out," Long Boy said. He took his foot off the gas and fastened his eyes on the rear-view mirror. I looked back. When we first slowed, the black shadow came closer, but as we moved slower and slower, it kept its distance. When we were barely rolling, Long Boy said, "Hol' yo' hat, baby!" He slammed the car into gear and slammed his foot down on the gas. The big car gobbled up the road like a hungry bobcat. We must have been hitting seventy when the car behind us showed lights. It was well over one hundred yards behind us now, and I watched as the distance grew every second. Then I heard the siren—*errrRRRRRRRWHAEEEeeeeee*.

I don't suppose there's a scarier sound in creation than a siren meant for you. My heart jumped and I looked at Long Boy. His face was grim. He took his foot off the gas. "Don't stop!" I said. "Keep going!"

"Won't do no good, honey," he said. *errrRRRRRRRWHAEEEeeeeee*. The car was gaining on us fast. Long Boy began to brake and it shot past us and skidded to a stop, blocking the road. Long Boy stopped the car and leaned over and patted my knee. "Ain't nothin' t' worry about, baby girl," he said. "Everything's goin' t' be all right. Let me do th' talkin'."

It was a black touring car with the top up. Two men were in the front seat. The driver stayed in the car but the other man got out and came walking back to us. He was wearing a Stetson hat and had a sway-backed walk. For a moment I was sure it was Jess Hardin. Then our headlights caught him and I knew he had to be Jess's deputy-sheriff brother. He had Jess's freckled face and hard expression, but he was older and heavier. He was wearing khaki clothes and there was a silver badge on his chest and a big pistol riding low on his hip. He was carrying a big flashlight. He shined it in our faces and looked us over good before he spoke. He kept his voice low, but somehow it sounded loaded as a gun. "Playin' games with us, mister?"

Long Boy gave a little apologetic laugh. "Well, I didn't know who was back there, so —"

Deputy Hardin didn't let him finish. "Risky thing t' do. Might git yo' tires shot off." He let that sink in before he said, "Out mighty early, ain't you?

"Sure am," Long Boy said cheerfully. "Me 'n' my little girl thought we'd make an early start."

"Startin' fer where?" Deputy Hardin asked.

"Down south. Eutaw," Long Boy said.

"Live there?"

"Nearby," Long Boy said.

Deputy Hardin put his foot on the running board and casually shined his flashlight around in the back seat of the car. "What's yo' business?"

"Livestock," Long Boy said. "Mules and horses mostly. Some cattle."

"Funny," said Deputy Hardin, and his voice got lower still. "I heered you was a bootlegger."

Long Boy laughed like that was a big joke. "Not me, friend," he said. "Nosir! Mus' be some mistake."

"Mebbe," Deputy Hardin said. "Mebbe not." He stood looking at Long Boy for what seemed a long time before he turned and walked toward the back of the car. He took his time getting around to my side, shining his light in the back seat, at the tires and along the folded top. When he stood beside me, he casually reached out his arm and opened the glove compartment. It was plain as could be he knew what he would find. He must have searched the car while we were in bed. He pulled the two straw-covered bottles out and said mildly, "Foun' th' ol' nest egg, didn' I?"

Long Boy's laugh sounded forced. "That's for a friend. I was takin' . . .'

Deputy Hardin didn't even look his way. He called out to the man in the car. "Aw raht, Bo. C'mon. I foun' what I was a-lookin' fer."

EIGHT

As you grow older, you begin to appreciate that not all bad experiences cause regrets. You probably know what I mean. Sometimes an experience is so bad that you wouldn't go through it again for all the bluebirds in spring, yet you're still not sorry you did it once. Maybe it's made you wiser or foxier or more understanding. But there are other times when an experience is so ugly or scary or hurts so much that it seems as pointless as a bad joke—what old country folks used to call God's cruel jest. All you can do about a bad experience like that is try and forget it.

That's pretty much how I've always felt about the night Long Boy and I got into so much trouble in Winston County. It's why, to this day, I don't know the name of the town where Deputy Hardin took us. I've never bothered to find out. It did seem we drove a long time. Deputy Hardin led the way in the black touring car. Long Boy drove our car and the man Deputy Hardin called Bo sat in the back seat behind us. I couldn't tell much about him as he climbed into the car, except he was big and ungainly—and silent. He didn't say a word as we drove through the dark night, but I could sense him looming at my back. Every time he shifted his weight or made a snuffling sound, I felt a little chill.

I do know the town was tiny—rows of one- and two-story buildings facing a small square or park that had a monument of some sort in the center. At that time of night, of course, everything was deserted and dark. Only two or three of the buildings even showed dim night lights. Deputy Hardin drove halfway around the square and parked at the curb in front of one of the darkened buildings. As soon as Long Boy pulled in alongside him, he yelled over, "Be sure you git 'is keys, Bo." Bo leaned forward and reached out a big hand and Long Boy gave him the car keys. It struck me how silly that was. I always carried an extra set of car keys in my purse. Long Boy mislaid his at least twice a year.

As soon as we reached the sidewalk, Deputy Hardin motioned us toward a doorway at a corner of the building. "Go ahead an' git th' lights, Bo," he said. We waited while Bo clumped up a flight of stairs and switched on a light at the top. They were steep stairs and after we climbed them, Bo went ahead of us down a corridor, switching on lights. There were two or three closed doors along the corridor, and behind one of them, my nose told me, was a dirty toilet. Bo had opened the door and turned on the lights to an office at the end of the corridor. He stood outside, waiting for us. I was surprised to see he was only a hulking old tanglefoot country boy. The door to the office had a frosted-glass pane. On it was painted a big silver star with a line of black letters underneath: CLEEDY HARDIN, DEPUTY SHERIFF. The office wasn't much to look at. Paint was peeling off the walls and there were big brown water stains on the ceiling. It was sparsely furnished with four or five old chairs that didn't match and a stained and dented pine table that was used as a desk. In one corner was a squat black wood stove that furnished heat during the winter. Deputy Hardin pointed to a chair against the wall near the door. "Sit over thar, little girl," he told me.

Deputy Hardin motioned Long Boy to a chair in front of the table. He walked around and plumped himself in a chair facing him. He was carrying the two bottles of straw-wrapped whiskey, and for a long time he sat there holding them against his chest and staring at Long Boy. He was older than I thought and his face was gray and drawn and unhealthy-looking. Somebody had sold him a bad set of false teeth. He had a habit of pushing the lower plate halfway out of his mouth when he looked at you. It made him look like a sickly bulldog. Suddenly he leaned forward and thumped the bottles down on the table hard. "Wal, Mr. Bootlegger," he said, "treed you good, didn' I?"

Long Boy did a fairly good job of forcing a laugh. "Aw, shucks, I ain't no bootlegger, man," he said. "Like I tol' you, that whiskey's for a friend. I didn't see no harm in buyin' a coupla bottles of—"

Deputy Hardin interrupted him with a snort. "Jes' a coupla bottles—no harm!" he said sarcastically. He looked over at Bo, who was sitting on the windowsill with his arms folded. "Hey, Bo, you hear 'at? This big bootlegger heah claims he don' know th' law." He glared at Long Boy and snorted again. "Humpf! Bet you know it better 'n me." His lower plate went jut, jut. He put his arms on the table and leaned forward. "Wal, jes' in case you ain't up on the particulars, you jes' listen t' me good! I don' need no coupla bottles t' make a case agin you, Mr. Bootlegger. Law says all I need is one drap!" He leaned back and drawled it out with satisfaction. "Jes' one li'l ol' drap!'

He looked at Long Boy like he was expecting him to say something. When Long Boy stayed silent, he said, "Now, I'll tell you what kinda mess you got yo'self in, Mr. Big Bootlegger. You kin jes' kiss 'at big purty ol' car outside goodbye. It's done been confeescated. Ain't no ifs, ands and buts 'bout that. Law says you transport alkyholic beverages in a vehicle an' said vehicle is confeescated t' be sold at public auction."

Long Boy said, "Oh, hol' on now. Seems t' me that's pretty rough jes' because—"

"Purty rough!" Deputy Hardin broke in. "You call 'at purty rough? Why, man, you ain't even let me finis' yet!" For a moment, it almost seemed he was about to smile. Instead, he pushed his bottom teeth out and sat there looking at Long Boy. He leaned forward and said, "Looky heah, big boy, I don't think you been listenin'. You're in real bad trouble an' you better jes' start thinkin' on it. I done got cases agin you fer possessin' and transportin' whiskey, an' I reckon if I try I kin think of a few other things." He pointed to the whiskey. "Them bottles ain't got no likker stamps. If I was a min' to, I could git th' Alkyhol Tax Unit boys over heah an' let them have a go at you."

He gave a snort that was almost a laugh. "Why, man, we got a li'l ol' prosecutor up heah 'at's gonna eat you up alive. Big ol' fancy bootlegger like you's jes' what he's been a-lookin' fer." He looked toward Bo. "Ain't 'at right, Bo? Ain't li'l ol' Roney Ware gonna have 'im fer breakfust?" Bo shuffled his feet. Deputy Hardin looked at Long Boy. "Rooney teaches men's Bible class. He hates whiskey worse'n sin."

I saw the back of Long Boy's neck flush. "Lissen," he said, "maybe we oughter talk

189

'bout me makin' bail."

Deputy Hardin sounded surprised. "You ain't gonna git no bail. Ain't no need fer it. This heah ain't th' city. We keep our court calendars up t' date. 'Bout sun-up I'm gonna run you over t' th' county seat an' book you. 'Roun' ten o'clock you oughta be in court." He paused and looked at Long Boy. "You might as well face it, you're gonna be up in these parts fer quite a spell—workin' on th' county roads. If you're real lucky, you jes' might git off with six months. Seein' as how you took it on yo'self t' come up heah lookin' fer trouble, I figger you'll git the whole twelve months. Might be a lot more if ol' Roney thinks he kin bring more charges."

That scared me half to death. I knew Deputy Hardin was telling the truth. Long Boy must have felt the same way. He said, "Maybe you 'n' me could work out somethin'."

Deputy Hardin looked disinterested. "Don' see whut thar is t' work out," he said. He nodded toward the whiskey. "Thar's th' evidence," he said. He looked at Long Boy. "An' thar's you. Don' need nothin' else."

He threw one leg up on the table and tilted back his chair and looked up at the ceiling. He sat there pushing his teeth in and out of his mouth, appearing to be thinking. " 'Course," he said after a while, "don' please me much t' see you end up on th' road gang. Allus have felt sorry fer them pore devils. Out in all kinds o' weather. Gittin' nothin' t' eat 'ceptin a li'l fatback an' cornpone. Don' like t' send a man t' th' road gang. Never have. Ain't that hardhearted."

He took his leg off the table and leaned forward. "Tell you whut I'll do. Can't do nothin' 'bout findin' 'at whiskey in th' car. You gotta stan' trial on 'at. But it'll make a heap o' difference if I don' testify you're a bootlegger. If you kin persuade ol' Roney an' th' judge you had 'at whiskey t' drink you might git off with a fine. Can't hardly git more 'n thirty days at th' worst."

He sat looking at Long Boy. Long Boy said cautiously, "I'm obliged t' you."

Deputy Hardin settled back and his voice was almost pleasant. " 'Course, I can't hardly overlook th' fack you're a bootlegger long's you got a mess o' whiskey hid away. Reckon you're gonna have t' tell me whar it's stashed. Bo an' me'll run out thar an' pour it out. 'At way my conscience won't bother me none.''

Long Boy said, ''There ain't no whiskey.'

Deputy Hardin's face turned mean. ''I know differunt,'' he said.

Long Boy said, ''I'm tellin' you, there ain't no whiskey. I tol' yo' brother —''

Deputy Hardin rared back in pretended surprise. ''My brother? Now, whut th' Sam Hill's my brother got t' do with this?'' He raised his voice. ''You hear 'at, Bo? I try an' he'p this heah man an' he drags my fam'ly in on it.'' He looked at Long Boy and his eyes grew so mean I thought he was about to explode. But after a while he turned away and said, ''Suit yo'self, boy. It's yo' funeral.'' He sat there mulling something over before he stood up. ''Bo,'' he said and nodded toward the hall. Bo followed him outside.

As soon as they left the room, Long Boy turned and gave me a smile and a wink. But it was a weak smile and he looked frazzled out. I guess he had never before been in such a squeeze. As far as I could see, he was in for the same bad trouble whether he did or didn't convince Deputy Hardin there was no whiskey hidden away. If he told the truth — well, knowing Deputy Hardin, it was plain he would be asking for more trouble than he had already. The more I thought about it, the more upset I got. We were always passing gangs of prisoners working on the road, and just the thought of Long Boy swearing away in the hot sun while some old potbellied guard with a shotgun cussed at him almost made me cry.

Deputy Hardin's low voice droned away in the hall for four or five minutes before he and Bo came back in the room. Deputy Hardin's face was grim and determined. As soon as he sat down he said, "Aw raht, big boy, le's cut out this ring-'roun'-th'-rosy! Whar's 'at whiskey?"

Long Boy said, "You gotter believe me, there ain't no whiskey."

"You're lyin'!" Deputy Hardin said.

Long Boy's voice sounded weary. "No, I ain't. There ain't no whiskey an' there never was."

Deputy Hardin glared at Long Boy and started breathing hard. "You off yo' haid! You gonna go t' th' work gang on accounta a few cases o' whiskey? Why, you mus' be crazy!''

Long Boy said, "I'm jes' tellin' th' truth."

Deputy Hardin's eyes were mean enough to kill. "Why'd you say thar was some whiskey?"

"I thought there would be," Long Boy said. "It never got delivered."

"You're th' wors' no-account liar I ever seen," Deputy Hardin said. But for the first time he didn't seem as sure of himself. Some of the meanness went out of his eyes, but when he spoke his voice was vicious. "You think on it. You jes' sit thar an' think on it. I'll give you a few more minnits an' then I reckon I'll jes' have t' git rough." He tilted back his chair and put one leg on the table and looked away.

After a short silence Long Boy said, "Look, I'll make you a deal."

Deputy Hardin tried to sound disinterested but his eyes were alert. "What kinda deal?"

"Well," Long Boy said, "you think I got twenty cases o' whiskey hid away, right? I ain't, but jes' t' prove it, I'm willin' t' give you th' price of that much whiskey—five hundred dollars. I don't have that kinder money on me now, but I can get it when the banks open."

Deputy Hardin took his foot off the table and brought his chair down with a bang. He tried to pretend he was indignant. "You tryin' t' bribe me, bootlegger?" he asked loudly. He looked toward Bo. "You listenin', Bo? You hearin' this?" He slapped his hand down on the table. "Man, you really are in a peck o' trouble now. Tryin' t' bribe a peace officer."

Long Boy said, "I wasn't tryin' t' bribe you. I don't know how else I can convince you I don't have no whiskey."

Deputy Hardin was still blustering. "You mus' be 'bout th' baldes'-face scannel I ever run acrost. Tryin' t' pass a bribe when you're already up t' yo' neck in trouble." He made a show of fuming and looking mad, but it was plain Long Boy's offer had planted doubts about that whiskey. He sat there sliding his teeth back and forth. Casually, too casually, he took out his pocket watch and looked at it. He stood up and said to Bo, "Gittin' on t' five. Somebody oughta be stirrin' over at th' cafe. Think I'll step over thar awhile. Come out in th' hall a minnit 'fore I go." He scowled at Long Boy. "You be thinkin' on whut I tole you."

When Deputy Hardin left the room, I knew we didn't have much time. It was plain as could be that he was on his way either to telephone or meet his brother. I had rolled it around in my mind before, but it was right then that I decided there was only one way out of the boggle we were in — pick up and run. Up until that time I suppose I still had some hope that Long Boy would talk us out of it, like he always did. But it was clear he had reached beam's end. I saw what he was up to when he offered to pay Deputy Hardin for the whiskey, but it had only half worked at best. Deputy Hardin might have doubts about whether there was any whiskey, but he hadn't given any signs that we could buy ourselves free. I opened my red pocketbook and put my hand inside and clutched the extra set of car keys. I squeezed them hard, hoping that somehow they would help me think of what to do.

Bo was out in the hall with Deputy Hardin for a long time. When he came back into the room, he didn't look at us but went behind the table and sat down in Deputy Hardin's chair. He propped his feet up on the table and began poking at his teeth with a matchstick. I looked him over good. He wore a special deputy's badge and had a gun strapped on his hip, but he was the same kind of shuffling, almost handsome old country boy I had been meeting all my life. He was the kind of boy that pumped gas in filling stations and worked behind soda fountains in drugstores and did odd jobs around hotels. I knew he was shy and unsure of himself, not too bright and probably too young to have a real mean streak. He had to be scared to death of women. Trixie could have had him lowing and eating alfalfa in two seconds flat.

I sat there and thought of all sorts of ways to throw him off guard, like pretending to faint or throw a fit and then hit him over the head. But I knew that wouldn't work. Besides, I only wanted to rattle him enough so he wouldn't think clearly for a few seconds. Finally, I thought of something. It wasn't much but I had to take a chance. I clutched the keys tight and slipped them out of my purse. I stood up and walked over to Long Boy and made my voice as whiney as a sleepy four-year-old's. "Daddy, I need to go the shit house."

Long Boy's mouth fell open and his eyes couldn't have been more amazed if I had suddenly sprouted pin feathers. Bo shifted his feet and a red flush started up his neck and covered his ear. He looked up at the ceiling. When I just stood there, he cleared his throat and made a jerky motion with his thumb. "Thar's, uh — place down th' hall."

I tried not to look at the silly expression on Long Boy's face, but grabbed his arm and whined again. "Daddy, I'm a-scared. You come stand by the door." Long Boy looked at Bo, but he still had his eyes on the ceiling.

"All right, baby girl," Long Boy said, "I'll go with you."

As soon as we got out the door, I stretched my arm across the front of my body and found Long Boy's hand and pressed the keys in his palm. He drew back a little. "Let's go!" I said through gritted teeth. He hissed under his breath, "Are you cra . . . Wait, hon . . . wait! . . ." But I kept walking down the corridor, looking straight ahead. As I passed the toilet door, I broke step just long enough to push the door open and close it with a bang. Then I really flew. Long Boy had been dragging behind, but he must have made up his mind to come along in a hurry. He was right behind me when I reached the stairs. You'll never believe what a racket our feet made on those staris. It sounded like two new-shod mules kicking down a barn.

When I reached the sidewalk I was running as fast as I could. I don't know how Long Boy got in the car, but I jumped on the running board and tumbled in head first. Long Boy must have hit the starter, reverse gear and the light button all at the same time. We roared backward, stopped and took off with a jerk that seemed to stretch my neck two ways at once. I managed to catch just a glimpse of the lighted window above us. It was empty.

Long Boy was muttering to himself, "This is th' craziest dang thi . . ." I guess we both saw Deputy Hardin at the same time. He was running toward us along the edge of the town square. Without hesitating, he leaped into the middle of the street and stood there, holding his arms wide. It was either the dumbest or bravest thing I guess I ever saw. There was no way of going around him. Long Boy gave a little groan and started slowing the car. I reached forward and grabbed the throttle on the dashboard and pulled it as far as I could. The motor seemed to take a deep, shuddering breath before the car leaped forward so fast it almost seemed to leave the ground. "Wha . . . wha . . . wha . . ." Long Boy grunted in surprise.

"He can jump!" I yelled.

Jump is what he did. For an instant or two his white startled face seemed to be hovering right over the car's radiator ornament before he turned and dove headlong for the curb. Long Boy pushed the throttle in and managed to straighten the swerving car. "Lord above," he said in an awed voice. Then he got mad. He bawled me out good, but I didn't pay much attention until he started running down and kept saying, "You might have killed him! . . . You might have killed him . . ."

I said, "Well, he ain't dead."

Nobody ever left a town faster than we did that one. The first signs of daylight were just beginning to show around the edge of the sky, so there were lights in a few houses we passed. They flew by zip, zip, and, quicker than you can tell it, we were in the dark countryside. Long Boy was driving too fast to take his eyes off the road. Every few seconds he would ask, "Are they comin'?"

I had turned around so I could watch the road behind us. "Not yet," I'd say.

We must have gone more than a mile before I heard the siren in the distance. Long Boy heard it, too. His face was grim. "We ain't goin' t' make it, honey," he said.

"Yes, we will," I said.

Long Boy shook his head. "Not in this yellow car we ain't. It was a real crazy thing t' do. I should have stopped you."

"It's better than you going to jail," I said.

" 'Fraid we jes' delayed that awhile," he said. "We can outrun them, I reckon, but come sun-up we ain't goin' t' have no place t' go. Ever' two-bit lawman in Alabama's goin' t' be watchin' out for this car."

"Maybe we can hide out in the woods," I said.

Long Boy grunted. "Might have t' do that, but what—" He brought the car to a skidding stop and slammed it into reverse and backed up. We had run through a crossroads. The sign pointing to the road we had been traveling said JASPER. It was the same road we had been on the night before. Long Boy muttered, "Sure don't want t' go that way." He swerved the car around in a cloud of dust and looked at the other signs. As we sat there with the motor idling, we could hear the siren coming closer and closer. Long Boy cocked his head and listened to it, his face serious and intent. Suddenly he gave me a big grin. "Well, le's give 'em a good run for it anyway, sugar." He threw the car in gear and we took off down a side road with the tires squealing.

It was a funny thing about that siren. It must have been the way the road curved or something. Sometimes we wouldn't hear it for as much as two or three minutes at a time. Then for the next few minutes it would come through as clear as if it was right on our tail. I kept looking back, trying to see lights, but after ten or fifteen minutes there wasn't much point in that. It was getting light enough to see the yellow dirt road clearly, and if I stared hard enough I could make out the landscape. We were traveling through scrub forest land, and as well as I could make out it was completely deserted. I hadn't seen a glimmer of light anywhere since we left the main road, and none of the shadows in the distance looked like houses or farm buildings.

Long Boy was bent over the wheel, not looking right or left. Most of the time he had the gas pedal jammed against the floor, or close to it. We were eating up the miles fast when we turned a curve — and ran into bad luck. Chugging along ahead of us, covering the narrow road completely, was an old open truck. There must have been two dozen men standing in the back, and from the way they were dressed I guessed they were construction workers being hauled to their jobs in the game reservation. Long Boy hit the brakes and said, "Oh, Lordy."

We trailed along behind the truck for probably a minute before I got too jumpy to stay quiet. "Maybe if you blow your horn," I said.

Long Boy's face was tight. "Won't do no good," he said. "How can he pull off the road?"

I peered out and looked at the road and felt foolish. Since I had last paid any attention, we had started up a grade. The shoulders of the road fell away four or five feet in most places, and in others the height was too high to judge in the half light. We crept along for another hundred yards or so, and the truck almost came to a halt as the driver shifted into a lower gear. The men in the bed of the truck thought it was a big joke that we were eating their dust. They were laughing and making faces and cutting up like grade-school children.

I don't know how long we trailed along behind that truck before I just sat back and gave up. I realized if I stayed keyed up and anxious much longer I was going to wet my pants. Every so often Long Boy would pull the car to the edge of the road so he could look ahead of the truck and see if a place to pass was coming up. At first, every time he did this he would grunt and say, "Nothin' doin'." Soon he stopped saying anything. I guess he didn't think I was interested. I just slumped back, trying not to think how slow we were creeping along and how fast Deputy Hardin was coming after us.

I thought I had myself pretty well under control until I heard the siren. That made me realize I was only fooling. I sat up as fast as I could and looked behind us. Long Boy kept turning his head to look over his shoulder. "See anythin'?" he would ask. "Not yet," I would say. I couldn't see any lights, but there was no mistaking that the siren was coming closer all the time. The men on the truck heard it, too. They were nudging each other and looking down the road and squinting over the back of the truck trying to get a look at us through the glare of the headlights. The siren sounded so close I was almost afraid to look around. Suddenly two or three men on the truck began pointing down the road and saying something to the others. As many men as could crowded to the end of the truck so they could see over the tailgate.

I swallowed hard. "He's coming," I said.

"I know," Long Boy muttered.

Long Boy drove to the edge of the road and pulled up so close to the truck that he was almost nudging it. He drove like that, craning his neck so he could look around the truck, for maybe another fifty yards or so. I heard him say, "Well, might as well," like he was talking to himself. He turned to me and his voice was tense. "Hol' on tight, sugar." He slammed his foot down on the gas and we went jouncing off the road.

I was so scared it took me a second or two to realize what Long Boy was up to. I guess you know what a road cut is. It's a place where a road is cut through the top of a mountain instead of going over the top of it. Usually the sides of the cut are sloped off so they come down to the edges of the road at about a forty-five-degree angle. Well, Long Boy had been studying the cuts we passed through while dragging along behind the truck. He had decided that if he was forced to, he would drive up the side of one of them and go around the truck. Naturally, I didn't know anything about this. When I caught my breath and looked up, it seemed we were headed right for the pink sky of dawn. We went up and up until the wheels of the car began to spin, then Long Boy gave the steering wheel a twist and we went careening across the face of the cut. We slid and bounced and kicked up so many rocks that it sounded like a crew of men were beating on the bottom of the car with sledgehammers. We bumped back onto the road about ten feet in front of the truck.

The whole thing took maybe twenty seconds. It was a lot longer than that before Long Boy tried to pretend he wasn't breathing hard and asked, "You all right, baby doll?"

I was still trying to catch my breath. "Sure," I said.

Long Boy laughed. "Well, we threw a hobble on 'em for a little while, anyway."

We drove for maybe fifteen minutes and, all of a sudden, daylight was all around us. It was the strangest thing. It was just as if somebody took a big feather duster and, whisk, whisk, all the shadows and dark places had disappeared. Long Boy looked worried. "We gotter get off this road, honey. If we don't find a side road pretty soon, we're goin' to end up in a town for sure."

But there weren't any side roads. On both sides of us, as far as we could see, was miserable-looking scrub land. Once or twice we passed sagging, half-rotten old rail fences, but it was obvious they dated back a hundred years. Once a few folks at least had tried to farm the land. It probably was so sorry and rock-strewn that they finally moved on. Or maybe it finally killed them. We were passing through a small wooded hollow when Long Boy stopped and began to back up. Near the side of the road, half hidden by undergrowth and drooping tree branches, was a small road not much bigger than a trail. He studied it for a while and said, "Le's try it for size, honey."

After he pulled into the road, he stopped the car and went back and used his foot to smooth over the tire tracks we had made in the shoulder of the main road. He took out his handerchief and dusted over the area good before he came back to the car.

The road was not nearly as bad as I expected. It was rough, of course, and sometimes so rutted that we scraped the bottom of the car, but I had gone over lots of roads that were worse. We had ridden along for what seemed a long time, but probably wasn't more than ten minutes, when Long Boy looked off into the woods and gave a grunt. "Looks like we're goin' t' meet somebody soon, hon," he said. He was right. We drove a few hundred yards farther, and there, sitting near the edge of the road, was an old lopsided dog-trot cabin made out of split rails. Behind the cabin, across a yard strewn with all the junk in creation, was a barn. It was twice the size of the house, but even more lopsided.

Long Boy drove into the yard and stopped near the sagging front porch. "Anybody t' home?" he yelled.

After a while the door squeaked open. An old man with weak, sleepy eyes and thin hair standing straight up stuck his head out. He looked at us and without a word closed the door again. I looked at Long Boy. He grinned and said, "Gotter put his pants on."

Maybe a minute passed before the door opened and the old man came out on the porch. He was tall and skinny and barefoot. He was wearing overalls over a pair of stained and dingy-gray long johns.

"Howdy," said Long Boy, putting a deep-country twang in his voice.

"How-do," said the old man. He showed

no curiosity at all, just stood there looking at us.

"Law's chasin' us," Long Boy said. "Thought you might he'p us."

The old man didn't change expression. He rubbed one hand slowly over his stomach. "Whut you done?" he asked.

"Hauled some whiskey," Long Boy said.

The old man must have been thinking that over, but his face looked as dreamy and uninterested as ever. He hooked an arm around an upright on the porch and lowered himself to the ground and walked over and stood in front of the car. He looked it over good, rubbing his thumb along the gray stubble on his chin. "Gotter git this heah car un'er kiver," he said.

"Sho do," Long Boy said.

The old man turned and walked toward the barn. It was built in two parts, with a hayloft extending over a runway down the middle. There was all sorts of junk in the runway, including an old one-horse buggy that had a sagging leather top and one shaft missing. The old man grabbed the one remaining shaft and begun pulling the buggy out of the runway. Long Boy drove the car close to the barn and got out and helped. The old man waved his arms, indicating that Long Boy was to drive the car into the runway. It was a tight fit, but Long Boy managed it. When we got out of the car and came outside, the old man was gone. He came around the corner of the barn a minute or so later, dragging a big rolled-up cloth ground cover, the kind that's used to protect seed beds. It was so rotten it was about to fall apart, but Long Boy helped him spread it and it covered the car completely. The old man climbed up into the loft and threw down maybe half a bale of hay. He and Long Boy scattered it over the ground cover and pushed the buggy back into the entrance of the runway.

The old man stood outside the barn and looked things over. "Might do," he said. As he turned to walk away he said, "Yawl come in th' house."

Stepping into that house was like going back to wilderness days. There was a big stone fireplace that almost covered one wall. It was used for cooking. Something was simmering over the fire in a black iron pot hanging from the end of a swinging iron tripod. Smoke-blackened pots and pans were stacked on the hearth and dishes and cutlery were scattered along the mantelpiece. A table that had been used so long it had a finish like satin was in the middle of the room. Four chairs with split-willow seats and backs were grouped around the fireplace. There was an unmade corn-shuck bed in one corner and an old kitchen safe with a tin front in another. On the walls, either hanging from or supported by wooden pegs, was the oddest conglomeration of things you ever saw. Everything from tintypes to rifles to rusty steel traps.

The old man stood in front of the fireplace and slapped the broad floorboards with one bare foot. "Got mah root cellar down un'er heah. Anybody comes nosin' 'roun, yawl kin hide thar."

"I'm obliged," Long Boy said. "Aimin' t' pay you for yo' trouble."

The old man gave him a calm look. "Don' take silver fer he'pin' folks," he said. "Agin the Book." He motioned to the chairs. "Sit."

After we were seated, the old man studied

the fire before he asked, "Whut name you go by?"

"Pray," Long Boy said. "This here's my little girl, Addie."

The old man nodded slightly. "Name's Jackson. Mos' folks call me Dock." He looked at the fire some more and said slowly, "Been know t' cook a leetle whiskey mahself."

"I figured," Long Boy said.

Old Dock thought about that. "How'd you figger?" he asked.

"Saw that stack of slow-burnin' wood down by the road," Long Boy said.

Old Dock rubbed his chin with his thumb. "Been meanin' t' move 'at wood," he said. He looked at Long Boy under his brows. "Say, you got purty good eyes, ain't you?"

"Mister," Long Boy said, "where I come from you gotter know revenuer signs afore they'll give you a name."

Old Dock digested that and his mouth twitched in a slight smile. The smile became a grin. He began to cackle with laughter. He swiped at his eyes with his hand and slapped his bare foot against the floor. " 'At's good," he said. " 'At's sho good!" He

looked at Long Boy. "Whereabouts would'
at be?"

"Down south," Long Boy said. "Coffee
County."

Old Dock's face was vague again. "Don'
know 'at," he said. "Never one fer gittin
'bout much. Been livin' heah all mah life an'
mah daddy 'fore me. An' his daddy an' his
daddy. Mah great-granddaddy come heah
from Tennessee. Reg'lar b'ar of a man, so
they say."

"You all alone?" Long Boy asked.

Old Dock nodded and gazed in the fire
with a faraway look. "Buried mah woman
two year ago September," he said. He
paused. "Good woman she were, too.
Married near fo'ty-seven year, an' nevah
raised her voice oncet." He paused again.
"Don' seem right somehow. Miss her."
After a silence he looked up and asked,
"Yawl et?"

"Not since last night," Long Boy said.

Old Dock pointed a bare toe at the iron
pot over the fire. "Got some squirrel stew
a-cookin' thar. Ain't much, but plenty of it."

"Thankee," Long Boy said. "Sounds

good. Don't recall I ever ate squirrel this time o' year."

Old Dock stood up and started taking bowls off the mantel. "They's all raht ef'n you don't take the sows," he said. "Get sow squirrels carryin' young'uns an' th' meat's kinder sharp."

The stew was good—tender pieces of squirrel cooked in corn meal with a handful of dried red peppers. After we had eaten, Long Boy and I went outside and walked slowly around the yard. I kept waiting for him to say something, but when he didn't I asked, "What are we going to do now?"

"I don't know, sugar," he said. "Haven't figured it out yet." He shook his head. "Ain't never had my tail caught in this kind of crack before." He looked disgusted. "It's that dang car. Minnit we hit a highway in that thing, we're goners. Might as well be drivin' 'roun' in a fire wagon."

"Maybe we can sell it," I said.

Long Boy looked bleak. "Worth a try, I reckon, but don't think we've got a chance. Not in these parts. Take that cart to a dealer, and the law'll be 'roun' faster 'n the shake of a lamb's tail."

"Well, we'll just have to leave it," I said.

"Be kind of hard walkin' out here, honey," he said. "We got t' have some way of travelin'." We walked awhile and he said, "Reckon you know we're goin' t' have to leave the state for awhile. Warrants are goin' t' be out for us everywhere." He grinned. "We snapped ol' Deputy Hardin's galluses pretty hard. Probably take some time for things to simmer down."

"Where will we go?" I asked.

"Well, Tennessee's the closest," he said. "If we don't like it up there we can go someplace else. They say Mississippi's a good place t' do business."

When Old Dock came outside, we walked over and sat on the edge of the porch and talked with him. Long Boy said, "Like t' sell that car out there."

Old Dock blinked a little. "Purty car," he said.

Long Boy smiled. "Know anybody might wanter buy it?"

Old Dock sounded puzzled. "You mean 'roun' heah?"

"That's right," Long Boy said.

"Why, ain't nobody 'roun' heah got no

money," Old Dock said. "Nevah has had."
He pondered that awhile. "Hear tell things
is hard ever'whar now. Reckon 'at's a fack?"

"It's a fact all right," Long Boy said.
"Maybe I could swap th' car."

"Swap fer whut?" asked Old Dock.

"For another car," Long Boy said.

"Oh," Old Dock said. He sat and
thought. "Hankins boys gotter truck. Ain't
much."

"Where do they live?" Long Boy asked.

"Ovah near Hankins' Springs," Old
Dock said. "Purty fur piece."

"How can I get in touch with 'em?" Long
Boy asked.

Old Dock thought some more. "Reckon I
kin git th' young Gaylord boy t' walk ovah
thar," Old Dock said. "He he'ps me out
sometime, stirrin' mash an' like that.
Gaylords live t' other side 'at hill yonder."
He pointed to a low hill in the distance.

"Be grateful," Long Boy said. "Will he
be goin' near a store?"

"Lokey's Store, I reckon," Old Dock
said.

"Mebbe he can get us a load o' groceries,"
Long Boy said.

Old Dock sat musing. "Could use some syrups," he said. "Had me a sweet tooth fer some syrups fer a week er two." He stood up. "Go call th' Gaylord boy."

"How you goin' t' do that?" Long Boy asked.

"Ring mah bell," Old Dock said.

We followed him around the cabin. A rusty rim from a wagon wheel was hanging by a chain from a chinaberry tree. Old Dock picked up a short iron rod and whammed it half a dozen times. It sounded as loud and clear as a church bell. "He'll come a-runnin' direckly," Old Dock said. "Down at th' branch a-fishin'. Allus is at this time o' day."

In about fifteen minutes we saw the young Gaylord boy coming across the field. He was as scrawny as a young boy, but he had been old enough to shave for at least twenty years. As far as I could tell, all he was wearing was a faded pair of overalls, held together here and there with pieces of twine. He had a vacant look and lots of teeth missing. Old Dock and Long Boy took him off and explained what they wanted. After a considerable time, Old Dock handed him a croaker sack and Long Boy gave him money for groceries.

We had more squirrel stew for lunch. Afterwards we went out on the porch with Old Dock, sitting with our backs against the wall and our legs stretched out in front of us. Before anybody could say anything, we all were fast asleep. The young Gaylord boy came back about three o'clock, sweating but happy. "Jeff Lokey gave me a stick o' candy when I buyed th' provisions," he said. "The Hankinses 'lowed they'd be ovah 'fore sundown. Leroy's be'n drunk agin." Long Boy gave him a dollar and he went away stunned.

After he left, Old Dock said, "None o' mah business, but that air car ain't stole, is it?"

"No sir," Long Boy said. "Paid cash for it an' got th' papers t' prove it."

"Jes' a-wonderin'," Old Dock said. "The Hankins boys are kinda mean when they think somebody's puttin' somethin' ovah on 'em. Reckon Leroy Hankins is jes' mean aller time."

For supper we had fried fatback, greens and hoecake. Old Dock poured sorghum syrup over everything. We had scarcely

219

finished before we heard a loud rattle and wheeze out in the yard, and we knew the Hankins boys had arrived.

You'll have to believe me, I never saw worse trash in my life than the three Hankins brothers. All of them were dirty and needed shaves and their overalls were so grimy that they could have stood in a corner by themselves. Those men smelled like a pack of wet hounds that had been lapping whiskey. They were more rangy than bulky, but any one of them was big enough to stand flatfooted and spit over a cow shed. Clovis and Asa Hankins were whoopers. They kept wide, idiot grins pasted on their faces, and they laughed at nearly anything that was said. Leroy, the youngest brother, had a mean, sulky expression that never changed. There was something about his eyes and his way of moving that.made you uneasy when he got at your back.

The Hankinses' old Dodge pickup truck looked almost as sorry and patched together as they did. When Long Boy looked at it his face froze a little. He pushed at the battered top and kicked a frayed front tire that had a funny bulge on the side, but didn't say anything. He led the Hankinses out to the barn and Old Dock gave him a hand as he took the ground cover off the car. He let the Hankins boys get a good gawk before he got behind the wheel and started the motor. He raced it awhile and slid out from under the wheel and stood on the running board. He made his voice real country. "Aw raht, boys, thar she is, good as new. She sells for better 'n twen'y-seven hunnert dollar, and she ain't got but six hunnert and seventy-nine miles on th' gauge. Wouldn't git shed o' her for nothin', 'ceptin' th' law's chasin' me for haulin' whiskey an' a few other things. Know I can't git away in her. She's too big and purty. Law'll be on me like a chicken on a June bug." He slapped his hand down on the door. "Look at her good."

Clovis and Asa Hankins looked at each other, and Clovis said, "Whut you a-askin'?"

"Ain't puttin' no price on her," Long Boy said. "Couldn't git what she's worth anyhow. What I'm a-lookin' for is a swap. Onliest thing I ask is you give me three days' head start 'fore you take her out on th' highway. Dock Jackson heah'll give you th'

221

keys an' papers then."

Clovis and Asa looked at him blankly. Leroy was scowling. "Well, c'mon, boys," Long Boy said. "Whut you offer? I'll take that ol' beat-up truck out thar as a starter."

Clovis and Asa looked at each other disbelievingly before Asa gave a little whoop. They both broke into wide grins and began slapping each other on the shoulder. Leroy had the same scowl. As far as I could see, nothing about the car seemed to impress him anyway, except the chrome spotlight. He kept running his hand up and down it and turning the handle that shifted the beam. He gave his laughing brothers a dirty look and spat on the ground. He turned his mean eyes on Long Boy and asked sullenly, "How we know th' car's your'n?"

Long Boy said, " 'Cause I got th' papers, man. They's right thar in the dashboard. All I gotter do is fill out a form on th' back and th' title's transferred t' you." He turned to Clovis and Asa. "Aw raht, boys, whut you offer 'sides th' truck?"

"We got four dollar," Asa said.

222

"I'll take it," Long Boy said. "Whut else?"

"I gotta good deer gun," Clovis said.

"Don't want it," Long Boy said. "Can't use no guns. Don't want no furniture neither. Whut else?"

Asa whispered something to Clovis and Clovis nodded. "We got two bales o' cotton," he said.

"Will they fit in th' truck?" Long Boy asked. Clovis and Asa nodded. "I'll take 'em," Long Boy said.

"Ain't gonna swap 'at cotton," Leroy said loudly.

Long Boy barely glanced at him. "Whut else, boys?" he asked.

Leroy made his voice louder and uglier. "Ain't gonna swap nothin'." He glared at Long Boy and his brothers, who had stopped grinning. He spat again. "Car ain't no good nohow."

Long Boy looked at him levelly. "Whut's wrong with it?"

"Can't haul nothin' in it," Leroy said.

Long Boy's tone showed how foolish he thought that was. "If that's all that's botherin' you," he said, "you can sell this car an' buy yo'self two trucks." He turned to Clovis and Asa. "For that matter, I reckon this car's got more space in it than that ol' truck."

"Ain't gonna swap!" Leroy said loudly. He turned and walked out of the barn. His brothers looked at each other in alarm and hurried after him. They overtook him when he was about halfway to the truck. We watched while they put their arms around his shoulders and talked to him earnestly. After a while he shrugged their arms off angrily and stalked away. Clovis and Asa stood there looking bewildered until Leroy started up the truck and began backing out of the yard. They both shot glances toward the barn, then turned and ran and got in the truck with Leroy.

As they drove away, I was so disappointed I was just heart-sick. Old Dock grunted. "Wal, 'ats 'at." Long Boy didn't say anything. His face was calm. While he was helping Long Boy put the ground cover back on the car, Old Dock said, "Right peeculiar folks them Hankinses air. Clovis an' Asa ain't so bad, 'ceptin' when they's likkered up. Reckon they take atter their daddy. But 'at Leroy, he's like 'is mama. Snappish as a vixen with kits, 'at woman. Allus in a fume. Oncet ol' man Hankins come home drunk an' give 'er a lick er two. She bided 'er time till he fell asleep, 'en built a fire un'er th' bed. Cooked him up somethin' awful, so they say."

That night we slept in the second room of the dog-trot cabin. Long Boy had a bed, but Old Dock fixed me a corn-shuck pallet on the floor. I was so sleepy my head was about to fall off, but I couldn't get what had happened off my mind. "Don't worry, honey," Long Boy said. "They'll be back."

"What makes you so sure?" I asked.

"Well, don't forget there's two against one," he said. "That's one thing. The other thing is Leroy wants that car jes' as bad as his brothers. He won't admit it because he's mean an' contrary. He can't he'p it. It's his nature."

Of course, Long Boy was right. About mid-morning we were sitting on the front porch when the old truck came rattling and wheezing up the road and pulled into the yard. Clovis and Asa got out with wide, foolish grins. Leroy looked as disagreeable

225

as ever. Clovis said, "Like to look at 'at car agin."

Without a word, Long Boy got up and led them back to the barn. After he and Old Dock had taken the ground cover off the car, Clovis and Asa walked around it slowly, grinning with delight. Leroy stood in the doorway glowering. After a few minutes Clovis and Asa went over to Leroy and took him outside. We could see them arguing with him furiously. Leroy didn't say a word, and nothing they said changed the mean, stubborn expression on his face.

It was probably fifteen minutes before the Hankinses came back into the barn. Clovis and Asa started circling the car again. Leroy stood near the door, but this time he kept scowling at Long Boy. It was plain there was something about Long Boy's calmness that stuck in his craw. He moved over and stood close to Long Boy and put his hand on the car's spotlight. "Car ain't no good," he said.

Long Boy gave him a brief glance and looked away.

Leroy's mouth tightened and he began twisting the handle on the spotlight. He made his voice jeering. "Reckon I'll jes' he'p mahself t' this heah spotlight, anyhow."

Long Boy turned and looked at him steadily. His voice was low but hard and cold. "Do," he said, "an' I'll skin you alive."

Leroy's scowl grew darker but he didn't say anything. He stood there with his hand on the spotlight until Clovis and Asa motioned him outside again. As soon as they were gone, I said to Long Boy, "You're going to start trouble if you're not careful."

Long Boy smiled. "Look, sugar, I was raised amongst hog-wallow scum like the Hankins boys. Let one of them trod yo' foot, an' first thing you know, all of them are stompin' you t' death."

This time the conference out in the yard seemed to go on forever. Clovis and Asa had Leroy cornered near the chinaberry tree. They were talking away with all their might. Occasionally one or the other of them would kick up a cloud of dust or throw his hat on the ground in disgust. Leroy was scowling, as usual. Looking at him, I realized Long Boy had sized him up perfectly. In his mean, contrary way, he

227

probably was enjoying himself. Finally, they came slouching back into the barn. Clovis and Asa had lost their grins. Leroy was unchanged. Clovis said to Long Boy, "Reckon we'uns hafta think on it some more."

"Sorry, boys," Long Boy said, "deal's off. I been offerin' you a brand-new car for a lotta junk, an' I got no more time to waste." He turned to pick up a corner of the ground cover.

That drew them up short—Leroy included. For an instant or two the glare in his eyes gave way to something else. He looked at Long Boy and turned to look at his brothers. He shuffled his feet. His expression grew meaner than ever. He said loudly, in the same jeering tone he had used earlier, "Rassle you fer it!"

Clovis and Asa began laughing and nudging each other, and at first I thought it was some kind of silly joke. But Long Boy turned around and looked at Leroy. "Rassle for what?"

Leroy said, "Fer that air spotlight agin th' swap."

"What kind o' rasslin'?" Long Boy asked.

"Cotch as kin," Leroy said.

"Shoes or barefoot?" Long Boy asked.

"Makes me no nevah mind," Leroy said.

"Barefoot," Long Boy said.

Clovis and Asa began whooping and pounding each other. I stood there too surprised to move. Even after the men began to leave the barn, I still couldn't believe it was happening. I hurried after them. Long Boy was stooping over untying his shoes. I marched up to him and said, "Are you crazy!"

"I'll take care of this, baby doll," he said. "Maybe you'd better go in th' house."

"I won't go in the house!" I said. I stuck out my bottom lip and glared at him, but I was about to cry.

Long Boy took off his shoes and socks and stood up. Leroy had kicked off his brogans and stood about ten feet away, pawing at the ground with his dirty bare feet. Clovis and Asa were behind him, almost rolling on the ground as they whooped and hollered and swatted each other. Old Dock stood off to one side, working his jaw in a chewing motion, he was so excited.

Long Boy began rolling up his sleeves. "Now, le's get this straight," he said. "If Leroy wins, he gets th' spotlight on th' car. If I win, he agrees t' swap th' truck, two bales o' cotton and four dollars for the car. Right?"

"Thass right, boy!" Clovis yelled. "You said it, boy!" Asa whooped. They fell in each other's arms laughing.

"Le's go then," Long Boy said. He began walking toward Leroy. Leroy spread his legs and crouched low, the knuckles of one hand dragging the ground. He looked like a big monkey. Asa yelled, "Make 'im say calf rope, Leroy!" Clovis pounded him on the back and almost fell on the ground laughing.

When he was about five feet from Leroy, Long Boy began circling him, looking over his right shoulder. Leroy shifted around slowly so he could keep facing him. Suddenly, he fell to the ground and, supporting himself on one arm, lashed out with his feet, trying to kick Long Boy between the legs. It was so fast and vicious I caught my breath. "That ain't fair," I yelled. "You stop that!" I was close to Old Dock. I moved over and tugged at his overalls. "Make him fight fair," I said.

Old Dock didn't hear a word I said. He was working his jaw fast and his old eyes had a bright gleam. "Don' git in th' way, little lady," he said, not taking his eyes off Long Boy and Leroy.

It seemed to me that Long Boy was circling Leroy a lot faster. I was surprised to see how smoothly and gracefully he moved. Somehow I had never thought of Long Boy as a fighter, only as a talker. For the first time I realized that for a middle-aged man, nearly thirty-five, he had a lot of prance left.

Leroy blinked and shook his head. Trying to follow Long Boy from a crouching position was making him dizzy. He stood up and, holding his arms wide, started moving toward Long Boy. Without slackening his pace, Long Boy said, "Don't step on that rake, Leroy." Leroy stopped and turned his head to one side and looked down. Long Boy took a half step forward and gave him a hard backhanded clout right across the Adam's apple. Leroy's eyes seemed about to pop out of his head. His face turned red, then purplish. He tried to draw a deep breath and made a noise that sounded like *Heeeeee.* He bent double, gagging and choking. Long Boy took dead aim with the side of his foot and kicked him as hard as he could under the chin. Leroy flew backwards and hit the ground like a two-hundred-pound sack of wet manure.

Clovis and Asa were laughing so hard they could hardly walk. They staggered over to Leroy and knelt beside him. Long Boy smiled at them and asked pleasantly, "Fair enough, boys?"

"Fa'r enough, fer sure," whooped Asa.

Clovis was twisting Leroy's head from side to side. "Fa'r as could be," he yelped.

All I could do for a while was stare at Long Boy. What I really wanted to do was go over and hug him but, of course, I couldn't do that. So I decided it was better to laugh than cry.

We pulled out in the old truck about an hour after dark. Long Boy was wearing a pair of Old Dock's overalls and he had taken the band off his hat and punched it out of shape. I wore my tackiest dress and a poke bonnet that had belonged to Old Dock's wife. Our suitcases were squeezed down between the cotton bales in the back of the truck and covered with croaker sacks. Old Dock came out to wave us off, but his mind wasn't on it. Long Boy had made him take a twenty-dollar bill, and he held it in his hand and kept staring at it. I guess it was the most money he had ever had in one piece in his whole life.

The old truck ran pretty well for a couple of hours. Then we hit a steep grade and it began to heat up and boil over. We had to stop and Long Boy got out and cussed and fussed and unscrewed the radiator cap. Watching him in the dim headlights brought back a pleasant memory. When he got back in the car, I asked, "Long Boy, we don't have much money, do we?"

"We got enough t' do us for a while," he said.

"But we don't have much?" I said.

"No, I reckon not," he said. "We spent a lot on that dang car, an', uh, other things."

He laughed. "We may have t' start sellin' Bibles again 'fore this is over, honeybunch."

Somehow that made me feel better than ever.

NINE

Maybe you remember a song they used to sing back in the thirties? I can't recall the name of it, but it had a line that went:

Five-cent cotton, fo'ty-cent meat,
How in the world kin a pore man eat?

It wasn't anything to smile about, really, except in a sad way. All farmers had their ragged behinds slam against the cold ground back then, but your average little cotton farmer was the one who was hurting for rations. He was near about desperate enough to eat the harness right off his mule. Looking back, I've often wondered if Long Boy and I weren't the only two people in the whole world who were making money out of cotton at that time. If President Franklin D. Roosevelt hadn't started a program that made farmers plow under every third row of cotton, I guess we would have made a million dollars. That program was supposed to cut the cotton crop and raise the price, but all it—but that's what I want to tell you about.

We didn't intend doing business with cotton when we came chugging up from Alabama in the old Dodge truck. Long Boy calculated later that we traveled only about 125 miles, but what with the truck boiling over and two punctures and one blowout, it took us all night long. It was good daylight when we reached the Tennessee line and I was curled up asleep. Long Boy had promised to wake me up, because it was the first state line I had ever crossed. When he shook my leg and said, "Here it is sugar! Here's Tennessee," I sat up right away.

I don't know what I expected, but whatever it was, I was disappointed. Tennessee looked exactly like Alabama, as far as I could see, except maybe the road was a little better. I sat looking around, yawning and blinking, for a mile or two before I asked, "Can't we stop pretty soon? I'm tired."

"In a little while, baby," Long Boy said. "I'd like to try an' sell that cotton first. We can get rid of this old truck 'most anywhere."

236

"How do you sell cotton?" I asked.

"Dogged if I know," Long Boy said. "Never sold any. Only money crop I know much about is peanuts. Maybe we can find out when we stop t' eat."

We stopped for breakfast at a roadside place. After we had eaten, Long Boy spoke to the fat man behind the counter, making his voice suit his faded overalls and beat-up hat. "Whar kin a man sell some cotton 'roun' heah?"

The man shook his head in sympathy. "Don't hardly pay t' bring it in, does it, mister?"

" 'At's a fack," Long Boy said.

The man said, "Mos' folks use th' spot market up near Pulaski. Reckon it's as good as any. 'Bout six miles straight up th' road. Great big ol' warehouse on th' right. You can't miss it."

"Thankee," Long Boy said. "Whut they payin'?"

"Middlin' ain't bringin' but a nickel a pound," the man said. "Won't do much better 'n that with Good or Strict Middlin'. 'Course, they'll start out by offerin' you three or four cents a pound."

" 'Course," Long Boy said.

Finding the warehouse was no trouble. It must have covered three or four acres. A big sign across the front said: HALSTEAD BONDED WAREHOUSE. As early as it was, four or five wagons and a couple of trucks, loaded with cotton, were lined up at a long platform before a rear door of the warehouse. We got in line and waited our turn. It probably took the better part of an hour before we reached the platform. Two big colored men, carrying hooks, stepped into the truck and tussled the two bales of cotton onto the platform. A huge scale was built flush with the floor. A potbellied old man, wearing glasses pushed down on his nose, was behind a stand-up desk near the warehouse door. When he saw the two bales of cotton, he reached up and took two long green tags out of a box on the wall near his head.

One of the colored men grabbed a bale of cotton and went *Huuff!* and pushed it onto the scale. He waited until the needle stopped quivering on the big dial and called out, making a song of the words, "Fo'r hundret an' eigh'y-nine, raht on th' line!"

238

"Four hundret an' eigh'y-nine," the old man repeated, writing it down on both ends of the green tag. He handed the tag to the colored man, who fastened it to one of the metal bands around the bale.

When it was his turn, the other colored man shoved his bale onto the scale. *Huuff!* He sang out, "Five hundret an' twen'y-six, tuk an awful lotta licks!"

"Five hundret an' twen'y-six," the old man repeated. He scribbled and handed the tag to the colored man. He looked at Long Boy. "Sellin'?" Long Boy nodded. The old man turned to one of the colored men and said, "Git 'im samples, Jim."

The man named Jim had an ugly, sickle-shaped knife dangling from a long cord tied to his belt. He grabbed it by the handle and ripped the sacking on the side of one of the bales. With one quick twist, he stuck the knife into the bale and whacked out a handful of cotton. He went around to the other side of the bale and did the same thing. He tore the bottom half off the green tag and stuck it between the two handfuls of cotton and handed the wad to the old man, who had taken a sheet of brown paper from

239

a shelf under his desk. The old man twisted the paper around the cotton so it looked like a big ice-cream cone. He did the same thing with cotton and the tag from the other bale and handed the two cones to Long Boy. When Long Boy just stood looking at him, he said, "Take them samples an' co'pons 'roun' ter th' front awfice. They'll give you yo' receipts."

We were going down the platform steps when we saw a tall young man coming up the driveway toward us. He was the best-looking thing, all dark in the brow and white in the teeth. He was wearing a crisp linen suit and a wide-brimmed Panama hat. I could have died because I was wearing that old dress and poke bonnet. The young man took off his hat and smiled at us. His voice was so deep and melodious it lingered in the air. "Good mawnin', suh. Good mawnin', young lady. Sellin' yo' cotton today?"

"Aimin' to," Long Boy said.

"Well, suh, Domingus and Son would 'preciate yo' patronage," the young man said. "We buy for th' bes' mills an' pay top prices. Our office is right ovah yonder." He

240

pointed to a row of small frame buildings across the road from the warehouse. "If you step by after you get yo' receipts, mah father will 'tend to you personally."

"Thankee," Long Boy said. "We will."

We drove around to the front of the warehouse and went in the office. A dark-haired young man, standing behind a counter, had just finished waiting on a tall old farmer with his arms filled with samples. Long Boy went over and the young man asked, "Name, please, suh?"

"O.C. Johnson," Long Boy said, giving one of the names he had a lot of identification cards for.

The young man wrote the name on one of the receipts in a big square book. He reached out and fished around in one of the samples Long Boy was carrying and found the green coupon. After copying down the printed number on it as well as the scribbled weight, he pushed the coupon back into the cone under the cotton. He did the same thing in filling out a second receipt and asked, "You sign, Mistah Johnson?"

"Sho kin," Long Boy said. The young man turned the book around and showed

Long Boy where to sign. He tore the pinkish receipts out and handed them to him and dropped carbon copies in a drawer. He said, "Warehouse charges start at noon today, Mistah Johnson. Unless you make assignments to a buyer, you're liable for all charges."

"Fair nuff," Long Boy said.

The pinkish warehouse receipts were like oversized bank checks and kind of impressive. When we got outside, I took one from Long Boy and looked at it. Across the top was printed the name and address of the warehouse, and below was a line that said, *U.S. Government Bonded.* Using an indelible pencil, the young man had filled in a form that certified O.C. Johnson had, on that date, stored a bale of cotton, tag number so-and-so, that weighed so much. He had signed his name in the right-hand corner over a line marked *Officer.* Long Boy's fake signature was in the other corner over a line marked *Owner.*

We walked across the road to the row of buyers' offices and found the small frame building with a sign DOMINGUS & SON over the door. There was only one room inside. A plump red-headed girl sat at a desk in the rear. Mr. Domingus had one haunch thrown up on a scarred table near the door. He looked like his son, gone to seed. His linen suit was wrinkled and he had a whiskey nose and needed a shave. His sharp old trader's eyes were bloodshot. "Mawnin'," he said.

"Howdy," Long Boy said. "Like t' see 'bout sellin' mah cotton."

Mr. Domingus reached out lazily and took a handful of cotton from one of the cones Long Boy was carrying. He squeezed it and ran his fingers through it for maybe thirty seconds, then pulled off a piece about the size of a walnut and handed the rest back to Long Boy. He began to stretch the small piece of cotton between his thumbs and forefingers, discarding a little at a time until only a few strands were left. Cocking his head to one side, he studied them critically before he blew them away. Without a word, he reached out and took another handful of cotton from the second cone and went through the same procedure. He shook his head slowly. "Wal, color's not very bright, as you can see for yo'self.

Staple's nuthin' special, an' it's kinder trashy, too." He thought awhile. "Reckon I can go as high as four cents."

Long Boy shuffled his feet like a chaw bacon. "Kinder hopin' fer more 'n 'at," he said.

Mr. Domingus shook his head again. "Wal, neighbor, can't pay for quality when it ain't there. Rather not handle anythin' 'ceptin' Middling or better, but try t' accommodate folks with Strict Low Middling like yo'self."

Long Boy appeared to be thinking that over. He said, "Reckon I'll try somebody else." He turned to me. "Le's go, honey."

Mr. Domingus waited until he was sure Long Boy was serious before he said, "Might raise it to four an' a quarter."

Long Boy didn't look back. "Thankee," he said.

We were almost through the door when Mr. Domingus said, "Wal, c'mon back in heah. Give you four an' a half. Ain't nobody gonna beat that price for that cotton. Stake mah reputation on it."

Long Boy paused and thought before he turned. "Take it, I reckon," he said.

Mr. Domingus didn't appear to be either pleased or displeased. He nodded toward the redheaded girl. "Lady back there'll take care of you." He called over his shoulder, "Four and a half cents, Annie Jo."

The girl had a real sweet way about her. She took the warehouse receipts and the green coupons and clipped them to a white form. Like the young man had done, she asked, "Do you sign, Mr. Johnson?"

"Yessum," Long Boy said.

She made a cross on the form and pushed it over to Long Boy to sign. "This is an assignment giving us ownership of the cotton," she said. While Long Boy signed, she turned to an adding machine and punched it. After she got the total, she gave Long Boy a smile and said, "Giving you four and a half cents, one thousand and fifteen pounds comes to forty-five dollars and sixty-eight cents. Is that right?"

Long Boy nodded. " 'Pears 'bout right."

She opened a large checkbook and wrote him out a check.

As we were leaving the office, Long Boy said to Mr. Domingus, "Be bringin' th' rest o' mah crop in tomorrer."

"Fine, fine," Mr. Domingus said. "Always glad t' do business. Treat you right."

When we got outside I said, "What did you tell him that for?"

Long Boy gave me a big grin and wink. " 'Cause I meant it, sugar," he said. "Wait till we get to th' car n' I'll tell you about it." He was in such high spirits that he took my arm and practically picked me up as we ran across the road. As soon as we were in the truck, he turned to me and his eyes were shining. "Hon," he said, "we jes' stumbled on somethin' that's goin' t' make us rich. I mean real rich! Why, do you know that man in there jes' gave me forty-five dollars for a few handfuls o' cotton?"

"Why, no, he didn't," I said, "he—"

Long Boy didn't let me finish. "But how did he *know* we had any cotton? How did that young fellow in the warehouse office *know* we had any cotton, 'cept that ol' man an' them two colored fellows in th' back of th' warehouse."

"Well, they know no old farmer's going to cheat them," I said.

Long Boy laughed. "How 'bout

somebody who ain't no ol' farmer?" he asked. He sat grinning at me until I got his point and looked at him. He laughed again. "Look, honey," he said, "this whole sellin' operation's based on th' fact that pore dirt farmers are th' most honest people there is. That—an' th' fact that a big old bale o' cotton ain't hardly th' kind o' thing you shuffle aroun' an' play skin games with. Nowadays, I reckon it's hardly worthwhile stealing one. But there could be a lot o' money in cotton if all you had t' do was sell it like we did today."

"Forty-five dollars doesn't seem like a lot to me," I said.

Long Boy said, "That's 'cause you ain't thinkin' big enough, sugar." He took out a pencil and his small notebook. "Now, le's figure this way," he said. "I reckon almost any little ol' one-mule farmer ought t' bring in about ten bales o' cotton a year. That wouldn't be much of a money crop. Well, le's say me 'n' you, dressed th' way we are now, drivin' this ol' truck, were t' call on two cotton buyers every day an' sell each one of 'em our whole crop o' ten bales. It would take us maybe an hour or two, and we'd be selling twenty bales o' cotton a day. A bale of cotton averages out to five hundred pounds. That means we'd be sellin' ten thousand pounds a day. If we didn't get but four and a half cents a pound like we did today, that would give us four hundred and fifty dollars a day. If we took Saturdays and Sundays off, that would give us two thousand two hundred and fifty dollars a week."

My mouth must have fallen open. I felt breathless. It took me a while before I saw what was wrong with the plan. "Well, just tell me one thing," I said. "Where are we going to get the warehouse receipts and samples?"

Long Boy waved his hand airily. "Oh, th' samples ain't important. We can get a little cotton anywhere." He looked thoughtful. "The way I figure it, th' warehouse receipts ain't th' most important. The whole thing depends on gettin' those tag coupons. With coupons and a coupla handfuls o' cotton, we can go to the front office and get receipts. With receipts, we can go on and do business with buyers. But, first, we got t' have those coupons."

"Where will we get them?" I asked.

Long Boy smiled. "Well, I'll do some more thinkin' on it, but seems t' me th' easiest way is jes' to take them. Come nightfall, I aim t' slip 'roun' to th' back of this ol' warehouse an' get myself a supply o' those green coupons."

He scared me. "You'll get yourself shot, too!" I said.

He laughed. "Who's goin' t' shoot me? Look, baby doll, nobody's goin' t' be guardin' a warehouse full o' cotton. Cost more t' haul it away than it's worth. They got an automatic fire system. I saw it."

"Suppose they discover they're missing," I said.

"They won't," he said. "I won't take 'em right off th' top o' th' stack." He started the truck and turned and smiled at me. "Whut you've got t' remember, hon," he said, "is that nobody in the world thinks those coupons are important right now, 'ceptin' you an' me."

We drove into Pulaski and registered at a hotel. After taking baths, we fell into bed and slept until suppertime. I guess it was just as well the daytime staff at the hotel had gone off duty when Long Boy and I came down to the dining room. If they had recognized us at all, they might have thought it funny that a farmer in old overalls and his tacky little daughter could suddenly appear looking like city folks. I wore my favorite green dress and Long Boy was wearing his blue suit that made him look like he might own the biggest automobile agency in town. After we ate, we walked down the main street, looking in store windows, and Long Boy stopped in a drugstore and bought a small flashlight that fitted into his coat pocket.

About ten o'clock we got in the truck and drove out to the warehouse. It was as dark and deserted as Long Boy had said it would be. In fact, it was so black and shapeless and silent that it gave me the shivers. I had expected Long Boy to go sneaking up to the back entrance like a burglar, hiding in the shadows, and maybe even slipping off his shoes so he wouldn't make any noise. Instead, he didn't even turn off the lights on the truck. He drove right around the building and parked at the platform as unconcernedly as if he owned the place. He left the lights on and the motor running. As he stepped out he said casually, "Be back in a minnit, sugar."

The big sliding door to the warehouse was closed, but there was a small door built into it. Long Boy shook the handle a few times and muttered to himself and used the flashlight before he got it open and stepped inside. I sat there fidgety as a sore-footed hoot owl. Every time I saw the lights of a car on the highway, I held my breath until I was sure it wasn't going to turn in at the warehouse. After about five minutes I was afraid to look toward the shadows all around me. I saw somebody standing there every time I did. As time dragged on and on and Long Boy still didn't come out, I began to imagine all sorts of things. Suppose somebody had caught him? Suppose he had fallen and hit his head and was lying in there unconscious?

Finally, when it seemed like the shadows were about to reach out and grab me, I couldn't stand it any longer. I pushed open the door of the truck and went running up the platform steps. The little door was open just a crack. I leaned close to it and

251

whispered, "Long Boy." When there was no answer, I pushed the door and stepped inside. My heart almost stopped when I saw a light and somebody standing only a few feet away.

It was Long Boy, of course. He had turned on his flashlight and was bent over the stand-up desk near the warehouse door. I suddenly felt so mad I wanted to bite him. "Come out of here!" I said. "Are you crazy?"

He turned and I saw a flash of white as he grinned. "C'mon in, honey," he said.

He had a tall stack of the green cotton tags on one corner of the desk. He was taking them one by one and scribbling numbers across the top and bottom. He nodded toward them. "Foun' a whole box o' these durn things. Thought I'd use the ol' man's marking pencil, long's it was handy."

"Let's go!" I said, still furious. "You've been in here half the night!"

"Jes' a few minnits more, baby," he said absently. He motioned over his shoulder. "Grab some of that cotton. We'll be needin' samples." One of the bales must have split open. There was a big pile of cotton about fifteen feet away from the sliding door. I went over and pulled out my skirt and filled it with as much of the cotton as I could. I stood there, first on one foot and then the other, fretting, until Long Boy marked the last of the green tags. "There!" he said. He reached under the desk and took a pile of the brown wrapping paper and folded it around the tags. He came over to where I was, and before I could stop him he took off the coat to his nice new suit and began piling cotton on it.

When we got back to the truck I was still sulky. Long Boy grinned at me. "Aw, c'mon, baby doll, smile. I ain't taken close count, but I think we raised ourselves about fifty bales o' cotton tonight."

We were up at daylight the next morning. Long Boy wore his overalls and beat-up hat and I had on my old dress and poke bonnet. We stopped at an all-night drive-in for doughnuts and coffee. After we got back to the car we sat there making up cotton samples, putting the green tag coupons between two handfuls of cotton and wrapping them up in brown paper. After we had eight of the cones stacked on the dashboard I said, "That's enough."

Long Boy said, "Aw, honey, one or two more."

"That's enough!" I said firmly. I was still nervous about the numbers on the coupons. I felt sure somebody was bound to notice they were out of order. Long Boy tried to reassure me. "There ain't a chance they'll notice," he said. "When that ol' man needs more tags, he jes' reaches in that box and grabs a stack. Besides, I betcha big growers wait till they've delivered ten or even twenty truckloads o' cotton to th' warehouse before they take their coupons 'roun' and get receipts. An', anyway, like I tole you, those coupons don't mean a thing to anybody, 'ceptin' you 'n' me."

There was already a line of wagons and trucks at the back platform of the warehouse. Long Boy pulled the truck to the edge of the driveway and stopped. "Le's let them heat up a little bit," he said. After about twenty minutes, when the line had grown longer and three or four big loads of cotton had been delivered, Long Boy started the truck and grinned at me. "Le's go ramify 'em, hon." We drove around the warehouse, past the platform, and parked in front of the office at the same spot we had the day before.

Two farmers were ahead of us at the counter. Both had their arms loaded with samples. When it finally was Long Boy's turn, the dark-haired young man didn't show any signs of recognizing him. "Name, please, suh?" he asked. When he reached out and fished around and took the first coupon, I held my breath. But he copied it down without a word. He made out eight receipts and asked in his usual polite back-handed way if Long Boy could write his name.

Long Boy said he could, and after he signed the last receipt he asked, "Whut's yo' name, young fellow?"

"Halstead, suh," the young man said. "John Halstead."

"You don' own this heah place, do you?" Long Boy asked.

Young Halstead seemed shocked at the idea. "No suh, that's mah Uncle Clyde."

"Clyde Halstead," said Long Boy musingly. "Any kin t' th' Halsteads down near Ardmore?"

"No suh, not as I know of," young Halstead said.

"Wal, fine folks, anyway," Long Boy said. "Now, save me some mor' o' them thar receipts. Be seein' you ever' day this week. Ol' truck won't haul but so many bales at a time."

Young Halstead said primly, " 'Preciate yo' business, Mistah Johnson."

Mr. Domingus was sitting at the same place we left him the day before. The gray stubble on his chin was a little longer, and maybe his eyes were a bit more bloodshot. He slid off the table and said, "Mawnin'."

"Come t' sell you mah bes' cotton today," Long Boy said.

Mr. Domingus didn't say anything. He took the samples from Long Boy and put them on the table. He went over them carefully, testing the staple of each between his thumbs and forefingers. After he had finished, he pushed five samples to one side. "Staple on this heah batch is fair," he said, "but th' color's poor. Reckon I can go as high as four an' a half cents." He pointed to the other three samples. "Now, that cotton thar is real trashy. Lots o' bolls an' stems in

256

thar, an', besides, it's plumb dirty. Ain't the quality I'm lookin' for, but I'm glad you came in heah, so I'll give you four."

Long Boy shook his head. "Nawsuh." Sounding like he knew what he was talking about, he pointed to the five samples and said," 'At thar is Middling cotton, an' I'm goin' t' tote it aroun' till I git a nickel a pound." He put his hand on the other three samples. "Now, this heah is th' same kinda cotton I sol' you yesterday. Reckon it oughter bring th' same price today."

"Whut'd I give you?" Mr. Domingus asked.

"Four an' a half," Long Boy said.

Mr. Domingus rubbed the side of his nose with his finger. He picked up the five samples and walked back and put them on the redheaded girl's desk. "Five for these, Annie Jo," he said. "Four an' a half for t' other three." He said to Long Boy, "Step back heah, an' th' lady'll take care of you."

In her sweet way, Annie Jo had Long Boy sign an assignment form and made him out a check for $193.21.

When we got outside, I felt so good I wanted to skip, but all Long Boy could manage was a small grin. After we got in the truck I asked, "Well, what's wrong now?"

Long Boy shook his head. "Doggonit, it jes' ain't enough, sugar. Eight bales o' cotton seems like a lot somehow, but a hunnert and ninety-three dollars sure ain't a lot o' money."

"Why, it is so," I said, getting a little mad. "It's almost two hundred dollars. That's a lot of money to earn in one day. It wasn't too long ago when we thought we were lucky if we made twenty dollars." The more I thought about, the hotter I got. I said, "Let me tell you, not many folks make two hundred dollars in one day. I bet President Franklin D. Roosevelt himself doesn't make that much!"

Long Boy smiled. "Now, now, honeybunch," he said, "simmer down. I wasn't complainin'. I was jes' thinkin'. We've got us a fine way of doin' business, but it's still got a lot of flaws in it."

"Like what?" I asked.

Long Boy said, "Well, we got th' whole day ahead of us. Wouldn't it be nice if we could sell another eight or ten bales o' cotton?"

"We could go to another buyer," I said.

Long Boy sighed. "That's jes' it. There's plenty of buyers, but we have t' go to th' same place an' the' same man t' get receipts. I miscalculated bad. 'bout that. Coupons will get you receipts all right, but not an unlimited supply." He rubbed his chin. "I'll have t' think about it."

He sure did think about it—hard. I'll say that for Long Boy. When he had a problem on his mind, he didn't think about much else until he found a solution.

The next day was Wednesday. We wrapped up ten samples and took them to the warehouse office. We took our receipts to a buyer named Lon Bates, who had an office down at the end of the row from Domingus & Son. He was a sour-faced old man with an abrupt manner. After testing our samples he said, "Give you five cents. 'At's th' top price th' mill lets me pay. Take it or leave it."

"I'll take it," Long Boy said.

"Fine," Old Man Bates said. "Tard o' hearin' folks complain cotton ain't wo'th

259

raisin'. Commission I git don't make it wo'th buyin' neither." He sat down and wrote Long Boy a check for $248.80.

On Thursday we took in another ten samples to the warehouse office. As soon as we crossed the road with our receipts we heard Old Man Bates yelling in his office. "Don't you go callin' me no robber, y'hear? I ain't gonna take that kinder talk from nobody!" He was standing behind his desk, facing a gawky freckle-faced farmer who looked as mad as he did. "You got any complaints," Old Man Bates said, "write to them perfessor fellows up in Washington. They's the ones that's runnin' things, not me."

The farmer eyed him coldly. "You write 'em, mistah," he drawled. "All I'm a-tellin' you is nobody's buyin' 'at cotton for no nickel a pound. I'm a-drivin' up t' Memphis whar a man can git a square deal." He turned and stalked out.

Old Man Bates was so mad and his hands were shaking so, he could hardly test our cotton. "Five cents," he snapped.

"I'll take it," Long Boy said. Old Man Bates wrote him out a check for $237.17.

When we crossed the road to the warehouse parking area, the gawky farmer was standing beside a huge empty flatbed truck. Long Boy went over to him. "Did I hear you say you aimed t' sell yo' cotton in Memphis, mistah?"

" 'At's right," the farmer said. "Brung me in a load o' Good Middling cotton. Ain't gonna let them robbers ovah thar buy it same as it war Middling."

"Can you sell receipts on this warehouse up in Memphis?" Long Boy asked.

The farmer looked at him closely to be sure he wasn't kidding. " 'Course you can," he said. "Bonded warehouse receipts is good anywhar. Why, I reckon most folks 'at got cotton stored in this warehouse goes somewhar else t' sell it. Most has got a reg'lar buyer close t' home. Some'll drive two hundred miles lookin' for a better deal. Man goes whar he gits th' bes' price.'

"Sho didn't know 'at," Long Boy said thoughtfully.

"Lookit, friend," the farmer said, "they's one thing you gotta remember in dealin' with buyers at a li'l ol' spot market like this one heah. Them robbers ovah thar is nearly

261

all workin' on commission for th' big mills. Lots of 'em'll make you think you got Good Ordinary cotton, then squeeze out a few dollars extra by tellin' the mills they paid you the proper Middling price."

"Is 'at so," Long Boy said.

" 'Course all buyers ain't like 'at," the farmer said, "but it's pert near wo'th drivin' anywhar t' git one who'll treat you right. Buyers who work direct for th' mills is bes'. Far as whar yo' cotton is stored, buyers don't give a dang, long's it's in a bonded warehouse. Mill's gotta send trucks 'roun' t' pick up cotton at all the warehouses anyway."

Long Boy nodded thoughtfully. "Wal, thankee kindly," he said. "I learnt a lot talkin' t' you." He didn't say a word as we drove back to town. When we reached our room he stretched out on his bed and stared at the ceiling. After maybe thirty minutes, he sat up and said, "Addie, baby, we got t' go back to th' warehouse an' get some more receipts this afternoon."

"No!" I said.

"Look, hon, it's important," he said. "We won't take many samples, maybe five."

"You're pushing your luck," I said.

"I know it," he said. That surprised me. When Long Boy was doing business it usually took all I could to to make him show some moderation. "Why does it have to be this afternoon?" I asked.

"I wanter study one of those receipts good," he said. "I think maybe I got an idea."

"What idea?" I asked.

He lay back down on the bed. "Well, there's no use talkin' about it till I see a receipt. I'll tell you then."

After lunch we got in the truck, and drove out toward the warehouse. About halfway there Long Boy pulled into a dirt side road and parked and we made up five samples. "Reckon this'll be th' last batch," he said. I couldn't tell whether his voice was sad or thoughtful. He started the car. "String would have run out tomorrow anyway," he said. "Guess I made a mistake when I made sure that Halstead boy knew me. Otherwise we might have gone on for a few more days."

When we parked outside the warehouse office he said, "You can wait in th' truck if

263

you wanter. Won't be but a few minnits."

"No, I'll go with you," I said. I knew he was up to something, and I didn't intend to let him out of my sight. But I was mistaken. As young John Halstead wrote out his receipts, Long Boy said, "Wal, this heah load winds it up. Won't see you till next year."

"Made yo'self a good crop, Mistah Johnson," young Halstead said.

"Fair," Long Boy said. "Yo' Uncle Clyde come 'roun' much these days?"

"No, suh," young Halstead said, "he spends mos' of his time out at his place near Aspen Hill. Crazy 'bout them walkin' horses he's raisin'."

When we got outside Long Boy went directly to the truck. He sat behind the wheel and studied one of the pinkish receipts for a long time, looking at it back and front. He seemed a little disappointed, but I couldn't be sure. He reached in the cotton samples and took out the green coupons and put them with the receipts. He handed them all over to me. "Put 'em in yo' pocketbook, hon," he said.

"Now, what . . ." I began.

264

He smiled. "I'm not goin' t' tell you a thing till I see if this works. You'll find out when we get back to th' hotel."

He drove back to town as fast as the old truck would go. As soon as we reached the room, he went over and picked up the telephone and said to the operator, "Honey, can you ring me Halstead's Bonded Warehouse, out on Highway Sixty-four?" He hummed under his breath until the connection was made and said, "Halstead's Warehouse? Could I speak to Mr. Clyde Halstead, please?... Oh, he is. Well, ma'am, this is John Boggs at Boggs Printers. I wanted t' talk to him 'bout maybe gettin' some of his printin' business. . . . Oh, he does? . . . Yes, ma'am, I see. Well, maybe you could tell me who does his work now?... Stationery and bills o' lading, yes, ma'am. Do they do his receipts and bale tags, too?... Oh, I see. . . . Down on South Street. . . . Well, thank you, ma'am. I'll try to call Mr. Halstead next Wednesday. Goodbye."

He hung up the telephone and gave me a big wink. After a few seconds he picked up the receiver again and said to the operator, "Honey, now can you get me Polk's

Printing Company, on South Street?" He cleared his throat, and when the connection was made he made his voice low and respectful and sort of prim. "Could I speak to Mistah Polk, please? . . . Oh, it is. Mistah Polk, this is John Halstead, out at Halstead's Warehouse. . . . Fine, Mistah Polk, an' yo' self? . . . Glad t' hear it, suh. Mistah Polk, Uncle Clyde asted me t' call an' tell you we're gettin' low on receipts an' bale tags. . . . Yes, suh, he said th' reg'lar order. . . . Well, suh, we need 'em as soon — . . . Saturday at three? Yes, suh, I reckon that'll do. . . . No, suh, he's not. Out at his place near Aspen Hill. Crazy 'bout them walkin' horses he's raisin'. . . . Oh? Well, it musta slipped his mind, Mistah Polk. . . . Yes, suh, I'll sure do that, Mistah Polk. . . . Yes, suh, I'll send th' cash 'roun' with this order. . . . Receipts and bale tags, yes, suh. . . . Thank you, Mistah Polk. One of th' warehouse men will come 'roun' at three o'clock on Saturday. Goodbye, suh."

Long Boy hung up the receiver and looked at me. His face was serious. "Now how 'bout that? That man don't pay his printin' bills." Then he gave a whoop and

266

threw himself back on the bed, laughing.

I looked at him, grinning. I was so excited I couldn't keep my feet still. "Do you think it'll work?" I asked.

" 'Course it'll work," Long Boy said. "Why, it's already worked." We sat there talking and laughing for maybe an hour, and Long Boy said, "There's something else we've got to tend to."

We went downstairs and got in the old truck and drove it to a garage down the street from the hotel. Long Boy talked to the owner and his two mechanics. "I don't want you to touch anything on the outside of this junk pile," he said. "But you've got till noon Saturday t' do anything you can t' fix it up on the inside an' make it run better. I don't care how much it costs. Jack it up an' put a new car under it for all I care." He took four $50 bills out of his pocket and handed them to the manager. "This heah is earnest money. Buy parts and new tires all ' round and anything else you need. I'll tack an extra fifty dollars on the bill t' be split amongst you, if I like th' job you do. You got two nights an' almost two days to make this ol' truck run like new." He slapped the side of the truck. "This heap's got a lot o' travelin' t' do in the next month."

The three men stood there with their mouths open before they started grinning. Back in those days people who talked like Long Boy just didn't come driving into garages.

I guess the next day was one of the happiest, most carefree Long Boy and I ever had. That night I even got Long Boy into a picture show. I still remember parts of it. It was called *Son of a Sailor,* with Joe E. Brown. I thought Long Boy would die laughing when one man said to wide-mouthed old Joe E. Brown, "I oughta cut your throat from ear to ear," and another man said, "Somebody's done it already."

It was on Saturday morning that we started getting nervous. We tried to act casual, but we bumped into each other a lot walking around the room. Long Boy called the garage to be certain the car would be ready, and we picked at our lunches and went around there about one o'clock. Those men had sure taken Long Boy at his word. They had found a nearly new wrecked 1933

Dodge somewhere and stripped it of its engine, mohair seats and whatever other parts they needed. The inside of the cab even smelled like a new car. The motor sounded like a mama cat nursing six kittens. It cost Long Boy $340, counting the bonus.

Before we checked out of the hotel Long Boy put on a suit of white coveralls he sometimes wore when we did business with wallets. We drove down South Street until we found the printing office and parked down the block. We were forty-five minutes early, but after twisting and drumming his fingers for about fifteen minutes, Long Boy said, "Maybe they're ready. I'll see." He wasn't in the printing shop long. He came out carrying a big box and a square package. When he got in the truck he said, "Cost me thirty-eight dollars and sixty-one cents. Le's see if it was worth it." He handed me the package and ripped open a corner of the box. It was crammed full of green warehouse tags. I tore the paper off the package. There were a dozen big square books. Long Boy took one and riffled the pages. There, a dozen to the page, all crisp and new-smelling, were 120 pinkish

Halstead Bonded Warehouse receipts.

For a breathless moment or two Long Boy and I just looked at each other. He started laughing first. He jammed his foot on the starter and said, "Move over, John D. Rockefeller — heah we come!"

TEN

I wish everybody in the world could be rich, at least for a little while. Oh, I'm not so dumb that I thinks lots of money necessarily makes folks either happier or better. All the same, there's no doubt in my mind at all that spreading some money around would cure more human ills and miseries than penicillin. And what I do know is that when you have more money than you know what to do with, the world becomes a brighter, simpler place. I can't explain this exactly, but it sure isn't just the money. Money isn't important at all when you don't need it. Maybe it's like the old-timey saying goes—heavy purse, light heart.

Long Boy and I didn't waste any time in getting rich. When we left Pulaski on Saturday afternoon, neither of us thought we would start doing business with the books of receipts before Monday. But when we got to Lawrenceburg, about twenty miles away, we registered at a hotel and I sat down right away and began practicing copying John Halstead's neat, rounded handwriting from the five genuine receipts we had. After about thirty minutes I had it down so pat that Long Boy looked at it and gave a low whistle. "It's pert near perfect," he said. "Why don't we give it a try?"

"Now?" I asked.

He grinned. "Why not? Ever'thing stays open late on Saturday."

He went down to the drugstore and bought a whole box of indelible pencils for me and a heavy marking pencil for himself. He marked the green tags while I copied out ten certificates. We made up samples and found a stocky, cheerful cotton buyer who had an office upstairs over a grain store. He tested our samples and offered us a nickel a pound. A quiet, gray-haired lady who worked in the office made us out a check for $250.96.

When we got back in the truck, we grinned at each other for a minute, and Long Boy drummed his fingers on the steering wheel. "Well, it's still sort of ear..." he began.

I looked at him and laughed. "Let's!" I said.

We hurried back to the hotel and made up ten more samples. This time we found a grumpy old buyer, who had his bottom lip crammed full of snuff, in an office near the railroad station. He was an old crook and didn't offer us but four cents a pound. Long Boy got him up to four and a half and took it. We came away with a check for $224.19.

Well—would you believe it?—we tried it one more time before we called it a day. It was almost nine o'clock when we sold our third batch of ten samples to a buyer who had his office right off the main street. I guess we might could have hit a couple more buyers if we hadn't been tired. At least, when we called it a day, there were farmers still walking around carrying samples. Our profit for the afternoon was $721.95.

On Sunday morning Long Boy sat down and scribbled weight numbers on a pile of tags, and I almost wore out my fingers writing out receipts. I had filled out more than half the receipts in one book before I finally had to quit.

We got up early Monday morning and set

out to do business in earnest. I just can't recall all the names of the towns we hit and the county lines we crossed in the next four or five weeks. We always did heavy business in the bigger towns, like Waynesboro, Savannah, and Selmer, of course, but we didn't pass up smaller places, like Pinger and Leapwood and Hornsby. We never sold less than thirty samples a day. On an average day we sold forty, but there were lots of days when we traveled fast and sold fifty. We always took in better than $700 a day, and after a while we didn't think much of it when we had a $1,000 day.

Never once did we have a buyer question our receipts. The only time one ever gave us a bad minute or two was in a little town called Pocahontas. We were doing business with the buyer for a mill there when he picked up one of our receipts and said, "Pulaski, eh? Why'n't you go to th' spot market there?"

"Did," Long Boy said. "Didn't like th' price they offered.'

"Who'd you see?" the buyer asked.

"Fella named Domingus," Long Boy said.

The buyer grinned. "Ol' Cal Domingus?"

"Reckon 'at's th' one," Long Boy said. "Tried t' cheat me."

The buyer laughed. "That's ol' Cal, all right. Know 'at ol' scutter!"

Oh, we had some problems. After the first couple of weeks, getting enough cotton for samples slowed us up two or three times. Long Boy slipped around to the back door of a warehouse one night and got us a small pile. Another night he found some on the platform of a cotton gin. We finally solved the problem when we discovered some cotton buyers didn't keep their samples but threw them out back of their offices. We'd drive around after dark and Long Boy would pick us up a supply. Lots of times we sold buyers samples they already had paid for and thrown out the back door the night before.

Cashing our checks was the biggest single headache we had. Long Boy didn't want to mail checks to his bank in Eutaw, because he knew that sooner or later they would be traced. He always cashed them and sent money orders to his bank. As long as we did business with a buyer while the banks were still open, cashing his check was no problem. But most days we still were doing business after the banks closed. Sometimes we had too many checks on the same little bank to dare cash them all. What we did then was go around to a mercantile or feed store and get them cashed. Long Boy would mosey in like a farmer who had just gotten his hands on some money and to buy something he needed in a hurry. Before long, we always had bales of hay and sacks of mule feed or churns and post-hole diggers in the back of the truck. After we got too big a load, we would stop alongside a pasture somewhere and leave everything in a pile for a farmer to find.

I liked it best when we cashed checks late on Saturday night. Most always then we went into a mercantile store and joined other farm families who were ordering a week's supply of groceries. Sometimes we went to two or three stores before we got all our checks cashed. We would have the truck pretty well filled with sacks of flour, grits and corn meal, slabs of sowbelly, and gallon cans of syrup. We always waited until we found a sorry, rundown old shackle somewhere, and we would stop and stack everything on the front porch. Lots of times everybody in sight, children and grownups alike, would run and hide indoors when we drove up. We wouldn't see a sign of them while we unloaded the groceries. But sometimes a worn, empty-eyed woman would come out on the porch and watch us. She always had a baby straddling her hip, and there would be a cluster of wide-eyed, runny-nose young'uns peeking from behind her faded, ragged skirt. I don't recall any of them, white or colored, ever said a word to us. They just stared while we unloaded the groceries. "They're all yours," Long Boy would say, and we would drive off. I always looked back. Usually they pounced on the groceries as soon as we left. But often they still were standing there, staring, when they passed out of my sight.

I think the thing that made me maddest was how crooked some cotton buyers were. Some of them would offer us three or four cents a pound for the same samples honest buyers paid us a nickel for. Long Boy always laughed when I fussed and fumed about them, especially when I used to say I was going to try and find out if there wasn't some place I could report them. It was a long time before I realized myself how funny I must have sounded.

It was really surprising how busy we were. Of course, I had to sit down almost every night and make out a new supply of receipts. Before long I could write like John Halstead from memory, but it still was boring work and I hated it. We took a lot of weekends off, of course, and I usually went to the picture show and bought just anything I took a fancy to. But it was funny—having all that money didn't seem to make me want more. Long Boy was the same way. On weekends he usually went out and found a pool hall, or did other things I didn't inquire about, but the only thing he was interested in spending money on was that old truck.

I guess you might say that truck got to be his hobby. It all started when he first discovered the new motor in the truck made it faster than a lot of cars we met on the road. He loved to pull up alongside a respectable-looking car at a stop light or railroad crossing. When the way was clear, he would slam the truck into gear and run off leaving the other car like it was standing still. Sometimes drivers stared bug-eyed, they were so surprised. Almost every time we had a day off, Long Boy would take the truck to a garage and ask the mechanics to fiddle around and see if they couldn't make it run faster. I don't know about things like that, but it seems to me the truck finally had more than one carburetor and something called an overdrive. I know it could scat like a turpentined cat when Long Boy wanted it to.

All the same, the truck still looked awful and I sometimes wished we didn't have to keep it. I felt the same way about wearing tacky dresses and a poke bonnet all the time, but I consoled myself that doing the kind of business we were doing made it tolerable.

To show you how little we knew about cotton, we had done business in four or five counties before we discovered we still hadn't reached the real cotton-growing section of Tennessee. You see, the bulk of the state's crop is grown in fifteen or sixteen counties, all well within 150 miles of Memphis. We had some vague intention of going to Memphis, but when we began to hit such rich cotton-growing counties as Hardeman and Fayette, we got sidetracked completely. Everywhere you looked there was a wagon or truck loaded with cotton. Cotton gins and warehouses were working night and day. Cotton buyers were as easy to find as fleas on old dog Tray.

My, we really did sell those receipts! I don't guess there was hardly a place in west Tennessee we skipped—from Chewalla to Hollow Rock to Golddust. One night when I was making out receipts I said, "We'll be starting on the last book tomorrow." Long Boy had his feet propped up, smoking a quarter cigar. "Well, I guess it's jes' as well, hon," he said. "Season's almost finished anyhow. We'll sell twenty or thirty more samples an' head into Memphis."

"What do we do when we run out of receipts?" I asked. Long Boy was feeling relaxed and prosperous. "No need t' do anything, baby doll," he said. "Seems t' me we don't need t' work but a couple of months a year from now on." He took a puff on his cigar. "May as well take it easy till cotton-pickin' time rolls 'roun' again. Then we'll get ourselves a big load of receipt books on another warehouse an' start doin' business again. Maybe down in Mississippi."

I've thought about that conversation lots of times since then. I guess there's one thing you can be sure about in this life. When things are going good and you don't have a single worry, that's the time to expect real trouble. I was too young to know it then, but Long Boy sure should have known better.

We had used only a dozen or so receipts out of the last book when we took Highway 70 and drove down to Memphis. I really expected to find that town in pitiful shape. Everybody said that between the low price of cotton and a bare trickle of shipping on the Mississippi River, Memphis was barely clinging to the vine. But it didn't seem that way to me. It looked like a big busy city, except maybe the people strolled along like they weren't in any particular hurry. Most folks were well dressed, too, especially the crowds along South Main Street, in the heart of town. The longer I looked at them, the more conscious I became of Long Boy's limp faded overalls and my ugly old dress. "We can't go to a hotel looking like this," I said.

Long Boy had been looking the crowds over too. "Yeah," he said, "I guess you're right." We drove for another block and he said, "We'll go down to the railroad depot and use the rest rooms to change in. I'd like to go to th' Gyoso Hotel, if we can. I hear it's real nice. We can drive the old truck into the parking lot an' go 'round to th' front door."

That's what we did. And Long Boy was absolutely right about the Gyoso Hotel. I guess everybody knows about it. It was old-fashioned and well worn, but it had beautiful old polished furniture and thick carpets and crystal chandeliers. It was the most elegant hotel I had ever stayed in. There was a genteel hush about it, if you know what I mean. All you had to do was look around like you wanted something, and there was somebody right there to help you. I just loved it.

We relaxed for a whole day before we set out to do some business with samples. We had left our country clothes in the truck out in the parking lot. Long Boy took off his coat and tie and pulled his overalls on over his trousers and put on his old hat. All I had to do was slip into a pair of rundown shoes and put on my poke bonnet. We drove down to the cotton market on Front Street. That place was just teeming. Huge trucks loaded with cotton were parked everywhere, and people were thronging in and out of the dinky little offices buyers had in all the rundown buildings up and down the street. There were lots of farmers carrying samples, but we saw plenty of big growers, too. They wore white linen suits and broad-brimmed Panama hats, and most of them carried canes. You didn't see them bothering with samples. They had whole warehouses loaded with cotton, and the buyers went out there and graded it. The big growers just came in to dicker over the price or pick up their checks.

We had ten samples with us and another ten in the truck. We didn't have any trouble at all in selling them at a nickel a pound. About the only difference was, there were several buyers to an office. After one of them had graded your cotton and a price was agreed on, the buyer made out a slip and took it with the coupons and receipts to a cashier's cage at the back of the office. You had to wait in line while your check was made out.

After we sold our last samples, we walked down Front Street and looked over the waterfront. The old Mississippi looked to me to be as broad as the ocean. If shipping was slow then, it must have been some sight when it was normal. Big boats and barges were tied up at all the wharves for as far as we could see. Others were passing up and down the river constantly. We saw one single line of barges being towed past that looked as long as a freight train.

We followed pretty much the same pattern for the next few days. We would drive down to Front Street in the morning and sell twenty samples. Afterwards, we would drive back to the parking lot and change into our good clothes before we went back into the hotel. I don't know what all Long Boy found to do, but I enjoyed just sitting in the lobby, watching all the different people come and go. I think it was the third day after we arrived that something exciting happened.

I was sitting in a large leather chair in a corner of the lobby when I felt something poking into my side. A letter, written on a single sheet of expensive folded stationery, had slipped down between the seat and the side of the chair. The letterhead was in large engraved type: JAMES WILKERSON & COMPANY. MINING ENGINEERS. SAN FRANCISCO. It had been sent to: "Colonel Rupert Culpepper, Sea Breeze Plantation, Biloxi, Mississippi." As well as I can remember, it read:

Dear Colonel Culpepper:

Attached herewith is all data pertinent in our survey of your mining property, Lost Mine #4, near Dugway, Utah.

As you will see, our fee for restoring Lost Mine #4 to full operational capacity will be $1,435,867.00. This fee includes the cost of all vehicles, but not the cost of two light airplanes, which we suggest you purchase for the convenience of yourself and associates who may be as busy as you are.

From previous experience, we know you

prefer to finance your mining operations by yourself, or with the aid of a few close friends and associates. However, if you wish additional financing, we will defray all costs of restoring Lost Mine #4 to full operational capacity for a one-quarter interest. Our geologists feel it has an unlimited potential.

The letter was signed by the president of the company. I sat there swallowing hard and looking at that figure again and again to be sure it really was for well over a million dollars. Then I jumped up right away and began looking for Long Boy. I couldn't find him anywhere. After I looked every place I could think of, I sat down and tried to compose myself while I waited for him. But I was scared to death Colonel Culpepper would come looking for his letter. I was sure of one thing. I wasn't going to hand the letter in at the desk — not until Long Boy read it, or I got a look at Colonel Culpepper so I could point him out later. Finally, I was too jumpy to wait any longer. I sneaked another look at the letter and memorized as much as I could and went over to the desk clerk. "Is Colonel

Culpepper staying here?" I asked.

The desk clerk didn't even have to look it up. He gave me a smile. "Magnolia Suite, fourth floor, little lady."

I took the elevator to the fourth floor and walked down the hall until I found a door with a brass plate on it: MAGNOLIA SUITE. I gave my skirt a yank and smoothed down my hair and knocked. A nice-looking colored man, wearing a starched white jacket, opened the door.

"Is Colonel Culpepper here?" I asked.

The colored man smiled. "Yes, he is, young miss. Who do I say is callin'?"

I was about to give my name when I heard a man's voice say, "Who is it, Richard?" The door opened wider, and Colonel Culpepper himself was standing there. The colored man gave him a big grin and nodded toward me and went away.

Colonel Culpepper looked like a millionaire, all right. He wasn't a tall man—in fact, I guess you might say he was on the short side and sort of plump, but he held himself real erect. He had snowy-white hair, lots of it, that he wore long and brushed back. He had the merriest bright blue eyes that I ever saw. But it was his face that made him unusual. It was as open and happy-looking as a baby's. It made you feel that he had never had a bad day in his life. He was wearing a beautiful beige pongee suit and expensive-looking brown-and-white shoes. A crisp white linen handerchief flared out of his breast pocket. For just a moment I got the impression he was a little taken aback to see me.

"Are you Colonel Culpepper?" I asked.

He smiled at me like we were sharing some secret joke. "So they tell me, lamb," he said.

I poked the letter at him. "You must have dropped this," I said.

He flipped the letter open and glanced at it. "So I did," he said. "Didn't know it had gone astray." His voice was light, like there was a bubble of a laugh in it that might break at any time. "Well, thank you, my..."

He stopped, because I had forgotten my manners completely. I had been looking past him into the room. I suppose it was the most beautiful room I had ever seen, leastways in a hotel. It had a fancy yellow-and-red carpet on the floor and furniture that fairly shone it was polished so well, and genuine painted pictures on the walls. But what had stopped me in my tracks was a silver bottlelike thing that Richard, the colored man, had just brought in and was putting on a sideboard with some ordinary bottles and glasses. I had seen them dozens of times in picture shows and they fascinated me. You know, you push a lever and water squirts out? Sometimes in comedies several people would pick them up and squirt each other in the face. I pointed and asked, "Is that one of those things that squirts water?"

Colonel Culpepper looked over his shoulder. "You mean my genuine Mayfair siphon," he said.

"I always wondered what they were called," I said, beginning to get embarrassed because I had acted like Ruby Rube. I felt my face flush. "I . . . I see them in picture shows a lot," I mumbled.

Colonel Culpepper's humorous expression didn't change but his mouth quirked a little. "That's a small doodad I picked up in England," he said. "Would you care to see how it squirts?"

I smiled at him. "Could I?"

Again he looked like he might laugh, but he didn't. He said, "Come in, little chicken." We walked over to the sideboard and he picked up the silver siphon and a glass. "The secret," he said, "is aplomb. Use enough pressure, but not too much." He pushed the lever, and *phhuutt!*—water shot out and half filled the glass. He handed me the glass and motioned for me to drink. "Cheers," he said. He lifted his eyebrows and waited while I took a sip of the bubbly water. It had a burning, strong taste and I made a face. Colonel Culpepper's eyes twinkled and he handed me the siphon. "Try your luck," he said. I pointed the nozzle at the glass and pushed the lever. *Phhuutt!* The stream almost knocked the glass out of my hand and water went flying everywhere. Colonel Culpepper's eyebrows shot up in pretended surprise, and Richard almost doubled up laughing.

I turned the siphon in my hand. "How does it work?" I asked.

Colonel Culpepper took the siphon out of my hand. "Well, you see . . ." For the next five minutes it seemed he didn't have anything in the world more important to do than show me how that siphon worked. He took it apart and showed me the little tube of gas that made it work and pointed out how the bottle was covered with a handmade lattice of heavy silver. He had the funniest way of talking, using big words but making everything he said sound like he was joking.

He put the siphon back on the sideboard and looked at the row of bottles with fancy labels. Whiskey, I guess. He turned to Richard. "Can we manage some . . . uh, softer refreshments for a small investor, Richard?"

Richard grinned. He seemed to find it real amusing that I had come calling. "Anythin' she likes, Colonel," he said.

Colonel Culpepper looked at me. "I wouldn't mind a strawberry Nehi," I said.

"Bring us two flagons, Richard," Colonel Culpepper said.

Again Richard burst out laughing. "Won't take but a few minutes, Colonel," he said.

While we waited for our drinks, I sat on the sofa and Colonel Culpepper took an overstuffed chair opposite me. He was so friendly and nice that I decided to ask him a serious question. "Tell me something," I said. "You're a millionaire, aren't you?"

His mouth quirked just the slightest bit. "So?" he said.

I asked, "How does it feel?"

His eyes brightened. "How does if feel to be young and pretty?"

I could feel myself blushing. "Aw . . ." I said. "Aw . . ."

He smiled. "It feels capital. Really capital!"

"The reason I asked," I said, "is that I'm aiming to be a millionaire myself."

He nodded, like what I said didn't surprise him a bit. He asked, "You're fond of money, are you?"

"Oh, it's not that so much," I said. "I really don't care an awful lot about the money. What I figure is, if I make a million dollars, I can do what I like and never have to worry about money."

He smiled and shook his head. "Ah, but it doesn't work like that, little pullet. There are hard rules to the game. You have to learn them before you can play well. To acquire huge stacks of money, you must be quite passionate about it. To keep it growing, or even safe, you must worry about it all the time."

I thought about that. "Well, I wouldn't like that," I said. "There's lots better things to worry about than money."

He nodded. "Quite true." He smiled. "You should also consider that there are better things to do than make money. Acquiring money and manipulating money is a game for people who don't have a talent for doing more worthwhile things. Making money is really a dull game for dullards. The only way an imaginative person can enjoy it is to make more money than anybody else, or take greater risks — or take money away from people who think it's so precious."

I looked at his open face and twinkling eyes. I said, "You seem to enjoy it."

He chuckled. "Oh, I'm an unusual millionaire. Most unusual. I'm constitutionally unable to take anything too seriously." He looked at me and his blue eyes fairly danced. "I work on the premise that nothing is very important, and most things aren't important at all."

I was still mulling that over when Richard brought our drinks. He poured them into glasses and added ice and stood grinning while Colonel Culpepper tasted his. It was plain he didn't care for it much, but he didn't say a word. He ran his tongue around the inside of his mouth and put the glass on the coffee table. Richard shook his head disbelievingly and walked away. Colonel Culpepper said, "I didn't ask your name, bunny."

"Addie Pray," I said.

He seemed to like my name. He repeated it softly and smiled. "Sounds scriptural," he said. "Are you staying here with your parents?"

"Just my daddy," I said. "My mama's dead."

"And what is your father's business?" he asked.

I tried not to hesitate too long while I thought of the best thing to say. "He sells things," I said. "Lots of different things, like cotton."

"How is business?" he asked.

"Fair, I reckon," I said. I knew it was

time to go. I tried not to look like I was gulping my drink, but I finished it as fast as I could. I stood up. "Well, I have to go now. Daddy'll be wondering where I am."

Colonel Culpepper walked to the door with me. I said, "Maybe you can meet my daddy sometimes. He knows a lot about business."

"I'd like to," Colonel Culpepper said. After he opened the door for me he gave me one of his funny crinkly looks and said, "Well, Addie, little pigeon, I hope you make your million dollars soon. And when you do, don't forget to come back to see Richard and me." I heard Richard laugh.

I could hardly wait to find Long Boy. I talked as fast as I could as I told him about the letter and everything that happened. He gave a low whistle. "Sounds like he's a real big mule, honey. Probably got his hand in everythin'."

"Maybe we could do some business with him," I said. "He's real sweet, but he's got so much money it really wouldn't matter."

"Sure wouldn't," Long Boy said. "Wouldn't even miss it." He looked thoughtful and said, "The only thing I don't quite un . . ." He stopped.

"What?" I asked.

"Oh, nothin'," he said. "I'll sure do some thinkin' on it. Maybe we'll meet him 'roun' th' hotel an' you can introduce me."

I was hoping that would happen, too, especially when the weekend rolled around and Long Boy and I both sat in the lobby a lot. But after three days passed, I almost gave up hope of running into Colonel Culpepper accidentally. I kept hoping Long Boy would come up with some scheme so we could get in touch with him.

We both were up early Monday morning, so we decided to drive down to Front Street and sell our samples as soon as the market opened at seven o'clock. That was a mistake right there. There were only a few people around that early on a Monday morning. But, of course, that's hindsight. We had never had any trouble before and we weren't anticipating any. We even picked out a buyer's office that wasn't busy.

I'll never forget the buyer we had that day. He had a cheap wooden nameplate on his table: JEREMIAH POSS. He was one of those meddlesome little men who always try to make any job they do more important than it is. He looked like a chesty squirrel with a gold front tooth and horn-rim glasses. After he tested the staple on our last sample, he said to Long Boy, "Coulder got another eighth outer that if you'd poured on more fertilizer, friend."

"Might could've," Long Boy said.

"What kinder fertilizer you use?" Poss asked.

"Reg'lar fertilizer," Long Boy said.

Poss popped his eyes at him. "Well, what kinder regular fertilizer?"

"Reg'lar chemical fertilizer," Long Boy said. "Bought it at th' feed store."

Poss stared at him for a while and sniffed. "Give you five cents," he said.

"Take it, I reckon," Long Boy said.

Poss collected our receipts and coupons and started making out a slip for the cashier. "How many acres you gonna plow under?" he asked.

I didn't know what he was talking about. From the way Long Boy hesitated for a moment or two, I knew he didn't either. He said, "Same as allus, I reckon."

Poss popped his eyes again and got a

sharp tone in his voice. "What you mean, same as always?"

"Same as this year," Long Boy said.

"Same as this year?" Poss said like he couldn't believe his ears. "Man, I'm talkin' 'bout the new cotton quota program. Where you been, anyway?"

"Oh," Long Boy said. He put on his chin-scratching act. "Wal, ain't decided yet."

Poss stared at him like he was an idiot. "You don't decide," he said. "Depends on how many acres you had planted this year. How many . . ." He broke off and, suddenly, his pop eyes got shifty. He gave a sniff and slowly finished writing out the cashier form. He raised his eyes and said, "Hey, what's that on yo' hand?" He reached out and caught Long Boy's sleeve and pulled his arm across the table and swiped at his hand a couple of times. "Wasn't anything, I guess," he said. "Thought I saw a spider." He got up and made his voice pleasant. "Take this to th' cashier."

As soon as he left, Long Boy said low,

under his breath, "We got t' get out of here quick."

"Why?" I asked in the same low tone.

Long Boy said, "That little act he put on—he felt my hand. He knows I'm no farmer."

I looked over my shoulder. Poss had his head and shoulders stuck in the cashier's cage and seemed to be talking away four feet to the yard. "You're right," I whispered. "Let's go!"

"Not yet," Long Boy said. "Le's mosey up to th' front first." We had almost reached the front counter when Poss took his head out of the cage and turned around. He showed his teeth and made his voice real friendly. "Might be a little delay on yo' check. One of th' machines broke down."

"Thankee," Long Boy said. "We'll wait."

We leaned against the counter while Poss went back to his table. He fussed around and pretended he wasn't keeping an eye on us. Fortunately, three or four farmers came in with samples, and one of them went over to Poss. He could hardly take the man's cotton he was so busy looking at us. Long Boy sauntered over to the door and looked up and down the street. I stood right next to him. Long Boy said, "What's he doin' now?"

I looked over my shoulder. "Pulling staple," I said.

Long Boy grunted, "Now!"

We stepped out the door and started up the street as fast as we could without running. The truck was about a half block away. We had almost reached it when we heard somebody holler, "Hey! Hol' on!" Neither one of us looked back. We got in the truck before we saw Poss standing in the doorway, beckoning to us. Long Boy threw the car in gear and we zoomed down the street right past him. Out of the corner of my eye I saw him standing on the sidewalk, waving his arms.

Long Boy's voice sounded calm. "We sure tore it good an proper that time," he said. "That little squirrel-headed rascal was purty smart."

I was beginning to relax. "Well, I guess that finishes Memphis," I said.

"Worse 'n that, hon," Long Boy said. "It finishes us, unless we can ditch this truck purty soon. He got a good look at it." I looked at him and was surprised to see his face was tight and worried. He said, "You're forgettin' this here is a big town. They got radios in police cars. In a few minutes ever' policeman in Memphis is goin' t' be watchin' out for us." I swallowed hard.

We turned into South Main Street, and—wouldn't you know it?—we were caught right in the middle of the early-morning traffic. We barely crawled along. Long Boy found every hole and cheated on every red light possible, but it was stop and go, stop and go. Long Boy's face got tighter and tighter. I was almost afraid to look at the policemen directing traffic we passed. After about fifteen minutes, when we were caught in one jam, Long Boy wiggled out of his overalls and pushed them under the seat. I changed shoes and took off my poke bonnet.

Long Boy had been thinking. "When we get to th' hotel," he said, "we'll leave the truck in the parking lot. We'll scoot in an' get our things an' go to another hotel. I don't think we bes' go to th' train depot or bus station jes' yet. They'll be watchin' out for a man an' a little girl." He shook his head. "Sure hate t' lose this ol' truck."

It took a long time, but we finally made it to the hotel parking lot. The truck had hardly stopped rolling before Long Boy was out the door, pulling on his coat and vest as he hurried around to the front door. I was right at his heels. Our things were scattered all over our room. And, of course, with the excitement and all, I simply had to go to the bathroom. When I opened the door, Long Boy was strapping up the last bag. We ran down the hall to the elevators. When we reached the lobby, two bellboys came rushing over and took our bags and Long Boy went to the cashier's desk to pay our bill. There were four or five people standing in line ahead of him. I could tell by the way Long Boy shifted his feet and kept straightening his bow tie how nervous he was. I was just as bad. I stood near the front door where the bellboy had put our bags, first on one foot and then the other.

Suddenly somebody touched me on the shoulder and said, "Good morning, Addie Pray." I almost jumped out of my shoes.

It was Colonel Culpepper. His eyes were as blue and twinkling as ever. He was carrying a cane and a Panama hat, and he had on a white suit that looked like silk. He smiled. "Did I startle you?"

I was so flustered I almost couldn't find my tongue. "Oh, no ... no," I said.

He said, "I was leaving, and when I saw..." He stopped and lifted his eyebrows. "Is something wrong, dear?"

I must have been looking over my shoulder, or maybe I was just fidgeting. "Oh, no ... no," I said again, giving a silly giggle. And because I couldn't think of a single thing else to say, I said, "My, isn't it hot today?"

He smiled and said, "Yes, it certainly is." He stood looking at me for a second or two before his face got that amused crinkly look. "Well, nice to see you again, dear," he said.

He had barely turned away when two things happened. First, Long Boy came striding across the lobby, stuffing the hotel bill in his pocket, and took my arm. "Le's go," he said. Second, two men appeared from out of nowhere and stood in front of us.

One of the men was old and had a hard, red face with small, cold eyes. The other was young, and he might have been nice-looking, except he had a sullen expression and a close, tight mouth. You didn't have to see the bulge on their hips and the heavy leather belts showing through their open coats to know they were policemen. They wore their hats and carried themselves like cops. The older man said, "Mistah Johnson? Mistah O. C. Johnson?"

Long Boy looked cool as mint custard. He even did a fairly good job of smiling. "Nope, not me," he said. "My name's Pray."

The young man said, "Don't you own that truck out back?"

"Truck?" Long Boy said, looking bewildered. "I don't own any truck."

The older man said, "What you say yo' name is?"

"Pray," Long Boy said. "Moses Pray." He put his hand on my shoulder. "This is my little girl."

The older man said, "Warn't you two down on Front Street this mawnin'?"

Long Boy shook his head. "Nope, not us. Don't know where Front Street is."

The younger man said, "Down at the

cotton market. Didn't you sell some cotton?"

Long Boy looked bewildered again. "Nope," he said. He smiled. "Say, what's all this about?"

The older man said, "Mistah Pray, do you have any iden . . ." He didn't have a chance to finish, because a voice said, "Ah, there you are, Pray. All ready to go?"

Long Boy and I turned at the same time. Colonel Culpepper was standing there, looking as happy and grand as a three-tailed rooster. I shot a glance at Long Boy's face. I couldn't tell what he was thinking — or what he might say. I said quickly, "Colonel, these men think we're somebody else."

Colonel Culpepper raised his eyebrows and looked at the two policemen. The younger one asked "Do you know this man?"

"Know him?" Colonel Culpepper said. "Of course I know him. He's the manager of my mill." He looked from one policeman to the other. He asked, "Who are you?" His voice was pleasant enough, but somehow he made it clear that they had better have a good answer.

"Police off'cers," the older man said. He turned back the lapel of his coat and flashed a badge pinned to the underside. "Whar is yo' mill?"

"Tupelo, Mississippi," Colonel Culpepper said. "We're going there now. There's my car out front." He raised his cane and pointed. A long shiny Pierce-Arrow was parked at the curb right in front of the door. Richard, wearing a blue chauffeur's uniform, was sitting propped up against the front fender. Colonel Culpepper took a big expensive wallet out of his inside coat pocket and found a card and handed it to the older man. "My card," he said.

The younger policeman craned his neck so he could read the card. He shuffled his feet and said, "Well, thanks, Colonel. Routine checkup."

The older man had a tiny bit of bluster left. "Kin we reach you at th' mill, if we need to?"

"Certainly," Colonel Culpepper said.

As the policemen walked away, Colonel Culpepper turned to us with a smile. "Ready to go? Where's your luggage? Ah, over there. Well, have the boys bring it outside." Under his breath he said, "Easy does it now." Raising his voice again, he said to Long Boy, "Very interesting conference, wasn't it, Pray?"

Long Boy said, "It sure was. Very interesting."

We waited on the sidewalk while Richard helped the bellboys load the baggage and came around and opened the door for us. He gave me a big grin. As soon as we were in the car, Colonel Culpepper leaned forward and said, "Make decent haste, Richard. We have a couple of fugitives with us."

Richard laughed. "Sure will, Colonel."

Colonel Culpepper settled back and gave us one of his quirky smiles. "Now, tell me, what outrageously criminal act have you two perpetrated?"

Long Boy had been sizing up the colonel. He smiled. "Oh, I think those fellas had us mixed up with somebody else."

Colonel Culpepper chuckled. "No doubt. Do you have a car around someplace?"

Long Boy shook his head. "Jes' an ol' truck back of the hotel. Don't think we'd better go near it."

"No, I shouldn't think that would be wise," the colonel said, still sounding amused. "We really are going to Tupelo. Be glad to drop you anywhere you like. I'd advise waiting until we've gone some distance."

"Sure 'preciate it," Long Boy said. " 'Preciate how you stepped in back there, too. Don't expect people to he'p complete strangers like that."

"And you're wondering why in the world I did it," the colonel said.

Long Boy smiled. "It had sort of passed through my mind."

Colonel Culpepper studied him with an impish expression. "Well, I'll tell you, Mr. Pray, I'm not overly fond of policemen. They have their place, naturally, but when some capital crime is not involved, it gives me pleasure to thwart them." He smiled at Long Boy. "That is, of course, when I don't run any risk. And, besides, you're not complete strangers. Your daughter and I are friends. Didn't she tell you about our very pleasant meeting?"

"I told him," I said.

Colonel Culpepper chuckled. "I'm sure

you did, little pullet."

I was still trying to figure out what he meant when Long Boy said slowly, "I jes' hope those fellas don't come nosin' 'roun' your mill an' cause you trouble."

Colonel Culpepper laughed. "Oh, come now, Mr. Pray, you don't really think I have a mill."

Long Boy grinned. "No, didn't think so — not for the last five minutes, anyway. Jes' wanted to find out."

Colonel Culpepper laughed again. "I've been in this business for thirty-five years," he said. "There aren't many worthwhile places I haven't operated in. But I do believe you're the most ingenious pair I ever met." He looked at us with his eyes sparkling. "Why, it was an hour after Addie left the other day before Richard and I realized we had been cased."

I still hadn't put everything in place, but I couldn't let that pass. "What did I do wrong?" I asked.

"You didn't do anything wrong, dear heart," Colonel Culpepper said. "No honest person in the world would have suspected anything. Not when it took a couple of old kit men an hour to realize that a little girl wouldn't have brought that letter up in person. She would have turned it in at the desk or given it to her parents."

"I wondered 'bout that letter," Long Boy said.

The colonel raised his eyebrows. "Naturally, Mr. Pray. It wasn't meant for you." He smiled. "I hope your name really is Pray."

"That's right," Long Boy said. "Moses Pray."

"Good," the colonel said. "My name is Lee. Major Carter E. Lee."

I just stared at him, and he looked back at me with his eyes twinkling. "Aw," I said, "I wish you did own Lost Mine Number Four."

"But I do own it, lamb," he said. "I own any number of mines, and I've got the deeds and leases to prove it."

ELEVEN

It seems to me that all the folks I've ever known have shared one experience. Somewhere along the line they have met up with one unforgettable person who made them aware of things they had never thought about before. Sometimes it caused them to grab their life by the nape of the neck and shake it up good. Sometimes it changed them only a little, for better or worse. But after meeting that one person, life was never quite the same again.

That's the way it was with Long Boy and me after we met Major Carter E. Lee. The three months we traveled around with him did more than show us a way of doing business we didn't know about. It whetted down a lot of rough edges we never knew we had. It made us conscious of the way of doing things Major Lee called "class." "Everyone is better off with some class," Major Lee said once, "but if you're phony it's absolutely mandatory."

It's not hard to understand why we liked

Major Lee. What's always amazed me is why Major Lee found Long Boy and me so fascinating. He sometimes acted like we were the greatest combination since black and white. After we got to know one another well, he would sit down for hours at a time and make Long Boy and me tell him about when we did business with Bibles and pictures of the deceased and things like that. We hit it off from the very first. There wasn't much groping around at all before we were acquainted, and Long Boy was telling him the truth about why we were leaving Memphis in such a hurry. When he heard how many warehouse receipts we had spread around Tennessee, Major Lee sat back in the car chuckling, saying, "Wonderful . . . just beautiful . . . simply beautiful." He reflected on it. "You scalawags have hit on the most artful little dodge I've heard about in a long time. You're right, Mr. Pray — who would expect anybody to play fun and games with something weighing five hundred pounds and costing only twenty-five dollars?"

"Yeah," Long Boy said. "Too bad little Poss put his foot in the churn."

"Oh, I wouldn't be too downhearted," Major Lee said. "Cotton warehouse rafters may rattle for a few months, but after a year or two you can resume operations, just as if nothing had happened."

"You think so?" Long Boy said.

Major Lee's eyes twinkled. "I know so, old boy. Human gullibility is dampened from time to time, but it's never been quenched yet. Good thing too. Otherwise people like you and me and little Addie would have disappeared about the time of the Pharaohs. It all—"

Richard said from the front seat, "City limits comin' up."

We stopped talking and looked out until we passed a big sign: YOU ARE NOW LEAVING MEMPHIS, THE CITY OF CHURCHES. COME AGAIN SOON.

Major Lee said, "Well, you two criminals have escaped the Memphis pokey, anyway. What are your nefarious plans now?"

"We have to do business for a car first of all," I said.

"And how do you do that?" Major Lee asked.

After Long Boy told him, Major Lee

shook his head. "I didn't realize there were places where you still could use that old thimblerig," he said. He smiled. "If I can offer some advice—don't do it. It might be worth the risk if you were strapped for funds, but you're wonderfully solvent at the moment. Besides—if you'll excuse my candor—it's silly to ever have voluntary relations with the police."

Long Boy said, "Well, to tell th' truth, I'd 'bout decided that myself."

I couldn't help protesting. "But it's so easy!"

Major Lee gave me one of his crinkly looks. After a moment he said, "Maybe I can help solve your transportation problem." He looked at Long Boy. "How would you like to purchase a new automobile for—oh, say, twenty-five cents on the dollar?"

"What kind of car?" Long Boy asked.

Major Lee shrugged. "Any car you fancy. Go to a dealer of your choice."

Long Boy grinned. "Well, it all depends…"

Major Lee laughed. "Oh, it'll be perfectly legitimate and above board. At least, as far as you're concerned." He settled back in the seat. "You see, one of my firms is the PruYea Company. Over the last six months or so I've sold PruYea stock to a considerable number of physicians in Mississippi and Arkansas. I took their personal checks for half of the purchase price and accepted promissory notes for the balance. Up until recently it was a fairly easy matter to discount sound promissory notes to banks—that is, they bought them from me at an amount somewhat less than the face value." He smiled wryly. "Unfortunately, as you know, banks have now fallen on hard times. They shy away from unsecured paper, no matter how sound it is. That's left me rather burdened with promissory notes."

He looked at Long Boy. "There are still some places where they are accepted at face value. The large automobile financing corporations, for example. Any one of them will relieve me of a promissory note in payment of a new automobile."

Long Boy said hesitantly, "Well, I . . ."

Major Lee raised his eyebrows. "Oh, come now, Mr. Pray. I wouldn't put the kibosh on you for such a small amount.

There's no reason why some nice doctor shouldn't pay most of the cost of your new car. I insist on it. We'll discuss it later."

"What's PruYea mean?" I asked.

Major Lee said, "I'm glad you asked, chicken. PruYea is a new and revolutionary breakfast delicacy." He got that bubbly, laughing tone in his voice. "Ah yes, PruYea is a wholesome mixture of tree-ripened prunes and active yeast, nutritious when ladled over cereal, stirred in milk, or spread on toast. Soon a large jar of PruYea will be as familiar a sight on American breakfast tables as jam or marmalade. And it's far more healthful. For not only does it contain valuable and essential nutrients, it is positively guaranteed to promote regularity."

"What does it taste like?" I asked.

"Awful," Major Lee said in the same tone. "Perfectly horrible. In fact, I long ago abandoned the idea of trying to blend prunes and yeast into a palatable mixture. Instead, what I put in my jars is some very expensive imported currant jam, with only a few spoonsful of prune juice."

Long Boy had been listening intently. "But how do . . ."

Major Lee smiled. "Oh, I don't market the stuff. Heavens no. All I do is sell stock in the PruYea Company, legally incorporated under the laws of the state of Delaware. The quart jars of PruYea I have on hand are made up as samples for prospective shareholders—all doctors, as I mentioned. Physicians love it. Most of them fall over themselves to buy stock. They are convinced millions of constipated Americans will gobble it up by the carload. Some of them consider it the greatest innovation in breakfast food since old Will Kellogg discovered corn flakes."

Long Boy said, "Well, I'll be dogged."

Major Lee was amused by the expressions on our faces. He said, "The PruYea Company is one of my oldest enterprises. Still one of the most profitable, too. I started it when I was only a lad, otherwise I'm sure I could have thought of a better name." He looked out of the car window for a while, with a musing smile. "I went into a barber shop in Connersville, Indiana, one morning," he said, "for a

317

haircut. One of the barbers was stirring something vigorously into a glass of milk. I asked him what he was doing, and he said he always took a cake of yeast in milk in the mornings for constipation. An older man, getting a shave, said if he would eat prunes for breakfast he wouldn't have to worry."

Major Lee chuckled. "You know, that was the first time it struck me that, along with such things as hate, love, avarice and generosity, one of the great human verities was constipation. I reasoned that if both prunes and yeast were popular remedies, they would be twice as effective and popular if mixed together. Well, as I mentioned before, I was never able to mix up a concoction that had any appeal. After I incorporated the PruYea Company I began using my currant jam for samples when I called on prospective stockholders. Actually, I had only middling success until I decided to restrict my shareholder list to doctors."

"My reasoning at the time was that doctors, more than anybody else, were aware of how preoccupied most aging people are with their bowels. But I discovered I had stumbled on a gold mine for two entirely different reasons. In the first place, doctors know absolutely nothing about business and they believe anything you tell them. More importantly, no matter how true they are to their Hippocratic vows, they are crazy about money. For many years now doctors have been contributing heavily to my support."

"But don't they ever kick up a fuss?" Long Boy asked. "It looks like . . ."

Major Lee raised his eyebrows and looked bland. "I don't know, dear boy. I never wait around until unpleasantness develops. I always tell them frankly that it will take between a year and eighteen months to launch the company properly and start production. Before that time I have vamoosed—moved on to new territory." His mouth quirked slightly. "Now that you mention it, I doubt if many of them do kick up a fuss. Most people are aware that starting a new business enterprise is a risky business. I should think that most of them are sensible enough to decide that they took a gamble—and lost—and they accept it philosophically."

"I'll be dogged," Long Boy said again.

When we got to Tupelo, we bought a new black Packard 12 sedan. It seemed awfully big to me, but Long Boy's eyes got all shiny when he saw it and I didn't object. It cost $3,675, but all Major Lee would take from Long Boy was a check for $900. It was about the easiest thing I ever saw. After we picked out the car we went up to Major Lee's hotel suite and told him what it would cost. He put through a long-distance call to a doctor in Yazoo City, Mississippi. All he said was, "Doctor, Major Carter Lee here. One of my PruYea purchasing men needs an automobile. I'm discounting your note to General Financing Corporation to pay for it. Thought I'd let you know. Yes, Doctor, thank you. Goodbye."

That night we had supper—I mean dinner—with Major Lee. We had almost finished eating when he said to Long Boy, "I have a couple of medium-size deals going that I'd like to close out within the next two or three weeks. I was planning on asking an old associate to come up from New Orleans and assist me. But if you still don't have other plans, perhaps you'd like to lend me a

320

hand. I'll cut you in for a third. That should amount to close to thirty-five hundred dollars." His eyes twinkled. "More if you prove to be a good bargainer."

I could see how proud Long Boy was, but he looked at me first. Of course, I was beaming. Long Boy said, "I'd sure like to give it a try."

Well, that's the way we started working with Major Lee. I didn't have a whole lot to do in the deals — Long Boy did all the work — but it was an education in itself just seeing how Major Lee did business.

The way the deals worked was this: A few weeks before, Major Lee had breezed into two small towns in Mississippi in his long, shiny Pierce-Arrow with Richard driving. One of the towns was Delhi, in Madison County, and the other was Vail, in Sunflower County. In each place Major Lee called on the president of the biggest bank. That was the way he always worked. He introduced himself as Elmer Winthrop, president of the Rosecraft Paper Company of Wilmington, Delaware. Major Lee said he had been looking over Mississippi for a site for a new paper mill and their town was the most promising spot he had found yet. He asked the bankers to set up a meeting with town officials, the president of the Chamber of Commerce and other leading businessmen so they could discuss the possibilities.

That was normal procedure, of course. I guess you know towns always make a lot of concessions to attract new industries. Back in those hard times, most little towns would have wrapped a pink bow around city hall and given it to any company that came in with enough jobs and a big enough payroll. A meeting with a town's leading businessman always gave Major Lee a good idea of how big a bite he could put on them, but, just as important, it gave him a chance to use his kit.

Major Lee had kits made up for all his companies. You just wouldn't believe how slick they were. Take the Rosecraft Paper Company, for example. Like all of Major Lee's companies, it was legally incorporated under the laws of the state of Delaware. That was because it was easier and cheaper to get a corporation charter in Delaware than any other state. Naturally, the

Rosecraft Paper Company didn't exist except on paper. But to look at Major Lee's kit you would have thought it was one of the biggest, most profitable paper companies in the country. In the first place, Major Lee had bought a few rolls of toilet paper, some paper towels, napkins, plates, stationery and other paper products and repackaged them in bright-blue wrappers and boxes that had *A quality product from the Rosecraft Paper Company, Inc.* printed on them. He also had a supply of Rosecraft's annual financial reports for the last few years, copies of advertisements and sales brochures, and even a batch of reports about Rosecraft from all the big financial reporting firms that make it their business to keep clients informed about how business concerns are doing.

That wasn't all. Major Lee also had clippings of stories about Rosecraft from big newspapers like *The Journal of Commerce* and *The New York Times* that carried his picture as Elmer Winthrop, president. He also had a clipping of a picture and write-up that appeared in *Forbes* magazine and copies of lots of pictures and articles that had appeared in different trade journals.

Every blessed thing was a fake, of course. Major Lee ordered the material for his kits from a man named Cannonball Wells, who owned a printing shop in Evanston, Illinois. Cannonball Wells specialized in turning out counterfeit reports and clippings, and he could copy anything. Sometimes when Major Lee read an article about a big executive or mining operator in a magazine like, say, *The Saturday Evening Post* or *Liberty,* he would send it along to Cannonball Wells and ask him to make him a few copies for one of his kits, substituting one of the names he used and his picture for those of the real man. It must have cost Major Lee an awful lot of money to make up his kits, and one time I mentioned it to him.

He smiled. "It's worth every cent, lamb," he said. "The whole purpose of a kit is to stop trouble before it starts. If you can supply the answer to every question anybody might conceivably ask, they won't go prying around on their own." He chuckled. "Besides, I write it off as an operating expense."

After Major Lee had let them get a good look at everything in his kit and had mentioned that his new mill would employ nearly two hundred people, with a payroll of about $24,000 a month, most local businessmen were ready to promise him anything he wanted on the spot. He refused to be rushed. He had a list of the concessions he wanted typed out on a sheet of stationery with a Rosecraft letterhead. One of the things he expected absolutely gratis was a sizable tract of land for a mill site. Major Lee always specifically mentioned the tract he wanted. This was important. Otherwise, as soon as word got around that a paper mill might be built in the area, everybody who had land for sale would take it off the market, hoping it might be selected as the site. Major Lee asked the town officials and businessmen to study the site of concessions and write him a letter, either formally accepting or rejecting them.

He had a smart way of taking care of that, too. In fact, the executive offices of all of Major Lee's companies had the same address: 2100 Holly Street, Wilmington. I never did know whether Major Lee had somebody sitting in a little office up there, or what. I do know that once a week he got a big envelope from Wilmington, mailed special delivery, that was filled with letters sent to his various companies. When telegrams were sent, somebody called him long distance and read them over the telephone.

Major Lee had decided the little towns of Delhi and Vail were ripe enough to pluck the night he asked Long Boy to lend him a hand. After we had finished dinner we went up to his suite. To give you some idea how carefully he planned everything, he had sent away for geodetic survey maps of the Delhi and Vail townships. He told us how he had set everything up, then spread the maps on the coffee table. "Now, I told the good people of Delhi and Vail that I wanted to build my mill here and here," he said, pointing to an area on each of the maps. "But where I finally have decided to put it is here and here." He pointed to areas outlined in red pencil on both maps. He chuckled. "Naturally, I won't tell them about my change in plans until you've secured a ninety-day option to buy both tracts of land. It's been up for sale for some time, so that won't be any problem. I'll give you the names of the owners presently."

"How much land is it?" Long Boy asked.

"There are fifty acres outside Delhi and sixty-one acres outside Vail," Major Lee said.

Long Boy asked, "How much is it worth?"

Major Lee smiled. "Oh, not much. I don't intend to bite too hard. At present market prices I'd say not more than two hundred and fifty an acre for the tract outside Delhi, and possibly a bit less than that for the Vail parcel. But don't quibble too much about any price they ask that won't arouse suspicions about your good sense. After all, we don't intend to exercise our options. Actually, the higher the price you agree to pay, the better your bargaining position when the town fathers of Delhi and Vail come around to buy you out. Naturally, it will be good business to get the options as cheaply as you can, but I wouldn't haggle too much over them either. The main thing is to get the options."

Two days later we set out for Delhi and Vail. We had stopped over in Jackson for a day while Major Lee had a lawyer he used regularly draw us up option forms on the two tracts of land. Major Lee had also given Long Boy $1,000 in cash to buy the options and cover any other expenses that might come up. Long Boy was using one of his phony names, L. C. Bailey. He was supposed to be a timber speculator who had just recently struck out on his own. If anybody started asking too many questions, he was to say that for the last ten years he had been working as a timber cruiser for the East Shenandoah Lumber Company of Wilmington, Delaware, one of Major Lee's companies.

We didn't have any trouble at all. The owner of the land outside Delhi was a sharp-eyed, snaggle-tooth old man named Yule Bastrop, who owned a dinky stockyard. When Long Boy told him what he wanted, he said, "Ain't much in'erested in options. Nothin' but a nuisance. If you want th' lan', why don' you jes' buy it?"

Long Boy said, "Well, to tell th' honest truth, I'm not a big enough operator t' swing a deal this size without some help. Need a few weeks t' raise th' money."

Old Bastrop's eyes narrowed. "Wal, 'at lan's gonna be valuable someday. Been holdin' it for an investment. Couldn't let it go less'n four hundred dollars an acre."

I thought he might have a stroke when Long Boy said, "That sounds fair enough. S'pose I give you two hundred dollars for a ninety-day option t' buy at that price?" Old Bastrop went along, docile as a tadpole, to a justice of the peace, where he had the option signed, witnessed and notarized.

The land outside Vail was owned by a dentist named Zebulon Gates, Jr. He was a pink, plump, youngish man with rimless eyeglasses. He looked so grateful when Long Boy told him why we had called that I was afraid he might offer the land for practically nothing. "My granddaddy left that piece of property," he said. "We've been tryin' t' sell it for years."

"What do you want for it?" Long Boy asked.

Dr. Gates hesitated. "Well, we've been

askin' two hundred dollars an acre. You think that's too much?"

"Sounds fair," Long Boy said. "I'll give you one hundred dollars for a ninety-day option."

As soon as we had Dr. Gates's option signed and notarized, we left for Jackson. We were supposed to meet Major Lee at the Hermitage House hotel, but he had left word at the desk that he had been called away on business and would be returning on Sunday. That didn't leave us much to do, except sit around our suite for three days. We had been taking suites ever since we met Major Lee. It was the first change he made in our way of living. It surprised me how much it improved hotel life. Besides giving you a comfortable place to sit and read, having a suite at a hotel makes everybody, from the desk clerks to maids, just a bit more anxious to please.

Major Lee blew in Sunday afternoon, looking as grand and happy as ever. He said to Long Boy, "As long as I had your help, dear boy, I thought I'd set up a few more towns." When we started telling him about what we had done, he held up his hand.

"Wait until I bathe and change. We'll discuss it at dinner."

It was plain that he was pleased at the way we had handled things. As Long Boy told him about it at dinner, he kept saying, "Excellent . . . excellent." He sat back and smiled at us. "I'll run down to Vail and Delhi with my maps tomorrow and tell them that they have landed my mill, providing they furnish the new site my engineers recommend." He chuckled. "I should think you'll be hearing from them almost immediately after that. Now, what we must discuss is our profit for the venture." He looked at Long Boy. "Have you any suggestions?"

"Some," Long Boy said. "From the size of my cut you mentioned, I figure you meant to make about a hundred dollars an acre on that land."

Major Lee nodded. "That was a preliminary estimate. I shouldn't mind making a bit more—or a bit less, for that matter."

Long Boy said, "Well, it seems to me we ought to make a lot more. Looks t' me like we got 'em over a barrel good an' proper. If

I'd bought them options as a legitimate timber man, I'd squeeze 'em till they hollered."

Major Lee's eyes twinkled. "You're absolutely right. We do have them over a barrel. Unfortunately, however, you're not a legitimate timber man. That handicaps us considerably. We can't take our case to court, for instance." He smiled at Long Boy. "I'm sure I don't have to tell you that small-town businessmen operate under a most peculiar code. They won't begrudge you a profit. Mercy no! They know that profits make the world turn and keep the Republic strong. In their hearts, they'll even envy you because, of what appears to be a fortuitous coincidence, you have secured something they need very badly."

Major Lee chuckled and shook his head. "But what keeps small businessmen from becoming big-time entrepreneurs is that they don't know what it means to make a killing. Large profits frighten them. That makes them somehow consider them immoral. If you squeeze them too roughly, I know by sad experience that they scream, 'Why, that's highway robbery!'—and they can get very ugly and self-righteous indeed. Among other things, they could pressure the owners of the land we need to repudiate our options."

Long Boy grinned. "Well, I didn't aim to rub them so hard the skin came off. But you don't mind if I try to kick the ante up a little bit, do you?"

Major Lee said, "Not a-tall, my boy. I hope you do." He smiled. "If you begin to feel twinges of greed, however, I hope you'll remember the world is very wide—and many towns are hungering for paper mills."

Major Lee left early Monday morning. We had made plans to meet him in Hattiesburg as soon as we sold our options. It wasn't far to Vail, but even so I was surprised how soon things began to happen. About two o'clock the phone rang in our suite, and after a while I heard Long Boy saying, "Nosir, I'm jes' not interested. . . . Nosir, I've got big plans for that land. . . . I wouldn't even think of it. . . . Well, you'd jes' be wastin' yo' time. . . . Come ahead, then, but I'm tellin' you now it won't do any good. . . ."

After he hung up he grinned at me. "That

was a fella named McDavid, president of the Vail Chamber of Commerce. He tried to get me to name a price for my option. He's comin' up to see me at ten o'clock tomorrow morning."

We had just sat down at breakfast the next morning when a bellboy came in the dining room and told Long Boy there was a long-distance call for him. After about ten minutes Long Boy came back, not looking too happy. "That was the town attorney of Delhi," he said. "Rivers, I think he said his name was. He offered me three hundred dollars for the option. When I told him I wasn't interested, he asked me to come up and see him. I told him it wouldn't do any good, and he said the town could condemn the land and take it over if it had to, something called eminent domain." He looked at me. "Do you reckon they could do that?"

"I don't know," I said.

"Doggonit, I don't think so," Long Boy said. "That land ain't even inside the town." He thought a moment and shrugged. "Well, anyway, he's comin' t' see me tomorrow afternoon."

It wasn't one man that came to see Long Boy from Vail, but three. They were all on the heavy side and too genial for me. They slapped each other on the back and laughed at everything that was said and made a big fuss over me. I went into the bedroom while Long Boy got down to business with them. I heard them talking and laughing for the longest time before I dozed off. When I woke up it was 12:30 and they were gone, and so was Long Boy. I thought they might all be down in the dining room, but when I went down to lunch they weren't there. Long Boy came back about two o'clock, beaming and smoking one of his quarter cigars. He took a certified check out of his pocket and handed it to me. It was for $6,200. "Couldn't get but a hundred dollars an acre out of 'em," he said, "plus the price I paid for th' option." He stood there, looking proud of himself. "They weren't bad fellows," he said. "Enjoyed doing business with 'em."

It wasn't like that with the town attorney from Delhi. He was a chesty, cocky little man with fighty eyes. I won't bore you with all the details, but he and Long Boy wrangled for two days. Long Boy looked grimmer and more frazzled out every time I saw him. But to show you how strange things work out sometimes, when the lawyer finally left, Long Boy had a certified check for $6,450—$125 an acre for the land, plus the $200 he had paid for the option.

Subtracting the cost of the options, that made the total profit on the two deals $12,350. Long Boy's share was a bit more than $4,100, and he really earned it. Major Lee was as pleased as could be over the way Long Boy had handled things. He just couldn't get over how Long Boy had insisted on getting the option money back; apparently nobody had ever done that before. After we'd had a good laugh over everything, I said, "I bet they'll be hopping mad when they finally find out they're not getting paper mills."

Major Lee raised his eyebrows and looked bland. "Why, no, lamb," he said, "I shouldn't think so. Disappointed certainly, perhaps even chagrined, but not angry. I told them several times that final approval of the mill had to be given by my board of directors." His eyes twinkled. "Of course, I did say that was a mere formality, but in that I made a mistake. They'll be receiving a telegram from Wilmington in a few days saying that I've been overruled by my directors. I'll admit that I made a serious misjudgment and apologize for it. As businessmen, they'll understand such things happen."

We did business with four more towns for paper mills in the next two months. Major Lee always had other deals going on his own. I never knew what they all were about, but every time we stayed in a hotel for more than a day he planted letters about his various mines in chairs in the lobby. I believe he sold a lot of PruYea stock. He couldn't stand to be idle. One time he said to me, "You know, Addie, chicken, I've never believed that I'm more larcenous by nature than most men. I simply thrive on the excitement of making deals. My fatal flaw is that I get bored if I do the same thing over and over again. Otherwise, I might have made a highly respectable businessman."

I loved it when Major Lee let me help him with his deals. It started down in Laurel,

Mississippi. I guess you've heard of Amos Bohacker, the famous multimillionaire oil man? Well, he had a big winter estate down there, right on the edge of town. Major Lee had registered at the Laurel Hotel as Colonel Clifton Bohacker. Every morning I'd go up and sit in his suite until one of the men he was making a deal with would arrive. Major Lee would introduce me as his niece. After a few minutes he would say to the man. "I have to drive my niece home. Do you mind too much? We can talk in the car."

We would get in the Pierce-Arrow and Richard would drive us out to the Bohacker estate. Just before we got there, I would say, "Uncle Clifton, let me out at the gate. I want to stop by the stables and feed my pony."

Major Lee would chuckle. "All right, dear. Now, tell Granddaddy I'll be out to dinner at the usual time."

By this time the man Major Lee was putting the kibosh on would begin to look a little bug-eyed. He'd say something like "Bohacker . . . Bohacker? Why, I didn't know you were kin to Amos Bohacker."

Major Lee would say casually, "Oh, didn't you? Yes, Amos is my older brother. We've always been very close — in business and everything else."

I would get out at the main gate to the estate and walk slowly until Richard drove away. Then I'd turn around and walk down to the main road where there was a filling station. I'd telephone for a dime taxi to take me back to the hotel. It got to be a regular thing, me helping Major Lee. Nearly every place we went there was some big millionaire everybody knew. Major Lee usually made me take $200 for helping him, but once he must have made an especially big deal because he insisted I take $500.

What I liked best was to sit with Major Lee and talk. He was the first person I had ever met who talked about — well, things. Long Boy and I usually talked about where we were going to eat, or what hotel we were going to stop at, or how we intended to do business. Major Lee would talk about famous people, or tell me about foreign places he had been, or discuss books. It was because of Major Lee that I discovered there was a place to get things to read besides the magazine racks and lending libraries in hotel lobbies. I almost went wild when I first found out I could walk into bookstores and buy books like *Little Women* and *A Tale of Two Cities* and my most favorite of all, *Gone With the Wind*. Pretty soon I had the trunk of the car so filled with books that Long Boy used to groan every time he opened it.

Major Lee helped me in other ways, too. At first he would just smile and say, "Addie, lamb, I believe there are too many bows on that dress," or, "You're too young to use red nail polish, chicken." But one time he sat me down and we talked about clothes and the way to dress seriously. "The thing to remember, lamb," he said, "is that rich little girls don't buy their clothes at cheap chain dress shops. Always go to the best stores in town when you shop. If you're in doubt, go to some saleslady who looks like a lady and ask her to help you make a selection. At your age, quality is the most important thing." He smiled. "When you get old enough, or rich enough, you can dress as outrageously as you like."

I never resented anything Major Lee said

to me, except one time. We were discussing doing business when he said, "Ah, lamb, you don't realize how unique and how fortunate you are. You truly don't know the difference between right and wrong. You'll grow up without any complications or neuroses at all."

I felt myself flushing. "Why, I'm not bad," I said.

Major Lee smiled. "I didn't say you were, chicken. You have a keen awareness of the difference between good and evil, thank heaven. I meant that it never occurs to you to consider whether society regards what you are doing is right or wrong. You should be glad you're so lucky. I envy you."

Major Lee had one bad habit. He drank. About once every two weeks he would stay in his suite for a couple of days and get drunk. I never saw him like that. He asked Long Boy and Richard not to let me see him, but Long Boy used to go up and sit with him. He said that all Major Lee did was sit around in his underwear, singing songs and making jokes while Richard kept 'him supplied with drinks. What few things we ever learned about Major Lee's past,

Long Boy found out when he was drunk.

One day Long Boy came in, looking astonished, and said, "You know, he really is a major—or was. He went overseas with the Rainbow Divison in nineteen seventeen. He jes' showed me a boxful of medals he got."

Another time Long Boy came in and asked, "Honey, do you know anything 'bout a school named Yale?"

"Sure," I said. "It's a real famous college. It's up in New York somewhere."

"Are you sure it's in New York?" Long Boy asked.

"Well, maybe not," I said. "I know it's up north somewhere."

"Major Lee says it's in Connecticut," Long Boy said. "He says he went there. He's sittin' up there singin' a song 'bout baa-baa sheep that he claims is a Yale song." He shook his head. "It sure don't soun' like a college song t' me."

We stopped traveling with Major Lee in November. Long Boy had just finished selling another option on a paper-mill site, and we were all having dinner at a hotel in Pascagoula, when Major Lee said, "It saddens me to say this, but I've decided to go to Europe for a change of scenery. Richard and I are sailing from New York Wednesday week."

I guess our faces showed how sorry we were. He smiled at us. "I've been giving a lot of thought today to the future of you two scamps. I've been wondering what you'll do next. Perhaps you can think it over and let me know before I leave. Maybe I can help in some way."

Long Boy and I talked it over for a long time that night. The next morning we went up to Major Lee's suite, and Long Boy said, "We've been wonderin' if you'd min' if we started doin' business with mine letters."

Major Lee said, "Why, certainly not, dear boy. I don't have a patent on that old dodge." He thought it over and smiled. "It's capital!" he said. "Simply capital! If we get you a suitable identity, you should make a fortune." He paused. "We will have to fix you up with a mine first, of course."

Long Boy grinned. "Do we really have to have one?"

Major Lee's eyebrows shot up and he got his bland look. "Why, naturally, you have to own a mine," he said. "How can you sell an interest in a mine if you don't have one?" His eyes twinkled. "It so happens that my mining holdings are rather extensive. Perhaps I could sell you one. What kind of mine were you considering? Gold? Silver? Copper? Lead?"

I asked, "What kind of mine is Lost Mine Number Four?"

Major Lee gave me one of his crinkly looks. "Why, that is a silver mine, lamb. A very valuable property. Would you consider purchasing it?"

I looked at Long Boy and he looked at me. "Well . . . maybe it's too expensive," I said.

Major Lee chuckled. "It certainly is. I believe I paid sixty dollars for it." His mouth quirked. "That included forty acres of rich salt desert, of course."

When I grinned at him he said, "Sold!" He looked at Long Boy. "You can reimburse me for my sixty dollars, but on the bill of sale we will put the price as one dollar and other valuable considerations. That will take care of any embarrassing questions about its actual valuation. I'd suggest you say you acquired it from your rich old uncle, Colonel Rupert Culpepper. It will cost you another five hundred dollars a year to obtain the services of James Wilkerson and Company, mining engineers."

Long Boy said, "Do you mean there—"

"Oh, yes, indeed," Major Lee said. "They are a well-known firm in certain circles." His mouth quirked again. "I haven't examined their mining credentials too closely, but for your five hundred dollars they will mail you a reasonable number of letters to scatter about. Better still, they are there to furnish impressive answers to any inquiries from prospective investors."

"I'll be dogged," Long Boy said.

We spent most of the next day and a half making plans for our new way of doing business. I never saw Major Lee more bubbly and happy. It was his idea that Long Boy should be R. H. "Tex" Harper, a Texas oil and cattle millionaire. "There are two decided advantages to such an identity," he said. "In the first place, anything to do with Texas is associated in the public mind with vast amounts of money. Secondly, you can let down your guard all you please, dear boy." He smiled. "Texas millionaires have a reputation for being—well, shall we say, flamboyant and rough-hewn." He looked at Long Boy speculatively. "You'll have to have a suitable wardrobe, of course." He paused. "Tulsa! That's the place. They have emporiums there that will furnish everything you need. You must drive over to Tulsa and get outfitted." He chuckled. "It won't matter how bright your plumage is as long as it's the most expensive made."

I sure did hate to tell Major Lee goodbye. But as soon as we went to a lawyer's office and got a legal bill of sale for Lost Mine Number Four, and Major Lee and Long Boy sent off a letter and money to the mining engineers for our letters, we left for Tulsa. We had more fun picking out Long Boy's new clothes. You just wouldn't believe how handsome he looked in his tight-legged suits and fancy boots and big $30 Stetson hats. We had an elegant suite at the Frontier Hotel, and we lolled around and took it easy for a week until we got a large unmarked envelope from the mining engineers with twelve letters inside. They were exactly like the letter I had found in Memphis, except they were addressed to "R. H. 'Tex' Harper, Lazy S Enterprises, Amarillo, Texas."

We both were itching to get started, so I went down to the lobby early the next morning and put one of the letters in a large straight-backed leather chair. Well, right from the beginning it was the easiest way of doing business we had ever found. Long Boy always said it was like fishing for catfish. "All you gotter do is sit back lazy-like," he said, "an' wait for somethin' t' swallow yo' bait." The very first week we did business with three investors for $1,000 each.

The only minor problem we ever had was when somebody turned one of the letters in at the hotel desk. Of course, then we had to move on to another hotel or find another place to drop our letters. We couldn't take a chance on two people handing the same letter to some nosy desk clerk. It was a rare thing when somebody did take the letter to the desk. Most people wanted, at least, to get a look at R. H. "Tex" Harper.

It was always easy to tell the gawkers

from the prospective investors. The gawkers wouldn't come inside. They'd stare at us wide-eyed and peek over our shoulders at the suite and go away. The prospective investors were a different thing altogether. Sometimes they almost knocked me down getting inside the door.

I guess you might say the whole secret of doing business with mine letters was not to do anything at all. Long Boy was wonderful; he was so casual in a friendly way. He always thanked the investor for bringing the letter up, but he wouldn't mention it again. The investors, of course, didn't want to talk about anything else. Every time they would mention the letter or the mine, Long Boy would change the subject. I never realized he knew so much about how Texans talked. After a while he had a few spiels down pat. He would tell a funny story about how his new oil well blew in a gusher after he had about given up hope. Or maybe he'd talk about some of his best cattle coming from "one of mah li'l ol' spreads that ain't but a hunnert and fifty thousand acres." He'd give a lazy laugh and say, "It jes' goes t' show size ain't ever'thing."

After fifteen or twenty minutes of this, investors almost always would say something like, "I sure would like to get in on somethin' like that mine," or, "How can a fella go 'bout buyin' into yo' mine?"

Long Boy would give them one of his slow grins and say, "Mah ol' daddy used t' say a man traveled th' fastest when he traveled by himself. 'Ceptin' a few close friends, I don't have stockholders in none o' mah enterprises. Too much danged trouble. Means you gotter write letters an' hol' meetin's, an' all that truck."

The investors would begin to tell him how they appreciated that. They'd say that if they were in a venture with a busy man like him, he'd never hear a word out of them. Long Boy would loll back, smiling, not saying a word while they sold themselves. No matter how much they insisted, we would never close the deal the same day. Major Lee had warned us against that. "If you do," he said, "fifty percent of them will go home and sleep on it and return the next day, asking for their money back. But if you let them dangle at least overnight, they'll be more eager than ever." I'm sure he was right. We never tried it the other way, but I don't recall that a single investor ever failed to come back.

What Long Boy always finally did was say he would think about letting them have a piece of the mine. But he did it in an offhanded way, like he was only getting rid of them. He wouldn't see them or talk to them over the telephone for at least a full day. When he let them come back up to the suite, he would act reluctant again until they had built up a full head of steam. Finally, he'd say, "All right, but I ain't goin' t' sit 'roun' no lawyer's office all day. I got better things t' do. I'll give you all th' rigamarole 'bout the section an' th' township whar th' mine's located, an' you get yo' own lawyer t' draw up th' papers."

That was something else Major Lee said we should always do. "You own the mine legally," he said. "There's no earthly reason why you can't sell an interest in it legally. Let the investor spend the time and absorb the fees for the sale." It did mean that lawyers would telephone from time to time, asking questions. Long Boy always cut them short and got rough. "Now, dang it, you listen t' me!" he'd say. "I didn't want t' have no dealin's with that fella. I wouldn't have, 'ceptin' he pestered me so. Now I'm sorry I did. Right this minnit th' deal's off! Off!" He would hang up.

That always brought the investor running, apologizing for how dumb his lawyer was. Three or maybe four times it brought lawyers running, trying to get a piece of the mine. I was willing to let them in. It seemed to me it would serve them right. But Long Boy said there was no use taking any risks. I suppose he was right. We could afford to be choosy.

When an investor got down to talking money, Long Boy always got grandly casual about how much the mine was worth. " 'Cordin' to th' offer the minin' engineers made, it's worth a lot more 'n four an' a half million as it stands right now," he'd say. "But if I let a few o' mah friends in, I reckon I'll jes' say th' value is a roun' million. I want 'em t' get fat an' happy, an', anyway, ain't no use me payin' more taxes. I'm workin' for th' govermint 'bout ten an' a half months outer th' year now."

Most investors wanted to put in either

351

$1,000 or $2,500. I don't know why those figures were so popular. We did business for $5,000 only twice. Nobody ever wanted to invest $2,000, $3,000 or $4,000. It always seemed to me that getting only one tenth of one percent of a mine for $1,000 would have scared some investors off. But it never did. We never took in less than $3,000 a week. The most we ever took in was $9,500.

We spent Christmas that year in Oklahoma City. I suppose you think it was the happiest Christmas we ever had. Well, it wasn't. When I walked down the street and saw families doing their Christmas shopping, with their faces so bright and their clothes so shabby, it almost broke my heart. I wanted to stop every little girl and buy her the biggest, prettiest doll in town. And I wanted to buy every little boy the fanciest, reddest bicycle. I couldn't, of course. They were hard-working, proud people and they would have been offended. We had all that money and I couldn't do a thing. It's awful, isn't it? We never can help folks until they're so desperate they have to take charity. Or until they've been poor so long pride has been ground out of them.

Long Boy tried to surprise me on Christmas Eve by having some bellboys bring a huge decorated Christmas tree up to the suite. He gave me lots of presents, but his special one was a gold locket, inset with a real diamond, that had his picture inside. I gave him a pigskin military brush set. We had a big Atwater Kent radio set in the suite, and he turned it on real loud so we could hear Christmas carols being sung in cities all across the country. I tried not to show it, but I was so blue and miserable I wanted to go off somewhere and bawl. Instead, I went to the big windows in the suite and looked out. We were 'way up high and it seemed the lights of the whole town were spread out right at my feet. It wasn't anything special, I know. But I never will forget exactly how it felt standing there, listening to "Silent Night" on the radio and feeling sorry for myself and the whole world.

On Christmas Day I sat down and wrote Major Lee a long letter. I felt like he and Long Boy were the only family I had. I always wrote to him every week at his Wilmington address, telling him where we were and where we were going next and how we were doing. During the first month he was in Europe he sent me three picture postcards, two from London and one from Paris. I didn't hear from him after that.

We worked Oklahoma for almost three months before we moved over to Arkansas. I suppose you've heard stories about how poor Arkansas was back then. Well, just forget them. Ordinary folks were poor enough, but lots of people had so much money that they hadn't bothered to count it for years. It seemed to me everywhere you looked there was an oil well, a natural-gas field, a coal or bauxite mine. Why, we did business in Little Rock alone for a month. Hot Springs was even better. Lots of rich people went there to soak in the mineral springs, or gamble, or carouse around in the wide-open roadhouses. So many people were always coming and going in Hot Springs that we probably could have settled down there for years, but we got bored after a month and moved on.

We began working Arkansas systematically, starting at El Dorado in the south, crossing over to Texarkana and back again to Camden, Fordyce and Pine Bluff. We did good business everywhere. It was almost two months before we got to Siloam Springs, up in the northwest corner of the state. We had heard it was a good little town to do business in. We never found out. When we went into the hotel to register, a telegram was waiting for us. It was from Major Lee down in New Orleans. It said: NEED YOUR ASSISTANCE MULTIMILLION DEAL. MEET ME ST. CHARLES HOTEL SOON AS POSSIBLE.

TWELVE

I guess you remember when they called New Orleans "The City of Sin." Wasn't that laughable? I never have decided whether folks were big hypocrites in those days or simply ignorant. It was always someplace away from home that was bad. Nobody would admit that in their own little town people could find all the things to do that human beings do everywhere.

I never saw any any signs that New Orleans was so wicked. I think the only reason it got that reputation was because of those old girls who lived in tiny houses called cribs down on Iberville Street. They had signs on the door like "Toronto Rose," or "Fifi from Paree," and "Broadway Bessie." They were a regular tourist attraction as they stood behind shutters in their kimonos, calling out to men passing by. What went on in Iberville Street never struck me as being so sinful as it was sad and dumb. Those girls must have known that they'd never do business with anybody except seamen and trash and country boys on a toot. When big spenders went tomcatting in the thirties they wanted privacy and soft pink lampshades and songs like "Stardust" and "The Sweetheart of Sigma Chi" playing low on the phonograph. It must be awful to know you can't make it in a business that doesn't take any more brains than hustling.

Now, let me tell you something strange. As soon as Long Boy and I crossed the new Huey P. Long Bridge and started driving into New Orleans, all jumbled up with my first impressions was this feeling that I was going to be real unhappy there. It was so strong it was almost scary. As it turned out, I had never been more right in my life. I'm only sorry I forgot all about it as soon as I saw Major Lee.

He was as grand and twinkly as ever. He even looked like somebody special when he walked through the lobby of the St. Charles Hotel. With all those fine and elegant people, that took some doing. Of course, he had one of the finest suites in the hotel. As usual, Richard was moving around in his smiling way, making it seem like a private home. We were dying to hear about the big deal Major Lee had, but he wouldn't talk about it. "It's a long and involved story," he said. "Get some rest first, and then we'll go to dinner. Afterwards, we'll come back here and I'll tell you all about it."

Naturally, Major Lee took us to dinner at Antoine's restaurant. That was where everybody who could afford it went on special occasions. He insisted we have pompano fish cooked in a paper bag, a dish Antoine's is famous for. I don't like to be critical, but it tasted like ordinary good fish to me. What interested me most was a French way they had of cooking potatoes so they puffed up and were all hollow inside. It was almost ten o'clock when we got back to the hotel and settled down in Major Lee's suite to talk. Richard had gone for the night, so there were just the three of us.

"Now, dear ones," Major Lee said, "this is one of those rare once-in-a-lifetime deals. I've already spent more than a month scurrying around, laying the groundwork. It involves millions — millions now being tightly squeezed by a miserly old woman named Amelia Sass."

"That's a funny name," I said.

Major Lee smiled at me. "I hope you can continue to be amused, lamb," he said. "It will make matters easier for all of us. Amelia Sass is not only extraordinarily rich, she's an extraordinarily unpleasant old woman. She has a genius for making people hate and fear her. Sass is her married name. She was born a Goldsborough and her fortune comes from her family. The Goldsborough name carries great weight in these parts. They were one of the first American families to settle here when New Orleans became part of the United States after the Louisiana Purchase in eighteen hundred and three."

There was a report of some kind, bound in blue paper, on the coffee table. Major Lee turned a few pages. "To keep the record straight," he said, "the first Goldsborough to settle here was named Thaddeus. He was a rich cotton broker and Amelia Sass's grandfather. Like most wealthy early Americans, he built a magnificent home in a section of New Orleans then known as Faubourg St. Mary. It is called the Garden District today. It has begun to deteriorate slightly, but it still is the most expensive, and in some respects the most exclusive, residential section in the city. Amelia Sass still lives there in the ancestral mansion."

Major Lee settled back. "Now, Thaddeus Goldsborough left a great deal of money. But it was his son, Louis, Amelia Sass's father, who made the family fortune spectacular. He was a member of the New Orleans Commodity Exchange. He was a plunger and dealt in anything. Some of his deals are legendary. Old Louis had a son named Felix, but apparently his daughter Amelia was, as they said then, the apple of his eye. He proved that when he died in 1885. Felix, his son, had died about three years before, at an early age, leaving a son. Old Louis made respectable provisions for this grandson, but he left the bulk of his fortune, some twelve million dollars, to his daughter Amelia."

Long Boy gave a low whistle. Major Lee smiled. "Yes, indeed," he said. "And you must remember that twelve million in those days made Amelia, at age twenty-five, one of the richest people in the country."

He gestured toward the blue-bound

report. "I haven't been able to learn a great deal about Blaise Sass, whom Amelia married the year after her father died. I get the impression he was somewhat older than she was. He died himself, in 1896, after they had been married ten years. At any rate, he's not important to our story, except he gave Amelia Sass a child—a daughter. Her name was Madeleine. She is most important—both to our story and to our deal.

"Madeleine Sass was born in eighteen ninety, when her mother was thirty years old. Everyone who knew Madeleine speaks of what a lovely, quiet, self-contained person she was. She and her mother were very close—inseparable. Most people believed that Madeleine was completely dominated by her mother. Later events indicate that this may not have been strictly true. Perhaps she simply had no reason for opposing her mother. In any event, throughout her childhood and even as a mature woman, she allowed—perhaps a better phrase is depended on—her mother to direct her life. She dutifully made her debut. One season she was a lady-in-waiting at one of the Mardi Gras balls. But she had no interest in social activities. Strangely enough, during this period Amelia Sass was deeply immersed in good works. She is still remembered for her philanthropic activities. Among other things, she donated a ward to Charity Hospital and endowed an orphanage in New Iberia. Madeleine assisted her mother in these activities, serving on committees, visiting social-welfare projects, and so on."

Major Lee sighed. "Madeleine Sass sounds as if she was an extremely dull young woman. People who knew her say otherwise. Perhaps it was necessary to know her to appreciate her unusual personality. The only interest she had on her own was painting. She was a rather gifted amateur, I gather, and quite conversant about art and artists. When she was thirty-two, already an old maid by New Orleans reckoning, through her interest in art she met a painter living in the French Quarter named Ferenc Kodaly. He was twenty-eight, four years younger than Madeleine."

Major Lee chuckled. "Now, Ferenc Kodaly was a young man one can appreciate. He seems to have had all the attributes of a great artist, except unusual talent, but—who knows?—given time, he may have proved that he had that. He was unconventional in his dress and personal habits, temperamental, dogmatic, argumentative . . ." Major Lee paused and smiled. "What have I forgotten? Oh, yes, he professed to have no use at all for money and to have contempt for those who soiled their souls making it. Madeleine apparently saw a great deal of young Kodaly before, eventually, she brought him home to meet her mother.

"Amelia Sass detested Kodaly from the start. For one thing, she is a Southern aristocrat to her bone marrow and Kodaly was a Yankee, and not even a pedigreed Yankee. He was born in New Jersey of Hungarian immigrant parents. Besides, he wore soiled corduroy suits and had paint under his fingernails. Worst of all, he either hooted or disagreed violently with almost everything she said." Major Lee smiled. "I will tell you directly how I know all these secret details. For Amelia Sass did keep her keen dislike of Kodaly to herself for some time. After a couple of months, when Madeleine continued to see him regularly—was seeing him more and more, in fact—she spoke out. She forbade Madeleine to see him any more. For the first time in her life, Madeleine failed to accede to her mother's wishes. Instead, she announced calmly that she intended to marry Kodaly."

Major Lee's mouth quirked. "Amelia Sass took to her bed—I mean, she actually took to her bed. She didn't remain there long. When she saw Madeleine was unimpressed, she rose fighting. As the rich always do when they quarrel with their children, she first threatened to cut Madeleine off without a penny. This was a rather empty gesture because on Madeleine's twenty-fifth birthday she had set her up a sizable trust fund. She next threatened to take legal steps to stop the marriage. Since Madeleine was already thirty-two years old, this was ridiculous. Madeleine showed no signs she resented either her mother's threats or constant railings. People who saw her at the time say that her attitude was sweet and conciliatory, but that she went ahead with her marriage plans as calmly as if her mother approved fully. Naturally, Amelia Sass did not attend the wedding. The first thing she did after the ceremony was to try to revoke Madeleine's trust fund. This was impossible. The next thing she did was cut Madeleine out of her will."

Major Lee glanced at the blue-bound document. "Now, Madeleine and Ferenc Kodaly were married in May nineteen twenty-two. They remained in New Orleans until November, then moved to Captiva Island, a small island off the west coast of Florida, near Fort Myers. They bought a house there, added several rooms and a large studio. They both settled down to painting. Madeleine wrote to her mother regularly, at least once every two weeks. Amelia Sass never answered any of her letters.

"In February nineteen twenty-four Madeleine gave birth to a child — a girl. Two months later she came to New Orleans with the child and visited her mother while she was here. Obviously she hoped for a reconciliation. That didn't happen. Nobody knows what was said at the meeting, but

Madeleine remained in New Orleans for another week and didn't visit her mother again."

Major Lee looked at Long Boy and me. "Now we come to the tragic part of our story," he said. "Amelia Sass never saw Madeleine again after she returned to Captiva Island. Nor did Madeleine ever write to her again. She apparently had left New Orleans convinced that patching up things with her mother was out of the question. As far as anyone knows, Madeleine and Ferenc and the new baby were completely happy for the next two years. They had no close friends on the island. The only time they seem to have left their home-studio was about once a week when they took the ferry to the mainland and went into Fort Myers to shop."

Major Lee looked at Long Boy. "Addie is too young, but I'm sure you remember the great hurricane that struck Florida in nineteen twenty-six. Most news reports concentrated on the severe damage Miami suffered. However, the storm swept on up the west coast and completely devastated several islands, including Captiva. People were given a few hours' advance warning that the storm was coming. For various reasons, however, many did not make it to the mainland in time. They were killed. Among them were Madeleine, Ferenc and their baby. Their home-studio was smashed to bits by the winds and the ruins were covered by the high seas for several days."

"Oh, that's awful," I said.

Major Lee nodded and looked reflective for a moment. "Amelia Sass was prostrate when she received the news," he said. He made a wry mouth. "As well she might be, particularly since she had rebuffed all her daughter's efforts to reconcile their differences. When she took to her bed this time it was in earnest. And more than grief. Apparently she had a heart condition that she had not known about. It was at this time that she suffered the first of a long series of heart seizures that has since left her almost bedridden because of chronic heart failure."

"Well, it served her right," I said.

Major Lee's mouth quirked a little. "Perhaps," he said. "As soon as she regained some of her strength, Amelia Sass acted resolutely. She dispatched people to

Captiva to investigate and determine exactly what happened. What they learned made her accept the fact that her daughter and son-in-law had died. But it also convinced her that her granddaughter was still alive somewhere."

Major Lee looked at our surprised faces and lifted his hands in a small gesture. He said, "Who knows? Maybe she's right. Naturally, one is inclined to believe it is only wishful thinking on the part of a guilt-ridden old woman. Yet there are some hard facts that can't be blinked away." He settled back on the sofa. "The facts are these: About sixty people were rescued from Captiva and adjoining Sanibel Island before the worst of the storm hit. They were taken by ferry to Punta Rassa, a small settlement on the mainland. Among the refugees was a little blond girl about two years old. She was alone and too young to tell anyone who her parents were or what had happened to them. There is no doubt at all that the child was there. At least twenty persons have testified they saw her. About a dozen have sworn they spoke to her and tried to find out who she was.

"Unfortunately, there was a great deal of confusion at Punta Rassa. The gale was blowing harder all the time and the seas were fantastically rough and rising. Many people were distraught because it was perfectly obvious that their homes and other possessions were going to be swept away. All of them wanted to get farther inland, to Fort Myers, for safety. The last time anyone remembers seeing the little girl she had been taken in tow by a poor family—'a Cracker family' is the expression everyone used. This family consisted of a poorly dressed couple in their thirties and three or four small children. Nobody recalls seeing either the family or the little girl after they reached Fort Myers."

Major Lee leaned forward. "There are other facts that suggest Amelia Sass's granddaughter may have survived. It has been established that Madeleine and her husband did not die when their home-studio was destroyed. They were lost while trying to make it to the mainland by boat—a dilapidated, leaky, highly unseaworthy old craft that they had bought for fishing and pleasure cruising around the island. They undertook this reckless and foolhardy trip because the boat was the only way they could transport Ferenc's paintings. Their automobile was a small two-seater Stutz Bearcat." Major Lee paused reflectively. "I myself have spoken to the last person to see Madeleine and her husband alive. He's a nice old Captiva fisherman named Crump. On the day of the storm, entirely because of his own concern, he got in his flivver and drove around the island to make sure everyone had received the evacuation order.

"When Crump drove up to the Kodaly place, Ferenc was going back and forth between the studio and dock, loading paintings in the boat. Madeleine came out in the yard to meet him. He inquired whether she knew about the seriousness of the situation and she said that she did. She said, 'My husband and I are going in our boat to Punta Rassa.' Crump was quite distressed about that and pointed out how high the seas were and how dangerous the trip would be. He tried to persuade her to drive to the end of the island and take the ferry with the other evacuees. She said, 'You don't understand. These paintings are my husband's life's work. We can't leave them here to be destroyed.' "

Major Lee pursed his lips. "Crump is almost certain Madeleine said 'my husband and I.' He is positive he did not see a child around. Of course, that is not conclusive in itself. The child could have been indoors, napping perhaps. Amelia Sass believed otherwise. After hearing everything, she concluded that Madeleine had sent the child ahead, maybe with someone who lived nearby or someone who had driven by earlier. She contended it was not like Madeleine to subject her child to unnecessary risks. If the boat trip had been successful, Madeleine and Ferenc would have been in Punta Rassa in less than an hour, probably in time to meet their daughter when she disembarked from the ferry. Unhappily, it didn't happen that way. No trace was ever found of the boat, paintings or bodies."

Major Lee settled back. "If Amelia Sass's theory is correct, three mysteries have to be explained. The first is how the child became separated from whoever was caring for her. Naturally, one can think of several explanations for that. The important thing is, it could happen. After all, we know there was a lost child at Punta Rassa. Another mystery is why the poor Cracker family never came forward with the child. The answer to that might be stupidity and misguided compassion. The Cracker couple had no way of knowing they had a young heiress on their hands. The child was as wind-blown and bedraggled as everyone else at Punta Rassa. Perhaps they concluded the child came from a family as poor and downtrodden as they were. Maybe they did look for the child's parents and finally decided they had been lost in the storm. Rather than turn the child over to the authorities and have her end up in an orphanage, they simply made her a part of their own brood.

"The biggest mystery is what happened to the Cracker family. Up until four or five years ago Amelia Sass had several investigators working full-time, searching for the family and the little girl she believed to be her granddaughter. None of the investigators ever found a trace of either. Whether Amelia Sass eventually abandoned the search, I don't know. For reasons I'll explain shortly, no one has been truly privy to her affairs for several years."

He looked at us with the trace of a twinkle in his eyes. "Now, I know you two scalawags are curious how I know so much about the Sass family. More especially, how we all can benefit from my knowledge. You will remember I told you Amelia Sass had a brother, Felix, who died young, leaving a son. Well, that son's name is Beauregard Goldsborough. I have known him for a number of years, quite a number of years." He smiled and paused. "I'm not certain I know how to convey the full flavor of Beau Goldsborough's unique character. He is a lawyer by profession, but his chief interest in life has not been the law but the pursuit of money. Nothing else interests him much. That's odd in itself, for since childhood he has had more money than he needs. If pressed, I'd be forced to admit that Beau Goldsborough is greedy—yes, greedy and underhanded and not to be trusted too far. He is one of those sterling gentlemen who will bend and twist the law, sneak over and under it, but who are afraid to break it."

Major Lee chuckled. "As you know, I have no such scruples. Several times over the years Beau Goldsborough has called on me when he has found a deal where the profits are irresistible but the risks great. Our partnerships have been highly profitable and amicable enough, but to keep the record straight I want you to know I am not an admirer of Beau Goldsborough. His relationship with his Aunt Amelia is difficult to define. Considering her sour nature, it seems to me that she has always treated him quite handsomely indeed. Amelia Sass seems to have been upset, for instance, when her father shortchanged Beau in his will. As soon as she received her inheritance, she promptly set up a million-dollar trust fund for him. When he received his law degree from Tulane, she turned over to him property and securities worth at least another million.

"Beau Goldsborough does not feel that his aunt has been generous. What has always rankled him most is that Amelia Sass has never let him handle her money and business affairs. Oh, she has called on him to perform certain chores and handle specific projects through the years. He was one of the people she sent to Captiva to determine what happened there, for example. But for almost forty years Amelia Sass entrusted all her investments and the bulk of her legal work to Judge Achille Marigny, a shrewd and distinguished old Creole gentleman who was both a power in legal circles and an ornament in New Orleans society. Beau had one consolation. After Madeleine Sass's marriage, and more so after her tragic death, he felt certain he would be Amelia Sass's sole heir. All he had to do in the meanwhile was make himself agreeable and subservient to the old lady. That wasn't difficult. He is absolutely cowed by Amelia Sass."

Major Lee smiled. "I imagine Beau spent many anxious hours when it appeared that Amelia Sass's granddaughter might have survived the Captiva storm. As soon as that crisis passed, another one arose. About five years ago, toward the end of nineteen twenty-nine, old Judge Marigny fell overboard his yacht while sailing on Lake Ponchartrain and was drowned. He and Amelia Sass were quite close. In fact, he was one of the few friends she had ever had. His death quite literally almost killed her. She refused to see anyone for days, and finally she had one of her heart seizures. For weeks it seemed almost certain she would die. She recovered eventually—but not completely.

"Her illness left her with a marked personality change. But what she suffers from is not particularly rare among the senile rich. She imagines that everyone in the world is out to take away her money. Beau Goldsborough first became aware of it when, after her illness, he tried to discuss her business affairs. After Judge Marigny's death he hoped that, finally, she would let him handle her investments and legal work. She became quite agitated and said that she would handle her money herself. In the last several years her condition has worsened steadily. She haggles over the slightest expenditure. Apparently at times she suffers from delusions that she does not have enough money to keep her in her old age. She has millions, but she refuses to keep the family mansion in good repair. She lets bills go unpaid for months and then settles them grudgingly. For example, at one time she had not paid the doctor who attends her for eighteen months. He complained to Beau, who showed a rare and unusual flash of courage by mentioning it to Amelia Sass. She was furious. She said that the doctor charged too much, and, anyway, she intended to take care of him through a bequest in her will."

Major Lee chuckled. "Beau Goldsborough's primary concern for some time, naturally, was that Amelia Sass would deplete his inheritance through mismanagement. He has some knowledge of Amelia Sass's investments because of his conversations over the years with Judge Marigny. Millions are socked away safely so that Amelia Sass can hardly lose them unless she goes absolutely crackers. But there are other millions she could lose overnight. About two months ago Beau received a severe jolt. Amelia Sass informed him that he shouldn't expect to receive anything when she died, that he had enough money anyway. He couldn't get her to talk about what she intended doing with her money, but she made it clear she had already cut him off without a penny."

Major Lee leaned back and smiled at us. "It was at this point that Beau came to me with his problem. He asked me to devise some scheme—any scheme—that would relieve Amelia Sass of some of her money before she lost it, or left it to establish a home for homeless cats, or something equally as harebrained. He promised his full cooperation." Major Lee paused and looked at us. "Now that I have given you a full account of the Sass family history, it perhaps will seem that the scheme I have devised was obvious. But, believe me, it took—"

All of a sudden everything was clear to me. "I know!" I said.

Major Lee raised his eyebrows and gave me an impish look. "What do you know?" he asked.

"You want me to be that old woman's granddaughter," I said.

Major Lee chuckled and looked crinkly. "That's right, chicken. Can you do it?"

"Sure," I said. I paused to think. "Leastways, I think so. How old was the little girl?"

"She would be eleven, " Major Lee said.

"I'm twelve, going on thirteen," I said, thinking out loud.

Major Lee's eyes were twinkling. "I know, bunny. But you're not a large twelve."

"Oh, I can do it," I said, getting more excited all the time. "I know I can." I looked at Long Boy. He did not seem as pleased as I expected. He was looking at Major Lee thoughtfully.

He asked, "How long will it take?"

Major Lee gave a small shrug. "Who can say for certain? A few months probably. Not more than a year, certainly. Amelia Sass is seventy-five and incurably sick. Her doctor is amazed that she's held on this long."

"Old folks can fool you," Long Boy said. "Sometimes they go on for years."

Major Lee nodded. "Yes, I know. I think it's highly improbable, but it could happen. I've considered it in making my plans. We'll discuss it in detail later, but briefly, what we must do at the very beginning anyway is have Amelia Sass transfer a large part of her fortune to her granddaughter. The Louisiana inheritance tax isn't as great as it

379

is in some states, but it still takes a great bite out of any estate. I shouldn't think it would take much persuasion on Beau Goldsborough's part to convince his aunt that she should put most, perhaps all, of her money in her granddaughter's name before she passes on. Once the transfer is made, it won't be difficult to siphon the money off—even if we have to be satisfied with half a loaf."

"How much money is there?" I asked.

Major Lee raised his eyebrows and looked bland. "No one knows exactly. However, everyone does know that old Judge Achille Marigny was a very shrewd and clever financier. If he took control of an estate worth roughly twelve million in the nineties, he certainly must have doubled it during the flush days that preceded nineteen twenty-nine. Even taking into account Amelia Sass's gifts to Beau, her early philanthropies and the present sad deterioration in securities and property values, there's a great deal of money left. Let's be extremely conservative and pick a nice round figure of ten million dollars. My arrangement with Beau Goldsborough is that I will receive twenty percent of anything we get. I'll split that twenty percent down the middle with you two."

"Why, that's a mill . . ." I began.

Major Lee looked blander than ever. "That's right, lamb. A cool million for each share."

Long Boy and I looked at each other. He gave a low whistle and I swallowed hard. I said, "When do we start!"

Major Lee chuckled and settled back. "Patience, dear heart," he said. "Patience. The bigger the deal, the more carefully one must proceed." He looked at me with his eyes twinkling. "There's one detail I haven't mentioned. I don't think you're going to be particularly enchanted with it, but it's of great importance. It's a detail that will cinch our case."

He paused and looked at Long Boy and me. "You will recall that I told you that Madeleine Sass paid a visit to New Orleans when her child was two months old. She went to see her mother at that time, but her primary purpose in coming here was to take the child to a dermatologist. It seems that all the females in the Sass family are afflicted with a birthmark called a nevus." He smiled. "It is what we call a strawberry mark. Amelia Sass has one somewhere on her body. Madeleine had one on her shoulder that was removed when she was a child. Her baby had one on the back of her neck, near the hairline, which the dermatologist incised. The child had a bandage on her neck on the only occasion her grandmother saw her."

He looked at me. "I'm afraid, lamb, that you're going to have to undergo the minor inconvenience of having a small scar made on the back of your neck. It's absolutely necessary. It won't show. It will be covered by your hair, but you can be sure it will be the first thing Amelia Sass will look for. I've already found a nice, highly competent young doctor who will take care of the matter. The dermatologist who performed the operation on Madeleine's baby has since died. Fortunately, Beau got a full report from him, giving the size and location of the incision he made, at the time a search was being made for Madeleine's daughter."

"What's 'incised' mean?" I asked.

Major Lee's eyes danced. "It means to

cut, in this case to cut out. But, of course, that won't be done to you. All the doctor will do is make a small incision in your neck and sew it up again."

"I don't want to do that," I said.

Major Lee smiled. "Not even for a million dollars?"

I thought about it. "Will it hurt?"

Major Lee shook his head. "Not in the least. Depending on your healing qualities, the doctor has assured me it will be completely healed and forgotten within a few weeks."

I looked at Long Boy. He said, "It's up to you, honey."

I thought some more. "All right," I said. "I guess it's not much to do for a million dollars."

Major Lee smiled. "Fine. I'm sorry it has to be done, but, believe me, it's mandatory." He settled back. "There's something else I forgot to tell you. I think it's a fascinating story. Amelia Sass was born in eighteen sixty, a few months before the Civil War began. As was the custom in those days, all the servants in the Sass household were slaves. Two of the servants, a couple, had a two-year-old daughter named Mayflower. One of the first things old Louis Sass did after the birth of his daughter was sit down and make out a document, transferring ownership of little Mayflower to newly born Amelia. That seems heartless and highhanded today, but apparently it also was a custom among the rich at the time.

"The idea seems to have been that Mayflower would grow up as little Amelia's companion and playmate. Then, when they became older, Mayflower would become Amelia's personal maid. Of course, the Civil War ended slavery, so part of the plan went awry. But little Mayflower's parents continued working in the Sass household after the war and even took the name of their former master. So little Mayflower Goldsborough grew up with Amelia anyway. She's remained with her all these years." He chuckled. "I've never met Mayflower Goldsborough, but I've heard a great deal about her. I wouldn't want you to get the impression that she's a faithful-old-retainer-mammy type. Her official position in the household is roughly that of a housekeeper and companion to

Amelia Sass. But she wields considerably more influence and power than that. Apparently she's as formidable and tough as old Amelia. Beau Goldsborough is terrified of her."

Major Lee sat back looking at us, smiling slightly. After a silence he asked, "Are you in—for a million dollars?"

Long Boy and I looked at each other and nodded together.

"Capital!" Major Lee said. "We are going to be very busy for the next few weeks, so I suggest we all get a good night's sleep. Beau Goldsborough will be here at ten o'clock tomorrow morning to meet you."

As we stood up I thought of one more thing. "What was that little girl named?" I asked.

"Amelia, lamb," Major Lee said. "After her mean old grandmama."

Beauregard Goldsborough was nothing like I expected. It must have been Major Lee calling him Beau that fooled me. I guess I expected him to be like those dark, flashing-eyed, beautifully dressed men I saw in the lobby of the St. Charles every evening. Instead, he was a tall, portly man, with a bay window. He had a sallow, washed-out complexion and just a fringe of thin reddish hair that was beginning to turn gray. Big faded freckles were sprinkled on the backs of his fat hands and across the dome of his huge bald head. I suppose you could call him dignified-looking. He sure tried hard enough. He moved and talked like he was the most important person in the world. A heavy gold watch chain was stretched across his belly, and he was the first man I ever saw with white piping on his vest. It wasn't until you studied him awhile that you realized his pale blue eyes were so flat and cold that they looked dead. I've seen more kindly eyes on a salt mackerel. He had a bad habit of sucking at his thick bottom lip so it always looked wet and blubbery.

He didn't say more than two dozen words during the half hour he spent looking us over. He sat in a chair in Major Lee's suite, his hands folded over his big belly, sucking at his lip and studying Long Boy and me, mostly me. Major Lee asked me questions about Arkansas and Oklahoma, and I tried to answer sensibly, but I couldn't forget how Beau Goldsborough was staring at me with his ugly dead eyes. When he finally left, Long Boy laughed and said, "I sure wouldn't want t' play two-handed poker with that ol' boy." All I did was look at Major Lee.

He smiled at me. "You did beautifully, dear. You were perfect, in fact. He'll be calling from the lobby shortly."

Sure enough, in a few minutes the telephone rang. Major Lee answered it, and we heard him say, "Ah, that's a leg up for us." After a pause he said impatiently, "That's perfectly obvious, Beau. I'll take care of details like that. Yes . . . yes, I'll be in touch." He hung up the phone and turned to us with a smile. "Beau says that you have the exact coloring of Madeleine Sass. You could easily be her daughter." His mouth quirked. "He also mentioned in his usual pompous, stupid manner that you are much too well dressed and well groomed to be from the backwoods of Florida." He rubbed his hands briskly. "Now, let's get down to some details."

It always makes me laugh when

somebody mentions a big illegitimate deal and talks about what easy money it was. Let me tell you, doing business in a big-time way takes just as much planning as pulling off an honest deal. Maybe more. It sure takes as much work. You won't believe how busy we were for the next few weeks.

The first thing I had to do, of course, was go and have a scar made on my neck. The doctor Major Lee had picked to do the job lived across the river in a part of New Orleans called Algiers. Long Boy and I drove over there the very next night after we saw Beau Goldsborough. I was pretty nervous and scared, I'll admit, and so was Long Boy. A couple of times he told me I didn't have to go through with it if I didn't want to, that money wasn't everything. The old fool. I think that helped calm me down and made me even braver than thinking about the million dollars.

The doctor's office was clean and it looked to be equipped well enough, but it was in a rundown neighborhood. I guess the doctor was real poor and needed the money bad. Anyway, it was plain enough he wasn't too happy about what he was doing. That's why I'm not going to mention his name. He was a youngish, solemn man, and he had made up a story to protect himself. He looked my neck over carefully and said to Long Boy, "She has an oil gland clogged here. It has created a small sebaceous cyst. It should be removed." He looked at Long Boy and said slowly and distinctly, "Sebaceous cyst. Will you repeat that, please?"

Long Boy said it. The doctor nodded. "Please remember that."

I didn't even have to take my dress off. He had me sit on a high stool and draped towels around my neck and shoulders. He pushed my head forward and made fussing sounds. "I promised not to cut any hair," he said, "but it's going to be necessary to shave a small patch below the hairline. It won't be noticeable."

Well, I just shut my eyes tight and tried not to pay any attention. It really didn't hurt particularly, only a few teeny sharp pricks now and then. In no time at all it was all over, and he was putting a bandage on my neck. "It may itch some," he said, "but don't scratch it." He turned to Long Boy.

"Bring her back five days from now, next Tuesday, at the same time. If she has pain before then, call me and make an appointment."

To tell the truth, I never did have any pain, only an itchy, drawing feeling occasionally. Oh, I winced and made faces from time to time, but that was just to make Long Boy get a worried look and start asking me if I was all right. I figured I was entitled to that much attention. The worst thing was I had to stay in our suite for the next five days. Major Lee didn't think it would be wise for me to be seen around with a bandage on my neck. He thought it might attract enough attention to cause somebody to remember me in case I met them later as Amelia Sass's granddaughter. I moped around in my robe, reading, and called room service when I wanted something. It was boring for three days all the same. Then Major Lee called me on the phone and told me he was sending up five typewritten pages that he wanted me to memorize so well I could recite the facts without even stopping to think.

It was the true history of a family that

was supposed to have adopted me when I got lost during the Captiva storm. Their name was Isbell. They were trash for sure, but their story was so sad and so typical of what happened to some poor folks in those hard days that it was enough to break your heart. After I had memorized their story, Long Boy read it. We started a kind of question-and-answer game that went on for two or three weeks. My answers came easier and sounded more convincing all the time.

Long Boy would ask, "What's your name?"

"Addie Isbell," I'd answer.

"Where were you born?"

"I don't know. I was adopted when I was about two. Mama always said my own folks perished in a storm."

"Whereabouts was that?"

"I'm not sure. I was too little to remember. I think it was up around Fort Myers."

"What's yo' pa's name?"

"Ernest Isbell. Folks call him Ern."

"What does he do?"

"Nothing regular. He hires out by the day when he can find work. Usually he picks fruit during the season. He used to be a fisherman but he lost his boat."

"Tell me about yo' mama?"

"Mama's name was Ida. She died of swamp fever when I was around seven. She was always sickly with chills and fever. She was too bad off for us to take her to a doctor that last time, and we couldn't get one to come out to where we lived, so she just died."

"Whereabouts did you go t' school?"

"Well, I never went really. I started twice, once down in Nocatee and once at Alva, but we moved on in a few months. Pa never saw much use in school. He always said it was a waste of time."

"But you can read and write, can't you?"

"Oh, sure. I learned that all by myself. Earl and Alma couldn't read and write, though."

"Earl and Alma? Who are they?"

"Why, they're my brother and sister. They're older than I am. Earl must be going on fifteen, and Alma is sixteen. I had another brother about my age named Billy Sam. He broke out in sores and died when I was real little. Mama said it was winter sickness."

"What happened to Earl and Alma?"

"Well, Pa gave Earl a bad whipping one night when he was fourteen and he ran away. We heard once that he was working on a fishing boat up at Osprey, but I don't know whether that's true or not."

"And Alma?"

"Alma—now, she was the one! She just walked off one night when we were in a fruit camp near Arcadia. Pa always thought she took up with a Cuban fellow who was hanging around. Alma always was crazy about boys."

"How did you and yo' pa get on together?"

"Not so good, to tell the truth. Pa's real quarrelsome. Sometimes he's plain mean. He used to whip us children for almost nothing at all. I was aiming to run away myself when I got a little older."

There was lots more. I knew where Ernest and Ida Isbell were married, and, naturally, I knew where Ida was buried. I could rattle off all the places the Isbells had lived and visited during the last five years. I

393

knew what kind of old cars they had, and I even knew the kind of snuff Ernest dipped.

On the night after the doctor took the stitches out of my neck, Richard served all of us dinner in Major Lee's suite. We were leaving for Florida the next morning and that was really what we had to talk about. But before we did anything else, Long Boy and I gave a sample of our question-and-answer game. Richard listened grinning, and Major Lee leaned back chuckling, saying, "Marvelous . . . simply marvelous." After Long Boy and I had finished and I was sitting there, feeling proud of myself, Major Lee leaned forward and asked, "And where did you go right after the Captiva storm?"

I thought awhile and felt myself flushing because I just couldn't think of the answer. "I . . . I don't know," I said lamely.

Major Lee leaned back again. His eyes were twinkling. "That's the right answer, chicken. You don't know. How could you possibly know? You were only two." He smiled at me. "I purposely deleted three or four years of Isbell family history from the account I gave you. I wanted it to start at about the time you would have an awareness of your surroundings and your family's activities. If someone presses you on a point, don't try to be clever and improvise. One false story always begets another. Soon you will find yourself in over your head. Don't volunteer any information about the Isbells. Answer any questions as completely and straightforwardly as you can. But if you don't know, simply say so. Nobody will find that odd. After all, you're supposed to be only eleven. Adults don't normally expect children to remember as much as they actually do."

He paused musingly. "Not that I expect anyone to press you on any point," he said. "You have a great advantage. You're not expected to remember back more than a half dozen years. And you're not expected to know anything about the Sass family at all. Actually, I don't expect old Amelia Sass to investigate your background. For one thing, she is old and ill and certainly in no condition to make inquiries on her own. Besides, I don't think she'll question your identity. Not when she was so obsessed with the conviction that Madeleine's child was still alive. If she has any of her wits left, she should conclude that it's not to Beau Goldsborough's advantage suddenly to produce her missing grandchild."

Major Lee gave a slight shrug. "Nevertheless, one shouldn't take chances. That's why I think definitely you two should run down to Florida so Addie can see both the investigator who is supposed to have found her and old Ernest Isbell, her purported father. After all, if they are ever forced to back up their stories, it certainly will be necessary for them to know what she looks like. I've used the investigator, McFarland, on deals before. He's always been competent and discreet. About Isbell I know nothing, except his family's history is perfect for our purposes, and McFarland says he'll swear to anything for a suitable payment. But I'd like to offer a strong word of caution. Don't discuss anything about our little scheme with either of them. They both know only so much, and nothing more. Only the three of us and Beau Goldsborough know what we are up to. Let's keep it that way."

He looked at me and his eyes danced.

"Ah, but going to Florida serves a dual purpose as far as you are concerned, chicken. The doctor tells me that you heal amazingly quickly. Within a month the small scar he gave you will have reached a stage where a layman can't determine its age. Oh, it will be somewhat pinkish perhaps. But we don't mind a slight prominence, particularly when it's meant to impress an old lady with weak eyes. So you have about three weeks to bask in the Florida sunshine before you return here and make final preparations to meet your rich old grandmama. I want you to return as brown and freckled and tousle-haired as any little Cracker girl." His mouth quirked. "Now, experts advise me that the best way to get the deep tan we need is for you to douse yourself with ordinary cider vinegar when you sit in the sun. Perhaps it won't smell as pleasant as cocoa butter or other emollients fashionable ladies use when they tan themselves, but I understand it works marvelously." He raised his eyebrows. "Besides, a little vinegar won't hurt you. You're much too sweet now."

I looked at Long Boy. He was grinning at

me. "Aw . . ." I said. "Aw . . ."

We went to Tampa and saw McFarland, the investigator, first. He was a tall, spare old man, with a long face and wise eyes. When we walked into his tiny office Long Boy said, "This here is Addie Isbell." McFarland took his feet off his desk and said, "I getcha." He studied me good. He shook his head. "I don't know what you folks got in min', mistah," he said. "But if you want this little lady t' pass for an Isbell, you better take her out an' run her through a brier patch a few times."

Long Boy grinned. "Pretty country, are they?"

"Countrier'n razor-backed hawgs an' jes' as ornery," McFarland said. "Can't get an Isbell t' wear shoes less'n you sprinkle 'em full of sand."

We found out what he meant when we got to Bradenton and looked up Ern Isbell. I never saw such a no-account old man in my whole life. He had a mean face and bleary eyes. Snuff juice was caked in the corners of his mouth and running down his chin. It was plain he hadn't had a bath since the last time he got caught in a rain. He hadn't shaved in weeks. The little shack he had in a palmetto grove outside town was just as filthy and sorry-looking as he was. A self-respecting pig wouldn't have claimed it as home. When Long Boy told him I was Addie Isbell, old Ern gave me a hard look. "She ain't gonna stay heah, air she?" he asked.

Long Boy told him I wasn't, but I really didn't pay much attention to what was said. After I was sure old Ern had got a good look at me, I walked away and waited for Long Boy in the car. I've been told I'm wrong, but I've never been able to change my feeling that there are two kinds of poor people. One kind you feel sorry for and want to help all you can, and the other kind just naturally makes you feel they're getting exactly what they deserve. Some people are vicious and lazy and low-down, no matter how much or how little money they have. I'll tell you one thing, I wouldn't have had old Ern Isbell for my real daddy, not for all of Amelia Sass's millions.

Long Boy could tell how blue seeing old Ern Isbell had made me. He tried to be extra cheerful and sweet as we headed back toward St. Petersburg, where we meant to stay. After we had gone a few miles, I asked, "It doesn't make much difference where we go, long as I get some sun, does it?"

"Why, I reckon not," Long Boy said.

I said, "Well, I've been thinking I'd like to go go to that island where that little girl got lost. You know, Captiva."

Long Boy looked at me. "Why, honey, there's nothing for you t' see down there. I guess folks have near 'bout forgot that storm by now."

"Maybe so," I said. "But I'd still like to go there. Can't we?"

Long Boy thought about it and grinned at me. "Why not? One place's as good as another." The first chance he got, he turned the car around.

I've always been glad we went to Captiva. In those days Florida wasn't nearly as spoiled as it is now. Still, nearly everywhere you looked there were tacky little houses or ugly old fake Spanish-style buildings. Except for the Everglades, the area around Captiva was one of the few places left where things looked the same as they did when the

Indians lived there. To get to Captiva we had to take a tiny, comical-looking ferry over to another island called Sanibel. Then we had to drive the whole length of Sanibel and cross a causeway to get to Captiva. Oh, it was wild and thrilling country. Lots of times we saw alligators sticking their snouts up in pools beside the road. Now and again we'd surprise one crawling across the road.

There wasn't really a hotel on Captiva. It was a huge old clapboard boarding house. You know, they rang a bell for all the meals and everything was laid out family-style. But it was nice and relaxing and everybody was sweet. Long Boy was right about one thing. Most people seemed to have forgotten the storm. Maybe they just didn't want to talk about it. It was three days before Long Boy met an old man who could tell him where the Kodaly place used to be.

We got in the car late one afternoon and drove out there. I can't explain exactly why I felt this urge to go there. I guess maybe I just wanted to know that little girl better. Sometimes when you go poking around an old place you get a strange, silly feeling that you know all about the folks who lived there. It wasn't like that the Kodaly place. All we found was an old foundation overgrown with weeds and vines. A few pilings stuck out of the water where the dock had been. I walked around and tried hard, but I couldn't get any feeling at all about Madeleine Sass or her baby girl or her husband. Considering some of the things that happened later, I guess it was just as well.

Long Boy and I drove back to the hotel without saying a word. For the next couple of weeks I rubbed myself with vinegar and lay in the sun or walked up and down the beach looking for shells. Long Boy got up at daylight every morning and went fishing. It seemed to me he caught half the fish in the Gulf of Mexico.

THIRTEEN

Now, let me ask you something. Suppose you had a little grandchild who you thought had died in a storm, and, suddenly, she turned up alive and well. You'd be overjoyed, wouldn't you? Of course you would. Chances are you'd weep and carry on, and you'd hardly be able to wait until you could put your arms around that poor little child. That's the way a normal person would act. Right?

Well, I guess we all knew old Amelia Sass wasn't exactly normal. But the hardhearted way she acted when she heard her grandchild had been found shocked us all. It simply was something we hadn't taken into account. We thought we'd planned for everything. We'd gone over every other detail a dozen times. Maybe we were feeling a little cocksure and proud of ourselves on the afternoon we sat in Major Lee's suite, waiting, while Beau Goldsborough went out to break the good news to Amelia Sass. I know I was.

It's hard to explain, but for about a week I'd even begun to feel that I really was little Addie Isbell, who had been found during a terrible storm. I suppose it was because I'd learned the part so well. One night I sat down for almost two hours while Beau Goldsborough stared at me with his dead-fish eyes and shot questions at me, trying his best to trip me up. He told Major Lee later that I was a cool little article. I was too much of a lady to say what I thought of him. I do know I looked the part I was playing. When Long Boy and I left Captiva, I saw the ferryboat captain's children around the dock at Punta Rassa. One of them was a girl about my age. She wasn't a bit tanner than I was. I even had the same redbug and sand-flea bites on my legs.

As soon as Major Lee answered the telephone we knew something had gone wrong. He listened a long time and his voice was real quiet as he said, "I see . . . how strange . . . yes, I see." That went on for a long time before he said in the same quiet tone, "Yes, I understand, Beau. We'll do our best." He hung up the phone and for a second or two he was the closest to looking disturbed that I had ever seen him. Then he looked at Long Boy and me and raised his eyebrows and chuckled. "Well, there seems to be a slight complication," he said. "Dear Amelia Sass didn't do anything so mundane as question the identity of her long-lost granddaughter. She simply doesn't want her."

Long Boy and I looked at each other in surprise. "Well . . . why . . . wha . . ." I said.

Major Lee smiled and looked reflective. "Most peculiar," he said. He came and sat on the sofa facing us. His mouth quirked. "Beau is quite shaken. Old Amelia wasn't happy when he broke the news. Instead, she became extremely agitated. Apparently she said over and over again, 'It's too late! It's too late!' When she did calm down somewhat she told Beau that she didn't want the child. She said that caring for her would have to be his responsibility, that he would have to rear and educate her." He chuckled. "Knowing Beau, you can imagine his reaction to that."

Long Boy said, " It's all off then."

"Oh, no," Major Lee said. He paused.

"Not yet, anyway. Apparently Mayflower Goldsborough saved the day. I gather she spoke pretty roughly to old Amelia, told her that she was behaving foolishly, that, of course, she'd have to claim her own granddaughter."

I was seething. "She's the meanest old woman I ever heard of," I said.

Major Lee threw back his head and laughed. He gave me a crinkly look. "Yes, indeed. Imagine disowning her very own little granddaughter."

"I mean . . . oh, you know what I mean," I said.

Major Lee smiled at me. "Yes, I do know, bunny," he said. He looked thoughtful. "Very odd," he said. "Perhaps it's only a temporary aberration — the shock and all. We'll have to see." He looked at me. "I only hope it doesn't make it more difficult for you, lamb."

"I've already told her to come runnin' if things get too bad," Long Boy said.

Major Lee nodded. "Sound advice." He smiled at us and threw up his hands in a small gesture. "Meanwhile, we follow our regular plan. Beau ostensibly will be leaving for Florida aboard the Silver Meteor within the hour. You two will rendezvous with him day after tomorrow as scheduled."

It didn't take me long to get ready to go out to Amelia Sass's house. I put on everything new, from panties to an inexpensive black-and-white check dress that Long Boy and I had bought in Tampa. These were clothes Beau Goldsborough was supposed to have bought me for the trip back to New Orleans. Major Lee had found a cheap old worn cardboard suitcase somewhere. In it I put a blue dress I had almost outgrown and a couple of pairs of old socks and two changes of my oldest underwear. What worried me most was the way Long Boy was moping around. You would have thought I was going off forever. Every five minutes he made me promise to telephone him regularly or come running if things got too bad. We didn't bother getting the car out of the garage but took a taxi to the Union Terminal. We waited at the lower-level ramp like we were supposed to, and right on time, at 4:15, Beau Goldsborough's long black limousine pulled up. Before I climbed in, Long Boy gave my hand a hard squeeze. The old fool.

There wasn't any reason for me to talk to Beau Goldsborough. Everything had been rehearsed over and over. So I didn't bother. He didn't say anything for a long time either, but sat back sucking on his bottom lip and drumming his fat fingers on his knees. When we headed up St. Charles Avenue, he thought of a question he hadn't asked. He leaned forward and closed the sliding glass partition behind the chauffeur's head. He fixed me with his dull cold eyes. "How did you get that scar on your neck?"

I answered automatically. "I don't know. Mama always said I had a scar back there. Is it bad?"

He grunted and drummed with his fingers some more. "Be sure you don't talk too much," he said.

I looked at him coldly. "I know what to do," I said.

He didn't like that. His face got a little red and he said in a nasty tone, "Well, just make sure you do it."

I wish I had made Long Boy drive me by Amelia Sass's house before I finally went out there. It could have saved me an uncomfortable five minutes or so. In those days the whole Garden District was impressive, all quiet and secluded and shaded by wonderful old trees. Most of the huge houses had wide porches and tall windows and were set back in gardens that were just overflowing with tropical plants and flowering shrubs. But Amelia Sass's house — the old Goldsborough place — was something special. It sat off by itself, in a deep spacious garden surrounded by a tall faded bricked wall that was covered by vines. And what can I say about the house itself? When we first drove through the tall iron gates and I saw it, all I could think about was Scarlett O'Hara's house in *Gone With the Wind*. You know — Tara, it was called. It was just the same, huge and gleaming white, with high gables and lots of wide windows, and fronted with tall stately columns. Broad, high steps led up to a sweeping verandah.

It was beautiful and I was bowled over. Even after the car stopped and the chauffeur came around and opened the door, I sat there gawking until Beau Goldsborough snapped at me, "Well, get out!" That embarrassed me, so instead of entering the Sass house all calm and cool like I planned, I went in with my ears burning and feeling like a little Cracker Betty from the Florida swamps for sure.

Mayflower Goldsborough opened the door for us. Now, most times after you get to know a person well it's hard to recall exactly how they seemed to you at first meeting. But I don't have any trouble at all in remembering my first impression of Mayflower Goldsborough. She scared me speechless. She looked so huge and unbending and fierce standing there that she reminded me of one of those voodoo queens I saw in serials at the picture show on Saturday afternoons.

Oh, I do so much want you to know what Mayflower was like. She was large, as I said, tall and well fleshed, but not the least plump. Her features were broad and generous, and her skin was so black it seemed to have a tinge of purple. But Mayflower's cheekbones were so high and prominent, and her bright eyes were set in such a way, that if she had been a lighter color I do believe she would have looked

Chinese. Maybe one reason she looked so — well, exotic, I guess is the word — is the way she dressed. She always wore bright-colored, long flowing dresses, with a piece of the same material around her head. I don't mean a mammy kerchief, but what in New Orleans they called a *tignon,* a kind of turban, tied so it had a flaring bow at the front. Mayflower was seventy-seven years old, and when she was tired or napping in a chair, you could see lots of wrinkles around her eyes and the corners of her mouth. But she didn't seem old. I don't mean she was young for her age. She just walked and moved in an unhurried, calm way that made her seem ageless.

Unless she knew you well and liked you, Mayflower had a dignity that was downright haughty. I think that's one thing that impressed me most at first. I'd never known any colored people real well, honestly known them. Most of them I had met were working in jobs, or were in the kind of fix where they had to be smiling and bowing and agreeable whether they really wanted to or not. Mayflower didn't feel any compulsion to smile at anybody, simply

411

nobody at all, unless she felt like it.

I don't want to go on and on about Mayflower, but I may as well tell you right now, I loved her. I loved her so much. I think I knew I was going to love her just as soon as I got over my first fright. On that afternoon I walked into the Sass house, Mayflower stood there wearing a sparkling green dress and a matching *tignon.* Without changing her fierce and forbidding expression or saying a word, she stretched out her hand toward me. I crept forward, scared to death. She fell to her knees and put her hands on both my shoulders. Still without a change of expression, she looked into my eyes and face for what seemed a whole minute. Then her eyes lit up, and the light spread to her face, and, suddenly, she was giving me the brightest, sweetest smile I ever saw. She had the same lilt in her voice Creole people do. "I'm glad you came, child," she said. "We need you here."

She got to her feet and looked toward Beau Goldsborough. In a flash her expression was stern again. He had lit a cigar, or maybe he had it all the time and I hadn't noticed. Mayflower said sharply,

"Put that stinking thing out! You'll smell up the house." Beau flushed and looked like a bad little boy who had been slapped. He held his cigar up and looked from side to side for something to put it in. When he couldn't find anything, he turned and walked out the front door to throw it away. Mayflower looked down at me, and there was such a bright, mischievous gleam in her eye, I thought she was going to wink. Instead, she picked up my suitcase and put her hand on my shoulder and said in her lilting way, "Come along, *cherie*. Your grandma-ma is waiting."

Mayflower kept her hand on my shoulder as we climbed the broad curving staircase to the second floor and walked down a long hall. I learned to know that hall as well as the palm of my hand. On that afternoon all I was aware of was a jumble of old pictures in heavy tarnished gold frames hanging here and there on the gold-and-blue wallpaper and the thick carpet under my feet. Amelia Sass's room was at the very end of the wing and opened onto a glass-enclosed sun porch. Her door was open. It was always open. Mayflower didn't say a word, but gave me a little push across the threshold.

Well, I can say this—Amelia Sass didn't look at all like I thought she would. I was expecting to meet some sour-faced, fat old woman. Instead, the thing that struck me first was how tiny and frail she was. She was propped up high in a tremendous old bed that had a white, frilly canopy. She was wearing a fluffy white bed jacket embroidered with pink and blue flowers. You couldn't call her a pretty old woman. Her face was too thin and had too many sharp angles. But she looked like somebody—somebody real aristocratic. I'll have to give her credit for that. Her hair was beautiful, snowy white and soft-looking, and her eyes were so bright and dark that she reminded me of a tiny Jenny wren. It's funny, but to show how misleading first impressions can be, for the first few seconds after I stepped into the room, the thought that was uppermost in my mind was how sad she looked. I even thought part of the brightness in her eyes was caused by tears. Of course, when she spoke, I knew better.

Her voice wasn't exactly sharp, but it had an impatient, nagging edge to it. "Well, come in, child," she said. "Don't stand there like a little ninny." I took a few steps forward, and then her voice got that kind of half-laughing, mocking tone in it that I learned to hate so much. "No, over here — closer," she said. "Gracious! I won't bite you. Let's see what a hundred generations of fine ladies and gentlemen have produced."

I went and stood by the edge of the bed. There was a faint smell of sachet about her. She made a little grimace that I guess was supposed to be a smile. She didn't reach out to touch me, but just looked at me with her bright eyes. From close up, I could tell she never had been pretty. Nice-looking, maybe, or always just real grand, I don't know. Her face and neck were covered with a network of almost invisible, teensy wrinkles. Her white tiny hands were blue-veined and speckled with age spots. I thought her expression was about to soften, but she spoke again, and her voice really was almost sharp. "Don't stand with your hands dangling like a field hand. Fold them in front of you."

"Yes, ma'am," I said. I folded my

hands across my stomach.

She pressed her lips together so tight they almost disappeared. She made a little snorting, laughing sound. "Ah, you speak," she said.

"Yes, ma'am," I said again. I had begun to dislike her even more than I had before I met her.

"Don't keep . . ." She broke off and her face got tight and pale. I could tell she was holding her breath. She reached out one hand and found a small cardboard box on the bed near her side. She opened it and took out a tiny white pill and put it in her mouth. She lay back a moment or two, not speaking, and the color came back to her face. She looked at me again, just like nothing had happened, and said, "Don't keep ma'aming me in that abject way. I'm your old grandma-ma—" she made her little laughing, snorting sound—"such as I am. Can't you call me Grandma-ma?"

I didn't realize Mayflower was standing behind me until she spoke. I guess she had come over when Amelia Sass took the pill. She asked quietly, "Are you all right, Missy?"

416

Amelia Sass's voice changed completely. It got flat and self-pitying. "Of course I'm not all right," she said. "I'm an ugly, useless old woman." She put her head back on the pillows and looked straight ahead and mumbled something in what I knew right away was French. I was to find out she and Mayflower spoke French about half the time. All the time when they didn't want me to know what they were saying.

Mayflower answered her in French. Amelia Sass lay there, staring straight ahead. Finally, she turned and gave me a searching look with her bright eyes. She said in a voice that was almost nice for her, "Well, turn around so I can get a look at the back of you." I turned around, and gently, so gently I almost couldn't feel it, her hand parted the hair at the nape of my neck. She must have been satisfied with what she saw, and it must have given her another one of her attacks. It served her right as far as I was concerned. I heard the covers of the bed rustle and there was a small gasping sound. I didn't get a chance to see exactly what happened, because Mayflower put her arm around my shoulder and started leading me out of the room. Before we got to the door, Amelia Sass said in a kind of breathless voice that still had a half-laughing, mocking tone, "You're too much for your old grandma-ma, but we'll have dinner together."

We didn't though. It was a long time before Amelia Sass and I ate together. And I liked that just fine. Mayflower led me down the hall to my room. If I hadn't lived in some fancy hotel suites, I guess I would have been knocked breathless. It was beautiful — but much too stiff and elegant for a child's room. It had an off-white, rich-looking carpet and white and gold wallpaper, and it was furnished with graceful old furniture. It had a canopied bed so high that I always used a little stool to climb into it. When Mayflower unpacked my suitcase and laid out the few things I had brought on that big bed, they made such a pitiful little pile that I could tell she was touched. They even looked sad to me. She got silent for a minute or two and then put everything away in a tall highboy as carefully as if I had brought a full wardrobe. Then she took my hand and led me out to a small balcony overlooking the garden. It was so pretty—so quiet and peaceful and cool. There was an old iron fountain in the center, and flower beds bordered the gravel walks, but it wasn't a formal, prissy garden. Parts of it were almost a tangle of tropical plants and shrubs, and growing close to the vine-covered walls were banana trees and dwarf palms and oleanders. Mayflower pointed to a towering magnolia tree in the far corner of the garden. Up close to the trunk was a small stone bench almost covered with moss. "You see that old tree there," she said. "From the time she was a little girl, your mother used to go sit under that tree all by herself. She called it her 'thinking place.' "

When I didn't say anything, she looked down at me. She asked in her lilting way, "Are you not curious about your mother?"

I couldn't think of anything to say that wouldn't make me feel worse than I already felt, so I just nodded.

"You ought to be," Mayflower said. "You're exactly like her." she paused. "Except you've got more grit in your craw. Lots more grit. I don't know how you got it.

I don't think I want to hear about the time you weren't here where you belong. It makes me sad. But if that's what made you a tough little girl, I'm glad." She looked out over the garden with a brooding expression and put her arms around my shoulders and drew me close to her side. "There's no room for soft people in this family now."

I even had my own bathroom. It was every bit as elegant as my room, but real old-fashioned, with a huge old bathtub on ornate legs and gold fixtures shaped like fish and swans. It also had the first bidet I had ever seen in my life. You know, I had never even dreamed there were such things. I looked at the bidet for the longest time, trying to figure out what it could possibly be used for. Finally, I called to Mayflower. When she came to the door, I just pointed. I thought she was going to laugh, but she held it back, except in her eyes. She tried to make her face solemn. "Why, where have you been, *cherie?*" she asked. "That little thing's to wash your feet in."

I knew she was teasing. "Aw . . ." I said. "Aw . . ." She burst out laughing and pulled me close to her side in a big hug and told me what it was really for.

We were still laughing when we went downstairs. I had forgotten all about Beau Goldsborough. He was waiting in the family sitting room, which was different from the drawing room and music room and downstairs study. But I know I'll never be able to get you straight about all the rooms in that huge old house. Anyway, Beau got up as soon as we came in. He looked at Mayflower expectantly. I didn't see the look she gave him, but it told him that everything was all right. He tried to get jovial. "Well, now," he said, showing his teeth in a smile that didn't touch his fish eyes, "my little niece is home safely at last." He patted my head—I mean actually patted it. "You be a good girl, dear, and Uncle Beau will come to see you soon." He turned to Mayflower. "Maybe I should go up and see Aunt 'Melia?"

Mayflower got her haughty look. "She's not receiving today," she said. It was plain enough she didn't like Beau at all.

He flushed and sucked his bottom lip and said, "Ah, well, I'll come another day then." Before I realized what he was doing, he bent down and gave me a big soppy kiss on the cheek. I guess maybe he was acting his part well, but it made me so mad I felt like poking him in his big belly. I was glad, though, he was taking good news back to Long Boy and Major Lee.

I went into the kitchen and sat with Mayflower while she fixed dinner that night. That got to be a regular thing. Some of the best talks Mayflower and I ever had were in that kitchen. You wouldn't believe how immense it was, and you'd probably be shocked because it was so old-fashioned. It didn't have a single thing that might be called a modern appliance. The old black iron wood stove had an oven big enough to bake half a side of beef, but Mayflower said it had been there for as long as she could remember. The wide cast-iron sink had regular faucets, but there was still a hole where a hand pump had been. The walls and overhead beams were covered with pots and pans, but they all were so big that they hadn't been used in years. Now, I know old out-of-date kitchens were pretty common in rich homes back in the days when servants were cheap and easy to get. People are not apt to worry much about a kitchen unless they have to grub around in it themselves. But seeing Amelia Sass's kitchen made me first realize how stingy she really was.

As time went on, of course, I began to notice lots of other things. How the carpets on all the stairs were worn threadbare, for instance. It was several days before I realized there were big brown water marks in the corners of my room where the roof was leaking. I looked and found it was almost as bad in every room. The wallpaper was in pretty bad shape everywhere, especially in the halls. Even the house and verandah could have stood a coat of paint. When things broke, they never got fixed. Besides, there was the mammoth old garage standing out back empty. Mayflower said that once it had been filled with eight cars. Amelia Sass had sold the last one about three years before.

But, as I said, I began to realize what an awful skinflint Amelia Sass was on that first night when I watched Mayflower cooking on a cheap little two-burner electric grill. When I went to the icebox to get Mayflower some butter I was really shocked. The icebox looked as big and sturdy as a boxcar, but it was practically empty and there was a dinky little piece of ice that wasn't big enough to chill a capon's butt.

As soon as I could, I worked around to the subject with Mayflower. "Do you do all the work around here by yourself?" I asked.

"Oh, not all of it, *cherie*," she said. "Marie and Robear live out back. You'll meet them soon, tomorrow maybe. Robear hasn't been feeling well, so they haven't been around for a couple of days." She smiled. "Everything around this place is old—but Marie and Robear are creaky. When the other servants left a few years back, they stayed on. They were so old there wasn't any place for them to go. Robear works around the garden, and he keeps it up fairly well, considering. Marie helps around the house, laundry and cleaning, but she's really too feeble to do much."

"A big house like this needs lots of help," I said.

Mayflower gave a little laugh. "Ah, you came too late, child. When I was your age there were servants waiting on servants." She looked at me. "When your mother was a little girl, the quarters out back were full, and we had other help coming in by the day." She paused and thought. "There must have been twelve or fourteen people around altogether."

"Why did they all leave?" I asked.

"Your grandma-ma decided we didn't need them," Mayflower said. She gave me a quick look. "She was right, too." She shrugged. "Pouf! Two old women don't need all that help around. Always underfoot." Her eyes got brooding. "One old woman I should have said. I can take care of myself. And I don't mind taking care of your grandma-ma. *Mon Dieu,* she's taken care of me often enough. Besides, times are . . ." She stopped. After a pause she shrugged again and said, "Well, times have changed." She busied herself over her cooking for a moment or two and looked at me with her big bright smile. "And you're no trouble. You can help, is it not so?" She handed me a cup. "Like fetching me some water now."

That was one thing about Mayflower. She would never say anything the least bit critical of Amelia Sass. Oh, she didn't mind

425

letting Amelia Sass have both barrels to her face. But she wouldn't talk about her to anybody else. Sometimes when she knew Amelia Sass had given me a hard time, Mayflower would give me an understanding squeeze or hug, but she wouldn't say a word. I think I understood that. All you had to do was see Amelia Sass and Mayflower together to understand how close they were. They'd been together all their lives, and I guess after seventy-five years you learn to accept somebody's faults, no matter how bad they are.

We always took up Amelia Sass's big wicker bed tray before we ate ourselves. Mayflower would fuss over it, making everything look especially nice, because getting Amelia Sass to eat enough was a problem. Mayflower always fixed a soup, a main dish and a salad. Sometimes we had dessert, but Amelia Sass always finished her meals with a small glass of port wine that came out of dusty old bottles Mayflower brought up from the cellar. On that first night we started another custom. Mayflower carried the tray almost to Amelia Sass's door and handed it over to me. She had rehearsed me in what to say, so I walked in with the tray, trying to smile like I meant it, and said, *"Bonjour, Grandma-ma."* It was the first time I called Amelia Sass Grandmama, and from that time on I kept it up, saying it in the French way she and Mayflower did.

Grandmama Sass didn't seem to be too pleased. Maybe I surprised her. She didn't take her bright eyes off my face as I crossed the room and put the tray on the bed. She pressed her lips together tightly and just sat there while Mayflower came and arranged the tray. There was a book on the bed. Grandmama Sass picked it up and thrust it out at me and said sharply, "Read me something." I must have looked confused, because she said impatiently, "Read anything — start anywhere." I opened the book to the first page and started reading. It was an old book printed in the small type they used to use. I read a sentence or two before I realized it was *Alice's Adventures in Wonderland.* I had read it before, twice, in fact. I bought a copy because Major Lee told me about it. From what I've always been told, I must have been the only girl in the world who didn't think it was wonderful. Maybe I got to it too late. I thought it was silly.

Anyway, I read two or three paragraphs before Grandmama Sass made a waving motion for me to stop. Her eyes were sharp as she studied me. "They told me you had missed most of your schooling," she said. "How did you learn to read so well?"

I gave her my little spiel about how I had taught myself to read and how Earl and Alma couldn't. She didn't ask me who Earl and Alma were. Instead, she leaned back against the pillows and lifted the corners of her mouth in the little grimace she used for a smile. She looked at Mayflower. "Blood will always tell, won't it, Mayflower?" Mayflower had a slight smile on her face, but her eyes were dark and serious. She nodded slightly.

Grandmama Sass turned to me. "I've been worrying about your schooling. I see now it's not going to be quite the problem I thought. At any rate, it's too late to do anything about it this year. Before next fall, we'll have to get you enrolled in a suitable young ladies' academy."

Mayflower said, "She needs clothes."

Grandmama Sass didn't like that. She frowned and turned down the corners of her mouth. "Why, I thought Beau was going to tend to that," she said. She looked at me sharply. "Didn't he buy you anything?"

I made a motion toward what I was wearing. "He bought me these."

Grandmama Sass's frown deepened. "Oh, that dratted man!" she said. She turned to Mayflower. "Maybe we should..."

Mayflower said, "Eat your dinner. It's getting cold. We'll talk about it later."

Grandmama set her mouth tight and turned to her tray. It was plain that the thought of spending a few dollars to buy me some clothes had upset her. Maybe that's why most of her first spoonful of cream soup ran down her chin instead of going into her mouth. She leaned forward over the tray and grunted with annoyance. Mayflower made a clucking noise and picked up her napkin and handed it to her. Grandmama Sass wiped her chin and her face got beet-red.

I don't think I changed expression. I didn't mean to, but Grandmama Sass looked at me and asked in her half-laughing, mocking voice, "Well, what are you thinking, little Miss Big Eyes? How disgusting your old grandmama is?" She gave a snorting laugh. "Oh, your time will come, too. You may not believe it, but someday you'll be old and ugly, sitting in a bed with soup running down your chin."

Mayflower made a shushing sound and said, "Eat your soup, Missy."

Grandmama Sass's mouth twisted. "Oh, don't shush me, Mayflower," she said. "Why shouldn't she hear the truth? Gracious knows I wish somebody had told me when I was her age." She looked at me with her eyes glistening they were so bright. "Did they send you to Sunday school down there in the Florida bayous?"

I shook my head.

Grandmama Sass gave her snorting laugh again. "Well, thank heaven for that! Maybe there's some hope for you. Let me tell you, dear little granddaughter, old God Almighty is a great joker. Nobody ever says that, do they? And do you know what His great joke is? Not that He makes us all die. *Non, ma cherie,* God is far too cruel and subtle for that. His great joke is that He makes us old and ugly and useless. Ah, you'll find out. If you live long enough you'll discover that life itself is a cruel joke. All you'll have to do is continue breathing and you'll be punished with decay and sorrow and pain. Why, you—"

Mayflower said sharply, "Eat your dinner, Missy."

Grandmama Sass stopped and shrugged. "Oh, very well," she said. She took a sip of soup and turned to Mayflower and said something in French. Mayflower answered her back. Grandmama Sass's face got solemn. She shot me a glance out of her bright eyes and maybe there were tears in them. Maybe not.

Mayflower tucked me into my big bed that night. I know my real mama must have done that, but I had no memory of it. When Mayflower leaned over and kissed me on the forehead before she put out the light, it was all I could do to keep from throwing my arms around her. Wasn't that silly for a girl of twelve, going on thirteen? I lay there for the longest time, thinking. I kept telling myself I should feel good. Our deal was working perfectly. Besides, it wasn't Mayflower's money we were after. I felt sad and lonely and miserable all the same. And you know what? I discovered I missed Long Boy something awful.

FOURTEEN

For about a week after I went to live at the Sass house I kept waiting for somebody to sit me down and ask me all about my life with the Isbells. As much as I disliked being around her, I was hoping it would be Grandmama Sass. It made me feel bad to lie to Mayflower. But nobody asked me a thing. Leastways, not in the way we had rehearsed.

That struck me as strange at first. In fact, it made me a little nervous until, bit by bit, I learned from Mayflower that I—well, you know what I mean, the real little girl—had been all they talked about in that big old house for three or four years. Up until the time Grandmama Sass got sick and almost died, apparently they still felt hopeful that I would be found almost any day. After that I guess her illness became everybody's chief concern. She and Mayflower never seemed to have had any doubts that I had survived the storm. What worried them most was that I might have died because I was not cared for properly by the family that took me away.

It was almost as if Grandmama Sass and Mayflower didn't want to hear about how I had lived before Beau found me. Maybe it was like Mayflower said, it made them feel bad to think about it. Or maybe it was because they both were old, and a few years didn't seem like such a long time to them. Anyway, most of the time when they talked about the time I had been missing, it came up in a roundabout way. On the second or third day, for instance, after Mayflower and I took up Grandmama Sass's breakfast tray, she looked at me and said in her mocking voice, "Now, we'll have to do something about your name, won't we?"

I just looked at her and didn't say anything.

Grandmama Sass said, "Oh, don't look at me in that cool way, little Miss Alice-sit-by-the-fire. Addie isn't your real name, you know. It was given to you by — by those people. I find it a very country name."

I did something foolish. The way Grandmama Sass talked always got my back up, so I had a hard time remembering I was playing a part. "I like it," I said.

Grandmama Sass gave her snorting little laugh. "Oh, you do, young miss? Well, how nice for you!" She studied me with her bright eyes and her upper lip curled. "And how unusual. I always hated my name. When I was your age I wanted a nice musical name, like my Creole friends—Delphine, or Felicite . . . or Desiree." She looked at Mayflower. "Do you remember, Mayflower, how much I envied little Melpomene Burmudez?" Mayflower was solemn, but she nodded.

Grandmama Sass looked at me again and shrugged. "Well, I certainly wouldn't wish on you a name I didn't care for myself." Her voice got mocking again. "But Addie Kodaly . . . oh, dear! It's equally as unfortunate as Addie Isbell. Maybe you'll change your mind as you mature."

One afternoon when Mayflower had stepped out and left me alone with Grandmama Sass, she asked suddenly, "And why are you looking so pensive, child? Do you miss your . . . those people you lived with?"

I shook my head. "No, ma'am."

Grandmama Sass plucked at the bedspread and gave me a sidelong look with her bright eyes. "Didn't they treat you well?"

I shrugged. "Not all the time," I said. I went into my little speech about old Ern Isbell.

Grandmama Sass clamped her mouth tight and looked at me a long time. When she started to speak, her voice sounded almost nice for a change. "Well, child, I want you to know . . ." All of a sudden she stopped and gave her unpleasant little laugh. "Oh, well, you seem to have survived well enough," she said. She gave me a mocking look. "Very well, indeed, I would say."

I simply couldn't figure that old woman out. Oh, I'm willing to admit part of it may have been my fault. I tried, but I guess she sensed I didn't like her. I couldn't do much about my feelings toward her, knowing how she had treated her daughter and how stingy she was and all. But she really didn't have any good reason for disliking me, or treating me in her standoffish, mocking way. I know Mayflower spoke to her about it. Lots of times when she spoke to Grandmama Sass in French, it was plain she was telling Grandmama Sass to shut up, or watch what she was saying. One night when we had forgotten to put a knife on Grandmama Sass's tray, I went downstairs to get one. When I came back upstairs and was almost at the bedroom door, I heard Grandmama Sass saying, "Oh, I know, Mayflower. You're right. I try—honestly I try. I am glad she's here. But I simply can't . . ." She stopped when I came in the room. She did treat me extra nice that night. For her, that is.

If she hadn't been such a mean, bitter old woman, Grandmama Sass could have been real interesting. She told wonderful stories about the old days. One night I just sat fascinated when she told about the old French Opera House. When she talked you could almost see how grand and glittering everything had been. The people sat in gold gilt boxes arranged in a horseshoe shape, and the women wore flowing gowns and were just drenched in jewels, like diamonds and emeralds and rubies. The men were all handsome and dashing in evening clothes, with top hats and capes lined with crimson silk. Flowers were everywhere and big chandeliers were blazing and everybody was happy and chivalrous and romantic. Oh, it was like something out of *Gone With the Wind.* But suddenly Grandmama Sass twisted her mouth. "Gone!" she said bitterly. "Burned to the ground. Every last scrap of velvet and gilt gone to ashes. Ashes." She gave her mocking laugh. "Just as everything ends up, dear little granddaughter. Ashes!"

She didn't stay in bed all the time. She never came downstairs, but sometimes she put on a robe and slippers and sat in the sun porch next to her room. Now and then she would walk up and down the hall, leaning on a gold-headed ebony stick that had belonged to her daddy. One afternoon she came down the hall and found me sitting on the top step of the staircase. She gave her little snorting laugh. "I used to sit there," she said. "Mayflower, too, most of the time. Many's the night we sat right there. From the time we were big enough to walk until we were past your age." Before I realized it, she somehow had managed to sit down beside me. She wasn't much bigger than I was. She seemed as frail and fragile as cobwebs.

We sat there for a long time before she spoke. "Don't believe the lies you hear about storing up happy memories, child. When you grow old, happy memories tear your heart more than bad ones. Much more." There was a long silence before she said, "Mayflower and I would creep out here when there were parties downstairs. They weren't much as parties go. Times were hard then — but we didn't know it. We were too young and too sheltered. We never knew about hard times." She paused. "More's the pity."

She pointed with her stick toward the gigantic crystal chandelier that hung in the foyer. "You see that useless old piece of junk? It held a hundred and sixteen candles." She gave her snorting laugh. "There weren't that many candles in all of New Orleans." She turned and looked at me with her bright eyes. "You see, when old General Beast Butler and his Yankees came in, the people stripped the warehouses of everything the Yankees could use. What they couldn't carry away they spilled and destroyed. Ah, there was so much sugar strewn about, Papa always said it looked like a snowstorm had hit the city. Molasses overflowed the gutters. They burned twelve thousand bales of cotton, and more than two thousand belonged to Papa. He helped set the fires with his own hands. There were..."

She paused. "Oh, but I ramble like an old fool. I wanted to tell you about the chandelier. It was a point of pride with Papa to have it lit when he entertained. Old Ep—Mayflower's father—and the other servants saved every scrap of fat and tallow. And they foraged around for every tiny candle end or dab of wax they could find. They boiled everything down in a tub and poured a tiny bit in every holder in the chandelier and made wicks out of twisted bits of cotton cloth. Papa always had that chandelier blazing when he entertained, but, oh, how it did smoke!" She gave her snorting laugh. "Mayflower and I didn't know it wasn't supposed to do that. We sat here entranced, thinking it was beautiful."

She sat silently for a while. "Ah!" she

exclaimed suddenly. "But I must tell you about the ball Papa gave the night the last Yankee troops left the city. Fifteen years they stayed. Imagine! I was almost seventeen the night of that ball. There were real candles in the chandelier then. I had a pink ball gown, made by Madame Hachard, the most famous *modiste* in New Orleans. Watered silk, it was, with a long train fastened by velvet ribbons. Mayflower tightened my stays until I could hardly breathe. Oh, how we danced that night. We danced and danced! Mayflower sat here, and every time I got so breathless I couldn't dance another step, I came up and sat with her. Oh, how . . ."

Suddenly she stopped and sat very still. "All those beautiful people," she said in a low, sad voice, like she was thinking out loud. "All those dear, beautiful, vital, smiling people." Her voice got shrill. "Dead! All dead!" She stood up so quickly, I was afraid she would topple over. "Gone!" she said harshly. "All gone! Do you understand that, young lady?" She tottered down the hall toward her room, making a low anguished sound that could have been sobbing or cursing.

Grandmama Sass always spoiled everything. It seemed to me she was worse on Mondays, after Dr. Morphy came by to check on her. He was such a nice little man, plump, with tiny hands and feet and big soft brown eyes. Mayflower said he was a famous heart specialist and came from one of the oldest Creole families in New Orleans. He called on Grandmama Sass, just like he was an ordinary doctor, because he had known her all his life. He knew my moth — oh, Madeleine Sass — real well, too. The first time he saw me, he stopped and looked at me closely. "You're Madeleine's daughter," he said. I nodded. He smiled. "Ah, it's the eyes — those grave eyes." After that he always called me Yeux Tristes, which means "sad eyes" in French.

Grandmama Sass treated Dr. Morphy like he was a little boy. While he was there, she was always giving her snorting laugh or making a small hooting sound and saying, "Oh, really, Bernardo!" or "Come now, Bernardo!" Once after he left, Mayflower and I went in and found her propped up in bed with her eyes almost glowing they were so bright. She curled her upper lip and said, "Dear Bernardo has just told me that by the end of the century people will live to be a hundred years old." She made a little sound of disgust. "Now, I ask you, isn't that stupid? People live too long now — much too long." She paused and gave her harsh laugh. "If the doctors knew what they were about, they'd devise some method of making people die at the proper time. At the exact time — before they began to lose their faculties and withered up and became a burden to themselves and everybody about them."

Mayflower said shortly, "That's foolish talk."

"Why, it isn't, Mayflower," Grandmama Sass said. "Oh, if some old ladies want to live forever ugly and shriveled and useless, let them. But, in the name of His High Holiness, shouldn't people have a choice? Everyone knows when the time . . ." She stopped and looked at me. "Oh, gracious, child, don't look at me as if I'm dotty." She curled her lip. "You'll find out — yes, indeed, everybody finds out."

Things like that got my back up. But they

annoyed me more—maybe even scared me a little. I suppose I should be ashamed of myself, but I got especially uneasy when Grandmama Sass had one of her seizures. It happened two or three times a day. Sometimes it looked like she was going to die before she popped one of her tiny pills in her mouth and her color came back. I didn't stay around her any more than was necessary. At first, I simply dreaded Thursdays and Saturdays. Those were the days Mayflower went off to visit her niece. I didn't know about Mayflower's niece until the second week, because she had stayed home because of my arrival.

Now, I'll tell you right away, I always thought there was something peculiar about Mayflower going off like that. For one thing, she never would talk to me about her niece or tell me why she had to spend so much time with her. She would always leave real early in the morning, about five o'clock, and wouldn't come home until after six. I could tell how tired she was as I sat with her while she fixed dinner. But she never complained, and always she brought me home something special, like a piece of cherry pie or a chocolate eclair. We used to laugh because whatever she brought always got a little squashed on the way home.

Marie puttered around, doing the cooking and housework while Mayflower was away. She was such a poor old thing, toothless and almost blank-eyed. She was so shriveled and brittle-looking, she reminded me of a burnt match stick. But she was as sweet as could be. Some days she managed everything real well. On other days she crept and stumbled around, doing everything wrong, and muttering to herself in a language Mayflower said was gumbo French. Robear, her husband, was just as wrinkled and toothless, but a bit more spry. Most of the time he worked in the garden, but he came in and helped Marie with the washing-up and heavy cleaning.

I would take up Grandmama Sass's breakfast and lunch trays on the days Mayflower was away, but I always found some way to slip away as soon as possible. For the first couple of weeks I spent my time wandering around the house and grounds. There was so much to explore, and I guess I saw everything. At least as much as I could. About half the rooms on the second and third floors of the house were locked up tight. Mayflower said Grandmama Sass closed them off so the sunlight couldn't fade the furniture and rugs.

As stingy as she was, Grandmama Sass took especially good care of her beautiful antique furniture. Toward the end of my first week there a skinny man with frizzly white hair came out with two colored helpers and hauled away half a truckload of furniture to be refinished and reupholstered. Of course, Grandmama Sass raised a fuss about how much it was going to cost. As I was going up the hall to my room I could hear her haggling with the man. "You're a thief, Emile!" she said, raising her voice, and she didn't say it in a kidding tone. "You've always been a despicable thief."

Having to spend money almost broke her heart. Take my clothes, for example. It took almost two weeks for Grandmama Sass to get around to buying me some. Naturally, we didn't go shopping like ordinary people. Grandmama Sass called Maison Blanc, the biggest department store in New Orleans, and asked them to send out a collection of clothes for her to look over. A man and a woman came out in a small panel truck. Before you knew it, Grandmama Sass's sun porch looked like a small shop. She called me in but didn't ask whether I liked anything or not. She sat back on a wicker sofa, looking regal as a queen, tapping her cane and speaking French with the woman. The first thing she did when the woman showed her something was reach for the price tag and look at it. About half the time she would just wave her hand, meaning it was too expensive.

To be fair, though, what she finally picked out wasn't too bad. She bought me eight dresses, two pairs of shoes, a robe and slippers, two dozen pairs of panties and socks, and a dozen nightgowns and slips. I ended up with almost as many clothes as I had back at the hotel. She didn't hide the fact she wasn't happy about having to spend so much. When I put on an act and pretended to be thrilled and thanked her, she turned down the corners of her mouth. "Everything is much too costly nowadays," she said. "Even ready-made junk."

It was some time before I realized Beau Goldsborough telephoned Grandmama Sass every day. I don't know what they talked about, but I had a feeling Grandmama Sass didn't care for him any more than Mayflower did. It wasn't anything she said. Maybe it was because she didn't mention him much at all. I told Mayflower one time that I didn't like Beau. She smiled. "You have to stand at the end of a long line, *cherie,*"she said.

"You don't like him, either, do you?" I asked.

She gave a small shrug. "He's the only kin Missy has left." She thought about it and smiled. "He was a sneaky little boy, and he's a sneaky man. A sissy little boy, too. All I do is remember that, and he doesn't bother me."

On the day after Grandmama Sass bought my clothes, Beau came calling in person. He had phoned Grandmama Sass to say he was coming. When he appeared, smiling like a short-fanged alligator, Mayflower let him in without a word. As soon as he saw me, he went into his jovial-uncle act. "Ah, and how is my little niece? I can see you're blooming, dear. Blooming! Uncle Beau brought you something." He held out a cheap little child's puzzle book like it was a diamond lavaliere. I thanked him nicely, and, like Mayflower had asked me to, I took him up to Grandmama Sass's room. The closer we got to her door, the more jovial he got. It was "Uncle Beau" this and "My dear little niece" that. Grandmama Sass held up her cheek for him to kiss, but she didn't seem especially happy to see him. I started out of the room, but she said, "Stay, child."

It was the kind of conversation you would expect a nephew to have with his aunt. She asked about his family, and he inquired about her health. They mentioned a few people they both knew. He was real respectful, saying, "Yes, Aunt 'Melia," or "No, Aunt 'Melia." Only one time did Beau get around to talking about money. He cleared his throat and said, "Er, Aunt ' Melia, I was wondering if you have any American Lead shares? It's been doing quite well the last few weeks."

Grandmama Sass curled her upper lip slightly. "Gracious, Beau, why are you so tiresome—always wanting to talk of business or money. You weren't reared that way."

Beau flushed and sucked at his bottom lip. "Well, I, er, ah, thought I'd mention it," he said. He tried a feeble laugh. "After all, we all aren't quite as well, er, situated as you are, Aunt 'Melia."

Grandmama Sass just looked at him grandly.

After he had given Grandmama Sass another peck on the cheek, I took him back downstairs. When we were halfway down the hall he hissed at me in a whisper so furious it was crackling. "You little fool! Why didn't you leave?"

I was so surprised I couldn't think of anything to say. I didn't even begin to get really mad until after he left. I had wanted to ask him about Long Boy and Major Lee. But seeing old Beau made me determined to do one thing. The next day was Saturday, and Mayflower was going to visit her niece. As I lay in bed that night I planned exactly what I meant to do.

As soon as I took up Grandmama Sass's bed tray the next morning I got out of the room as soon as I could. I flew downstairs and went into the study. I lifted the telephone real carefully and called Long Boy. It was a risky, foolish thing to do, I knew. I held my breath, expecting any moment to hear a click when Grandmama Sass lifted the phone in her room. She didn't, though. When Long Boy finally answered the phone and heard my voice, he sounded so happy I do believe he would have come crawling right through the telephone wires if that had been possible. I shushed him and whispered and hung up.

That was one of the longest days I ever spent. But, finally, two o'clock came rolling around. I moseyed down to the gate and opened it and ran most of the way to St. Charles Avenue. Long Boy was parked, waiting, and, oh, it was so good to see him! We drove out St. Charles Avenue and turned into Audubon Park and parked near the golf course. We talked and talked. Naturally, I told him every single thing that had happened. He told me how much business he had been doing selling PruYea stock with Major Lee. Then he told me how Beau had started complaining about our deal. Now that it was working so slick, he was always around whining that 20 percent for our share was too much. Long Boy laughed. "Major Lee lets him whinny a time or two, then he lifts his eyebrows an' gives th' curb bit a good twist. Ol' Beau's sure met his match."

When we started back up St. Charles Avenue, Long Boy asked, "How much longer will it take? How's th' ol' girl holdin' out?"

You know, that just brought me up short. I sure didn't like Grandmama Sass, but talking about her dying in such a coldblooded way seemed terrible. Of course, two weeks before I'd been doing the same thing without giving it a thought. I tried to be businesslike. "She's pretty strong," I said, "except when she has one of her attacks."

Long Boy said, "I was afraid of that. Well, it hasn't been long. I guess you'll have to hang 'roun' a few months before we start worryin'."

"I guess so," I said. Suddenly I felt just awful.

Meeting Long Boy on Saturday

afternoons became a regular thing after that. He'd park and wait for me, and we'd always drive out to Audubon Park and talk. It was surprising how fast time went by. One day I looked up and realized I'd been living at the Sass house for six weeks. I hadn't lived any one place that long since my mama died. Things would have gone on like that until—well, for quite a little while, if the old toilet in my bathroom hadn't gotten stopped up.

I really didn't have anything to do with the toilet getting stopped up. That may seem unimportant, but it does help explain why I acted the way I did. The other reason may be that I was feeling blue and moody. I had seen Long Boy the day before, and every time I saw him it took about twenty-four hours for me to settle down again. Anyway, the toilet had been gurgling and acting funny from the time I moved in. On that Sunday morning it suddenly clogged and started overflowing. I mopped up the best I could, and when I went downstairs I told Mayflower about it. She said she would send Robear up to look at it. I didn't give it another thought until

Mayflower and I took Grandmama Sass's luncheon tray up.

As soon as I walked in the room Grandmama Sass looked at me with her eyes flashing. Her voice was harsh. "Well, young miss, Robear tells me you've stopped up the plumbing in your room."

"Why, I didn't . . ." I started.

"How can you be such a little simpleton?" Grandmama Sass asked, her voice even harsher. "Don't you know it costs a fortune to have repairs made nowadays? How could you have done such a thing?"

I put the tray on the bed and faced her. "I didn't," I said. "It was—"

"Of course you did!" Grandmama Sass said. "It didn't simply happen. You threw something down there that—"

"I did not," I said, beginning to burn.

"There's no use in denying it!" Grandmama Sass said, her voice getting high and shrill. She was simply furious. Her eyes were burning and her hands were trembling slightly.

Mayflower said sternly, "That's enough, Missy."

Usually that would have stopped

454

Grandmama Sass, but she was too mad. She barely glanced at Mayflower. "You listen to me, young miss," she said, curling up her upper lip in a little snarl, "if you're such a little savage you've never learned to operate a commode, ask someone to help you. I don't have the money to —"

It wasn't what she said that made me so mad. I don't even think it was her tone. It was just the thought that she was so mean and stingy that something like a toilet getting stopped up could make her snarl and cause her hands to shake. Everything I'd been holding against her suddenly rose up and began to choke me. I guess it was the maddest I'd ever been in my life. "No, you listen to me!" I said. "You stingy, dried-up old nanny goat! I don't care one little jaybird fart about your old toilet. I didn't stop it up, but I wish I had! I'll go around and stop up every toilet in this old house if it makes you spend some of your precious money! You fool with me, and I'll push you down a toilet, you . . . you stingy, miserable old . . . old turd head!" I ran out of breath and stood there glaring at her, almost panting.

Was she surprised! Her mouth fell open—I mean really fell open. It looked to me like her chin was on her chest. "Oh! . . . Oh! You make me sick!" I said and turned and stalked out of the room.

I went down the hall to my room, so mad I couldn't see straight. I started to throw myself across my bed, but I realized I didn't want to cry. I was just plain pure mad. I went over to the window and stood there, saying every cuss word I knew.

After a few minutes the door opened, and Mayflower came in. Her face was stern, but her eyes weren't. "You shouldn't speak to your grandmama that way," she said.

"Oh, you always take up for her," I said. "You know she's wrong."

Mayflower stood looking at me for a long time before she went over and sat on the edge of the bed. She held out her arms. "Come here, *cherie.*" I went over and she put her arms around me. "You don't understand your grandma-ma," she said. "Haven't you ever been scared?"

"Not scared of dying, like she is," I said.

Mayflower said quietly, "No, I don't mean that." She paused. "Your

456

grandma-ma's not scared of dying. She wants to die, I think." She paused again, and her voice was thoughtful. "I never thought of it exactly that way. But I guess what's always scared Missy is not dying but living. Living has been one big hurt. She's had a hard life, about the hardest life of anybody I know about."

She drew me closer and sat silently for a while. When she spoke, her voice was soft. "It was always hard — always, from the time she was a little girl. Oh, her mama and papa loved her. They weren't bad people, and they bought her things and spoiled her. She was just a little pet who amused them when they weren't too busy. Trouble was, they were always busy. Her papa was busy making money, and her mama was busy having clothes fitted and calling on her friends and going to parties and balls. Every night they were out somewhere. Missy was a scared, lonesome little girl. When we were small, my mama used to take us both in her lap. Missy would lie there, not moving, she was so thankful and blissful. All because somebody took the time to love her. I mean, just took her in their arms and loved her, didn't buy her things, or treat her like a cute little poodle dog."

Mayflower's eyes were brooding. She gave a little sigh. "It wasn't better when she got older. I know Missy has told you stories about all the exciting and gay things that went on when she was a young girl. It wasn't like that. Missy's forgotten." She paused. "Maybe she doesn't want to remember. I don't know why young men didn't take to Missy. She was so sweet and gentle, it always seemed to me they ought to have clustered around like flies after honey. Missy would come home and cry and . . ." Mayflower broke off and sighed again. "Oh, but why talk about it, *cherie.*" Her eyes got dark, and she said, "And Blaise Sass." Her lips twisted with distaste. "Thirty-five years old, and still a selfish, spoilt mama's boy. He wouldn't have married Missy if old Mrs. Sass hadn't made him do it. Missy wouldn't have married him, except . . ." She stopped again and shrugged. "What does it matter now?" She looked at me. "Those were hard years, *cherie.* Hard, bad years. It was a blessing for all of us when he became a drunkard. At least, he stayed in his room most of the time with a bottle. When he did come out — well, on the day they took his body out of this house, the servants would have held a jamboree in the quarters if I hadn't stopped them."

Mayflower looked at me. "Then there was your mother."

I said, "Grandmama Sass didn't treat her right."

Mayflower didn't change her expression. "Who told you that?" she asked.

I hesitated. "Well . . . I . . . I figured it out."

"Then you've figured wrong," Mayflower said. "No human being ever loved another more than Missy loved your mother. Your mother was smothered with love." She looked away. "By Missy and by me. That was the mistake. You shouldn't love and shelter somebody too much. It makes them helpless." She turned and looked at me again and there were tears in her eyes. "Maybe Missy didn't act right when your mother wanted to marry your daddy. I don't know. How could anybody know? I thought Missy was right at the time." She paused. "I don't want to say

459

anything against your daddy. But he had had two wives before he met your mother. He had left them both, and him not yet thirty years old. He was selfish and demanding — and hard. Maybe artists have to be like that. All Missy and I were concerned about was your mother. She was so . . ." Her lips began to tremble. She stopped and looked away again. After a while she said, "But that's not what I want to talk about. I want to try and make you understand why your grandma-ma is scared to take you into her heart." She looked at me and her voice was soft. "Don't you understand, *cherie?* She's old and tired and she's been hurt so much. She doesn't want anybody to become so close to her that she can ever be hurt again." She paused and sighed. "Besides, there's somethin' . . ."

I said, "Maybe you're right. But she wouldn't have so much trouble if she didn't worry all the time about her old money."

Mayflower said, "There's no money."

I just looked at her, not understanding.

Mayflower said again, "There's no money." She gave a small shrug. "That was what I was about to tell you. There hasn't

460

been any money in — well, since near the end of nineteen twenty-nine. The man who took care of your grandma-ma's money stole it all. Then he killed himself."

I was simply stunned. I knew there had to be some mistake. I said, "Aw . . . I . . . Why, nobody could steal that much money!"

Mayflower looked at me levelly. Her eyes were serious, but the corners of her mouth turned up in the tiniest smile. "I didn't know you were so interested in money, child," she said. She sat looking at me in the same level way for a second or two before she stood up. She said, "You come with me."

She took my hand and, not saying a word, led me down the hall to her room. She opened the doors of a tall antique wardrobe and rummaged around in the bottom of it. When she turned around to face me she was holding a letter. "This is Judge Marigny's letter," she said. "Your grandma-ma thinks I burned it. I don't know why I didn't. Maybe I knew you'd come along someday and want to know about it."

She handed me the letter. There were two sheets of heavy paper, covered with the kind of smallish, old-fashioned handwriting that looks almost like printing. I sank to the edge of the bed and read it:

Amelia, ma cherie —

When these lines reach you, I will be gone — yes, dead, my darling 'Melia. My mind has been in such a feverish whirl — I have thought and schemed and worried so much, all these weeks and months and years — that all I crave is rest, sweet, unending rest, and there is only one place I can find it.

Oh, 'Melia, if you knew the anguish I have felt all these years — the guilt that tore my heart each time I looked into your trusting face — perhaps you could forgive me in some small measure for the way I have betrayed you. Nothing I can say will change the ignoble fact that I have been a thief and a parasite, nor will anything alter the truth that for 22 years I have lived a life of deceit and hypocrisy. But, believe me, dearest 'Melia, I did not wish it to be so, nor have I had a moment's peace in all those years.

Yes, it was in 1907 that I began stealing

from you. Do you even remember the financial panic in that sad year? I lost more than $2,000,000 of your money. It was not lost through dishonesty, nor do I believe it was poor management. Far wiser and cleverer men than I were wiped out in that crash, 'Melia. Oh, if only I had told you the truth! My pride prevented it, and pride laid the groundwork for my years of deceit and misery.

Your "Untouchable Portfolio," supposedly so filled with low-yield bonds and securities that I boasted to you were secure from all market fluctuations — it never existed, 'Melia. It was a myth, a device I used to account for the monies I lost or stole. Yes, as time went on, I stole from you increasingly — to maintain my style of living or for my own speculations.

There were periods when I thought I might recoup part, perhaps most, of my defalcations. It drove me to take greater risks and speculate more wildly. Always I lost, 'Melia — always I lost. I myself was appalled at how rapidly your "Untouchable Portfolio" grew over the years. Over the last year, when it reached the sum of

$6,500,000, I have stayed at the point of desperation, nearly at the edge of madness, trying to find the monies to cover the interest it was supposed to yield.

Last week's market crash ended the painful farce, 'Melia. Yesterday, in a desperate effort to answer a call for more margin, in a vain blind attempt to save something, I forged a check and plundered $30,000 from your personal checking account. It was all that was left of your fortune. Now, it is gone.

All is gone. Your great fortune—gone. My honor—gone. My life—gone. My hope of Heaven—gone.

Oh, try to forgive me, my dearest 'Melia. I beg you, in the name of Our Blessed Lord, please

> *Forgive your*
> *Achille*

I put the letter down slowly and looked at Mayflower. "Oh, that poor man," I said.

She nodded slowly. "He was the best friend your grandmama ever had, next to me. She would have trusted him with anything. It almost killed her when he drowned himself."

"Did he really steal everything?" I asked.

"All but a little utility stock your grandmama had almost forgotten about in a safe-deposit box," Mayflower said. "It brings in six hundred dollars a year."

"But how do—I mean, how have . . ." I began.

Mayflower smiled slightly. "How do we live? We manage somehow. I work at Thompson's Cafeteria downtown two days a week. I get two-fifty a day. That almost feeds us."

I felt like I wanted to cry.

"Then you don't have a niece?" I said.

Mayflower shook her head. "No, *cherie,* I didn't want you to know about things—not for a while." She smiled at me. "When we have to have money for something special, we sell furniture. Those rooms locked, they're all empty. We sold some furniture to buy your clothes."

That really hurt. I swallowed hard. No wonder Grandmama Sass had been so upset about the old toilet. "But why didn't you tell anybody?" I asked.

Mayflower smiled. "Tell who?" She gave

a short laugh. "Beau? What good would that have done?" Her face got serious. "Anyway, your grandmama didn't want anybody to know about Judge Marigny. All the time she was so sick we thought she might die, she begged me not to tell anybody about him. Everybody thought his death was an accident."

"But this big old house," I said. "Why haven't . . ."

Mayflower drew herself up, and her voice was firm, almost stern. "This house belongs to me," she said. "Your grandmama signed it over to me when your mother got married. She didn't want your daddy living here. We keep this house. Your grandmama and I were born in this house, and we both intend to die here."

I sat there thinking. I thought so hard, I almost forgot about Mayflower. When I finally got up, I was halfway to the door before I remembered her. I ran back and gave her a hard hug. "You've got to trust me, Mayflower," I said. "I'll be back in a little while. Just trust me." I didn't look at her face as I ran out of the room.

I ran downstairs to the study and

telephoned Long Boy. I was so lucky he was there. As soon as he answered, I said, "You get out here right away — as fast as you can. Come to the house. I'll meet you at the front gate."

"Wha . . . why . . . wha," he stuttered. I hung up the phone and ran out of the house. I didn't want to talk to anybody until I'd seen Long Boy.

It seemed like it took him forever to get there, but really I guess he broke all speed records. His face was worried when he drove up. As soon as I opened the door I began talking. At first his face got longer and longer, then he began to smile. By the time I had finished, he was laughing. "Well, how about those old sisters," he said. "They sure pulled a fast one."

That irritated me. I don't believe I ever saw him act so silly. "They did not," I said. "They haven't done anything. They didn't ask us to come messing around."

"Yeah," Long Boy said. "Yeah . . . I see what you mean." He grinned at me. "Well, let's go back to the hotel, honey. No use you hangin' 'roun' any longer."

That really burned me. "I will not," I

467

said. "I'm not going to leave until I get things straightened out. We've got to help them."

Long Boy smiled. "Help them how, sugar? 'Course we can give them some money if you want. But I don't . . ."

"Oh, don't be so dumb," I said. "They won't take any money from us. We've got to figure out a way to help them so they don't have to worry any more." I looked at Long Boy and said firmly, "I'll tell you one thing — Mayflower's not going back to that cafeteria ever again. Not if I have to go around and do business with cashiers every day."

Long Boy grinned at me. "All right, baby girl, simmer down. We'll help 'em. I'll study on it. But I've sure got t' get back to the hotel an' tell Major Lee what's going on."

"I don't want you to tell him," I said.

"Oh, now, whoa," Long Boy said. "You can't double-cross a partner when you're doin' business."

I thought about it. "All right," I said. "But I'm not leaving that house until we figure out something. You can call me there."

Long Boy let me out at the front gate. Just as I expected, I found Mayflower in Grandmama Sass's room. They both looked up when I came in. They stared at me, not saying a word. They looked so old and trusting sitting there that all of a sudden I realized how much I loved them — loved them both. I said briskly, "All right, girls, first I've got to tell you something."

FIFTEEN

Sometimes if you go down to New Orleans, I wish you'd go around to the newspaper offices. Ask them to let you look at the editions for May 4, 1935. You'll see what I was like when I was twelve, going on thirteen. Oh, I was big news that day. Every single paper carried my picture and a story about me on the front page. The story I liked best was in the *Times-Picayune.* It carried a big headline that asked: IS THIS THE RICHEST LITTLE GIRL IN THE WORLD?

It was funny about that story. The skinny man who wrote it didn't look like anything at all. His coat was wrinkled and bunched up in back, and his fingers were brown with tobacco stains, and his eyes were so bleary and bloodshot that he looked like he had been on a toot for a month. But, my, how he could write! I still remember how he ended his story. It said, "Will her vast fortune of $50,000,000 bring this clear-eyed, flaxen-haired gentle little girl happiness?

Will she find her Prince Charming and live happily ever after? Or will she become the prey of a dissolute titled foreign fortune-hunter and live a life of disillusion and despair? Only time will tell. Time tells all."

Wasn't that nice? Of course, the $50,000,000 was just made up, but I was partly responsible. When the reporters asked me that day how much I was going to inherit, I really didn't know what to say. So I tried to make my voice sound like Grandmama Sass's and said, "Gracious, I'm sure I don't know. I wasn't reared to talk about money."

Sending the reporters out was Major Lee's idea. It was the first thing he thought of when we got busy—right after I told the whole story to Mayflower and Grandmama Sass. While I talked, I simply couldn't tell what they were thinking. Sometimes Mayflower would smile a little, but then her face would get stern and fierce-looking. Most of the time Grandmama Sass lay back looking stunned, but now and again her eyes would almost burn they got so bright. When I finished, there was a long silence, before

Mayflower looked at me with her face serious and said, "You should be ashamed of yourself. Fooling us that way. We've had enough trouble."

I said, "Oh, Mayflower, I am. Believe me, I am." I went over and put my arms around her. "I wouldn't have done it for anything if I'd known . . . well, if I'd known how everything was."

Grandmama Sass made a low moaning sound. "So Beau has betrayed me," she said. "How could he have done such a thing? How could he have been so ungrateful after . . ."

"Oh, hush, Grandmama," I said. "You knew Beau was a big crook. All you have to do is look at him to know he's crookeder than a dog's hind leg."

Mayflower laughed and pulled me closer. After a while Grandmama Sass gave her snorting little laugh, too. "You're right, child," she said. "I've always known Beau was . . . undependable. He's very much like his mother's family. The Colsons were always a shifty lot — very shifty."

"Now, the first thing I'm going to do," I said, "is get you two straightened out. I'm going to see that you never have to worry about money again."

Mayflower looked at me with a little doubting smile. "How are you going to do that, *cherie?*"

"I don't know yet," I said, "but I have two of the smartest men in the world working with me on this. We'll think of something. You can be sure of that."

It was maybe an hour before Major Lee called. He was chuckling. "So our beautiful operation has gone up in smoke, has it?"

"It sure has," I said.

He asked, "Is there any way Beau could have heard about it?"

"Oh, no," I said. "Not a chance."

"Excellent," he said. "I think we all should have a conference. I don't think I should risk a visit to the Sass home—not yet. Suppose you meet us at the place you've been meeting Long Boy in half an hour."

Richard drove Major Lee and Long Boy out in the Pierce-Arrow. I told them all about how Mayflower and Grandmama Sass had taken the news, and Major Lee asked me a few questions about Judge Marigny's letter. He sat back, saying,

"Amazing . . . unbelievable . . . simply incredible." When we reached Audubon Park, Richard drove in and parked near the golf course.

Major Lee looked at us with his eyes twinkling. "Well, dear ones," he said, "I dislike sounding so unimaginative, but at times like this I always think of an old adage—when someone hands you a lemon, make lemonade. I propose that we do that."

"I don't want anything," I said. "All I want is to help Mayflower and Grandmama Sass."

Major Lee looked at Long Boy. "Do you concur?"

Long Boy nodded and smiled at me. "Anythin' Addie wants is fine by me," he said.

Major Lee settled back and said, "Capital! I really don't think it would be ethical for me to put the kibosh on Beau. After all, we are partners in this venture." His mouth quirked. "There also is the chance that Beau may offer me some attractive deals in the future." He smiled. "On the other hand, Beau has been very naughty the last few weeks—very naughty.

He has made numerous efforts to wiggle out of our agreement. He even grumbled when he had to reimburse me for expenses I was put to in setting this deal."

He looked at us and his eyes danced. "No, I won't put the kibosh on Beau, but I'd be most agreeable if someone else diddled him soundly. He needs to be taught a lesson." He chuckled, "If two dear old ladies did the job, I'd be delighted." He gave me one of his crinkly looks. "Long Boy and I have been discussing this, and we also agree, lamb, that you should be rewarded with something for your fine work — a handsome gift, perhaps."

"I don't want anything," I said. "All I want . . ."

They both laughed. "Yes, we know, lamb," Major Lee said. He looked thoughtful for a while. "Now, what we must do first," he said, "is establish firmly that there is a Sass fortune — with everyone." He looked at me. "At the same time, bunny, we will establish your credentials as an heiress, in case you have to operate on your own. The best way to do that is through an anonymous call to the newspapers." We sat there for about an hour going over what I was to do.

When I told the girls we were working on a plan to do business with Beau and how we would start, Mayflower burst out laughing and said, "Tell me what to do, *cherie.*"

But Grandmama Sass curled her upper lip and said, "Reporters! Oh, gracious, must we? We've never let reporters near the house."

"Well, it's time you did," I said.

Grandmama Sass snapped her bright eyes at me. "I know you're trying to help us, young miss," she said, "but I have some misgivings about all this scheming. Do you think the plan these gentlemen are working on will be . . . will be honest?"

I said, "Grandmama, will you please stop acting like you're still rolling in millions. I don't know what you mean by honest. Just look at it this way—you gave Beau an awful lot of money. Now you need some of it. You know he won't give it to you. It seems to me you've got a right to get some of it any way you can."

Grandmama Sass lay back thinking about that. "Why, yes, indeed!" she said.

"It is my money, isn't it?" She gave her hooting laugh. "I certainly have a right to take some of my own money." From that time on I never heard a peep out of her. Sometimes it seemed to me she was enjoying herself more than the rest of us.

Well, as I mentioned, meeting the newspaper reporters and photographers was no trouble. They arrived in two bunches, but so close together that it was like a real press conference. I sat in a chair in the drawing room. Mayflower stood by my side, looking haughty and fierce. The only thing I was really worried about was that one of them might know something about the time I was supposed to have been lost and living with the Isbells. Major Lee didn't want anything said about that. He was afraid it might start somebody snooping around. I was just to pretend that my mother and daddy had been lost in a storm. But none of them asked anything about that at all. What they really wanted to do was get a look at me and take my picture and check out the tip Major Lee had phoned in that I was heiress to one of the biggest fortunes in the country. Most of their questions were kind of silly. When they asked where I went to school, I told them I was being tutored at home. I had white spots in front of my eyes for at least an hour after the photographers shot their flashguns in my face.

We had more fun when those papers came out. We spread them out on Grandmama Sass's bed and read parts of the stories to each other and laughed and laughed. Grandmama Sass had her tiny gold-rimmed reading glasses perched on the end of her nose. "I do wish you would listen to this," she said. She read a line that said her fortune was so great that perhaps even she did not know exactly how much she was worth. "Hah!" she said. "How ridiculous! I know exactly." She put the paper down and looked at us and made a sound that sounded almost exactly like a giggle. "I counted every penny this morning when I gave Robear ten cents for the iceman."

We were still laughing and cutting up when Major Lee called me on the telephone. "Beau has just left here," he said. He chuckled. "He's upset over your publicity—very upset. I tried to reassure him it was of no consequence, but he's on

478

his way out there. You know what to do."

"Sure," I said. "I'll handle him."

Old Beau really was upset. He was pink in the face and had a pinched look around his nose and mouth. His eyes had as much life as two cold poached eggs. He didn't bother with his jovial-uncle act. He shot me a hard glance and said to Mayflower, "I came as quickly as I saw the papers. Aunt 'Melia must be furious—all this . . . this unfortunate notoriety."

Mayflower gave him her usual haughty look. She said simply, "She's not receiving. She's not well."

Beau said, "I shouldn't wonder." He sucked his bottom lip. "Most unfortunate... terrible." He shook his head. "The family has never had this sort of cheap attention before." He sucked his lip some more and looked at me. "Ah, little niece, perhaps we can take a walk in the garden. Uncle Beau wants to speak with you."

As soon as we were through the French doors, he turned on me furiously. "You stupid little brat! What are you up to?"

I looked wide-eyed and innocent. "Nothing," I said. "What have I done?"

"You know what I mean," he said, getting red even on top of his big bald head. "Why did you talk to those newspaper people?"

"Well, what else could I do?" I asked, sounding injured. "They came to the house and asked me questions."

He studied me with his cold, dead eyes. "Did you send for them?"

"Of course not," I said. "Why would I do something like that?"

He glared at me for a long time before he began sucking his lip. "Aunt 'Melia must be beside herself," he said.

I gave a little shrug. "Well, she didn't like the picture of me in the *Item* much. She said it made me look too thin in the face. But she thought the one in the *Times-Picayune* was good."

He didn't know what to say. He stood there looking at me with his fish eyes and opening and shutting his mouth. Finally, he got red in the face again and said, "You listen to me, you little sharpie! Don't you try any tricks with me. You do exactly as you're told—and nothing else. Don't you ever speak to a newspaperman again. If they come to the house, have Mayflower send them away."

As soon as he left, I ran upstairs and gave Mayflower and Grandmama Sass an imitation of how he had acted. After we laughed awhile I called Major Lee. "Fine... excellent," he said, sounding like he was having the time of his life. "Now, ask Amelia Sass if I may call on her tomorrow night — rather late, say, ten o'clock."

"I don't have to ask her," I said. "Grandmama never goes out at night. You just come ahead."

Well, I wish you could have seen those two together when I introduced them. Both so genteel and elegant, saying all the proper things, but sizing each other up right to the fillings in their teeth. When I saw they were hitting it off together, I went downstairs and sat with Mayflower. Major Lee was up in Grandmama Sass's room for more than an hour. When he came downstairs, he was beaming. "Charming woman, your grandmama," he said. "Utterly delightful. Very knowledgeable about financial matters, too." He gave me one of his crinkly looks. "Still, lamb, I don't think it would do any harm if you rehearsed her rather thoroughly in the lines she has to say. I've given her a typed memo with the main points to be covered. She must be line-perfect if our little deal succeeds."

I did try to rehearse Grandmama Sass. I tried every way I knew. Mayflower helped all she could, too. All of us even sat down and wrote out a speech for Grandmama Sass to say that covered all the points in Major Lee's memo. But Grandmama Sass was just one of these people who can't act, or maybe I should say lie. Everything she said came out so stiff and unnatural-sounding that it wouldn't have fooled an idiot child. Finally, I just threw the speech away and made sure she memorized the memo. She got tired of me pestering her. "Oh, I'll do it right, child," she said. "I'm not in my dotage completely, you know. All I need is . . . well, the proper audience."

To tell the truth, I doubted if she could pull it off. On the afternoon she sent for Beau, I was as nervous as a walleyed fox. As soon as he walked into the room and found Mayflower and me there, Beau knew something was up. He was so silly, fawning on everybody one minute and acting pompous the next, that he made me sick. I could tell how nervous Grandmama Sass was when she cleared her throat. Looking more at me than Beau, she said in a high, unnatural voice, "Beau, I am aged and infirm and I . . ." It was the speech we had thrown away! I thought I would die. I pressed my lips together tight and shook my head as much as I dared. Grandmama Sass stopped and muttered, "Yes, of course. Yes . . ." She turned down the corners of her mouth and thought. Then she looked at Beau and almost yelled in the same high, unnatural voice, "Beau, I have decided to leave you everything I own."

Beau was so surprised he jumped a little. He got red in the face and sucked his bottom lip. He said, "Ah, well . . . I . . . I . . ."

Seeing Beau so taken aback must have steadied Grandmama Sass. She gave her short, snorting laugh, and from then on she was fine. Wonderful, in fact.

Beau recovered quickly. He said pompously, "Well, naturally, I'm pleased and grateful, Aunt 'Melia." He gave one of his alligator smiles. "But I am sure it will be many, many years before we have to think about your demise."

Grandmama Sass said impatiently, "Don't be a fool, Beau." Her dark eyes seemed to snap they were so bright. She said, "In any event, my demise has nothing to do with it. I want you to take charge of my estate now. What time I do have left I want to spend with my granddaughter." She paused. "I've been too deeply concerned with business affairs these last few years. I fear it's made me a hard, parsimonious old woman." She gave me what she thought was a fond smile. "I want to forget business completely and live a happy full life with my grandchild."

I do believe she got Major Lee's memo right, word for word.

Beau's ears were pink, and he was sucking on his bottom lip so hard it looked like a piece of raw liver. "I think you're showing very good judgment, Aunt 'Melia," he said. "For years I've been urging you—"

Grandmama Sass didn't let him finish. "Now, what I have in mind is a guardianship," she said. "Because of my

484

years, that shouldn't be difficult to set up."
She was reciting the memo perfectly.
"I want to be relieved of financial
responsibilities and have them removed
beyond my control." She gave Beau a sharp
look out of her bright eyes. "Can that be
done?"

Beau said quickly, "Oh, yes, indeed,
Aunt 'Melia. Indubitably—if that's what
you want."

"Now, in becoming my guardian, I also
want it stated explicitly that you are
becoming the guardian of dear little Addie."
Her upper lip curled. "Despite those stupid
newspaper accounts, I have no intention of
having her burdened with the responsibility
of an independent fortune while she still is a
child. I know from sad experience how
much of a strain that can be."

Beau said, "Well, of course, if I become
your guardian, it's underst—"

Grandmama Sass said sharply, "I want it
stated explicitly, Beau. Quite explicitly. I
want it clear that you are assuming full
responsibility for her and for her debts and
'obligations until she reaches her majority. I
want it stated. Do you understand?"

Beau flushed. "Oh, yes, Aunt 'Melia," he said quickly. "I'll do exactly as you say." He looked at me with his ugly eyes and showed his teeth. "I was only going to assure you that you could trust me to care for my dear little niece. I would treat her as my own child."

Grandmama Sass's eyes flashed. "Oh, yes, Beau," she said. "No one who has ever known you has doubted your generosity."

I held my breath. That seemed to be going too far. But old Beau sucked at his bottom lip and looked down at his big belly. "Well, so I've been told," he said, trying to sound modest.

Grandmama Sass said, "I wish you'd draw up the papers as quickly as possible, Beau. As far as I am concerned, from this time on you are in control of my estate. I will refer everything to you."

Beau looked so pink and full of himself, I really don't believe I would have been surprised if he he had crowed. "You can depend on me, Aunt 'Melia," he said. He paused. "Could you—well, that is, er . . . can you give me some approximation of the size of your holdings?"

That wasn't in the memo. Grandmama Sass turned down the corners of her mouth. Her eyes got bright and she gave her snorting laugh. "Gracious, Beau, I've never sat down and added it up. The idea!" She gave a little hoot and waved her hand airily. "It's probably three times larger than it was when I got it from papa."

That shook old Beau so hard he forgot to suck his lip. He gave a little grunt and swallowed two or three times.

"There's one other matter we must take up," Grandmama Sass said. "I don't recall whether I've ever mentioned it to you. Several years ago I gave Mayflower the deed to this house. She was born here, as I was, and I wanted it to remain her home if I predeceased her. Naturally, I have made provisions for her in my will. Since I will have nothing to leave once the guardianship papers are signed, I want first to set Mayflower up a modest trust fund. We've discussed it, and agreed that the income from a trust fund of one hundred and fifty thousand dollars will be adequate for her needs. So I wish you would take care of that as your first order of business."

I was watching old Beau closely. His eyes narrowed a little when Grandmama Sass said she had given the house to Mayflower. He didn't like it, but there wasn't a thing he could do. He said, "Why, certainly, I can arrange that, Aunt 'Melia. However, if I may suggest . . ."

Grandmama Sass waved her hand for him to be quiet. "What I had in mind is a trust fund similar to the one I set up for you after papa died." She fixed him with her bright eyes. "That was quite satisfactory, I take it?"

"Oh, yes, Aunt 'Melia," Beau said. "Quite satisfactory."

Grandmama Sass paused, and I knew she was trying to think whether she had forgotten anything. She glanced toward me. I blinked my eyes. She had covered everything perfectly. There was just one more tricky little detail to be taken care of.

Grandmama Sass said, "Well, that's all, Beau. You're a lawyer. Draw up the papers. Take care of Mayflower's trust fund first." She leaned back against the pillows and her eyes got so bright they were glowing. "I feel a great weight off my mind already," she said.

Beau stood up. He put his hands flat against his big belly and said pompously, "As well you might, Aunt 'Melia. You have had a great responsibility for many years. I can only say that I think you have made a wise decision. You know looking after the family's interest will always come first with me. Ah, indeed, if I have to devote full time to it." He paused. "Now, about the funds for Mayflower's trust fund. If you will . . ."

Grandmama Sass's eyes flashed with annoyance. She said, "Gracious, Beau, take care of that yourself. I'm certainly not going to bother myself with a detail like that now. Set up the funds and you can reimburse yourself after you take over the estate and acquaint yourself with my holdings."

When Beau stood there, sucking on his bottom lip, she gave him a dark look and said sharply, "I presume you do have the funds to take care of such a small matter, don't you?"

Beau said, "Of course, Aunt 'Melia. I . . ."

Grandmama Sass leaned back against

her pillows. "Well, do it then," she said. "At once."

Mayflower left the room with Beau to let him out. I felt like giving a big whoop, but since I couldn't, I gave Grandmama Sass the biggest grin I could manage. She looked so proud of herself. Without thinking, I ran over and threw my arms around her. She gave a little gasp, "Gracious . . . oh, gracious." She hugged me back—tight—and stroked my hair. Would you ever have thought that would happen?

Mayflower surprised me. When she came back, her face was long and sad and she sat down heavily. When we just looked at her, she said, "I can't believe it. All those worries. I can't believe they're going to end."

It was late that night before I could reach Major Lee. He and Long Boy had been somewhere on a deal. When I told him what had happened, he laughed. "Beautiful," he said, "simply beautiful. Now, I want you all to sit as quietly as mice until the trust fund is arranged. When that is done, we will go into the second part of our little operation."

After that, I talked to Long Boy for a long time.

It didn't take old Beau but two days to set up Mayflower's trust fund. He even sent his car for her, so she could go down to the bank and sign all the papers. When she came back, she looked as proud and haughty as a queen — until you looked at her hard. All I had to do was cut my eyes at her, and she would hug me and laugh so hard she shook. She was so happy it made me want to cry. It was that night we had our real celebration. We sat in Grandmama Sass's room, laughing and giggling, almost until midnight.

Major Lee came out the next night. He was as grand and bland as usual, but every time he looked at Grandmama Sass and Mayflower and thought about them diddling old Beau, I could tell he had a hard time keeping a straight face. After we settled down in Grandmama Sass's room, he said, "Well, ladies, the first part of our plan has been an unqualified success. I want to congratulate you all. No matter what happens next, you are assured of an income that will allow you to live in comfortable, if not luxurious, style." He raised his eyebrows. "But what you have now is only a pittance compared with what you can obtain if the second part of our operation also is successful. Only a pittance."

Mayflower laughed. "I'm ready," she said.

"Yes, indeed," Grandmama Sass said. "You tell us what to do, Major."

Major Lee's eyes danced. "Very well, ladies," he said. "I am happy you are so enthusiastic. For the second part of our plan depends almost entirely on your enthusiasm — and boldness." He paused. "But before I go into details, I should like to explain at greater length why I proposed that Madame Sass ask Beau to set up a guardianship to take control of her interests. A guardianship is quite an interesting legal proceeding." He raised his eyebrows. "Most interesting. As you know, its purpose is to allow the courts to appoint a guardian to care for another person called a ward, or another person's property, or both. Most wards, as you also undoubtedly know, are persons under legal age, or persons who suffer some mental or physical condition which makes it impossible for them to manage their own affairs. Great lawsuits are often waged over whether or not persons actually are so incapacitated by age and illness, or insanity and alcoholism, and so on, that they need legal guardians."

He smiled at Grandmama Sass. "Of course, in your case there is no dispute. You have voluntarily requested Beau to relieve you of the management of your affairs because of your age and illness."

He settled back. "Now, I have mentioned these elementary points because a great many people apparently believe that guardians derive some direct financial rewards for managing the affairs of their wards. Perhaps the great lawsuits have left that impression. Actually, a guardian's role is often difficult and singularly one-sided. For one thing, a guardian assumes full legal responsibility for his ward. In specific cases, this includes responsibility for a ward's care and well-being, debts and other obligations."

Major Lee's mouth quirked. "On the other hand, a guardian is expressly forbidden to reap any financial benefits from a ward's estate. He must account for all profits and render all financial accounts before the court." He raised his eyebrows. "Now, Beau is eager to take on this unrewarding and time-consuming role because he believes eventually he will inherit your entire estate worth millions." He chuckled. "How eager do you suppose he would be if he knew the entire Sass estate consists of some public-utility shares bringing in six hundred dollars a year?" He looked at Grandmama Sass. "Their value is around twenty thousand dollars, I presume?"

"Seventeen thousand," Grandmama Sass said.

Major Lee nodded. "Just so. Hardly an amount to entice Beau to become your guardian and maintain you in high style." He looked at all of us. "The problem we face, ladies, is quite simple. The guardianship petition Beau presently is happily preparing will be complete in all but one important detail. He must either affix to it, or file separately, a complete inventory of his aunt's assets. Without such an inventory, the courts will not even consider his petition." He smiled. "Now, we know that Beau will not lay out unlimited funds for the support of his dear aunt if he learns her estate is not worth millions, but only seventeen thousand dollars. So we must not let Beau know the extent of the Sass estate. At the same time, we must affix a true and complete inventory to his petition, get it signed before reputable witnesses and then approved by a court. What we must do, actually, is have Beau legally declared his aunt's responsible guardian without him being aware of it."

Grandmama Sass asked, "But how can you do such a thing? I al . . ."

Major Lee's mouth quirked. "By being both highhanded and underhanded, madame," he said. He smiled at her. "You will play the highhanded role. I will discuss it with you presently. I will take care of having the petition filed." He paused. "I have an acquaintance who is beholden to me for certain small services. He is rather important in the Long machine, and—"

"Huey P. Long?" Grandmama Sass asked in a shocked voice.

Major Lee said, "Yes, madame."

"A horrid man," Grandmama Sass said.

Major Lee raised his eyebrows and looked bland. "Perhaps," he said. "I take no interest in politics. My acquaintance assures me that he can have a friendly judge approve Beau's petition and have it filed away quietly. It's a rather common practice, I gather." He looked at us. "Actually, the whole procedure is more or less a legal nicety. It is not essential to our operation. Still, it might prove to have considerable value. For one thing, it will create a legal obstacle if Beau ever seeks to recover any goods you ladies have purchased." He gave me one of his crinkly looks. "More importantly, it benefits lamb here. For, as you know, the petition also makes Beau fully responsible for her debts and obligations. He is not concerned over that. He knows her true identity and he thinks that you do not." He chuckled. "Perhaps we can surprise him. Her debts may be considerable."

He smiled at all of us. "We will discuss some operational details presently. But what I want to impress on you is, as of this moment, you have Beau hanging high and ready for plucking. He thinks he will soon be in control of a multimillion-dollar fortune." He looked at Grandmama Sass. "You have already told him you intend to refer all bills to him. How long he will hold still while you fleece him, I don't know. A great deal depends on how adroitly you handle him. But for the present at least, buy everything you need or want. Spend as recklessly as you please. Buy anything."

I asked, "Anything?"

Major Lee chuckled. "Anything you desire, lamb."

I looked at Mayflower. "The first thing we've got to do," I said, "is get some things for that old kitchen."

As soon as we served Grandmama Sass breakfast the next morning, Mayflower and I got ready to go shopping. Major Lee had brought out a suitcase of things I had told Long Boy to send me. Inside, like I asked, was an envelope with $300 in it. Mayflower made noises, but I made her take it as a loan. I knew she would be short of money until her first trust-fund check came. We telephoned for a taxi and went to Maison Blanc department store first.

I never was so surprised in my life. I'd

497

never realized so many people read newspapers. We had hardly got inside the door when a tall, bald-headed man in a dark suit, a floor-walker, I guess, came up bowing and smiling. It was "Yes, Miss Kodaly . . ." "No, Miss Kodaly . . ." and "Right this way, Miss Kodaly." People started turning around and gawking, and I heard them whispering, "Richest girl in the world . . . little heiress in the paper . . ." It really tickled me. I tried to keep a straight face, but what I felt like doing was smiling and throwing them kisses. Mayflower was just wonderful. She was wearing a long sweeping black and red dress, with a matching *tignon*. She walked along stiff and haughty, paying no attention at all to the whispering. By the time we reached the elevators, we had a little crowd of people trailing along behind us. As soon as we got off the elevator, a tall, beautifully dressed dark-haired woman came running up the stairs all out of breath and introduced herself as Miss Somebody-or-other. "Maybe I can be of assistance," she said. She joined the floor-walker and came along with us.

When we got to the appliance department, Mayflower didn't waste any time. She walked over to the biggest, shiniest electric refrigerator on the floor and put her hand on it. "I want this," she said. Then she and the dark-haired woman went over and fussed around stoves until Mayflower picked one she wanted. After that she bought pots and pans, all kinds of utensils, an electric egg beater and a coffee grinder, and I don't know what all. I was so busy looking at things, it was some time before I paid any attention to what was going on around us. Would you believe it? A whole crowd of people were gathered at the entrance to the appliance department, gawking at me. Two guards in blue uniforms had come from somewhere and were standing there with their arms folded. When I looked toward them, most of the people just stared, but a few waved. One fat, blondined woman kept snapping her fingers at me and saying, "Honey . . . honey . . . look at me . . . look at me, honey."

After Mayflower bought everything she wanted, we went down to the cosmetics department. This time the two guards came along as well as the floorwalker and dark-haired woman. It was the same thing all over again. While Mayflower bought all kinds of creams and colognes and perfumes she and Grandmama Sass used, people thronged the aisles and gawked at me. I never knew people could be so silly, especially women. They cooed and gurgled and waved to me like idiots. Two or three made like they were coming over to me, but the guards stopped them. When she had finished, Mayflower asked, "Is there anything else, *cherie?*"

I nodded. "I want to buy a radio—a big one."

Mayflower looked doubtful. "Missy doesn't like them," she said. "She won't have one in the house."

"Oh, that's crazy," I said. "She likes music. We'll get a combination radio-phonograph, with lots of high-class records."

We went over to the radio department, with everybody trailing along. I picked out the biggest, most expensive radio-phonograph they had. It was in a mahogany cabinet and was simply beautiful. I told the dark-haired woman Grandmama Sass liked opera and asked her to pick out some records to send out with it. Nobody had said a word about money, but I told the floorwalker, "Charge everything to my grandmama, Mrs. Amelia Sass—but send the bills to my uncle, Mr. Beauregard Goldsborough. He handles our business affairs."

We headed for the door then, the guards going ahead, and the floorwalker and the dark-haired woman walking with us and the crowd trailing along. By this time I was beginning to feel pretty grand. A guard called us a taxi. As soon as we got inside, Mayflower and I looked at each other and burst out laughing.

When we started up Canal Street, I asked Mayflower, "Don't you think we ought to have a car?"

She was still laughing. "Who'd drive it?"

"Why, we'd hire somebody to drive it," I said.

She looked thoughtful. "I've been thinking about asking a young couple I know about to come live out back and help

501

around the house," she said. "I suppose he drives."

"What kind of car does Grandmama Sass like?" I asked.

Mayflower shook her head. "I don't know, *cherie*. She's had so many."

The taxi driver was a short jug-eared man. I leaned forward and asked, "Mister, what's the best limousine you can buy?"

"Cadillac," he said right away. "Oh, sure, can't beat a Cadillac."

"Take us to a Cadillac dealer," I said.

There was a young, dark, kind of good-looking salesman in the showroom at the Cadillac agency. He looked bewildered when Mayflower and I came in. "I want to look at some cars," I said. He smiled and waved his hand. "Sure, go ahead, honey."

If Mayflower hadn't smiled, I probably would have told him who I was. Instead, I gave him a cool look and went over with Mayflower and started looking at the cars. Pretty soon, I noticed the people in the little back office standing up and craning their necks to look at us. A man came out of the office and walked over to the young salesman and said something. He almost stumbled over his feet getting over to us. I really gave him a cool look this time. "I don't think you have what I want," I said. "I want a black limousine."

"Oh, we have limousines upstairs, miss—ma'am," he said.

He led us up the stairs to another showroom. There was a big black hearse up there and three long black shiny limousines. I saw the one I wanted right away. It looked like old Beau's, with dove-gray upholstery and a sliding glass panel between the front and back seats. I asked Mayflower, "Do you like this one?"

She didn't know a thing about cars. She stuck her head in the front window and looked around. "It's very pretty, *cherie,*" she said.

I said to the salesman, "I'll take it."

He got so flustered and red around the ears I thought he was going to drop his salesbook. I gave him my spiel about charging it to my grandmother, but sending the bill to my uncle. I added, "We'll take it with us."

That really confused him. He gulped and fumbled and said, "Well, excuse me, ma'am—miss—I'll have to check and see if it's ready." He went away for a minute or two and came back with an older man, who gave me a big smile. "We can put a temporary tag on this car and let you drive it away, Miss Kodaly," he said. "But if it's convenient, we'd like to have it back overnight for a final servicing."

"Oh, that's all right," I said. "You can have it back right away. We just didn't want to ride a taxi home."

The young salesman drove us home. I was sorry about that. Mayflower and I had a lot of laughing and giggling to catch up on.

SIXTEEN

You may not believe it, but spending lots of money is an art. If you gave a rich person and a poor person the same amount of money, the rich person could spend his twice as fast. Folks who are used to having money know things to buy that poor folks haven't even heard about. I learned that by watching Grandmama Sass. Without leaving her room, she diddled old Beau better than I could have done if I'd gone on a shopping spree every day.

Of course, that big old house helped her. For about two weeks almost any time you looked in her room she was busy with a fancy decorator or a landscape gardener, a painting or plumbing contractor, or a roofing man. Her sun porch was overflowing with swatches of expensive drapery and upholstery materials, samples of thick carpeting and hand-blocked wallpaper.

But it was the little, casual ways Grandmama Sass spent money that impressed me most. She came out with them two or three times a day. "Mayflower, call that nice little Mr. Beamis and ask him to come out and restock the wine cellar. Tell him we want an ample supply of champagne. None of his bootleg wine—good vintage Krug. I'm so weary of drinking dear papa's old port." Or she might say, "Do you remember those delicious little partridges stuffed with pate we used to get from Jansen's, Mayflower? Find out if they still have them. Order a couple of dozen." Once she said, "Mayflower, I'm so tired of looking at napkins with frayed edges. Call that little shop that carries Belgian linen. Get a good supply—say, six dozen." At least twice a week she would say something like, "Mayflower, Emile called. He says he has a Louis the Sixteenth secretary almost exactly like the one we sold. I told him to send it out."

Grandmama Sass was like a different person. Not being half scared to death all the time because of money worries helped, I'm sure. It was more than that, though. I think having something to do, instead of lying in bed and feeling old and useless, was the main thing. She wasn't a bit nervous the afternoon Beau came out to get the guardianship petition signed. She got up and dressed and went downstairs for the first time since I'd known her. She looked so tiny and aristocratic, wearing a black silk dress, with jeweled buckles on her tiny black shoes and carrying her gold-headed ebony stick.

Major Lee had told Grandmama Sass to be sure and get highly respectable witnesses. They were so highly respectable they made me sick. You know, black suits and crackjaws and both dull as beetles. Mr. Sayre was a tax lawyer she used to use, and Mr. Lasalle had something to do with the trust department of a bank where she used to keep her money. They were already waiting with Beau in the library when Mayflower and I helped Grandmama Sass down the stairs and came in.

It didn't take long. After Mr. Sayre and Mr. Lasalle shook hands with us solemnly and Beau simpered around, we sat down in the stiff leather chairs and Grandmama Sass said, "Beau, first tell these gentlemen the agreement we have reached. Then you can read your document." Major Lee had told her to do that.

Beau was too long-winded and pompous, but he covered everything well enough. He explained to Mr. Sayre and Mr. Lasalle that Grandmama Sass wanted to be relieved of the responsibility of caring for her estate so she could devote more time to me. So, at her request, he was petitioning the court to declare him her guardian, giving as reasons her age and general poor health. Naturally, he was assuming all legal responsibility for her care. He showed his teeth at me and said, at the same time, he was petitioning the court to make me his ward. In addition to maintaining and educating me, he specifically would be responsible for all my debts and obligations until I reached my majority.

When he finished, he looked at Grandmama Sass. She nodded. "Now, read your document."

I didn't understand a lot of the legal terms, but it seemed to me the petition covered everything. It did say that because of her advanced age and infirmities,

Grandmama Sass was unable to take care of her estate, but I guess that was the way it was supposed to be.

When Beau finished, Grandmama Sass asked, "Do I sign anything?"

Beau said, "No, Aunt 'Melia."

Grandmama Sass asked, "Do you sign anything?"

Beau said, "When I file the petition, I will..."

Grandmama Sass said, "Please sign now."

Beau flushed and gave a nervous little laugh. "Well, it's most irreg..." He broke off and sucked his lip. "Very well, Aunt ' Melia," he said. He took out his pen and wrote his name at the bottom of the last page of the petition.

Grandmama Sass turned to Mr. Sayre and Mr. Lasalle and thanked them for coming. They made some solemn noises and shook hands all around, and Mayflower showed them out.

Beau got pink in the face and gave his nervous laugh again. "Really, Aunt 'Melia, it wasn't necessary to have them here. You see, the court—"

Grandmama Sass said, "I wanted them here."

Beau sucked his bottom lip. He showed his teeth in his alligator grin. He said heartily, "Well, if you wanted them, Aunt 'Melia, I'm glad they came. It certainly didn't do any harm for them to be, er, apprised of our agreement." He picked up the petition. "Now, what I must have from you is—"

Grandmama Sass held out her hand. "May I have the document, please?"

Beau looked surprised, but handed it to her.

She said casually, "I'll read it over carefully tonight."

Beau turned red up to the top of his bald head. "But, Aunt 'Melia, you can't—that is, you don't . . ." He broke off and sucked his lip." He tried his jovial laugh. "But you've heard it read already. I'll send you a copy from the office if you wish to, er, peruse it at your leisure. It would expedite matters if we could wind up everything today." He showed his teeth. "Perhaps I could read it to you again."

Grandmama Sass said with just a touch

of annoyance. "Oh, don't be tiresome, Beau. I can't understand all those whereases and wherefores. A day or two won't matter." Mayflower had come back and was standing near the door. Grandmama Sass said, "Come along, you two. Goodbye, Beau. I'll be in touch with you."

We walked out of the room and left old Beau standing there red-faced.

We didn't go upstairs, but cut through the butler's pantry and went into the kitchen. After we heard Beau's car leave, we came out laughing and giggling and waited on the verandah until Calvin brought the Cadillac around. Calvin and his wife, Rita, were the young colored couple Mayflower had hired to live out back and help around the house. We didn't take a long drive that day, just up St. Charles Avenue and through Audubon Park and back. But it was the first time Grandmama Sass had been out of the house in five whole years! Her eyes were so bright they snapped as she sat back, either exclaiming or fussing over the changes that had been made. Every now and then she would hold up old Beau's petition and shake it a little and we all would laugh like crazy.

Major Lee came out that night. Grandmama Sass gave him the petition and a list of her utility stocks, and Calvin brought up a bottle of champagne. I had a taste myself. Major Lee looked as happy as if he had pulled off a million-dollar deal. "A beautiful operation," he said. "Fabulous. When I have the petition filed by my helpful acquaintance it will be completed." He quirked his mouth. "To be candid, ladies, it has succeeded beyond my expectations. Because of your, ah, inexperience, I had anticipated some difficulties."

He smiled at Grandmama Sass. "How long it continues to be a success now depends entirely on you, madame. Beau undoubtedly will press you impatiently at times to return his petition and give him a list of your holdings. I do not expect that he will press too hard. Indeed, he will do his utmost not to alienate you for fear you will not leave him your millions. But the situation is somewhat trickier than it was when he first began to draw up the guardianship petition." He took a sip of champagne before he smiled at Grandmama Sass again. "I do suggest you avoid an appearance of sheer obstinacy. Perhaps the cleverest way to put Beau off is with, ah, feigned eccentricity and vagueness. After all, such characteristics are almost expected of wealthy ladies of mature years."

Grandmama Sass gave her snorting laugh. "You mean rich old nuts."

When Major Lee was ready to leave, I walked downstairs with him to let him out. "How long do you really think we can keep on diddling old Beau?" I asked.

He gave me a crinkly look. "Oh, indefinitely, chicken. Indefinitely." He chuckled. "I don't see a great deal of Beau these days. Seeing me distresses him. It reminds him of the stupendous commission he thinks he will owe me when he gets control of his aunt's fortune. Undoubtedly, he's hatching all sorts of dark schemes to avoid paying it. But that in itself is a sign he doesn't suspect a thing." He paused. "As I've said before, Beau has a great deal of money. I don't think he will complain about Madame Sass's expenditures too much. Not as long as he thinks he is coming into her estate worth upwards of thirty million." He hesitated. "Of course, there's another thing. Naturally, I never mention it to the others. What will restrain Beau most of all is he doesn't think he will have to pay his aunt's bills for long. He's had discussions with her doctor, and he's firmly convinced she won't live much longer."

"Well, she will!" I said firmly. "She's getting better all the time."

This was true—almost. Grandmama Sass probably had as many of her seizures as ever, but they didn't seem to bother her as much. Two or maybe three times a day she would get deathly white and seem to stop breathing. She would pop one of her tiny nitroglycerin pills in her mouth. After only a few seconds the color would come back in her face, and she would go on with what she was doing. I had become so used to her seizures that I really wasn't too concerned over them. I don't believe Mayflower was either.

We had such good times together that summer. For almost a month the house was a mess, with plumbers and painters and paperhangers tracking in and out. Every evening I would take one of Grandmama Sass's arms and Mayflower would take the other, and we would lead her down to see what work had been done that day. The house was simply beautiful when it was finished, painted inside and out, with new carpeting and wallpaper and draperies. It must have cost old Beau a fortune.

We practically lived in Grandmama Sass's room. Rita always served our dinner up there off trays. It tickled Grandmama Sass to think of all sorts of expensive and rare things to eat, because old Beau was paying for it. We had caviar and quail and pheasant, and everthing you can think of. Of course, Grandmama Sass and Mayflower always had wine with their meals—either champagne or a red wine called claret. They enjoyed everthing, but to be honest, it was almost a relief to me when Mayflower cooked on Thursdays, Rita's day off, and fixed things like gumbo and fried chicken.

And let me tell you about that radio I bought. When the men brought it in, Grandmama Sass grumbled and made faces and pretended to be horrified. But she kept it going from morning to night. We had so much fun listening to it. Every night before dinner we gathered around to laugh at

Amos 'n' Andy. Through dinner, we usually had on Kate Smith. After that, it was Edgar Bergen and Charlie McCarthy, or Fred Allen, or Ed Wynn. Sometimes we laughed so, we ran out of breath. Grandmama Sass was facinated by Walter Winchell, and we always sat up late to hear the Hit Parade.

Sometimes we were in the room when old Beau telephoned. Grandmama Sass handled him perfectly. "Oh, is that so, Beau," she would say, sounding vague. "Gracious, it doesn't seem that long. Time does go so swiftly when one is old. . . . Yes, I must get to it—I really must." Her voice would get a bit sharp. "Now, don't be tiresome, Beau. I have a great deal on my mind. . . . No, you haven't made me angry, Beau, but I do wish you didn't discuss business so much. . . . Yes, I'll do that. . . . Yes, I bought a few things there. . . . That amount sounds right. . . . I've never doubted that, Beau. . . . You've always been considerate. . . . Yes, I will. Goodbye, Beau." She would hang up the phone and give her snorting laugh.

Mayflower and I went shopping once a week. We always had a list of things we needed, but we would put our heads together and laugh and giggle and try to think of things to add, just so we could diddle old Beau. I loved those shopping trips. After a couple of weeks, people stopped recognizing me as the richest little girl in the world. Actually, I never caused much of a commotion but that one time. I guess that's when I first began to realize the truth about being famous. Up until then I thought people became famous. You know, because of what they did. Oh, I know people can become famous for a short while, like war heroes and people who climb mountains for the first time, but I didn't realize you had to work full-time at being famous, and work hard. You've got to keep your name before the public all the time. That's why some people who do really important things soon get forgotten, while big showoffs who run around working to get their names in the papers stay famous.

I met Long Boy twice a week—on Tuesdays and Fridays. It aggravated me so much because he wouldn't come to the house and meet Mayflower and Grandmama Sass. When I would fuss at him about it he would say, "Aw, I don't want to meet those ol' sisters, honey. We've got nothin' to say t' each other."

"They're not old sisters," I would say. "They're wonderful—both of them. You'll like them."

"Yeah . . . well, maybe someday," he would say.

I worried about him a lot. He still was selling PruYea stock and working with Major Lee on various deals and doing real well. Sometimes he was bubbling over after pulling off a big deal, but other times he was glum and quiet. Once he sighed and said, "I'll be glad when this is all over so's we can go off an' start doin' business for fun. Far's I'm concerned sellin' good stock or bad stock is about th' same. It's too much like workin' for a livin'."

I knew what he meant. I missed our old life, too. As much as I loved Mayflower and Grandmama Sass, sometimes when I hopped into the car with him I felt like telling him to just keep driving. I'll say one thing for Long Boy: he never once asked me to leave Mayflower and Grandmama Sass. As far as he was concerned, they were my

518

partners in a deal. You can't run out on partners until a deal is finished.

Now, I must tell you about my jewels. From the very beginning, of course, I had known Major Lee had some special plan in mind for me in his operation. That was why he wanted me made old Beau's ward and went to such trouble to file the guardianship petition. I wondered about it a lot at first, but as time went on I almost forgot about it. One evening when I went into Grandmama Sass's room, I could tell by how bright her eyes were and how Mayflower was smiling at me that something was up. Grandmama Sass said, "Child, Major Lee telephoned. He is coming out after dinner. He has a surprise for you."

"For me?" I asked. "What is it?"

Grandmama Sass gave a little laugh. "I think he'd better explain."

I looked at Mayflower. "Do you know what it is?"

She laughed, too. "Indeed I do, *cherie*. I think it's wonderful."

All through dinner I kept pestering them to tell me what the surprise was, but they only laughed and made teasing remarks. It was almost ten o'clock before Major Lee arrived. Even then it seemed to take forever for us to get settled down to talk about my surprise. Finally, after Calvin had brought up a bottle of champagne and poured everybody a glass, Major Lee gave me a crinkly look. "You will remember, lamb," he said, "that I said from the outset of our little operation that you should have some reward for your good work. At the time I had not met these good ladies. But they wholeheartedly agree you should reap some special recompense. In fact, they are most upset because you personally have not benefited from Beau's generosity. In our recent telephone conversations your Grandmama Sass has been most insistent that I do something about it at once." He smiled. "Accordingly, today I dropped in at Pierre Roget Sons, the jewelers, and introduced myself as a representative of your grandmama. I told them that she had decided you now are old enough to start a tasteful collection of jewelry. I chose a collection of rather chaste but expensive baubles which they will bring out and show to you tomorrow. Among them I hope you will find something that pleases you."

I was so disappointed. I've never cared a hoot for jewelry, and I would have been pleased lots more if my surprise had been a box of chocolate-covered cherries. But they all were smiling at me, and looking so pleased with themselves, that I knew I couldn't tell them that. I tried to sound happy. "Oh, that's lovely. Thank you very much." I waited a while before I asked, "Are you sure old Beau will pay a bill like that?"

Major Lee chuckled and said, "Right to the point, chicken." He raised his eyebrows. "No, I must confess I'm not sure. I think perhaps he might. Only time will tell."

When I just looked at him, not understanding, he chuckled again. "As you grow older and deal with them, lamb," he said, "you will discover that luxury jewelers operate somewhat peculiarly. They charge such exorbitant prices and make such huge profits on their trinkets that they are most lenient about the matter of payment. I explained to them that because of various problems of taxation, and so on, your grandmama wished payment for the jewelry deferred until you come into your inheritance as the richest little girl in the world. Since life is short, but business goes on and on, they readily agreed. Indeed, they were everjoyed to make a connection with you at such an early age."

I thought about that. "What you mean," I said, "is that you're not sure whether we're doing business with old Beau or with the jewelry people."

Major Lee smiled. "Precisely." He raised his eyebrows. "But since Beau is your guardian by law, I anticipate that someday he will either pay or there will be a resounding lawsuit." He got his bland look. "In any event, it is not a matter that concerns us." He looked at Grandmama Sass. "Does it, madame?"

Grandmama Sass gave her snorting laugh. "Most certainly not," she said.

Two men came out from the jewelry store carrying four or five black leather cases. My, they were so elegant and sleek, wearing black coats and striped pants and short hard collars, with pearl stickpins in their neckties. I told Grandmama Sass later that they reminded me of big important diplomats. She turned down the corners of her mouth and said they also looked like barbers from the St. Charles Hotel. And, do you know, she was right? Just notice sometime. Most diplomats look like barbers.

We all sat in Grandmama Sass's sun porch while they opened up their cases. They did everything with a flourish. They had some heavy cream-colored silk handkerchiefs and they handed them around to put in our laps while they passed out jewelry. The first thing they gave me was a pearl necklace with a little diamond clasp. It was pretty. I sneaked a look at the tiny price tag and swallowed hard and took a good look. It said $11,000. Grandmama Sass did all the talking. She would wave her hand and say, Too gaudy," or hold a piece up to the light to examine it better and say, "How many carats are there in the diamond?" I don't think I opened my mouth but once. Somewhere along the line, in between the bracelets and brooches and rings, they handed me a little beetle with gold legs and a diamond head and tiny rubies clustered together to make the body.

"Oh, that's cute," I said. The price tag said $4,500.

After a while Grandmama Sass said, "The pearls definitely—the matched strand." She had been putting pieces aside on the table by her side. She began picking through them, but, then, she waved her hand and said, "Oh, we'll take the lot."

That's how I got my jewelry collection—pearls, six brooches, a matching diamond bracelet and necklace. It cost more than $54,500. I'm not sure how much more. I never could find the price tag on a gold and emerald brooch shaped like a leaf. After the men left I thanked Grandmama Sass and picked up everything. "Where are you taking it, child?" Grandmama Sass asked. "Perhaps you should put it in the safe downst—"

"I've got a place to put it," I said. I went to my room and opened the closet and took out my Roi Tan cigar box. Everything fitted perfectly.

I've got to tell you one more thing. One night we were listening to the radio, and I said something—I don't remember what—but Mayflower and Grandmama

Sass burst out laughing. I'd never before heard Grandmama Sass laugh like that, natural and clear and happy. She said, "You're a joy, child. I don't know how we ever got along without you."

I've never forgotten it, because there came that night in August when we sat up late listening to the radio. Jessica Dragonette sang, I remember, because when I told Mayflower and Grandmama Sass good night and went to my room, I was wishing I had a voice like that. I had undressed and put on my nightgown when Mayflower opened my door. I'd never seen her look like that. Her eyes were wide and hurt. She said quietly, "You'd better come, *cherie*. Missy's sick. I've called the doctor."

I didn't bother to put on my robe and slippers, but just ran like I was. Grandmama Sass was lying back against the pillows with her eyes closed. Her face was deathly white like it got when she had one of her seizures. Mayflower reached out and took one of Grandmama Sass's tiny hands and clasped it in both of hers and 'stood there looking at her face. I said, "Her pills—did you . . ." I stopped, because

Mayflower shook her head slowly, not taking her eyes off Grandmama Sass's white face.

After a while Grandmama Sass opened her eyes. She looked at me and said, "Madeleine?"

"It's Addie, Grandmama," I said, swallowing hard.

"Oh, yes Addie," Grandmama Sass said weakly. She closed her eyes. She said so softly I almost couldn't hear her, "It seemed long—so long." After a short silence she gave a soft sigh. "But it wasn't long." She opened her eyes and looked at me. "Madeleine?"

"It's Addie, Grandmama," I said, beginning to cry.

Grandmama Sass closed her eyes again. Then she opened them and looked at me and turned up the corners of her mouth. She said, "Addie, you little devil." She closed her eyes and—and that was all.

Once Long Boy and I sold a white Bible to a sweet-faced woman who told me her husband and little girl "went away." I'd never understood what she meant. But that's what Grandmama Sass did. She went away. Her tiny, frail body was still there on the pillows, but she had gone away.

I cried out, "Don't go Grandmama! Oh, please don't go!"

Mayflower realized how it was, too. She leaned over Grandmama Sass with her face all twisted and tears running down her cheeks and whispered, "I'll be along soon, Missy. I'll be with you soon."

I thought my heart would break. I was too young to realize what had happened when I lost my mama. So Grandmama Sass was the first person I had loved who died. It almost—but what can I tell you? You know what it's like. Or if you don't, someday you will. I thought about all the things I wished I hadn't said—and the things I wished I had said. And all I could decide was we ought to love one another more, all of us. Love one another more, and show it and say it before it's too late.

Mayflower and I just clung to each other. After they came and took Grandmama Sass away, and while people came and went, we sat together and cried and talked. And somehow time passed. It always does.

We didn't go to Grandmama Sass's

funeral. Mayflower didn't want to go, and I wanted to stay with her. On that morning we sat in Grandmama Sass's room and talked for hours. Finally, at noon, I got up and kissed Mayflower. "I'll be back," I said. "Don't you worry about that. I'll be back." Mayflower held me close and said, "You've got to come back. This is your home, *cherie.*"

Calvin had already taken my baggage downstairs. I walked out of the door across the verandah into the bright sunshine. Long Boy was waiting. And would you believe it? He was driving that old Dodge truck. My mouth just fell open. "Wha. . . . why . . ."

He grinned. "Got a fella t' get it for me," he said. "He told them it was stole." He opened the door of the truck for me and said, "Thought we'd ride up to Kentucky. I've been studyin' on it, an' I've got an idea we can do some business with tobacco."

I got into the truck and — do you know? — it felt so good. Like I was home. I bent over and put the Roi Tan box under the front seat. Long Boy started the motor, and *VOOMmmmm* — that old truck took off

528

like Moochy's goose. I looked up, startled, just not believing it.

Long Boy cut his eyes at me. "Got me a V-twelve Cadillac engine in this ol' thing," he said. Then he turned and gave me the biggest, widest, sweetest grin. He said, "Figured you 'n' me still got a long ways t' go, honeybunch." The old fool.